CW01663079

MORGAN BROTHERS
BOOK TWO

Alec

NEW YORK TIMES BESTSELLER

MARGARET MCHEYZER

Alec

email: hit_149@yahoo.com

There's always

LIGHT

if you reach for it

Prologue

ALEC

"HAVE YOU GOT any idea how annoying she is? I don't want her here, Dean. She can go to hell." I huff in frustration as I wait for my physiotherapist to arrive.

"Why is she annoying?" my brother Dean, asks.

I want to tell him how mad she makes me. Serena always has a smart-ass remark whenever she's working on me. She gets under my skin and stays there for hours after she leaves. "She just is."

Dean narrows his eyes at me, and clicks his tongue. "Well, until the doctors give you the all-clear, pull your fucking head out of your ass and do whatever it is she needs you to do. You want to sit around and wallow? Do it, but if you don't do what she tells you to do, you can't come back to work."

Being a firefighter is my life. If she doesn't give me the all-clear to get back to work, my life will be ruined. I pick my water bottle up, start to take a drink, but instead I throw it in frustration. "This is bullshit!" Just what I need—Serena opens the door right as the bottle flies through the room.

She's got that stupid smirk on her face as she lowers her gaze to look at the water bottle. "Great. You're being a dick again, aren't you?" She sighs. "You're such a pleasure to help when you're being a dick."

"See?" I yell at Dean while pointing to Miss Smart-Ass.

"Oh, little brother needs to cry to big brother. Boohoo." She balls her hands into fists and pretends to rub them over her eyes. "Get over yourself," she challenges.

"Do you see what I have to deal with, Dean? She's not making it any better." I need to find another physiotherapist. She's driving me crazy.

"Why? Because I call it as I see it? Don't like to hear me call you out when you're being an ass? Sorry, buddy. I'm not pandering to your stupid emotions."

My jaw tightens and the muscles in my arms flex as I grab my thighs and squeeze. "I swear you take enjoyment from my pain. You probably walk out of here and pump your fist in the air because you've hurt me."

She frowns and sulks, "You're being a baby. You just don't like being wrong." Drawing in a deep breath, I lift my finger, pointing at her. "Put your finger down before I break it," she warns.

"Why do you even bother coming? It's obvious you don't want to be here." I say as I look to Dean for support. But then I notice the door is closed and Dean is gone. Typical. He's left me here to deal with her on my own. *Thanks for having my back, bro.*

"You know, if you put as much effort into getting yourself better as you do into whining, you'd be up and walking around a lot quicker." She stands with a hand on her hip.

There's a tightness in my chest. "Get on with it, will you?" I snap at Serena.

"No, I'm not doing anything for you while you're being an unappreciative dick."

I roll my eyes, and turn my head to look out the damn window. "Do you have any idea how frustrating it is to be a fireman who can't go to work because a fucking garage door broke my ankle? Not to mention, I have a mother who's babying me, and won't give me a moment of peace? Just, fix me," I say through gritted teeth.

"No!" Serena replies without hesitation.

I snap my head to look at her. "What the hell is your problem, Serena?"

"My problem?" she asks in a high-pitched voice. "My problem is you. You're this entitled little boy who thinks his job is the only important job in the world. And you think treating me like I'm the asshole is acceptable? Guess what, buddy? I treat you the way you treat me. My problem is *you*." She walks over and pokes me in the arm. "You're so spoiled." She pokes me again, this time in the chest.

I grab her wrist, and pull her down toward me. "You have no idea what you're talking about."

She tries to yank her hand back, but I pull her closer. Staring up into her wild hazel eyes, I can't help but look down at her beautiful lips. Shit, what am I thinking? This woman is the devil's spawn, there's nothing beautiful about her. Not even her plump, kissable lips. She attempts to pull her arm away again, but I bring her closer again. "Let me go." Her breath catches in her throat.

"Is that what you want?" I ask, my eyes flicking up to look into hers. She worries her lip between her teeth, and I find myself staring at her mouth again. "Is that what you want?" I repeat when I find her muscles loosen around my grip.

"I…I..." she stutters.

When I release Serena's arm, her eyes widen and she takes in a sharp breath. Reaching up, I grab the collar of her polo shirt and pull her mouth down to mine. "What are you doing to me?" I whisper just before our mouths collide ferociously.

She deepens the kiss while she straddles my thighs and roughly runs her hands through my hair, latching on as we attack each other's mouth. "Is this what you want, Alec?" She strokes her tongue against my bottom lip, then gently nibbles.

"Oh God, yes." I lace my fingers through her hair, keeping her mouth on mine. God, I want her. She slips her hand down my chest, and slides it into my pants. Teasingly she feels my hardness over my boxer briefs. "Jesus," I mumble as she grabs my dick and massages it in her hand. I'm fumbling to take her shirt off when we both hear the door.

She pulls away, leaving me wanting, needing her. Her eyes widen, and her mouth falls open. "Shit," she says as she covers her mouth. Serena's shaking her head in disbelief. "Oh my God. I can't believe I kissed you." She stands, and stumbles backward until she finds the lip of the huge window. Leaning against it, she brings both her hands up and rubs at her temples. "I'm so sorry," she says while shaking her head. "I'm so sorry."

"Serena, it's okay."

She holds her hands up while she frantically searches for something. Rapidly blinking, she reaches for her bag. A tear rolls down her cheek, and she wipes it away. "I'm so sorry," she repeats as she slings her bag over her shoulder and makes a dash for the door.

"Serena!" I call as she slams the door behind her while fleeing from me. This fucking cast is stopping me from going after her. I try to maneuver the wheelchair, but I know she'll be gone by the time I get outside.

The door flings open, and for a split second I'm hopeful she's returned so we can at least talk about that kiss. "Why did I see Serena bolting from here like her ass was on fire, Alec?" Mom snaps.

"It's nothing," I say as I try to get around her. "Can you move please, I have to go after her."

"She's gone. She got in her car and took off like she couldn't get away from here fast enough. What did you do to her?" Mom stands in front of my wheelchair, with her arms crossed across her chest. "What did you do to her?" she asks again, even angrier.

"Nothing! Just move, I have to get to her."

"No, I'm not allowing you to go anywhere near her until you tell me what happened? She ran out of here, crying. What the hell did you say to her?"

"I didn't say anything." I run my hand through my hair, and sit back in the wheelchair. Mom's not going anywhere until I tell her something. I feel like I'm fifteen again, not a twenty-eight-year-old man. "I kissed her," I say in a small voice.

"Oh."

"And she kissed me back."

"Oh," Mom says again. She narrows her eyes at me. "Then why did she run out of here crying, Alec?"

"I don't know. I think she panicked, and she ran."

"Right...um. Well, right, I'm...ah," she stutters. "I thought I was going to have to come in here and tell you you're being a cranky old shit, and to get over yourself. But, as it turns out, nope, I don't think I have to say that."

I let out a breath. "Yeah, you do. I've been a bastard to her, Mom."

Mom walks over to the bed and sits on the edge. "You better call her and apologize, son. Because whatever is going on with you two, you need to sort it out."

"I know, Mom," I yell.

Mom lifts her brows at me and tilts her head to the side. "I beg your pardon," she says in an eerily calm voice.

"I'm sorry." I let out a long breath and rub my fingers over my eyes. "I shouldn't have yelled at you like that, Mom. It's not an excuse, but I'm so frustrated with myself."

"Then you better call that woman and apologize to her. Look." She places her hand on my leg and gently squeezes. "I know firefighting is in your blood, son. But if you can't handle it when you get hurt, then I suggest you quit now. Because this is nothing." She waves her hand over my broken leg. "You can easily recover from this. But what happens if you *seriously* hurt yourself? You can't go into shutdown mode because you're feeling sorry for yourself. And Serena..." Mom points toward the door. "She's only here to help you keep your strength up, and get you through it. She's a damn saint for putting up with your bullshit, let me tell you, Alec. You've only been here for a short while, and I want to smother you in your sleep. You're being an ass. Get over yourself." She stands and walks to the door. "Now, get out here and say hello to everyone."

Mom's right, I've been an asshole. A self-pitying ass. "I will. First I need to send Serena a message."

"Make it a good one, because I like that one, and I want her to come back."

She walks out, leaving the bedroom door ajar. I reach for my phone, and bring up messages. Shit, what do I say? I type out many messages, and delete each and every one of them. I settle on the only thing I can say.

I'm sorry for being an asshole.

Slipping my phone under my leg, I head out to Thomas's belated birthday party. Dean sees me, and walks over. "So, that was interesting," he says as he hands me a soda.

"I need something stronger than a soda."

"Too bad. You're still on pain medication, and you shouldn't mix them together."

"Someone else running my life," I say sourly, as I look up at him.

"You're in a great mood. Can't wait to have you back on the crew," he says sarcastically. "Joanne and I copped an eyeful. You and Serena, huh?" he says about him and his fiancée.

"No, it's not like that. It was in the moment and we just kissed." I look over to Thomas who's playing with Tripod. I don't want to talk about me and Serena, because there *is* no me and Serena. It was a stupid, one-time kiss. "How's it going with Joanne and Thomas?"

"He's a good kid. I'm adopting him."

I look up to Dean. Fuck, he's fallen hard for Joanne and her son. I never thought my older brother would be a family man. He's always been such a loner, and introvert. "Congratulations." I hold my hand out, palm side facing up, and Dean slaps it with a high five. "Who would've thought, eh?"

"Who would've thought? You and the physiotherapist."

"That was nothing, man. We both lost our heads for a moment."

Dean snickers. "Okay then, keep telling yourself that. Maybe one day you'll believe it."

"What do you mean?"

"Dean?" Joanne calls. She gestures for him to come over to her.

"Duty calls, little brother. Duty calls."

"You're so pussy-whipped," I say before he leaves.

"Yep, and proud of it." He smiles brightly as he heads over to Joanne.

No woman in the world will ever tie me down the way Dean is. Nope, no chance in hell. I just can't wait 'til my leg heals so I can get me some sweet, sweet lovin.'

Chapter 1

SERENA

I DON'T HAVE time for his bullshit. He's such an entitled prick. I get how Alec is feeling sorry for himself because he's hurt and can't get back to work yet, but I'm not putting up with his bullshit. Nope. And what the hell was that kiss? And why did I react to him the way I did?

Driving home, I shake my head and slam my hand on the steering wheel. "You're an idiot, Serena. A damned idiot!" I shout at myself. Never in a million years would I ever kiss or get involved with a client, so why did I kiss Alec, of all people? *Hashtag jerk number one.*

Thankfully the drive from Mulberry Point to Faith Haven is less than fifteen minutes. But those fifteen minutes are filled with anxiety and me scolding myself for kissing him.

"You're not my type." I replay the scene over and over in my head. "Get your hands off me." I point out the windshield. "No, of course I don't want to kiss you." But I did, so badly. Alec was a temporary relief to a much bigger problem. One I have to manage on my own.

Pulling into my driveway, I stay sitting in the car for too long. I don't want to go inside. I'm afraid of what I'll find, or maybe I'm afraid of what I won't find. I look around the neighborhood, and my stomach tightens. I hate living here. I don't ever feel safe in my own home, I can't wait until I'm able to get out of here. If only to get away from the house down the street that's constantly throwing parties at all hours of the night, and any day of the week. Whenever I drive past, and the two guys who live there are outside, they both stop and stare as I drive into the driveway. They make my skin crawl with their creepy glares.

Looking around, I'm relieved to see they're not outside. I get out of my car, and head straight inside. The moment I'm in, I lock the front door, and double-check it. Turning, with my back against the front door I close my eyes for a moment and take a deep breath. "Jordan?" I call. A part of me doesn't want him to be here, but another part of me wishes he was. I'm met with silence, meaning I'm alone. My heart crumbles and I silently pray he's okay. Opening my eyes, I rifle around in my old, oversized bag for my phone. I check to make sure he hasn't called me. I notice the time, and I let out a long breath. I've got just over an hour before I have to start at my other job, giving me enough time for me to do a twenty-minute meditation. God knows I need it today.

I double-check that the door's locked, and I head down the small hallway off the tiny kitchen to my room. Shivering, I rub my hands up and down my arms. It's so cold in here all the time. Doesn't matter what the temperature is outside, it's always cold in my room.

Taking out the tin I have hidden at the back and top of my closet, I sit on my bed and open the lid. Lifting the most current photo I have before Mom and Dad passed away, I look at all the smiles on our faces. Dad's got his arm around Mom's shoulders, while Jordan is poking his tongue out at the camera, and I'm smiling like a goof. This picture right here is one of happiness, joy, and so much love. I wish we could all go back to this moment when we were all happy.

I slink off my bed and sit on the floor. Crossing my legs, I place the photo on my lap, and find the guided meditation on my phone. Pressing play, I straighten my back, place my hands, palm faced up, on my thighs and close my eyes. This next twenty minutes is only for me. For me to escape the pressures of having to look after my younger brother, while trying to provide food and utilities and everything else life demands of us.

By the time the twenty minutes is over, I'm feeling a lot more positive about what my future holds. I'm doing the best I can, and working on getting help for Jordan, and getting us out of this shithole. Standing, I look at the photo once more and let it fill my heart with all the love we once shared. Placing it back in the tin, I stand and hide it at the back and top of my closet along with my parents' wedding rings, and Mom's engagement ring. One day I'm going to meet someone who loves me as much as Dad loved Mom.

One day.

I grab my jeans from the dryer, and my work t-shirt, pull my light brown hair back into a ponytail, and apply some gloss to my lips. Looking at myself in the bathroom mirror, I can see the dark circles under my eyes. I need sleep. But I also need to focus on getting the money together for Jordan's treatment.

I hear the creak of the front door; my breath catches in my throat and my eyes widen.

"Serena!"

I let out a relieved breath, thankful it's Jordan. I rush out of the bathroom, and the moment I see him, my shoulders slump and my heart breaks. "Jordan." I keep my voice from trembling when I see all the spots on his face, and just how thin and sickly he appears. "Where have you been?" I ask.

He half shrugs. "Around. Got any money? I'm hungry and need food." He comes in for a hug, and I have to hold my breath not to inhale his filth. I balk when he pulls back.

He's not going to spend my hard-earned money on food. He's going to go and buy drugs with it. "Um, I don't. But there's food in the cupboards and the fridge. Do you want me to make you something quick to eat? I've gotta get to work though. Oh, the shower's free. And I've washed your clothes too, so you've got clean clothes on your bed."

"Yeah, thanks. Um, nah, I feel like getting food out. I'm gonna jump in the shower and then take off. I've got a buddy waiting for me."

I know exactly what he's going to do. He's going to wait for me to leave so he can go through my bedroom and take whatever he thinks has value so he can sell it for drugs. "Yeah? I'll wait and drop you off."

"Nah, don't worry. I'll walk. You go."

I hate leaving him here on his own, but I'm also nobody's fool. I learned from the first and only time he ransacked my bedroom and took everything he thought he could sell. Thankfully, he didn't find the tin, or he would've pawned the little I have left of our previous lives. I changed the door to a thicker wood, and have two locks on it. He lost his shit when he found out I did it, but now, he's come to terms with it. "I haven't seen you for days, Jordan, how are you?" He scratches at his arm, while frantically searching around for something. "There's no money here, and nothing you can take to sell for drugs."

"I'm not using no more," he says defensively. "I'm clean now. I promise." He crosses his heart while eagerly waiting for me to fall for his bullshit.

The scabs on his face, his erratic behavior, and crazy eyes all tells me he's had a hit recently and he'll start coming down soon. I smile at him, although my soul is crying. "I'm so happy to hear that. I'm really proud of you." My stomach churns with sorrow.

I reach out to place my hand on his shoulder, but Jordan pulls back. He lowers his gaze, and sighs. "Fuck, Serena, why do you have to judge me? I told ya, I'm fucking clean."

"All I said was I'm proud of you."

His face reddens as a sheen of sweat creeps across his forehead. Without any warning, he slams his fist into the drywall, creating a hole and making me jump in fright. He jerks his hand back, and clears his throat. "Fuck, now I have to fix this. Give me money so I can go buy stuff to fix it with."

Tears well in my eyes, but I hold it together. "I don't have any money on me, Jordan. I need to go to the bank to get some out." In my head, I'm already thinking I can't outrun him if he tries to make a run for it to my bedroom where my bag is. And I also know there's twenty dollars in my purse.

"How am I supposed to fix it if you don't have money? Just give me your card, and I'll go get the stuff." He holds his hand out to me for my ATM card.

If I give him that, then everything I've been saving to get him to the treatment center is as good as gone. Shit, I have to do something, or he may turn violent and take my bag or even my car. "Hang on." I hold a finger up to him. "Just wait here." I didn't want to do this, but he's left me with no other choice. I run into my room, grab my purse and take the twenty dollars out. "Here. I remembered I had this for milk and bread. But you'll get the stuff for the hole, right?" I know that money is gone and so will he be for the next few days.

He smiles triumphantly when I hand him the bill. "Yeah, I'll get stuff to fix the hole." His eyes are wired, and I can see the cogs turning with his enthusiasm to buy more drugs. "I'll be back later tonight, yeah?" he says.

No, he won't be. He'll walk out of here, and it might be a few days, or even a few weeks before I see him again. "Just, go have a shower first. I'll wait and I'll take you to your friends."

He's already heading toward the door. "Nah, it's okay. I'll grab a shower when I get to my buddy's place. I gotta go. Love ya, sis." He slams the door on the way out, and I'm left knowing I've bought my drug addict brother twenty dollars' worth of drugs.

He would've waited until I was gone and he would've kicked the door down to my bedroom. It was the only thing I could've done. I had no choice. He most likely would've found my tin, and our parents' jewelry would've been sold.

Feeling sick to my stomach, I look at the time, and know if I don't leave now to go to work, I'm going to be late for my shift. My stomach is twisting with fear that my brother is going to overdose, and it'll be the money I gave him that'll kill him. Leaning my forehead against the door, I close my eyes and pray that I haven't just murdered my brother. "Please, stay safe," I whisper.

When the knot in my stomach settles, I make sure my bedroom door is firmly locked before leaving the house and heading toward my next job.

"Welcome to The Narrow Table," I greet the family that enters the restaurant with a smile. But inside, I'm dying because I'm still so worried about Jordan. I realize, logically, that twenty dollars won't buy enough drugs for him to overdose. But I still hope he's okay. I'm hoping I haven't sent him to his death. I hate myself for giving him that money, but I really couldn't see any other way.

"We'd like a table please," the father says as he places his arm lovingly around his wife. Their two young boys hover close to their mother. I smile at them, trying to push this feeling of dread as far down as I possibly can.

"Sure, please follow me." I grab two menus for the adults. The kids are really young, maybe five or six, so I grab two coloring booklets and a bucket of colored pencils for them. I show them to their seats, and give the boys the coloring books. Both smile when I place the books and pencils in front of them.

"Thank you!" they chime in unison.

"You have beautiful manners, and you're so very welcome," I reply with a huge smile. "Your waiter will be with you in a moment."

"Thank you." Both parents look down at the menus while the boys happily color.

I walk back to the front of the restaurant, and I'm drowning with images of my afternoon. What if Jordan's trying to get clean, and I've sent him out with money to buy drugs? I'm doubting every single word of our interaction, but deep down inside, I know if I didn't give him the money, he would've found a way to break into my room.

"Hey, you okay?" Dani asks when she returns to the front with menus from a table.

"Yeah, just stuck in my thoughts. Anyway, I didn't know you were working tonight."

"Yeah, it's been crazy busy at Elle's Café, and here, but I'm saving up so I'll take any shift I possibly can."

"I have no idea how you can work two jobs and still have a social life," I joke with her.

"Says the chick who has how many jobs?" I hold up three fingers. "Three? And when do *you* get to have a social life?"

I snort and roll my eyes. "No time for that. Anyway, what are you saving for?"

Dani half shrugs. "Whatever, nothing in particular and everything I want." She smiles broadly. "Anyway." She gestures with her eyes that she needs to take another order.

The rest of my night is spent seating people, and worrying. At the end of service, I lock the door and walk over to the register to start tallying everything up. The other waiters return and all put the tips in the tip jar so we can evenly divide it among us. "I'll wipe down the tables," Shaun, one of the waiters says.

"I'll sweep and vacuum," Dani offers.

"I'll help in the kitchen," Simone calls.

"I suppose I'll mop once everyone is done." Great, this means I'll be one of the last people here other than the kitchen staff who have to clean the kitchen. I divide the tips between us, and lay a pile out for everyone to take. Ninety-four dollars is ninety-four dollars closer to the thirty-five thousand I need to send Jordan to the rehab center I found. It's by far the best one, but it's expensive and in Kentucky. Getting Jordan there will be a challenge in itself. But I only need seventeen thousand more before I can send him.

I pull my phone out of my pocket and look at the time. By the time I mop the floors, and leave it'll be close to eleven and I need to be out the door by eight tomorrow morning to get to my main job.

Crap, I have to come back here to Willow Heights tomorrow afternoon to clean the Morrison's house. The more money I earn, the quicker I can send Jordan into rehab. He needs it, but most importantly *I* need it for my peace of mind.

But for now, I need to mop these floors and get myself home so I can sleep. God, I'm so tired. But I have to push through. One day though, I won't need to work three jobs trying to save my brother's life. Because he'll be clean and sober, and together we'll be able to rebuild our lives.

I hope.

Chapter 2

ALEC

"YOU'RE GETTING AROUND a bit better," Mom says as I push myself out of the bedroom and into the dining room.

"Yeah, I'm feeling a bit better too," I reply.

"What time is Serena due today? Oh, I'm making you scrambled eggs."

"Can you make me some bacon with it?" I ask. "After all, bacon is the most important food group there is." She turns her head and narrows her eyes at me from over her shoulder. "I take that as a no then."

"You'll get eggs and juice. I'm not making you bacon."

"You're not a very good host, are you?" I tease. "I'll have to give you a negative review on the Airbnb website."

She turns and sticks her finger up at me. "Well, if you don't like it then you can cook for yourself. Oh no! That's right, you can't because you're a damned invalid!" she mocks.

"You're a nasty woman, Elise Morgan."

"Yes, yes I am. I'm so nasty I'm here looking after you. Get over yourself." She smiles. "I must admit, I'm glad to see that you're not such a grumpy bastard today."

Until Serena shows up. Thankfully I haven't seen her since last Saturday when Mom hosted a belated sixteenth birthday party for my nephew-to-be. "I'm kinda determined to be up and walking around as quickly as I can. I need to return to work."

There's a knock on the door, and I instantly groan knowing Serena has arrived. Mom stops cooking and looks at the time on the microwave. "Serena isn't due for another hour, is she?" She wipes her hands on the tea towel, then walks down the short hallway to the front door. "Oh, my favorite son!"

"Hey!" I protest.

"You're my other favorite son," she calls as she and Dean appear together.

"What are you doing here?" I ask.

"I've come for breakfast, I'm hungry." He rubs his stomach, then stretches.

"Joanne doesn't feed you?" I ask.

"Yeah, but she had to leave for work early today. She was gone before I got home from work. I just dropped Thomas off at school, and I thought I'd drop by and see how my little brother is doing." Dean drags out a chair, and sits as Mom continues making breakfast for the three of us.

"I'm doing okay." I pointedly look down at the cast on my leg. "I can't wait until I get this stupid thing off. Then, I'll be ready to get back to work."

Dean winces. "I've already told you, Alec. I'm not taking you back until the doctor and Serena give you the all-clear. I won't have you endangering yourself or the rest of the crew because you're sick of being here."

I don't want to endanger anyone either. "I just need to get back to work," I sigh. "I don't want to be the weak link on our crew, either."

"Then do what Serena wants you to do, and put aside whatever you two have going on between you," Dean says.

"Yes, well, keep it in your pants, Alec. You need to get yourself better first. But, let's face it, your history with women is fairly poor," Mom says as she brings over a plate piled with toast then walks back into the kitchen.

"It's not that bad," I try to defend myself.

"Yeah?" Mom asks in a high-pitched voice. "What's your longest relationship been? Five, or six months?" I flinch. "Come on, son. You're telling me you haven't had a relationship longer than six months?" She returns to the dining table with three plates stacked in one hand, and a huge bowl of scrambled eggs in the other.

"I get bored." I shrug. "They're all the same."

"Stop going after the same type of woman, then. That says more about you than about them," Mom barks. Dean chuckles as he grabs two pieces of buttered toast and starts eating them. "And just because the perfect woman fell into your lap doesn't mean you get to be an ass to your brother." She smacks Dean on the back of the head.

Dean lowers his eyes, but with a wide smile murmurs, "Sorry."

"Well, when I find her, I'll be sure to not let her go. Okay?" I ask Mom, trying to pacify her.

"You're an idiot, Alec." She clicks her tongue and shakes her head. "Anyway, eat your breakfast before it goes cold."

"Don't have to tell me twice," I say as I reach for the scrambled eggs that are slightly out of my reach. Dean sees me struggling, and he picks the bowl up goes to hand it to me, but pushes it further away. "Pass the eggs, Dean."

"Which? These eggs?" He points to the bowl.

"Yeah, those eggs."

"Sure." He picks the bowl up, and scoops up a huge amount, and mounds it on top of more toast. He places the now half-empty bowl down just out of my reach. "These are so good, Mom." He happily devours the food on his plate. I narrow my eyes at him. "Sorry, did you want some?"

"You're being a dick, Dean," Mom scolds.

I smirk and cross my arms. "Fine. Here." He hands me the bowl, and I empty most of it onto my plate as Mom offers the toast.

"Thanks, Mom." I smile.

"You're such a mommy's boy," Dean teases.

"Nah, that's Rhett," I reply.

"You know what? I don't like either of you at the moment." Mom points to me then Dean. "So yes, I do like Rhett better than the both of you." Dean and I laugh as Mom squirts some ketchup on her eggs and toast. "How's work?" She looks to Dean.

"It was so quiet last night. I think we ran drills for about two hours straight."

"And how's my grandson and daughter-in-law?" She instantly relaxes when she mentions Joanne and Thomas.

"They're really amazing, I'm lucky to have them." Dean smiles sheepishly.

"When are you getting married?" I ask as I shovel more breakfast into my mouth.

"We haven't set a date yet. But, soon I think. Joanne's been given this amazing opportunity, and if she goes ahead with it, I want us to be married before that starts."

"What's the opportunity?" Mom asks.

"Her boss, Hope, has bought some old buildings here in Mulberry Point and she wants to create a food court. Hope wants to put in a dessert bar and have Joanne run it. But Joanne's doubting herself, and she's not sure if she wants to do it."

"I'll help her!" Mom offers. "Tell her, I'm happy to leave my job and come work for her. I love baking. I'm not that good at it, but I'm good at..." She squints. "You know what, don't worry, I'll call her and talk to her about it."

"What? No, you can't do that."

"And why not?" Mom asks Dean. "She's my future daughter-in-law. And if she needs help, I'll be there for her."

"Mom, everything's been a bit overwhelming for her. First her husband died in prison."

"Pffft." Mom flicks her hand. "That beast stopped being her husband the moment he laid a hand on her."

"I said the same thing. But still, he was a part of her life. And now she's engaged. Give her some breathing space."

"Breathing space? Are you kidding me, Dean? This family doesn't do breathing space. We do in-your-face-suffocating. *Breathing space,*" she says again with a scoff.

Dean turns and whispers, though still loud enough for Mom to hear, "Help me out."

"Like you helped me out with the eggs? Nope."

"Prick," he mumbles. "So, you and Serena, huh?" He glances at Mom to see her reaction.

Now who's the prick? "Honestly, it was a momentary lapse of judgement. She's not my type."

"Yeah. Your type lasts three-point-four seconds," Mom says.

"Stop." I hold my hand up to her. "Serena is a bit chubby, and she's plain, and she's annoying."

"Wait a second." Mom lifts her finger to me while Dean sucks in a deep breath. "I didn't realize I brought up a man who looks at someone and judges them by their weight. You should be ashamed of yourself, Alec. Because let me tell you, I'm mortified those words even left your mouth." She stands abruptly, taking my plate and heading to the sink.

"I'm not done," I object while still holding my fork.

"Yes, you are. Because what you said about that woman's weight is atrocious. I never knew you to be so shallow. Now it makes sense why you can't keep a girlfriend, though. Because you choose them with your eyes, and not your heart."

"Mom, I'm sor..."

She swings around in the kitchen holding up a finger to me. "Don't even bother. And let me tell you, if you make her cry once more, you'll have me to deal with."

I look to Dean for support, but he shrugs and keeps on eating. "Thanks for the backup."

"Not from me." He shakes his head.

With Mom now giving me stink eye and the cold shoulder, I may as well wheel myself back to my room to get ready for Serena's arrival. It's not that Serena is fat, but she's certainly not petite. I prefer my women slim, and able to wear sexy dresses that make my head turn. I like it when I show up to take them out, and they're all dolled up with a beautiful, figure-hugging dress and lips so red that I can't wait to slide my cock inside their mouth.

"You look like you're about to rub one out," I hear the annoying voice of Serena.

"Ugh." I look over to her and roll my eyes. "Aren't you early? You're not supposed to be here for another half an hour."

"Well, aren't you lucky then? You get to see my beautiful face half an hour earlier."

Beautiful face? Who is she kidding? She's ordinary, and there's no way in hell she'd be able to pull off red lipstick. Or a figure-hugging dress. "Let's get this over and done with."

"My sentiments exactly." She places her bag on the floor, and comes to help me out of the wheelchair and onto the bed.

"I can do this on my own," I snap, already annoyed by her.

Serena steps back and lifts her hands as she watches me use my upper arm strength to move from the wheelchair to the bed. "Look at you go," she says without even cracking a smile.

"What's your problem, Serena? If you don't want to be here, leave. I'll find someone else to do what you do. You're not the only physiotherapist in Mulberry Point."

Her jaw tightens. Without a word she starts working on my good leg. She's a bit rough but I'm not going to complain, or she'll intensify what she's doing. When she's finished working on the front of my legs, she huffs and says, "Turn on your stomach." It takes me a moment, but I get on my stomach and she attacks the back of my legs with a lot of force.

"Hey," I finally say when she digs the palms of her hands into my calf.

"Remember you're always welcome to find one of the plenty of other physiotherapists in Mulberry Point," she swipes back with sass.

"Do you have any idea how annoying you are?"

"Do you have any idea how many people actually appreciate what I do for them?"

"Name one...your mama?" I say. She slaps the back of my leg. "Hey!" I protest as I crane my head to look at her. "What's your problem?"

"My parents died, you inconsiderate dick. Now shut up and let me work on you so I can get out of here before I give in to my impulses and kill you."

Shit. I didn't know. I lower my head and close my eyes, deciding to not say anything about the immense pain she's more than likely purposely inflicting on me. I should apologize. It's the right thing to do. I'm such an idiot. "I'm sorry, Serena."

She doesn't reply at first. Instead, I know she accepts my apology because her actions become a bit gentler. When she's finished with my legs, she steps away. "When you're ready, get yourself back in your wheelchair," she says. "Have you got weights here?"

"My brother does. Ask Mom."

Serena walks out of the room, and I feel like a complete dick when I see how sad she looks. She comes back in carrying two dumbbells and hands them to me. "You need to keep your upper arm strength up. Start today with three sets of ten repetitions."

"I can do more than that," I say.

She closes her eyes for a moment, takes in a sharp breath, holds it, and lets it out. "Start today with three sets of ten repetitions. Tomorrow move it up to three sets of fifteen repetitions. Keep increasing the reps by five every day."

She sits on the side of the bed, and waits for me to do what she's asked. She blankly watches as I do the first set. "Serena, I'm sorry about what I said." She gives me a tight smile and a small nod. She's still hurting and I feel like a complete dick for saying what I did. "Can we talk about it?"

"You're doing good. I'll be back tomorrow to bring you crutches, so we can get you more mobile. I worked on your leg muscles quite a bit, so you'll be sore tonight. But tomorrow, we'll start on more lower body strength exercises to keep you as toned as possible so you can return to work quicker." She doesn't even make eye contact with me.

"Serena," I say as she picks up her bag. "Please." I feel like I'm begging.

I finish with the reps, and she comes over to take the weights from me. "I'll see you tomorrow," her voice is dull and flat.

"Serena," I call as she walks out. No use in trying. She's in no hurry to return. I hear her and Mom briefly talking, although I can't exactly make out what they're saying. The front door closes moments later, and Mom comes into the room. I look at her, waiting for her to say something. "I can explain."

Mom narrows her eyes at me. "What did you do, Alec?" She places a hand to her hip.

Serena didn't say anything to her. I just dug my own grave with Mom. "We were..." I point toward the door. "She was..." I throw my hands up. "I said something stupid."

"If it's about her weight, so help me God, Alec..."

"No, it wasn't about her weight. We were saying stupid shit to each other and I said something about her mom, and she told me her parents are dead."

Mom smacks the palm of her hand to her forehead. "You're really good at pissing people off lately, aren't you?"

"I don't know what it is about her. She gets under my skin and claws her way into my head. She's so damned annoying, and she doesn't just do her work. There's always a side of sass, and...and...and..."

Mom smirks and gives me a nod. "Oh. I see." She scoffs and heads out of the room.

"What do you see?" I call after her.

"You're such a blind idiot."

"What? I'm not blind. What?" I yell a little louder, frustrated that Mom's talking in riddles.

She pops her head back into the room. "You like her," she says with certainty.

"No, I don't."

"You do. But your head is up your ass, and of course you're too self-centered to see it. Maybe when you grow up you'll see how perfect she is for you."

I want to say something, but everything I'm thinking in my head makes me sound like *I* am self-centered, and my head *is* up my ass. Instead, I turn and look out the window trying to ignore Mom and her stupid words of wisdom. *Wisdom, my ass.* More like clueless words because she has no idea what she's talking about.

"Yeah, I thought so." Mom walks away, and I'm left thinking about Serena and what I said to her. Well, I'm an ass for saying what I did about her mom, that's for sure. But as far as liking her, no way. She's so not my type. Not at all. Not only is she chubby, but she's super sensitive too. It's not my problem that she takes everything to heart. Not my problem at all. She needs to grow some balls and deal with it.

Then why do I feel like shit?

Chapter 3

SERENA

DRIVING OUT TO May's, I can't help but think about what Alec said. I know he wasn't aware of how both my parents had died. I know that, and I know in my heart he didn't mean to be such a jerk about it. He tried to apologize, but he's been a rightful dick from the moment I met him.

What's his problem? Actually, what's his problem *with me?*

I pull up at May's and sit in my car for a moment. I have a list of clients I have to get to today, and I can't do that if I'm not focused. Luckily, the next three clients are back at the hospital, so I don't need to make any more house calls today.

I take my bag and my portable table out of the car, and head up the steps to knock on May's door. "May, it's Serena!"

"You waiting for an invitation?" she calls out, making me smile.

What I love about May is that what you see is what you get with her. There are no hidden agendas, no maliciousness. She's just May. Opening the door, I head down the short hallway, past the kitchen and find her sitting in the family room watching wrestling. "Never took you for a wrestling fan." I start setting the table up.

"Who isn't?" she asks. "Move, you're in my way." She flicks her hand for me to shift. "Yes! Smash him, smash him, smash him!" she yells at the TV, gesticulating widely. Shaking my head, I reach over and take the remote, turning the TV off. "Are you kidding me right now?" she asks in a shrill voice.

"Come on, up you get."

May narrows her eyes at me, but pushes up from the sofa, and with a slight struggle, gets up on the table. For a seventy-year-old woman, she's still fairly sprightly, though the stroke she had has slightly mellowed her. "What's wrong with you today, Serena?"

"Nothing, why?" Except for Alec. He bothers me. I don't know if I should go back there, but I desperately need the money. Jordan doesn't have health insurance, so it all falls to me. Which means I need to come up with the thirty-five thousand for his treatment.

She lays on her stomach, and I work on her lower back. I can feel the knots around her sciatic nerve, and when I start working it, she flinches. "Hey, you're a bit heavy handed today."

"I'm sorry," I say as I try to lighten my touch. But Alec's words about Mom play over and over in my head. "He's so inconsiderate," I mumble to myself.

"Who's inconsiderate?" May asks.

"No one." I keep working on her lower back.

"What's this *no one* done?"

"Nothing."

She cranes her neck and looks at me. "Right. You'd better talk to me, because whatever is eating at you is bothering you enough to have you hurting me."

I step back and sigh. "I'm sorry, May. I'm...I'm, you know, I'm sorry." I don't really want to talk about all the pressures that are suffocating me. I'm here to help May, not the other way around.

"Who is he?" she finally asks after I restart on her lower back. "And don't think you saying 'no one' will make me stop asking you questions. You may as well make this easy on yourself, and tell me. Either way, I'll find out."

I smirk, because even though I've been coming out here for about eight or nine months, I also know May is incredibly respected in the community, and if she wants to find out something, all she needs to do is ask. She's like Hope River's very own confessor. Everyone tells her everything. But funny enough, she never speaks about anyone else's business. A confessor who's also a vault. "I've just got some personal things happening," I reply.

"Personal as in with your partner?"

"I don't have a boyfriend."

"A girlfriend then? I'm very open-minded. Had my fair share of fun when I was younger, so no judgement from me."

My eyes widen with her declaration, but hey, good for her. "No, not into women. I haven't tried, but I don't find women sexually attractive."

"You don't have to explain yourself to me. We are who we are. Tell me about this boy causing you troubles."

"He's a client." I shrug, not really wanting to tell her, because I don't want to breach his privacy.

"That's a start. Do you like him?"

"No!" I reply with too much force.

"Then what's the problem?"

I'm not entirely sure what it is either. "He gets under my skin, and he's a jerk." May chuckles. "He said something that I'm struggling with."

"If he's a jerk, he'll always say something you'll struggle with."

"Doesn't help that we've kissed."

May tenses beneath my touch, and waves her hand for me to stop. "Oh no. Nope, we're not doing this while you're working on relaxing my lower back. Coffee time. Come on." She pulls her t-shirt down and hoists herself to sit up.

"I haven't finished, May. You should lay here for at least another twenty minutes."

"No, no, no, no." She waves her skinny finger at me. "We're talking about what happened, because something else is going on here."

"Please let me finish." God, I need the money and if I don't do this, then I'll have to try and pick up another shift at The Narrow Table.

Nimbly, she gets off the table and walks toward the kitchen. She's still got it together for an old chick. "Consider this May's Intervention. Hurry up, get out here. We don't have a lot of time before you have to leave."

I'll have to see if I can pick up a shift for Sunday night at the restaurant. I'll ask the manager tomorrow night when I go into work. I pack my folding table up then follow the aroma of one of the amazing coffees May makes. I sit at the kitchen counter, and watch as May flutters easily around the kitchen making our coffees. "Do you actually need me? Because even with that cane, you move around quite well. You could save yourself a lot of money by not seeing me anymore."

She places her hand to her chest and gasps. "I'm shocked you think I could get by without you." She carefully hands me a mug with coffee, then she brings hers over and sits beside me. "Tell me about this kiss."

"It was nothing." I shrug.

"If it was nothing, then you shouldn't have a problem telling me about it." May's gray hair is loosely pulled back in an old-fashioned bun on top of her head. Her inquisitive eyes stare at me, waiting for my reply. May might be seventy, but she doesn't dress like a woman her age. She often wears jeans, and brightly colored t-shirts. She's the perfect mixture of modern and sophisticated. But boy-oh-boy, she's one hell of an observant woman. "Well, what happened?" She picks her mug up and takes a sip.

"Honestly, I don't know. From the moment I met him, I felt something. But I didn't know what it was. He was angry at me being there, and I don't take too kindly to working with people who don't appreciate me. So, I told him he was acting like an entitled ass. We seemed to butt heads from the moment we met. He'd say something and I couldn't control myself. I'd come back with a harsh comment" I chuckle. "I still can't control myself. I give as good as I get."

"Well done." May claps her hands once. "But how did you end up kissing?"

"He was being a dick. I poked him in the shoulder, told him to snap out of it. The next thing I knew, he had his hand around my wrist, and..." I slowly shrug. "I don't know how, but we ended up kissing."

"You don't know how?" May rolls her eyes. "Pffft. When two people like each other," she starts.

"But we don't like each other."

"Oh, goody!" She claps her hands together. "An enemies-to-lovers kind of romance. Oh, this is going to be fun!"

"We're not *ever* going to be lovers, so you can stop clapping now." I sip on my coffee.

"Did you kiss today? Is that what's put you in an interesting mood?"

Interesting? "No, it was last Saturday. It was dumb, and it shouldn't have happened. Anyway, it doesn't matter, it won't happen again."

"Obviously, there's something there if you kissed." Her mood has become less joyful, and more serious as she drinks her coffee and waits for my reply.

"For a moment I lost my head. I was caught up in a dream of something that could never be." A smile strains to stretch my lips.

"So, you do like him, then? Because now I'm confused."

"Being with someone isn't in the cards for me, May."

"Let me ask you this. When was the last time you had sex?"

My face instantly reddens. "Jesus, that's pretty personal." My hands tremble as I lift my mug to take another sip of coffee.

"Okay, I'll go first. I got my dirty on very recently. Why do you think my lower back has been hurting me? I'm not the pretzel I used to be. It's more missionary, reverse cowgirl, me on top, you know. I can't be sticking my leg up over my head anymore, or I'll break a hip. Then I'd really need you." What a conversation to be having. And what an image to get in my head. "I've shared, now it's your turn." She taps her fingers on the counter, waiting.

"It's been a long time, May. Long, long time. I've got other priorities right now."

"How old are you?" she asks.

"Twenty-seven."

"Twenty-seven and you're not having sex at least six times a day?" *A day?* She blows out her breath and shakes her head. "Girl, you're missing out. Now look, if you don't want a serious boyfriend, you at least have to do yourself a favor and taste what's on the menu. You have no idea the immense stress relief you'll feel once you've reached orgasm. All the worries in the world disappear, even if it's only for a few moments. You deserve it, Serena."

"What you've described is only achievable for people who have only one job and a stable life." I stand, pick up my mug and finish off my coffee. "And I don't have any of that. For now, it's all about working, and keeping my brother al..." Crap, I've said too much. "Thanks for the coffee, May. I've gotta head back to the hospital because I've got more clients."

"I didn't know you had a brother. What's going on with him?"

I lift my foldable table and my bag and start walking toward the front door. "I've gotta go. This time next week, right?"

"You know it. But, if you ever want to drop around for a coffee, then you're more than welcome," she says as I walk across the porch and down the front steps.

I hope May doesn't bring this up again. I don't want to talk about Jordan and his addiction with anyone.

Rushing home, I have forty-five minutes to get changed and head back out to Willow Heights. The Bishops have asked me to clean their house once a week instead of once every two weeks. Thankfully, they're incredibly accommodating and know I have two other jobs, so they allow me to come in late because they don't get in from work until late themselves. When I pull up at home, the guys down the road are outside, and watch as I park my car and walk into my home. I can feel their eyes glued on me as I walk to my front door, unlock it, and get inside. They give me bad vibes. I don't know what it is about them, but something doesn't sit right in my stomach.

"Jordan?" I call, although I can tell by the darkness he's not home. I unlock my bedroom door, and look around, making sure nothing's been disturbed. I check the window, and it's still locked, although he wouldn't be able to get in here because there are bars on every window in this house. Looking at my phone, I know I'm already late. Problem is, I'm going to be home late, and I need to be up early tomorrow to get to the hospital for my appointments. "You're doing this for Jordan," I say to myself over and over again.

I change in record time and make sure to lock my room, and double-check it as I leave. My eye catches the mail I brought in, and I quickly go through them in case something of importance is in there. A letter with the property management company's logo catches my eye. I rip it open, and begin to read the letter.

Dear Miss Whitaker,

RE: Termination of lease.

Please be advised the owners of the home request you vacate the property within three weeks date of this letter.

Kind regards,
Sharon Talbot

I stumble backward until my knees find the sofa, and I collapse on it. "What?" I say as I rub my fingers across my forehead. All the air leaves my body as I burst into tears. I didn't move here because I liked it, I moved here because it was cheap and I could save more to send Jordan to a rehab center. I don't know what to do. I can't come up with the remainder of the money for the rehab center in three weeks, it's impossible. And now I have to find somewhere else to live which is sure to cost a lot more than what I'm paying here. I wipe my eyes with the back of my hand, and try to push that out of my mind for now. I need to get over to the Bishop's house and clean it.

I'm not sure I can deal with anything else. I'm already struggling to breathe with everything on top of me. I need a break.

Chapter 4

ALEC

"Look at you, getting around with crutches now." Rhett pulls out the chair from the table and plonks himself down. "How are you feeling?"

"I'll be better when I get back to work," I reply.

"He's a miserable bastard," Mom says from the kitchen.

Rhett smiles at Mom. "So, he's normal then?"

"I'll be kicking you out of my place the moment I can drive. Don't get too comfortable. And you better not be having sex in my bed."

"I don't want to hear this, boys." Mom brings over a coffee, and a packet of cookies, and sits at the dining table opposite Rhett. "Why are you here?" She intentionally stares at Rhett.

"Dean will be here soon too," he replies, but doesn't actually answer the question. "Can I have a cookie?" He reaches across the table, and Mom moves the packet away from him. "Come on, Mom. Just one."

"No. These are mine."

"You're not her favorite anymore, I am." I proudly turn to Mom. "May I have a cookie please?" I hold my hand out, knowing she's going to give me one.

"No." She moves the packet away from me too. "And I don't have a favorite anymore. I now like Dean's dog, Tripod, and Thomas. Those two are my favorites."

"My dog is your favorite?" Dean asks as he walks into only part of the banter. His eyes light up when he sees the cookies, and reaches for one. Mom smacks his hand away and hides the cookies under her arm. "I only want one."

"Not happening, buddy. These are mine, and mine alone." Rhett chuckles, and Dean rolls his eyes. "Why are you all here? Is it family dinner night? Because I don't recall inviting either of you two here." She points to Rhett, then Dean.

"I didn't know we need an invitation now, Mom." Rhett's smile says he knows she's not serious.

"We're actually here to take this loser out for dinner." Dean points to me.

"Aww, now I like you two again." Mom stands and gives Dean a hug, then walks around to give Rhett a hug.

"What about me?" I ask.

"You, son, are a grumpy pain in the ass. You're wallowing around here because you were hurt at work, and you're pissing me off."

Rhett snickers, and Dean looks up the ceiling. "And this is why we're here, to take him out for a while. Get his head back in the game, so he'll stop acting like he has been," Dean says. "Get ready."

Grabbing the crutches, I stand and head to my room. I've been going stir-crazy surrounded by these four walls. But Mom's right. I've been so frustrated with myself that I'm taking it out on everyone. "Where are we going?"

"A burger place over in Willow Heights," Rhett calls then continues talking with Mom and Dean.

The only thing I can wear is sweatpants or shorts because of the cast on my leg. But I get ready, and crutch my way out to the dining table where Dean and Rhett are already standing, waiting for me. "I'll drive," I joke.

"Yeah right." Dean huffs. "Can you get up in my truck or do you wanna go in Rhett's car?"

"Your truck should be fine."

"Bye, Mom." Dean gives her a kiss while she dunks one of her cookies into the coffee.

"Bye." Rhett gives her a kiss too.

"I'll be back later." I give her a kiss on the cheek, then follow my brothers out. Dean opens the door of his truck, and I heave myself up, carefully moving my leg in. Rhett jumps in the back.

"Bye, boys," Mom calls before closing the door to the house.

"How is it living back at Mom's?" Dean asks.

"I think I'm sending her crazy."

"Why?" Dean asks.

"I'm struggling big time. I keep going over the fire and what I did wrong, and I'm frustrated with myself that I got into this situation." I hit the top of my casted leg.

"We were in a fire, and the roof collapsed, sending the garage door crashing down on your foot. You're lucky it's only a broken ankle. Shit like this happens, Alec. You have to stop beating yourself up over it," Dean recaps the incident that's put me out of action.

"I've been doing this long enough to know when a ceiling is bowing, and when I hear the crackling, I know it's going to cave." I'm so damn frustrated with myself. This all could've been prevented if I listened, and I used my instincts.

"Let's get out, and have some dinner and a few drinks, and forget about it for tonight," Rhett says from the back seat.

I know they're trying to snap me out of this self-pitying mood of mine. But I feel like I keep digging myself further and further into a hole.

"How's it going with Serena?" Dean asks.

"I'm keeping my mouth shut, if that's what you're asking. She tells me what to do, and I do it. I know she's only here to help, and I've made it hard on her. So, now I just do what she says."

"Is she helping?"

"Yeah, she is. I take my frustrations out on her, because she's an easy target. But holy shit, she's a spitfire. She doesn't let me get away with anything."

"No more kissing?" Dean asks.

"Wait, what? You kissed her or she kissed you?" Rhett asks.

I thought he knew. "We kissed each other, and only once."

"If you like her, you should ask her out," Rhett advises, but he really has no idea what he's talking about.

"Oh no. How's this, Rhett? Alec doesn't like her because according to him, she's chubby and plain."

"Please tell me you didn't say that to her?"

"Nah, he said it to Ma, who ripped him a new asshole," Dean proudly tells Rhett. "It was so funny; you should've been there."

"Do you honestly care about what she weighs?" Rhett asks in a condescending tone.

"I'm over this," I say even more frustrated. "I didn't come out with you two so you can roast me for what I like in a woman."

"But what you like is superficial. I mean, wouldn't you rather have someone who's loyal, and funny, and only has eyes for you?" Dean asks.

"I know I would," Rhett answers.

I turn to look at Dean and feel like punching him in the arm, but decide not to, considering he's driving. "Joanne's hot, so you can't talk."

"Sometimes I have to remind myself that we're actually related," Rhett says from the backseat.

I flip him the bird. "What's happening at work?"

"Not much. Usual stuff." I turn to Rhett who's playing on his phone, but shrugging too. "You know, just stuff."

"Okay, we're here. Do you need help getting out?" Dean asks when he parks his truck as close to the restaurant as possible.

"I'll be fine." I manage to get out of the truck, and slowly make my way up to the entrance where Dean and Rhett are already waiting because they're faster than I am.

"God you're inconsiderate, Alec. Always holding us back," Rhett teases.

When I get over to them, I push past as Dean holds the door open for me. "See, I'm a perfect gentleman for my date."

Rhett laughs loudly, and I can't help but smirk. Who needs enemies when you have brothers like mine.

"Dani?" Rhett says in a surprisingly high pitch.

"Rhett?" She's just as shocked to see him as he is to see her. "What are you doing here?"

"I didn't know you work here too. I thought you worked over at Elle's Café in Hope River."

"I work both here and there. But what are you doing here?" She looks at me, and her eyes quickly move to my cast, and my crutches.

"Getting some burgers."

"You're eating in?" she asks, hesitantly.

"Yeah," Rhett replies. Why is Rhett's voice a different pitch to normal?

Dani keeps staring at Rhett for a moment too long, before quickly blinking and turning away. Wait, have these two hooked up? She reaches for three menus, and as she walks away, she peeks over her shoulder at Rhett. I straggle behind Dean and Rhett, but I certainly see the look she gives him. Dani seats us toward the back and closest to the kitchen, places the menus on the table then glances down as she nervously tucks some hair behind her ear. "Um," she says with a voice crack. I can't help but notice how Rhett can't take his eyes off of her. "Your server will be with you in a moment."

"Thanks, Dani." Rhett smiles widely.

She leaves, but looks over her shoulder and smiles. "Have you two hooked up?" I ask as I reach for a menu.

"Who?" Dean asks, completely oblivious to what just happened.

"What?" Rhett dismisses me with a flick of his hand. "Don't know what you're talking about." He drags the last menu over and focuses on that rather than answering my question.

It dawns on me quickly. "If you had sex with her in my bed, I'm gonna kill you. I told you already, no sex in my bed."

"But your kitchen table is okay?"

"I'm gonna kick your ass," I warn.

"What? With your one gimpy leg?"

"Hello, and welcome to The Narrow Table, I'm your... Are you shitting me?" I look up to see Serena standing in front of us, ready to take our order.

"What are you doing here?" I ask.

"I'm working, Alec." She looks over to Rhett and gives him a tight smile, then smiles at Dean. She softly shakes her head then pulls in a long, slow breath. "Welcome to The Narrow Table, I'm your server, Serena. Are you ready to order?" her voice quivers.

Dean looks up and smiles at Serena. "We all having burgers?" he asks, looking at the two of us. Both Rhett and I nod. "Can we have three burgers, and three sides of fries please. I'll have a water."

"Soda please," Rhett says.

She looks to me, waiting for my reply. "I'll have a soda too."

She taps away on the tablet, then reaches for the menus. She's worrying her bottom lip between her teeth, and refusing to look at me. She walks away without saying another word.

I find myself tapping my fingers on the table. "Why would she be working here?" I ask aloud.

"Who knows. Maybe she likes it," Dean answers.

"Or maybe she has to," Rhett says.

I look over at him, questioning. "What do you mean?" Rhett shrugs. "Physiotherapists earn pretty good money, don't they?" I ask.

"I don't know, but you'd assume so," Rhett says. "Who knows why she's working here. Maybe she's saving for something and this is the only way she can get what she wants. I don't know. You can always ask her."

"The fact she's working two jobs says a lot about the person she is. It's a very admirable trait," Dean says as he nods his head. "Good for her. Working hard for what she wants. At least you know she doesn't sit around expecting anything to be handed to her."

"How do you know that, Dean? So what, she has two jobs. A lot of people do," I say. But it does leave me questioning why she'd need to work two jobs considering I'm fairly certain physiotherapists earn a good salary. Tipping my head back and crossing my arms in front of my chest, I try to think of every possible reason why she'd have this job, too.

"Your drinks." Serena carries over a serving tray with the two sodas and a water. She places them in front of us and barely lifts her gaze. She's deliberately avoiding me. "I'll be back soon with your food." She can't get away from us quickly enough.

"Brother, what have you done to her?" Rhett asks.

"What? I haven't done anything."

"Except be a jerk to her. She's probably terrified you're going to start something here," Dean says.

"I wouldn't do that."

"From everything you and Mom have told us, you take enjoyment in making Serena's life miserable when she's with you," Rhett says and lifts his brows.

"Yeah, but that's when we're together, I wouldn't do anything to cause her to lose her job. I'm not *that* much of a jerk."

Suddenly, we hear someone drop something in the kitchen, then a male's voice yell something inaudible. Dean, Rhett, and I all look toward the kitchen. The three of us straighten our backs, and are prepared to go in there if something's happening. Less than a moment later, Serena leaves the kitchen holding two plates and balancing another two on her forearms. She catches me watching her, and I notice her eyes are red like she's been crying. "Something happened," I say, instantly trying to stand so I can get to Serena and see what's going on.

"Yeah, I noticed that too," Rhett says, his voice hard.

She walks back toward the kitchen, and I call her toward us. Serena's shoulders slump, and she quickly wipes at her eyes. Her face and neck are flushed and she's rubbing her lips together. "Everything okay in there?" I ask as I pointedly look over to the kitchen.

"Yep," her voice squeaks unusually high. "Your burgers shouldn't be too long." Serena gives us a strained smile, then walks back into the kitchen.

"Something's going on," I say. "And she's not saying anything."

"She might be having a bad day; you don't know. Leave it alone, Alec," Dean says.

Nah, I have to know why she's like this. Is it because I'm here? I don't want her to lose this job because of me. And I don't want to put her in a bad mood for the rest of her shift either. I'll talk to her when she comes back to the house. Now's not the time to talk to her. Not here, and not with my brothers hanging around and listening.

"So, when's the wedding?" Rhett asks Dean. For a split second, I thought he was talking to me.

"Don't know yet. Soon, I think."

"I'm your best man, right?" Rhett asks. "I'm the better looking one."

"Here we go. I knew this was going to happen," Dean says as he pinches the bridge of his nose.

"Hey, if you want the dork, then go for it. I'm not gonna stop you," I say as I point to Rhett.

"It might be easier to elope then have you two in the wedding party."

"Mom would kill you," Rhett says. "And I wouldn't even try to stop her."

"I know." Dean throws his head back and groans.

"Here are your burgers," Serena says placing three plates down in front of us. "I'll be back in a second." She walks away, still not looking at me, but quickly returns carrying three baskets with fries. "Would you like anything else?" she asks as she looks down at the table.

"I'm good, thank you," I reply and try to catch her gaze so I can smile. But she doesn't lift her head. She doesn't even wait for Dean and Rhett's reply. She just leaves.

"Man, something's going on," Dean says then shoves half the burger in his mouth in one go.

"Dude, slow down. No one's going to steal your food," Rhett teases.

"It's good," Dean replies while chewing, and shoving fries into his mouth.

"If you choke, I'm not saving you," Rhett says. "And he's gimpy, so he can't save you." Dean starts chuckling while chewing. "And she's irritated by him, so she ain't helping either." He points toward Serena, then me. "So, don't choke."

Dean chews his food, then swallows. "You're an ass."

I can't help but be worried about what's happening with Serena. Dean and Rhett talk and try to include me in their conversation. Luckily, I can reply with head nods, and *aha's* when needed. But my mind is on Serena for so many reasons. Why is she working here to begin with?

At the end of the meal, Dean sits back and rubs his stomach. "You have to lose that or it's gonna get bigger," I say.

"Says the guy who's grown a second ass," he snaps back. "And don't even pull the sympathy card on us. It won't work."

"Way to deflect." I catch Serena walking out the front of the restaurant. Where did she go? She didn't have her bag over her shoulder, which means she's not leaving. Is she okay? "You ready to go?" I ask.

"Your shout, right?" Rhett slaps his hand on my back.

"Hey, I'm the sick one here."

"Yeah, sick in the head." Dean leans over and pushes on my head.

I take my wallet out of my sweatpants, and open it. I throw three twenty-dollar bills on the table, and try to get out to the front so I can see where Serena is. Maybe I can talk to her to see if she's okay.

"Sixty bucks? For three burgers and three fires? Are you kidding me? What are you, made of money?" Dean says as we walk out the front of the restaurant.

I'm searching for her, but I can't move fast enough to see where she is. "I tip well," I say.

"No, you don't. You're an ass," Rhett says.

"Whatever." I catch sight of Serena at the side of the building. She's talking to a guy who's taller than her. She's looking up at him and shaking her head. Dean and Rhett head for Dean's truck, but I'm standing watching Serena's body language. She shakes her head again, then steps back. She buries her face in her hands, before throwing them into the air and poking the guy in the shoulder. The guy steps forward and raises his hand. Fuck no. Not on my watch. As fast as I can, I get over to her. "Serena," I call.

She looks over to me, and her eyes widen as she turns and places her hands on her head. "Great!"

"What's going on?" I ask as I get closer. Dean and Rhett reach Serena only a second before I do. I stand in front of Serena, creating a barrier between her and this guy. He's way too skinny, and he stinks. "Are you okay?" I ask without turning away from the guy.

"What are you doing here, Alec? Just go." She tries to push me out of the way.

"What? No. Who are you?" I confront the guy while Rhett and Dean stand in position to go after him if he tries anything on Serena or me.

"Who the fuck are you?" he spits as he looks me up and down.

Judging by his clothes, and the number of sores all over his face and arms, I'd say he's a junkie who was probably trying to shake Serena down. "I suggest you take off, buddy," I say in a low tone.

"Hey. I don't need your help." Serena stands in front of me and points. "He's my brother," she says with a clenched jaw.

I do a double take, trying to see the resemblance. But I can't. "Are you sure?" I ask dumbfounded.

"Jordan," she sighs as she blocks my line of sight from him. "If you wait five minutes, I'll go inside and get you some food."

"Nah, I'm not hungry, I just need some money for cigarettes." He notices my crutches and narrows his eyes at me, then he sees Dean and Rhett standing protectively near Serena. "Fuck it." He throws his hands up and turns to walk away. "Thanks for the help, sis," he splutters sarcastically before breaking into a run to take off.

Serena lowers her head and runs her hand through her hair.

"We'll be back at the car," Dean whispers. He gives Rhett a small whistle and flicks his head to the side. They both walk away, but keep turning back to make sure her brother doesn't return and try something.

"Why did you do that?" she says as she turns to face me.

"He was about to hit you."

"He wouldn't have hit me. He was frustrated that I wouldn't give him money."

"He raised his hand over his head. He was about to hit you," I say again.

"Whatever. Look, I need this job, I've gotta get back in." She walks away, and I struggle to keep up with her. "Can you go, please?"

"Serena."

She turns abruptly and holds her finger up at me. "You don't get to come here and lecture me about my brother. You have no idea about anything."

"Then tell me."

She screws her face up, and sighs. Serena then straightens and pulls her shoulders back. "I'll see you at your next appointment. I hope you all enjoyed your burgers this evening." She smiles, then pivots and walks back into the restaurant.

What the fuck just happened?

The moment I'm in Dean's truck, I sit back, close my eyes, and rub at the tension across my forehead. "Before either of you ask, no I had no idea she had a brother who's a junkie."

"Better find out what's going on there, Alec. Because her brother is only one hit away from becoming violent with her. And that shit doesn't fly with me," Dean says.

"Or me," Rhett echoes.

"Don't you worry, I'm gonna get to the bottom of this." I just have to figure out how to broach the subject so she doesn't clam up.

What the hell is going on?

Chapter 5

SERENA

OPENING MY EYES, I look up to the ceiling and sigh. I haven't seen Jordan since that day last week outside of The Narrow Table. A part of me is hoping he hasn't overdosed and isn't lying dead somewhere, but another part of me thinks that's exactly what's happened.

I've been at my wits' end, trying to keep calm every time my phone rings. But there's a sick feeling brewing in the pit of my gut dreading *that* knock on the door. And today's no different.

Except I need to get ready because I'm seeing Alec again. I know he's going to try and talk to me, just like he has in our other sessions. It's bad enough that now he knows I also work at The Narrow Table. Thankfully he doesn't know I clean three houses too.

I push the thin blanket off my bed, and get up. Unlocking my bedroom door, I head to the bathroom.

Once I'm showered, I look at the time, and know I have a spare twenty-five minutes before my first client of the day, which, incidentally, is Alec. I should look for somewhere to rent considering I have only weeks before I have to leave. But I also need to meditate to get my head in a good place.

I lock my bedroom door again, and sit on the floor. I flick through the mediations on my phone and find one to calm my mind. I like this particular meditation, it always makes me feel good once it's done, although it only plays for fifteen minutes.

When the fifteen minutes are over, I feel calmer and more prepared for the busy day ahead. I have back-to-back clients, then I need to head over to the Royces' to clean, before doing the late shift at The Narrow Table. Only to come home, and try to sleep, and start all over again tomorrow. But, tomorrow won't be so bad, because I don't have any houses to clean, and I think I'm only at the hospital with no house visits. *Yes.*

Opening the calendar on my phone, I double-check that I do have Alec first up, then back to the hospital once I've finished with him.

I lock my bedroom door, and when I leave the house, I triple-check that the front door is bolted. Getting into my car, I notice the creepy guys aren't outside yet. It's too early for them. They were up until all hours last night with their music blaring.

I'm surprised to reach Alec's in reasonably good time this morning. Getting out of the car, I roll my shoulders and stretch before I grab my bag and head inside. I know Alec's going to ask me questions about Jordan, but I don't want to talk to him about it.

Reaching the front door, I take deep breath before I knock.

Alec's mom, Elise, opens the door with a large smile, holding a mug of coffee. Damn it, I didn't have breakfast and now my stomach rumbles when I see her with her mug. "You're bright and early today, Serena."

"Yes, I am. I've got a full day."

She steps aside, and I head inside toward the back. "Is he awake?"

"He's been awake for a while. He gets his cast off soon, and he's looking forward to it."

"I do have that written down. It means I'll increase my visits to twice a week."

"Come three times a week if it means I can get back to work quicker," Alec says as he smiles toward me. His smile makes my stomach twist, but I know he's only being nice because he saw me that night with my brother.

"Well, let's get you back to work as fast as possible," I say and give him a small nod. Alec's use of the crutches is now quite proficient. He easily moves around furniture, and is quite nimble. "Let's work on your lower body today. I haven't done a lot with your lower back, and I think once you get back to work, you're going to feel it. How heavy are those hoses?"

"They're heavy. Just the small ones can be forty-odd pounds."

"You've been in a cast for what, four or five weeks now, right?" He nods. "You would've lost muscle mass in that time. Not from your arms, because I can see you've been doing the exercises I've given you and keep up with the dumbbells." For a moment, I forget how much of a jerk he can be, and I take in the absolutely beautiful muscularity, his arms bulky and defined.

"Are you okay there?" Alec asks snapping me out of my perving on his strong, beautiful arms. God, *stop looking, Serena.* He's going to think I'm greedily drinking him in. I so am, but I don't want him to know.

"Yeah!" I say in a pitch that's way too high and obvious.

A small smile tugs at his lips and his eyes stay stuck on me. Oh crap, this is awkward. Why did I have to look at his arms? Why can't I come in here, do my job, and leave? I've successfully done it most other times, unless you count that time we ended up kissing. But that hasn't happened again, *thank God.*

"Want me on the bed?"

And naked.

Wait, stop. *No, no, and no.*

"Sure." There goes that stupid high pitch again.

Oh, my God. What's wrong with me? I know. I need to get laid, it feels like it's been forever. I'm probably a virgin again. *He's not your type, Serena.* He's arrogant, and cocky, and I bet he likes women who are all perfect and stuff. I could never be like them. I don't even *want* to be like them.

"Are you done?" Alec asks.

"What?"

"You're having a whole silent conversation with yourself, and I'm not sure whether you've finished or not. I didn't want to interrupt your staff meeting." I narrow my eyes at him. Alec chuckles. He lowers his sweatpants to the top of the curve of his lower back. "Is this good?"

"You have no idea," I whisper to myself. His ass is F.I.N.E.

"Is it now? Thank you."

"What?" Wait, did I say that out loud? No, I didn't…did I? I squirt some lotion onto my hands and start massaging his lower back trying to loosen the tense muscles.

"You said my ass is fine."

"No, I didn't."

"Yeah, you did. It's okay if you did. I don't mind."

"Of course, you wouldn't, because you're arrogant." I use the heel of my palm to go in deeper. He doesn't wince. Damn it!

"I'm not arrogant."

"Yeah, you are."

"No, I'm not," he protests.

"If you say so." He turns to look at me while I'm working on his lower back. "What?" I ask trying really hard not to keep staring at the tops of his pert ass cheeks.

"You think I'm arrogant?"

"Do you want the truth or a lie? I'm fine with whichever you want to hear." I stop for a second to squirt more lotion on my hand.

"I'm not arrogant."

"Okay." *Yeah, he is.*

"I'm not." I roll my eyes and slightly shake my head. "I'll prove it to you, ask me anything."

"I don't have to ask you anything, Alec. You've been overbearing, and you've shown me an attitude of superiority. I bet you haven't ever complimented a woman for anything beyond her looks."

I'm met with silence. Finally, he starts making a sound that loosely resembles an answer. "I..."

I leave it for a moment, waiting for him to form some type of coherent sentence. And when he doesn't, I say the only thing I know is true. "So, I'll add shallow to arrogant."

"I'm not arrogant," he says again.

"You're admitting to being shallow. Good for you. They say the first step to recovery is admitting you have a problem."

"Hey, you're judging me for liking women who look a certain way. I bet you like your men to look a certain way too."

"I don't choose looks over substance. Unlike you."

"You're quite judgmental for someone who thinks I'm arrogant." I press harder into his lower back, and he flinches beneath my touch. "You don't like being called judgmental?"

"You know nothing about me, Alec."

"I know you have a brother who's a drug addict."

I stop working on him, and squat down beside him so he can see my face. "You saw a glimpse of something and you think you know me." I scoff as I stand. "You have no idea."

"I've been trying to talk to you about it, but you're so closed off that you refuse to give me anything." He pushes up from the bed, and swings his legs onto the floor, his casted leg sticking out further than his other leg. "Give me something so I *can* understand."

"Why? So you can sit there and laugh at me, or judge me, or try to fix me? I don't need any of that, especially from you."

"I won't laugh at you, or judge you, or try to fix you."

"Then why is it important for you to know what's going on with my life. Why do you care? We've established that this," I stop talking and gesture around my body. "Is not what you like because we both know I'm not your type. We have no other relationship outside of me being here to help you get back to work. Again, tell me, why it's important for you to know anything about me?"

He stares at me blankly for a moment. "You think I find you unattractive?"

"Your exact words were: *you're judging me for liking women who look a certain way*. I don't fit your mold, Alec; I break it. I've got hips, and thighs, and boobs. I can almost guarantee, the women you find attractive don't look anything like me." He narrows his eyes, and drops his gaze for a moment. "Yeah, I thought so." I walk over to pick up my bag so I can get out of here before I burst into tears. It's hard enough not knowing where Jordan is, but I also have to be in a room with a man I can't take my eyes off of, who finds me ugly.

"Where are you going? We're not finished yet."

I swing around to look at him, and lift my finger before lowering it and stepping backward. Tears are brimming my eyes, and my breath is caught in my throat. "Yeah, we are."

I turn again, and head straight to the door. I reach for the handle, but Alec's strong arm slams the door shut from behind me. He pins me against the door with his body, his erection pressing into my lower back. "You send me fucking crazy, Serena. I can't think of anything but you." His mouth sucks on my earlobe before he pulls it with his teeth and nibbles.

Closing my eyes, I steady myself against the door. "We're not suited, Alec. I'm not what you want."

"But you're what I fucking need. I breathe you, Serena." He snakes his hand around to my stomach, and pulls me back into him. "Tell me you want me too," he whispers then peppers hard, fast kisses down the column of my neck. I tilt my head, giving him access and allowing him to kiss the tingling, heated skin down my neck. "Tell me."

"I..." I'm lost for words. He's an enigmatic force and he makes my head spin every time he's near. He thrusts into my butt as he slips his hand under my t-shirt and into the cup of my bra. I groan when he teasingly pinches, and tugs on my erect nipple. "Alec, please," I beg.

"I need you to tell me you want me as much as I want you." He pinches my nipple again, and I angle my body closer to his.

There's a strong flutter in my belly, and an even stronger sensation of desire between my legs. "Stop," I say in a small voice. Alec pulls his hand out of my bra, and steps back. Leaning my forehead on the door, I steady myself and take a few deep breaths. I can't allow myself to have feelings for him. It's not healthy or professional. Straightening my shoulders, I lift my chin up, but refuse to turn to look at him. "I'll see you in a few days."

"Serena, don't go," he demands as he closes me in against the door again.

If I don't get out of here now, I know I'll end up sleeping with him. I turn to look him in the eyes. His look is hungry as his gaze fixates on my lips. He brings his hand to my face, and gently he skims the back of his fingers across my cheek before running the pad of his thumb over my bottom lip. My stomach is in knots, and my breath is heaving rapidly. "We can't," I say trying to form an argument.

"Because you don't want me?" He trails his finger down the front of my throat. God, I love his possessive touch.

"Because you're my client."

"I don't care."

He moves his face closer to me, and licks my bottom lip with a hard, controlled stroke. I squeeze my legs together, trying to create friction where I'm desperate to be touched. "Please, I can't do this," I beg while shivers take over my body.

He steps away with both hands in the air. Closing my eyes, I let out a deep breath. "Look at me," he says with a low measured tone.

Opening my eyes, I find myself teary. "My life is anything but easy, and right now, I'm barely keeping it together." My smile wavers as I press my lips together. There's no pros or cons to whatever it is that's happening between us. "I simply can't do this."

"Let me in, Serena. Talk to me. Let me help you, let me take some pressure off."

I let out a humorless chuckle and softly shake my head. "Having sex with you will only destroy me, Alec."

"What? Why?"

"Because I'm the type of woman who'd give her soul for the right man. And you're the type of man, who wouldn't give a shit about my soul if it wasn't packaged in a size zero dress. And I ain't a size zero; more like a twelve." It's right at this moment, that his eyes take in my body from the neck all the way down to my feet. "Yeah," I say. "I thought so." Turning, I walk out of his room with tears in my eyes, and my breath caught in my throat. I hate that judgmental stare he gave me. I'll never be anything other than what I am, and I refuse to be fat-shamed by someone so shallow.

"Serena, are you okay?" Elise asks as I walk past her in the dining room.

I try to plaster a fake smile on my face, but I think the tears falling have given me away. "Yes, I'm done. I'll see you next time." I don't hang around for her to say anything. Instead, I rush out to my car and get the hell out of here.

Driving to the hospital where I work, I park on the street and lower my head to the steering wheel, just bursting into tears. My life at the moment is made up of stress, anguish, and uncertainty. My meditations are only masking the real problems.

Soon I'll be out of the cheap housing I've been living in, trying to save everything I can. Jordan has disappeared, and all I know is that he may be dead somewhere. The man I've been trying to help get back to work has somehow managed to crawl his way under my skin and stay there. And I don't have a minute to think about any of this, because I'm working my ass off to get my brother into rehab. Not to mention, I'm *so* fucking tired.

There's a knock on my window, and I startle. Looking up, I see Alec's brother Dean standing beside my car. I wipe my eyes before getting out of my car. "Hi," I say as I look around suspiciously.

"I thought it was you, Serena. How are you?" he asks.

Tired. Frustrated. Terrified. "I'm well, thank you." I look around again. "Are you okay?" I point toward the hospital.

"Ah, yeah. Just some routine stuff."

"Oh, right." I smile, but this is turning awkward quite fast. "I just came from your brother's," I say trying to muster some type of conversation to get rid of the weirdness.

"I'm sorry about him. He was dropped on his head as a child." I laugh out loud. "By me. Although, technically that would be difficult because he's only ten months younger than me."

"Ten months?" Wow, really?

Dean rolls his eyes. "Yeah, yeah, I know. He looks closer to Rhett's age than mine. It's a running joke in the family. But, yes." Dean's lightened my mood. "You know," he says. "Alec's been so frustrated with himself since he got hurt. He thought the garage door falling on his leg was his fault, something that he could have avoided. But it wasn't. And since then, he's been a moody bastard." So he's not always such a dick? "He blames himself."

And he's taking it out on me. "Thank you, it's helpful to know he's not always like he is now."

"He's a perfectionist, and he..." Dean looks around before continuing. "He has a..." he pauses again. "He...he's a good guy, Serena." Is he trying to set us up?

"I'll keep that in mind for the next time he's an asshole toward me."

Dean winces and lowers his gaze for a second. "Okay." He steps back further. "I'll let you go."

"Yeah, thank you." Dean walks away, but it's left me questioning so much. I know Alec and Dean are brothers, but why would he tell me what he did? There's a sick feeling in the pit of my stomach. I have to push Alec out of my mind, because right now, I need to get Jordan the help he needs. And the only way I can do that, is by making the thirty-five thousand I need to send him to that rehab center.

Everything else can wait.

Including Alec.

Who am I kidding though? We'd never work, even if I wanted us to. I'm not his type. Period. Done. Finished.

Chapter 6

ALEC

"LOOK AT YOU go!" Rhett says as I walk into Mom's without the cast. "What did the doctor say?"

"Obviously, I'm still on crutches, and I have to up my physio, but I already knew that. And I need to be reviewed in another two weeks to see if I can return to work."

"Yes!" Rhett holds his hand up so I can give him a high five.

"Oh, and you'll be moving out of my place and back in here. Because I'm going home."

"But you can't drive yet," Rhett replies with a hint of worry to his voice.

"What have you done?"

"Nothing. I swear. It's just that I like being out on my own. These last few weeks of being at your place, have really shown me that."

"Then move out of here. Mom probably wants her own peace and quiet."

Rhett screws his nose up. "You know Mom won't cope."

"What won't I cope with?" Mom asks as she arrives into the conversation at the most awkward of moments.

"Nothing," Rhett quickly replies and widens his eyes warning me not to say anything.

Mom looks to me to fill her in. "I don't know." I shrug. "I barely ever listen when Rhett's talking." I take a side glance over at him. "Shit, I didn't even realize you were here."

He smirks triumphantly that I've kept my mouth shut. "Anyway. Get on the phone to your brother and tell him family dinner here tonight," Mom says to Rhett.

"Actually, I can't make it. I've got something I have to do. And Dean and I are working tomorrow, so I doubt Dean, Thomas, and Joanne will be able to make it."

"Ah, okay. Well, what time is Serena coming over today?" Mom asks without even looking at me.

"She said I'll be her last client for the day." I'm hoping tonight we can get everything out into the open. She's avoided talking to me when she's been here, and I hate how cold she is toward me. Something's eating away at her, and all I want is for her to open up and tell me what it is. I suspect it has something to do with her brother.

And maybe the fact I had her up against the door with my hands all over her. I swear I can still smell the sweet scent of her floral shampoo.

"Good, maybe she'll want to stay for dinner then. Text her, Alec."

"What?" I ask. "You want her to stay for dinner?"

"She seems like such a nice young woman." *You have no idea.* "And I'd like to get to know her better." *Me too.*

"Sounds like Mom's already matching you two up." I shoot Rhett a *shut the hell up* glare. He chuckles to himself, then continues looking down at his phone. "Anyway, I'm out of here.

See ya, Mom." He stands, walks over to Mom who's in the kitchen making herself a coffee, and gives her a kiss on the cheek. "Loser." He flicks his chin at me.

I stick my middle finger up at him as he laughs again before leaving. Mom brings her coffee over and places it on the table, pulls her chair out, and sits. "I like Serena." Oh, here goes.

"Do you?"

"Yep. And I know you like her too."

Mom's like this super sleuth. Are all moms like this? No use in denying it. "I do like her, but I have a feeling she has a lot going on in her life, and she doesn't want anything else."

"Have you slept with her?" Mom lifts her coffee and takes a sip.

"No," I answer honestly.

"But you want to."

"You have no idea," I say before even thinking of a Mom-appropriate reply.

"Really?" She turns to look at me, her eyebrows high and a smile pulling up on the corners of her mouth. "Your father and I didn't have three boys without us being hot for each other."

"Oh, come on, Mom. Do I really need to hear about your and Dad's sex life?" Not a mental image I want to envision.

"Don't be a prude." She smacks me on my upper arm. "You can't tell me you're a damn virgin."

"No, I'm not. But talking about my sex life with my mother is kinda awkward."

She rolls her eyes and sighs. "I'm not asking about your sex life. I'm asking if you find Serena attractive and want to pursue some kind of relationship with her, or, if she's just another notch. Because I don't take Serena to be a 'notch' kind of young lady."

"Do you know she has another job? She waits on tables."

"I swear, I'm gonna slap you stupid if you're looking down your nose at her for waiting on tables."

"God no, no. No. That's not what I mean." I get up, and head over to the kitchen to grab a bottle of water from the fridge. "I mean, she's obviously accomplished and intelligent. But why would she be working at a restaurant, earning minimum wage when I thought physiotherapists earned good money?" I know it must have something to do with her brother.

"Maybe she needs the money, and she's doing everything she can to get it. If anything, you have to respect her more for working two jobs.'

I hobble over, and place the bottle of water on the table. "She's pushing me away."

"How?"

I sit again, and blow out a breath in frustration. "I'm trying to get close to her, and I know something's stopping her." Mom tilts her head to the side. "I kissed her again." Her brows rise. "Well, I nearly kissed her." Mom nods slowly. "It happened last week." Mom puffs her cheeks and blows out. "I know," I say as I tap my fingers to my temple trying to think how I'm going to get Serena to open up to me. "My head feels like it's going to explode."

"Have you tried talking to her?" I glare at Mom. "Okay, what..." she interrupts herself as she frowns. Mom lifts her finger, then brings it to her chin to tap. "Clearly something's going on with her. What else has she said?"

"She hasn't said anything. But, remember when Dean, Rhett, and I went out a couple of weeks ago?" Mom nods. "That was where we found out she also waits on tables. She looked like she was going to cry when she saw me. But, as we were leaving, we saw her talking to this tall, gangly looking guy, who went to hit her, and we all intervened. It turns out, it's her brother. He's an addict." I take in a deep breath. "It honestly looked like he was going to hit her, and when we stepped in, she wasn't happy that we did."

"Ah," Mom says as if she's figured the riddle of Serena. "She's working two jobs, and her brother's an addict. Maybe she's trying to get him clean somehow. Rehabilitation clinics aren't cheap."

"Wouldn't her insurance pay for it though?"

"If he has insurance. If he's an adult, he probably isn't covered by her insurance, and if he's a junkie, he likely isn't working a job that would give him insurance." I run my hand through my hair, trying to make sense of it all. "That girl is probably killing herself to get her brother help. And don't forget, drug addicts are controlled by their drug, not by logic or reason."

"She could talk to me though, tell me what's going on."

"Because you've been so accommodating to her, and shown her you're someone compassionate who she can trust?" Mom snidely snaps. I don't respond, because I know I haven't been a gentleman to her at all. "I take it by your silence you know you've been a dick." I look away, refusing to meet her harsh gaze. "So, what are you going to do about it, Alec? If you want to win her heart, you have to find a way for you two to connect. And if you only want her for a bit of fun, don't bother even trying to get to know her. Because she's not the one for you."

I hate when Mom's right. But I hate myself for treating Serena so poorly to begin with. I take my phone out of my pocket, and dial Serena's number. "Hello, Alec," she says in a clipped tone.

"Hey. I got my cast off," I say.

"Yes, I know. I'll be over at about six." There's a slight awkward pause. "Is that all?"

"I was wondering if you'd care to stay for dinner tonight? Considering I'm your last man, I mean client, ah, um..." Shit, I didn't think this through before calling. "I'd like for you to stay for dinner tonight." There's silence. I quickly look at the phone in case the line has dropped out. "Hello?"

"Um," she mumbles.

"Please?" I say too forcefully. This is now uncomfortable and weird. Mom hits me on the arm and when I look at her, she's glaring at me with a tight jaw and wide eyes. "Would you like to have dinner with me tonight, Serena?" I flick Mom's hand away, then turn so I can't see her scowl burning holes into my head.

"With just you?"

"No, Mom will be here too."

"I like your mom," she says.

"I'm not telling her that, her ego's big enough as it is." Mom hits me again, and when I catch a glimpse of her, she's still glaring at me.

"Thank you, I'd love to stay. But I have to be up early tomorrow, so I need to leave by nine."

"Okay, I'll see you in a few hours." I hang up and find Mom's now smiling and looking all cocky. "What?"

"You're welcome." She pushes the chair out, and walks into the kitchen. She opens the fridge door and yells over at me. "I have ground beef, turkey, American cheese, tomatoes, carrots, potatoes, chicken, pumpkin. What are you making?"

"I can barely stand!" I protest.

"I'll help, but I'm not doing it all on my own. What do you want to make?" she asks again.

"You said there's ground beef?" Mom nods. "I'll make my spaghetti and meatballs."

"Good choice, you do make a nice spaghetti and meatballs. Serena will love it, unless she's a vegetarian, or vegan, then she'll be watching us eat."

"Shit." I type out a quick message to Serena, now worried we'll be serving her something she doesn't eat.

Do you have any allergies, or are you a vegetarian, or vegan? Actually, it might be easier to tell me everything you don't eat.

I eagerly wait for her reply.

Not a vegetarian or vegan, and I have no allergies. Looking forward to dinner.

I smile widely. "What?" Mom asks.

"She's looking forward to dinner," I say.

"Huh. Look at that, treat her well and she's responsive," Mom mocks. "And I'm letting you know right now, if you're a jerk to her, I'll be kicking you under the table."

"Just kick my good leg, okay?"

"I want you out as soon as possible, so don't worry. I won't be aiming for your bad leg." She stops and evilly scratches at her chin. "Or will I?"

"I'll make the meatballs, then go take a shower."

Mom waves her hand in front of her face. "I was going to mention how you're a bit heavy on the nose, son."

"I am not." Am I? I lift my arm to sniff. Mom bursts into laughter. "Whatever," I murmur.

"You're going to be hurting tomorrow, but do the exercises I've given you, and that should help with the pain."

"You worked me over quite well today, Serena." I get up off the bed, and grab the crutches so I can head out to the dining room. Opening the door, Mom's already prepared the table, but there's only two place settings. "Aren't you staying?" I ask Serena. Truthfully, I'm disappointed I don't get to spend more time with her.

"I thought I was."

"Joanne called me and said she made extra dinner for me tonight. So, I'm heading over to their house. I won't be too long."

Mom says, grabbing her bag and slinging it over her shoulder. "What a shame I can't stay. Alec makes the best spaghetti and meatballs."

"You cook?" Serena turns to ask me.

"Yeah, of course."

"Growing up in a house with four males meant they had to learn how to cook, and clean, because I wasn't going to be a slave to any of them. Don't get me wrong, I'd look after my boys if something happens." She looks down at my leg. "Like this." She points to my foot. "But I refuse to be their maid. I taught them early on how to cook, do laundry, and clean. Anyway, I'm off to your brother's. I'll see you next time, Serena." She waves her hand over her shoulder as she heads out.

"Why do I feel like your mom did that on purpose?" Serena asks.

"Because she probably did." I take a breath and offer Serena an awkward smile. "Anyway, would you like a drink?"

"Let me get it. Fridge?"

"Yeah."

Serena walks into the kitchen, and double looks at something on the counter. "There's a bottle of wine here."

"My God. Can that woman be any more obvious."

"She's as subtle as a brick to the head." Serena chuckles, and I can't help but laugh too. "But, I'm driving, so no wine for me."

"There should be juice, water, or soda in the fridge."

She opens the door, and reaches in for something. "I'm good with water. You?"

"Water's fine." She walks over to bring the pitcher of water, and starts laughing again. I follow her line of sight and know exactly what she's laughing at. "Wine glasses. Oh, Mom. There are normal glasses in the cupboard beside the range."

"She's gone to all the effort to set up the table, let's just use these." She's so sweet. She sits beside me, and looks at the food.

"You really made this?" She looks at the serving bowl of spaghetti and meatballs.

"I did. My own secret recipe." I reach for the serving bowl, and put a good amount on her plate before I help myself.

"Why did you do that?"

"What did I do?" I ask as I grab the cheese, and offer it Serena.

"You put a serving on my bowl before you took your own."

Shit, did I? I've never done anything like that with any woman I've ever been with before. The only thing I can think of is that I want to please her. "I like making you happy, Serena."

She drops her gaze, and I notice her cheeks becoming pink. Bringing her hand up, she smooths her hair before her fingers trail across her throat. "Thank you," she replies with a slight crack of her voice. "Do you like being a firefighter?" She twirls some spaghetti around her fork, and lifts it to her lips.

Jesus, her lips. They're plump and succulent, and all I can do is stare at them while she chews. Wait, she asked me a question. I better answer it before she thinks I'm some kind of level five stalker, just sitting here staring at her beautiful kissable lips. "Love them. It! Love it," I quickly correct. *Stop looking at her lips, freak.* "This injury has screwed with my head though. I keep thinking if I looked up five seconds earlier, I would've noticed the bowing of the roof and I could've gotten out before it collapsed." I look over to her, and she's shoving more spaghetti in her mouth. My God, her damn mouth is so delicious. There's sauce on her bottom lip. I lean over and with the pad of my thumb, I clean it off and lick my thumb. She's staring at me. Why's she staring at me? Shit, I just did it again, didn't I? "I'm sorry." Right, no more looking at her lips.

"You didn't even realize you were doing it."

"Just so you don't think I'm some kind of perverted weirdo, I'm not going to look at your lips anymore tonight."

"It's my lips you like?"

"I like everything about you, but yes, ma'am, your lips are particularly delicious." I still refuse to look at her. Not because I'm embarrassed that I like her, but because I really want to kiss her.

"Delicious?" She laughs. "I've never had my mouth referred to as delicious."

"Then whoever you've been with was a fool."

"Ain't that the truth," she mutters under her breath. "Anyway, I don't want to talk about me or my past failures. What about you?"

I dare to look at her again, but make an effort *not* to look at her luscious lips. God, I want to kiss them. "Well," I start. "You were right."

"Of course I was." She cuts one of the meatballs in half with her fork, and pops it into her mouth. I think I have a fetish for her mouth. "About what, exactly?"

"I have only ever dated women who look a certain way."

She shoots me a surprised glance. "Really?"

"I have a type, and that type never works out."

"And why's that?"

"Because they don't challenge me. I get bored really fast, and move on. It's not their fault."

"No, it's yours," she toughly throws at me.

"A bit harsh, but yes. It is mine. Thing is, I've never really searched for substance. And the women I've gone out with, I think they only want a hot fireman."

"Now you're hot, are you?" She wipes her mouth with a paper napkin, smirking, and laughs loudly. "Wow, talk about conceited. Anything else you want to brag about?" she teases.

"If I'm being honest, I'm a damn good lover too."

"Should I ask one of the women you claim have no substance and only want a hot fireman?"

"You don't let anything go, do you?"

"If you say the words aloud, then it's all fair in love and war, Alec."

"Wait, is this love or war?" I point to her, then me, then back to her. Serena's cheeks redden and her cute pink tongue pops out as she licks her lips, which sends me fucking wild. I grip the seat of the chair, to stop myself from grabbing her. "You have no idea how badly I want to kiss you right now."

She sucks in a deep breath, and bites her bottom lip. There's an electric energy pulsing between us, but I don't want to give her a reason to run again. I'm going to wait until she kisses me. She leans close, and skims her fingers across the back of my hand. "Soon," she finally says before averting her gaze. I notice the happiness drains away rapidly. She straightens, and clears her throat. "All three of you are fire fighters?"

"Yeah. And Rhett's best friend, Penelope, she's in our crew too. And there's also Hugo, who's our newest recruit."

"Wait, Rhett, Penelope, and Dani all went to school together, right?"

"Yeah. Pen and Rhett have been inseparable pretty much since they were born. Pen's like a member of our family."

"She and Rhett aren't together?"

"God, no. They're like brother and sister. We tease them about it all the time, but both find it repulsive. You know what, if they ever did hook up, I think it would be strange seeing them all over each other." I shiver at the thought. "It would be like if Pen and I hooked up." I shake my head. "She's like my sister. No, thanks."

Serena laughs. "That's a hard no then."

"Yeah. Rhett and Pen are super tight. I mean, if either of them ever had a serious relationship, their partners would have to be strong and understanding. Those two are tighter than most families." I think now's a good time to broach the subject of her brother. "Is it just you and your brother?"

Serena's lips tighten as she nods. "Yeah. When my parents died, it was just me and Jordan. It's been only us ever since." She's become more rigid. This must be hard for her to open up. I'll have to be careful in what I ask.

"Tell me about Jordan." I opt for her to volunteer as much information as she wants as opposed to me asking her something that'll cause her to clam up.

"He's my younger brother. He's twenty-four, and as you know, he's gotten himself into a difficult situation."

"How are you coping with his *situation?*"

Her brows lift in surprise. "It's challenging on a good day, and soul-destroying on a bad day." Her eyes widen. "I can't believe I admitted that to you."

I reach for her hand, and place mine over hers, gently squeezing. "It's okay. You can tell me anything."

"I'm working three jobs so I can save enough to send him to rehab." Three jobs? Is she kidding?

"Three? When do you have time to yourself?"

She chuckles, though there's no joy behind the strained sound. "I meditate every day, and then I push on because if I don't, I won't be able to help him when he can't help himself. And before you say it, I know he's an adult and I shouldn't worry about him, but he's the only family I have."

"I wasn't going to say that at all. I think you're an incredible woman who's doing her absolute best." Her smile is strained, and her eyes are sorrowful with heartbreak. "Can I ask how much the rehab center is?"

"Thirty-five thousand. I've been saving everything I can, and I'm proud to say I now only need around fifteen and a half thousand more to send him."

"You've saved nearly twenty thousand dollars?" Holy shit, now that's impressive.

"Nearly, but soon, that's going to dwindle and I'll need to top it up. Which means, the more shifts I can pick up at the restaurant, and the more houses I can clean, the quicker I'll be able to get it back to that number."

"Wait, I'm confused. Why is it going to lower?" Is she okay? What can I do to help?

"It's a long story, but basically, I moved us to a crappy part of Faith Haven, because I thought the cheaper the house, the more I can save to send Jordan to rehab. But now, after two years and a bit, the property management company sent me a letter evicting us. I can afford for us to move somewhere nicer, but that means there's less money to go toward his rehab."

"I can give you the rest of the money."

"What? No! I don't want your money." She stands abruptly and moves away from me. "I don't want your money, Alec," she repeats.

"I'm sorry. I didn't mean to offend you, Serena." Shit, think quick. "What about a loan from the bank?"

"I've tried, but the most they'll lend me is ten thousand." She sits again. "I feel overwhelmed by it all. The thing that scares me most is that I'm afraid I'll be too late to save him." She buries her face into her hands, hiding away from me.

"Hey." I stand, balancing on one leg, and drag my chair next to hers. Wrapping my arms around her, I comfort her while she cries. "You're an amazing woman, Serena. What you're doing is remarkable."

"I'm not doing this to impress anyone, Alec. I'm doing this to save my brother."

"Then let me help you. I can loan you the rest of the money, and you can pay it back." She shakes her head. "What if I include interest?"

She keeps crying, but laughs at the same time. "Thank you, but no. I won't take your money. Jordan's not your responsibility. He's mine." She takes a deep breath. "Every time

I arrive at the hospital, I always check to see if he's in the morgue. I'm terrified that's where I'm going to find him one day."

"Then let me help you, before it's too late. I have the money; you won't be leaving me short."

I can see she's seriously considering it. But after a long moment, she shakes her head. "Thank you, but I simply can't."

She's got an unbreakable, white-knuckled grip on what she thinks she needs to do. I'll find a way to help her get Jordan into rehab. "So, tell me, what's your favorite color?" I ask as I gently rub my hands up and down her back.

"I love yellow, It's such a happy color. It's always been my favorite. What about you?" Serena wipes her eyes, and sits back breaking the amazing contact we were sharing. I want her back in my arms. She felt right, like she belonged there.

"Well, I am a firefighter," I say and give her a wink.

"Wow, talk about cringeworthy. Is that how you pick up women? You wink and tell them you're a firefighter?"

"In my defense, you have no idea how often that actually works." Now I feel like an idiot.

"I don't think I actually want to know." She seems a lot more at ease now. "And your favorite color?" she asks again.

"Before you say it's cheesy, I just want you to know that..." I slink my shoulders forward. "I know it is. My favorite color is red. Fire engine red to be specific." I close my eyes and rub at the center of my forehead. "Yeah, yeah, I know."

I hear nothing for a few seconds, then Serena starts laughing. I glimpse up at her, and she's holding her stomach with one hand, and wiping the tears with the other. I close my eyes again, slightly shaking my head. "At least you're consistent," she says.

"I'm moving away from the favorite color conversation now."

She finally stops laughing, and sits forward, crossing her arms on the table as she pushes her half-eaten bowl out of the way. "I must admit, tonight hasn't gone exactly how I thought it would. Thank you, Alec, I do appreciate everything. But I need to go. I've got a full day tomorrow. One of the houses I clean called me on the way over and asked me do an extra cleaning tomorrow. Which means I need to be gone by five in the morning, so I have time to get home, have a shower and get to the hospital."

She's working herself to the bone. "I need a house cleaner. Would you be able to clean my house?" She looks around and crinkles her forehead. "This is Mom's house." Shit, how much do I offer her? I don't want to pay her what everyone else is paying her, I want to pay her more. How much do cleaners earn? I have no idea. "I need the bathroom done. And the floors cleaned once a week. Say two hundred dollars?" Instantly I know I've given her an offensive number because she sinks lower into her seat.

"Sorry, Alec, I don't have time."

Why does she continue to block every offer of help I'm trying to give her? "Well, if you change your mind, I'd love the help around the house." She stands and picks up her bowl. "Please, just leave it. I'll do it." She lowers the bowl and smiles.

Serena walks over to the sofa and grabs her bag from where she left it. "Thank you for dinner, it was nice to have a home-cooked meal. I haven't had time in what feels like forever to eat anything other than something quick, or something from the restaurant."

"Can I cook for you tomorrow night too?"

"I can tell you right now, I'm going to be wiped out with everything I have going on tomorrow. But thank you for the offer, I'll grab something at the restaurant." She heads toward the door slowly, giving me enough time to grab my crutches, and follow her out. She opens the front door, before stopping and returning. She leans in and places a light kiss to my lips. "Thank you. For everything."

I want to grab her and kiss her like she's never been kissed in her life. I want her to lay beneath me while I lick my way all over her body, saving her lips until last. Tasting them while I push inside of her, and claim her as mine. Mine for now, mine forever. "You're welcome. Any time," I say while a vision of her naked below my body keeps teasing me with the promise of a perfect future.

In time, she'll become mine. And only mine. But for now, I need to figure out a way to give her the rest of the money she needs to save her brother, and stop working all these jobs.

I watch as she walks out to her car, unlocks it with the fob and gets in. I'm relieved to see her car is relatively new and not a heap of shit. Because there's no way I could stand by and have her driving around at all hours of the day and night in a car on the verge of breaking down. When she's a way down the street, I head back in to clean up and try to figure out this complication of her not wanting my money.

But I also need to figure out what exactly has happened between us. One moment she irritated the shit out of me, and the next, I fucking want her. And I want her bad.

Chapter 7

ALEC

"IT'S GOOD TO see you up and around. Are you here to help?" Pen asks as she sets up for the community cookout the station is putting on.

"As much as I can do considering I'm still on crutches."

"Then you're totally useless," she jokingly says.

"Hey, what are you doing here?" Dean asks when he sees me.

"Here to help." Dean eyes the crutches and shakes his head. "Can you man the grill?"

"Yeah, of course."

"Hey, Alec, you're getting around quite well," Joanne, Dean's fiancée, says as she comes over and gives me a kiss on the cheek.

"Not too long left on these things." I tap one of the crutches against the tar of the driveway. "I can't wait to be back here though." I glance over to the station.

"I bet. If you need anything, just call out and I'll help."

Joanne really is such a sweet woman. "Thank you," I say before she heads toward the storage shed to keep bringing out chairs. Dean places a table on its side, and swings out the legs to make it stand. "How you landed someone so nice still baffles me."

"I'm a nice guy," Dean says, trying to talk himself up.

I'll never admit it, but yeah, he is. "Is that how you fall asleep at night? Stroking your own ego?"

"Whatever."

"Why are you here?" I hear Rhett calling from behind.

"Thought I'd help."

"Doing what? It's not like you can walk around." Rhett looks at my leg. "How are you feeling?"

"I can't wait until I'm back here again, and I'm back in my own house. The moment I'm good, you're back at Mom's."

"Don't remind me."

"You should get your own place, Rhett," Dean says.

"Alec and I already had this conversation. I don't think Mom would cope without at least one of us there. You know she loves having us around."

"She might surprise you. Talk to her," I say.

Rhett half shrugs. "Anyway, it'll be good to have you back. Even if you're all gimpy and shit." A backhanded compliment. *So Rhett.*

"Let's get the grill fired up, because people will start showing up soon," Dean says.

"I'm on grill duty!" I proudly announce. Watching everyone working together is killing me. While I'd rather be more involved and mobile, I want to help, and I can work the grill.

The next two and a half hours fly by with a lot of the regulars turning up. Old Mr. Rickson shows up and sits at a table, talking with Joanne and her son, Thomas. People come and go, with most leaving a donation we can pass on to the shelter over in Faith Haven.

Whenever we put on community cookouts, homeless people always stop by, hoping to get fed. We've never turned anyone away. As I'm cooking the sausages and burgers, and handing them out, I see someone I instantly recognize.

Jesus, he looks like shit. "Hey," he says as he scratches at his arms while looking down at what I'm cooking.

"Hi." I've gotta try and have a conversation with him. "Jordan, right?"

He looks around suspiciously, his eyes darting everywhere. "Yeah, how did you know?"

He doesn't remember the day we saw him outside The Narrow Table, where he raised his hand to hit Serena. He doesn't recall how we intervened before he had a chance to strike. "I know your sister, Serena. She's a friend of mine." He turns back to look at me, narrowing his eyes with extreme paranoia and skepticism. "She's my physiotherapist," I quickly add.

He takes a breath, and nods. "Oh yeah." He relaxes, dropping his guard if only for a moment. He looks down at what I'm grilling and licks his lips. He looks like he hasn't eaten in a long time. He's even skinnier then when I saw him at the restaurant. "How much?" He gestures toward the food.

"You hungry?"

"A bit." He licks his lips again. Then shoves his hands into his dirty jacket pockets, then takes them out, and forces them back in again. Talk about fidgety. He lifts his right hand to scratch at his neck. He looks terrible. And he stinks. "Can I have one? I don't have any money."

I catch Rhett's attention and I discreetly signal for him to come over. He sees the back of Jordan, and walks up, creating a bit of barrier between us. "Hey, how's the leg?" Rhett asks as a cover up.

"It's starting to hurt. Do you think you can take over for a bit? My friend and I are gonna sit and have something to eat. Aren't we?" I look to Jordan who's jumpy and looking around.

"Yeah, yeah," Jordan says. "Whatever, man. Whatever."

I load a paper plate up with sausages and burgers, and while trying to balance them and use the crutches, I head over to two available seats. "Jordan," I call when I notice he's so uptight and he hasn't followed me.

"Yeah, yeah. Good, yeah." He gives Rhett a thumbs up, then comes over to sit beside me.

I have to breathe through my mouth, because the wretched odor coming off of him is going to make me gag. I move my seat back a bit, hoping the offensive smell will waft in the opposite direction. "Hey, would you like a drink?" Joanne offers happily.

"Couple of waters, please." I give Joanne a tight smile while silently messaging her to leave.

She catches on fast, and leaves to grab us two waters. From the small interaction Dean, Rhett, and I had with Jordan, I know he's capable of lashing out. The fact he's completely under the control of drugs, means he'll do anything for that next hit. Including fighting, stealing, and most likely selling himself. But I'm not here to judge, I'm here to try to figure out a way to help him.

I look over my shoulder, and notice both my brothers are close by, in case I need them. They give me an unnoticeable nod. No one else will know their eyes are on us, but I'll know. They've got my back.

I push the plate over to Jordan, who's eating like he's a starving man. "How you doing, Jordan?"

"Good, good." He shoves food into his mouth.

"Have you seen your sister?"

"Yeah, yesterday." I know this is a lie because she hasn't seen him for weeks.

"Yeah? How is she?"

"Good, good." He pushes more food into his mouth. "Do you have any money? She told me to get groceries, but I forgot my wallet at home. She'll pay you back." This is the drugs talking, not him.

"Nah, man. I'm out myself. I haven't been working." I point to the crutches and my foot.

"What happened?" I'm surprised, because this is the first glimpse of him being lucid and thoughtful.

"I'm a fireman, and while we were putting a fire out in a house, the roof buckled, and the garage door fell on my foot."

He looks back to the firehouse. "You're a fireman here?"

"I am. But I can't come back to work until my leg has properly healed."

His brows draw in together as he slows his chewing. "I wanted to be a paramedic before," he pauses as he stares down at the half-eaten plate of food. "But I don't think I can now."

"Why not? You don't want to do it anymore?" I'm being really careful in what I'm asking. I don't want to spook him, or send him off on a paranoid ramble.

He leans in closer to me, and I hold my breath so I can't breathe him in. "They're watching me."

There goes the moment of lucidity. "Who are?" I know his reply will be filled with incoherent ramblings of a drug addict.

He points up to the sky. "The government. They've been chasing me for a while, but I didn't do it."

"It's silly they'd think you did."

"That's right." Absentmindedly he starts scratching at his arms again. "They've put a location device in me, but I've got most of it out." He keeps scratching, the sores on his arms are vile.

All I can think of is poor Serena. "If you had the chance, would you become a paramedic?" I'm trying to force his mind toward something more positive.

He stares past me and zones out. Nope, he's done. There'll be no way he'll talk about anything that's not a conspiracy theory, his demented thoughts brought on by the drug abuse. How sad. Without another word, he nods as if he's been asked something, pushes his chair back, scoops up the remainder of the sausages and runs like he's being chased by the police.

I let out a long sigh, and shake my head. "What happened?" Dean asks as he drags out the chair Jordan was sitting on, looks at it and sees the brown stains. "Did he shit himself?"

"I think it's dirt more than shit. He stinks, though."

Dean tips the chair so no one can sit on it, goes over to the grill, grabs paper towels and antibacterial spray, and he wipes the seat down.

I look over to Rhett, and whistle to get his attention. He hands the tongs over to Penelope and comes to sit with Dean and me. "That was Serena's brother, right?"

"Yeah. He's in a bad state," I reply.

"What are you going to about it?" Dean asks. He clears his throat, looks to Rhett and says, "What are we going to do about it?"

"Serena is working three jobs trying to save enough money to send him to some rehab center that costs thirty-five K."

"Shit, that's a lot of money," Rhett says. "I've got about fifteen."

"I've got it all if you need it," Dean says.

"How's this, she's managed to save nearly twenty thousand by saving the expense of living somewhere decent."

"What do you mean?" Dean asks.

"She told me she's living in a shitty part of Faith Haven, not because she can't afford somewhere nicer, but because the rent is cheap and she can put more money into savings to help her brother."

"Nah, we can't let her do this. We'll give her the money," Rhett says.

"I offered it to her, and she shut me down. She won't take it."

"Brother, you're a smart person. Figure out a way to get it to her."

"I've been thinking about it. I'm going to find out which facility it is, and pay it. She'll lose her shit about it, but I can't have her working nearly eighteen-hour days just to get this money for her brother."

"What about a loan?" Dean asks.

"She said the most she can get from the bank is ten thousand. Oh, and she's being evicted too. She's damn proud though, and she won't accept my help."

Rhett stands and pushes the chair in. "Figure it out, and tell me how much you need. Pen's getting hammered, I'm going to go help." I hold my fist out, and he hits it with his own closed hand.

"Between the three of us, we can get that kid the help he needs without her having to kill herself working all those hours."

"I know." I scrub my hand over my chin, trying to figure this out.

"Is she yours?" Dean asks.

"Not yet, but she will be."

He stands and claps a hand to my shoulder. "Then she's family, and we don't let family drown."

"I know. But try telling *her* that."

"She of all people should know what we do for family. Look at what she's putting herself through for her brother, who has no idea of the pain he's causing."

Dean starts to walk away, but a thought pops into my mind. "Hey, Dean?" He returns and leans on the back of the chair he was sitting on. "Joanne was living out at Hope River wasn't she before she and Thomas moved in with you?"

"Yeah, and when their house is finished, we'll be moving into that, and I'll be renting my house out. But that won't be for another month or so. Do you wanna put Serena up at my place?"

That's a thought, or she could move in with me. But my house is even smaller than Dean's. "I'm thinking, where was Joanne living before she moved in with you?"

"May's house. Actually, it's a stable that was converted into an apartment. That could be a good fit for Serena. But, I have to say, I'm worried about the brother." He purposely looks toward the path Jordan took as he left. "I wouldn't put him there. Not with May. She's old, and frail, and I wouldn't put it past him not try to break into her house."

Closing my eyes, I rub my hand across my temple trying to figure all of this out. "If I can get him into this rehab place Serena wants him to go to, then we've got a fighting chance he'll come out clean."

"At thirty-five thousand, you'd hope it's more than a fighting chance." He claps my shoulder again. "Brother, I don't envy you at this stage. Just give me a figure and I'll have the money to you."

"Thanks."

He walks away, leaving me to think how the hell I'm going to swing this. Serena is too stubborn and proud to accept my help. And she'd be even more mortified if she knew I'd discussed this with my brothers. I somehow have to get Jordan into rehab, while trying to get Serena to see I'm doing this to help her.

I don't know what to do.

But, first things first. Pulling my phone out of my jeans pocket, I dial her number. "Hey," she answers nearly immediately.

"Hey. What are you doing?"

"Um, at the restaurant. I'm having a quick bite to eat before my shift starts. What are you doing?"

"I'm at the community cookout at the station."

"Oh, that's right. You told me about that the other day. I didn't even realize that was today. I was going to come help, but I'm slammed. I'm sorry, I can't make it. After my shift here, I need to get over to the Morrison's house to clean. I probably won't be home 'til late, and I have to keep packing too." I can hear it in her voice. She's frazzled and worried.

"Tomorrow you've got me, am I your last client for the night?"

"You are. And, when I'm finally home I'll either keep packing, or go to bed early. Yay me!"

"Well, can I throw a monkey wrench in the works for you?"

She sighs, and I feel she's overwhelmed through the phone. "Yeah, sure."

"Have dinner with me. The only catch is, you have to drive, because I can't do that yet."

She chuckles, which brings a huge smile to my face. "I've got a lot to do, Alec."

"I know, and I promise I won't keep you out for too long. Just a quick dinner. I'll have you home before curfew." She laughs again. "What do you say?"

"So, is this a date-date, or a 'let's eat because we both need food date'?"

"Um, I'm confused."

"Doesn't take much," she jokes.

"Hey!" I try to protest. "It's an '*I like you and want to take you out on a date-date*' type of date."

"Ah, so it's a date-date-date?"

"There are too many dates going on. Let me simplify this; I want us to go out and have dinner with you because I like you."

She laughs again. "Okay, I'd like that." Yes! I fist pump the air. "Crap, I have to go. I'll see you tomorrow."

"Bye."

"Bye," she says and hangs up.

Operation *Woo Serena* is in full force. Now, I need to enlist Mom's help with something else. I flick through my numbers and hit the green button to dial Mom's number.

"Yes, son," she says as she answers.

"I'm wondering if you can help me with something please?"

"Does it involve your brothers?"

"No, why?"

"Just wondering. Does it involve Serena?"

"Well, kinda, yeah. I need a chauffeur."

"What? Now? I only took you down to the firehouse an hour ago. I'm not picking you up yet."

"Not yet, later. But can you take me somewhere?"

"Where?"

"I need to go to the mall." There's silence on the other end of the phone. "Mom, are you still there?"

"The mall? As in the place where there's stores?"

"Yeah, why?"

"You hate going there." I nod in agreement. "And this is for Serena?"

"Yes!" I say again, with a touch of frustration.

"My boy is in love," she happily cheers.

I roll my eyes and shake my head. "I'm not in love. I just like her."

"My second favorite child is in love!" she cheers and claps her hands together.

"Hey? Second favorite? I should be your favorite."

"You're my equal second favorite, does that sound better?"

"Who am I equal with? It's Dean right? I'm equal with Dean?"

"You're equal with Dean and Rhett."

I scratch my head. "That means you don't have a first favorite. How does that work?"

"Because you all annoy the shit out of me from time to time. Anyway, you're in love with Serena. So, yes, of course, I'll take you to the mall. Are we buying her an engagement ring?"

"What? No! Mom, you're getting ahead of yourself!"

"Oh, so it's a promise ring. I'm fine with that too."

"What the hell is a promise ring?" I look around trying to find someone who can sympathize with me. Apparently, I'm on my own. Jesus, did Dean go through this when he and Joanne were seeing each other?

"It's fairly self-explanatory, son. You promise to marry her one day."

I hit my forehead with the palm of my hand. "Mom, listen, we're not anywhere near the stage of marriage yet."

"You said YET!" she screams the last word. "Oh, my baby! He's growing up into a real man. I'm so proud of you, Alec."

"This conversation isn't going where I want it to go. Can you take me to the mall when you come to pick me up? And no it's not for an engagement, wedding, or promise ring."

"Not yet it's not! Eeeek. I'm so happy for you. Serena is a perfect addition to our family."

"For God's sake, Mom."

"Alright, alright. Calm down before you give yourself a heart attack. Yes, I'll take you to the mall."

"Thank you." Whoa, that was like pulling teeth with no anesthetic.

"To purchase an engagement ring," she says so quickly I have to try and replay it in my head. "Bye, second-favorite son. I'll see you soon." She hangs up before I can say anything about the engagement ring saga.

I can't wait until I'm back into my house. Because I have a strong feeling, Mom's going to start preparing the wedding invitations soon. I let out a sigh, and tilt my head back, looking up at the sun as it slowly arches over the station.

Operation *Woo Serena* is moving forward like clockwork.

Chapter 8

SERENA

THE MOMENT I pull up in front of Alec's house and turn my car off, my phone starts ringing. I look at the number confused. My stomach contracts and I feel like I'm about to be sick. Is this the phone call I've been waiting for? "Hello?"

"Sis, have you changed the lock on the door?"

I clutch at my chest and let out a sigh of relief. "No, why?"

"Shit, my keys aren't fitting the lock." I hear the sound of the keys jingling in the background.

"Are you sure they're you're keys?" I ask the obvious.

There's a moment of silence, before Jordan yells in frustration. "Fuck, these ain't mine."

"Do you know where your keys might be?" I'm hoping that he didn't have our address on those keys, because if someone he's been hanging out with finds them, then I'm in a world of trouble.

"Yeah, I think so. Anyway, why aren't you home? I need you to come home right now," his voice is tense and urgent.

"Why? What's wrong? What do you need?" I'm completely prepared to go home and take Jordan straight to hospital to get him into a local rehab center until I can come up with the remainder of the money to get him into the one in Kentucky.

"I need some money." I close my eyes and lean my head against the glass. "I'm hungry."

I was really hoping he was going to say he wants out of his lifestyle and he needs help. But instead, he wants me to give him money. "Sorry, Jordan, but I won't be home for a while."

"Where the fuck are you, Serena? You whoring around somewhere?"

I purse my lips together, trying to hide the pain. Tears cling to my cheeks. I know this is the drugs talking and not my brother, but his words still hurt. "I'm working."

"I'll come to the restaurant then. I need money."

"I'm not at the restaurant, Jordan."

"You fucking slut, you're out having a good time, while you leave me starving and with no way to get inside the house. God, I fucking hate you." I hear him slam something. "Fuck you!" he hangs up, leaving me in a state of torment.

I drop the phone onto my lap, and rub the tension from the crown of my head. I was looking forward to going to dinner with Alec, but now, Jordan's completely ruined the small glimmer of happiness I was trying to hold on to. I should go home and try to smooth it over with Jordan.

A huge part of me wants to slap myself across the face and yell, 'Wake up, he only wants money for drugs.' But there's still that tiny part of me that needs to make sure he's okay. Because if I don't look after him when he can't look after himself, then who will? If not me, then who?

I'm conflicted about going home or staying here. But in reality, even if I do go home, and Jordan is still there, I'm not doing him any favors by giving him money to go feed his addiction. At least this way, by working, I can save and get him the help he desperately requires.

I know I'm stuck in my own head, and I need to get out of it before I fall into the rabbit hole of desperation. I lift my phone again, and find a quick five-minute guided meditation. Five minutes is better than no minutes.

Closing my eyes, I listen to the sound of my own breath, pushing any other thought out. Meditation is the only thing I have time to do for myself. And whenever I finish, I'm always calmer. When the meditation is complete, I open my eyes and find I'm ready to keep going with the rest of my evening. Including my non-date date with Alec.

I reach for my handbag and pull on it, only for the strap to break and the bag to fall onto the driver's seat. Thankfully, it's zipped up so nothing falls out of it. "It's okay, I need a new handbag anyway," I say to myself. Nothing is going to break my now peaceful mindset. *I will not implode. I will not implode.*

With my handbag wedged under my arm, and my phone and keys in the other hand, I walk up to Alec's Mom's house. Knocking on the door, I can hear the clacking of the crutches as Alec comes to open the front door. When he does, his face brightens as he smiles. "Hello," he says as he steps to the side to let me in. "Are you okay?" He quickly closes the door behind me and follows me to the back of the house.

"Yeah, why?" I ask as I turn to watch him slowly make his way toward me.

"You look like you've been crying, come here." He engulfs me in a massive hug. Holding me close to his body. I try to pull away, but he tightens his arms around me, and I'm surprised to find myself lifting my arms and wrapping them around him. "Is it Jordan?"

My body instantly melts, and I start crying again. The tears pour out of me and I'm sobbing into Alec's chest. He keeps holding me, refusing to let go, even just a little. "He called me," I say between the cries of Jordan's hurtful words. "He called me a whore."

"Aww, sweetheart." He kisses the top of my head while tenderly rubbing his hands up and down my back. "I admire just how strong you are."

"I feel like the weight of the world is on my shoulders, Alec. I'm trying so hard to move forward, but then something happens and I'm thrust back into a pile of shit."

"I know it's hard right now, but think of the end result. Jordan being clean."

I step back and wipe my eyes and cheeks with the back of my hand. I look around searching for a box of tissues. When I see them, I head over and take two out. When I glance over to Alec, his dark brown eyes are staring intently at me. "I'm sorry, I should've asked."

The left side of his lips pull up into a sexy smirk. "No, I like how comfortable you are with me." He hobbles over to the table, pulls out a chair, and sits. "Let me help you help your brother," he says.

"You offered the same thing only a week ago, and I refused it then," I say as I head into the kitchen and open the cupboard beneath the sink to find the trash. "I can't take your money, Alec."

"What if it's a loan? I'll charge you interest and everything."

I chuckle softly. I really want to take his money and get my brother the help he needs, but I'm torn about accepting this massive helping hand from someone I'm starting to have feelings for. "I'm struggling," I openly admit as I scratch at a microscopic piece of fluff on the table. I just don't want to look at him while we're discussing this. Because if I do, I know I'm going to burst into tears again.

"Why?"

"Because I'll feel like I have to work even harder to pay it back to you. I don't ever want you looking at me like I'm taking advantage of you."

"How can you be taking advantage if I'm shoving this money in your face? Look." He leans over, grabs the chair I'm sitting on by the seat, and pulls me toward him. Opening his legs, he pulls me so close, that both of my legs are inside his spread ones. He cups my face between his large, warm palms, and stares straight into my eyes. "You not paying this money back hasn't even crossed my mind. I see how hard you're working for the sake of your family. And I understand what it means to have a close family. And when one falls down, we all step up, hold our hands out, and offer help. It's what families do. It's what my family does, and it's what *your* family does." He leans in and places a lingering kiss to my forehead.

God, this feels so nice. I can't remember the last time someone wanted to help me. Or when someone even held me. I feel so pathetic. I burst into tears again. There's a tightening in my chest, and I notice my leg bouncing. "I can't do this, Alec," I say as I break away from his embrace, stand and start pacing.

Alec watches me walk back and forth while wringing my hands together over and over again. "Serena..."

I shake my head at him, and point my finger. "My life is spinning out of control, and I don't want you to be part of it."

"But I do."

No, he can't have a functional relationship with me. "I'm not normal," I say as I try to push him away with everything in me. "My happy family died the moment my parents died in that fucking car crash," I squeeze the words out of my core. "They died, and they took my family with them." Alec stands with difficulty, and tries to hobble over to me. But I back away from him. "I can't even get this right, Alec. I came here for a job, and now I'm falling for someone who is..." I shake my head and avert my gaze, staring at nothing.

"You're too hard on yourself, Serena. You can't do this on your own."

"I've been doing this on my own from the moment they died."

"Please, let me help." He leans against the counter, genuinely concerned for me.

My shoulders slump as I lower my gaze to stare at the floor. "I'm tired, Alec. I'm tired of fighting and not being heard."

Alec doesn't give me another moment of solitude. He embraces me, holding me hard against his body. "Sweetheart, I'm listening."

"I can't bring you down with me, Alec."

"Family is always there to help each other."

I look up at into his sinful dark eyes, and shake my head. "I'm not your family."

"No, not yet. But you will be, in time."

What's he talking about? "Stop talking in riddles, Alec. I can't deal with it. I've got too much going on and deciphering riddles is the last thing I want to do."

"You'll be mine soon, Serena. Which means, you're my family. And if you're my family, so is Jordan."

"These last few years have felt more like I'm falling further and further into a bottomless pit. Taking care of Jordan, and trying to save him from himself has sucked the life out of me. I'm not even sure if there's anything left to give you."

He lowers his head, his mouth scraping over my lips. There's a tingling in my chest and crazy, off-the-charts fluttering in my stomach. My mouth becomes parched as I desperately try to hold onto some form of distance. "Let me help you," he whispers against my mouth, his warm breath mingling with my own.

"I don't need saving." But damn it, I need to close this distance between us. I need this connection.

"No, you don't." He crashes his lips firmly to mine, shredding any insecurities I have about us. Alec expertly dominates this heated kiss. He's taken control, demanding I allow him to lead. Right now, all I want is to fall and let him catch me.

Our kiss is intoxicating, and sensual, without it being over the top or frantic. There's a carnal desperation to it, with our hands wandering, and our breath mingling. This is nothing like the first time we kissed. *This is more.*

Pulling away from Alec, I search his eyes, looking for some kind of signal from him. Was this nothing more to him than a fleeting kiss? Because to me, it was a beginning. "I love your lips," he says and swipes his thumb over them. "I love knowing I was the one who caused this perfect redness." He keeps grazing his thumb over my bottom lip, but stops when he grasps my chin, and moves my face up to look into his irresistible dark eyes. "You take my breath away, Serena."

I wrap my arms around him, and hold him so damn tight I'm afraid to let go. "Alec, please do me one favor."

"Anything for you."

"I can't survive losing you too, so please, don't let me fall for you."

He takes in a sharp breath. "There's no chance of that, sweetheart."

I could stay here forever, but I know I have a job to do. Taking a large gulp, I use all my willpower to break away from Alec's protective arms. "Right. On the bed," I order.

"Yes, ma'am," he happily replies. The mood is already shifting from all-encompassing heavy, to light and flirty. "Now, just a warning, but I haven't been with anyone for a while, so the first time might be over a bit quicker than I'd like it to be."

I laugh too loudly. "We're not having sex."

"What?!" Alec yells as he stops limping, and turns to look at me.

"Sorry, you've paid for a physiotherapy session, and I have to provide it."

"Oh come on." He throws his hands up in frustration. "Can't we skip that part and get to the good stuff?"

"The good stuff huh?" I stick my finger in my mouth wetting the tip, then run it over my lips.

His eyes widen and his mouth falls open as he watches me teasing him. "The good stuff. Like that." He points to my finger.

"I tell you what?"

"What?" he eagerly asks.

"Get on the damn bed, and let me do my job." I place my hands on my hips as I wait.

He clicks his tongue and rolls his eyes. "You're no fun."

"Shut up. I have a job to do."

"Fine, but I'm doing it under protest."

"Duly noted, and already forgotten. Stop your sulking, and let me get to work because you promised me dinner, and now I'm hungry."

"Fine!"

"Fine!" I retort in the same sarcastic tone. I can't help but laugh though. He's made my night so much better. And we haven't even gotten to dinner yet.

"I know I said we'd go out for dinner, but I've ordered pizza," Alec says.

"I was just thinking how I didn't really feel like going anywhere. I wish I had a bathtub though, so when I go home I could take a long, hot bubble bath. But, that's okay, maybe the next place will have one."

"You haven't found anywhere yet?" Using the crutches, Alec walks over and sits on the sofa. He pats the space beside him. "Actually, sit there, and give me your feet."

"Why?"

"Because I'm going to massage them."

What? No guy has ever massaged my feet before. Like, ever. "You don't have to do that."

"I know. But I want to. Please." He looks at the space, then back to me. "Pizza will be here in about half an hour. For now, let me take care of you." Aww, I think the ice around my heart is beginning to melt. I sit, take my shoes off and lift my legs. "Lay back," he says. "And close your eyes."

"You're not going to do something kinky with my feet are you? Wait, do you have a foot fetish? 'Cause I'm not into feet."

Alec starts laughing. "If you're worried that I'm going to suck on your toes, don't be. Because I'm not into feet either, unless they're yours."

"So you *are* going to suck on my toes?" I lean up on my elbows to watch, because that's some freaky-assed shit right there. Especially considering I've had shoes on all day. "Toe jam a delicacy for you?"

"You did *not* just say that?" He laughs even harder. "Please, trust me, no foot fetish at all. Now, lie down, will you? Let me help you relax." He lets out a loud, long sigh. "You make me work for it, don't you?"

It's my turn to laugh now. "As opposed to what?" Hang on, do I really want to know? "Wait." I hold my hand up stopping him. "I really don't want to know." He uses his thumb to really get into the balls of my feet, and I swear to God, my eyes roll into the back of my head. "Holy shit." I hear something pop, then I feel something cold on my foot. Opening my eyes, I look to see what he's doing. "Where did you get that from?" I ask when I see the lotion.

"Something you'll learn about me, I'm always prepared."

"You know what?" I lay back again, and close my eyes, just feeling all the pressure being massaged out of my feet. "I don't even want to know why you have that lotion, or when you use it."

Alec laughs even louder. "Ah, Serena, you are one funny woman. I freaking love it."

"Less talking, more massaging." The more he does, the more my body relaxes. Shit, I could get used to this.

"So, I have something for you?"

"Is it a lifetime of foot massages? Because, you could do this for me every night of the week."

"No, it's not. It's something else," there's a slight harshness to his voice.

And this worries me, because if he gives me money, I'm not entirely sure what I'll do. I don't want to take it, but if it means getting my brother the help he needs, then I might defy all my scruples and take it. But at the same time, I don't want to be put in this position with Alec. We're not there yet. We're not a couple with a joint account. Or joint anything at all. "I'm not sure I'll be able to take it," I finally say.

"It's not money," his reply instantly soothes me. "But I did buy you something."

With the amazing touch of his massage, I'm tempted not to open my eyes, to hell with it. "Do you have to stop doing what you're doing to give it to me?"

"At some stage."

I wave my hand around. "Then I don't want it."

He laughs. "How about I give it to you when the pizza gets here?"

"You know, I'm only about five minutes away from falling asleep on the sofa. And what would Elise think? Actually, where is your mom?"

"I think she's gone out with Vi and Richard. She said something about seeing a movie and going out for dinner somewhere. I don't know."

"Who are Vi and Richard?"

"Pen's parents," Alec replies. "Anyway, I'll wait to give you your present when the pizza arrives."

"Well, thank you. I already love it."

"You have no idea what it is. You could hate it."

Opening my eyes, I crane my neck and find a cushion behind me. I grab it, and slide it under my head. Watching Alec massage my feet is strangely exhilarating for me. "I'm going to be honest with you, Alec. No man has ever done this for me."

"It makes me happy that I'm the first man to care for you. Because you'll never want anyone else if I treat you the way you should be treated."

"You know why I know I'll love whatever you bought me?" He shakes his head. "I haven't received a gift in years. The last time someone gave me something was the Christmas before my parents died. And ever since then I'm..." I slowly shrug.

"Well, it's time we change that. I like doing things for you, Serena. And knowing I'm doing things that you've never had, like this." He glances down at my super moisturized feet. "Makes me want to do more for you."

"What happened to the Alec who was arrogant and self-centered?"

"He's still here." He smiles broadly. "But I realized something."

"What's that?"

"You said something that made me really think hard about who I am. You said you bet I had never complimented a woman past her body, and you were right. Dean's always been a bit of a loner, and never really interested in anything superficial. And Rhett has always had so many women who've adored him, and

I'm sure he's had a revolving door of meaningless relationships. But me, I've always wanted the perfect arm candy, but would get frustrated when the arm candy never challenged me in any way. And I thought it was them, but as it turns out, it's not. It's me. I was small-minded, and superficial."

I'm not entirely sure where he's going with this, and it's not comforting to know, I'm not arm candy. "Are you telling me arm candy is perfection? Because I'm not changing, I love my body, Alec. And I refuse to lose weight so someone can feel better about themselves. I love my size twelve curves."

"That's what I'm trying to tell you. You're the most amazing woman I've ever met, and not one of those women I've ever been with could hold a candle to you. I love how you keep me accountable and push back, and you don't let me get away with anything. But I love your smart mouth, and can't wait until it's wrapped around my cock. Your tits are fucking beautiful and I'm salivating at the thought of having them in my mouth. My God. I never in a million years thought I'd find myself crazy for someone who doesn't fit my mold. And let me tell you, I can't wait until we're together."

I pull my legs back, and sit up, staring at Alec. "I'm sure what you said was meant to sound endearing, but there were a lot of backhanded compliments in that verbal diarrhea."

Alec throws his head back, laughing. "See, like that." And right now, I can't help but love how he's such a male. I launch myself at him, straddling his legs and kissing his face. His hands are on my hips, tugging and pulling at my t-shirt. He tries to take it off, but I stop him.

"I'm not having sex with you now, Alec. I'm not ready for that."

"I just want to cop a feel," he honestly says.

"You're such a boy."

"You've got big boobs, Serena. And I love boobs. Love boobs so much," he emphasizes.

"No boob action for you." I grind against him feeling his erection through his sweatpants.

"Oh man, you're killing me, woman, you're killing me." He throws his head back, and places his arms over the back of the sofa, just letting me grind against him. "But keep going, and don't stop."

There's a knock on the door, so I throw my leg off of Alec, grab my purse from my bag and walk out to get the pizza. "What a gentleman, making me pay," I tease Alec.

"I can't exactly get up and follow you."

I laugh too loud as I open the door, give the driver the money and take the pizza back to where Alec is sitting with a huge hard-on. "Seems something crawled into your sweatpants. Are you okay?"

"You're a damn smart-ass, aren't you?"

I open the box and take out a slice, eating it while Alec stays on the sofa watching me. "Want some?" I tease.

"I've just discovered something."

"What?"

"I love watching you eat." I smile broadly. "But, I'm hungry, so bring it over here." I take the pizza box over to the sofa, and place it between us. Alec opens the lid, takes a piece, folds it and inhales it.

"Jesus, do you chew at all?"

"Pizza is life, Serena. You'll have to learn such facts for when you move in with me."

His reply catches me off guard. "I'm moving in with you, now am I?"

"Not yet. But soon."

"You're such a cocky bastard." I laugh at him.

"I think you called me arrogant. I prefer arrogant, thanks." How does one reply to someone who's so overtly confident? They don't. "Now, for this present I bought for you." He quickly shoves the pizza in his mouth, then stands, reaches for the crutches and heads in the opposite direction than his room. "I'm going to need a hand," he calls.

Jumping to my feet, I head through the galley kitchen. "Where are you?"

"Marco!" he calls making me smile.

"Polo!"

"Marco!" I find him in another bedroom on the opposite side of the house. It feels weird being in here, because I instantly know this is Elise's room. I stand at the door, not wanting to enter, because it feels like I'm invading her privacy. "Now, I can't carry it." He looks at a fairly large light yellow gift box on the king bed.

I look at the box, then I look to Alec. "Is that for me?" I point to the box.

"Yep. But I can't carry it. So, you have to." I look at the box again, and shake my head. I don't reach for it. Whatever he's bought is too much. I can't accept such a large present. It's not even my birthday yet. "You look like you're having a silent meltdown. What's wrong?"

"Whatever is in that box is too much, Alec. I thought you may have bought me some hand lotion, or a perfume, but that box is much too large for it to be either of those things."

"Maybe it's a box, in a box, in a box. But you won't know until you open it. But, if it'll make you feel better, you can open it when you get home."

Alec's proudly standing near the box, eagerly waiting for me to take it and open it. I lift the box and find it's not as heavy as I thought it was going to be. "Out in the living room?" I ask.

"Sure thing."

I take it out to the living room, and set it on the coffee table. "You remembered," I say as I look at the glossy box.

"Yellow is your favorite color." He sits beside me, and lays the crutches on the floor. The pizza box lid has now been closed, and is waiting for us to return to it.

Lifting the lid of the yellow box, yellow tissue paper hides the contents. I unwrap the tissue paper, and I can't help but smile. There's a candle, a teddy bear, peanut M&M's, a Swarovski pouch, hand lotion, Post-It notes, pens, scarf, bubble bath, picture frame, lip balm, a mug that says 'good morning sunshine,' Juicy Fruit gum, and a double-handled Ted Baker tote bag. But the thing that brings tears to my eyes is everything is yellow, except the Swarovski pouch. When I lift the pouch, I open it and slide out a pretty round, yellow pendant on a long gold chain.

"I didn't know your birthstone, but I saw this and thought you'd like it."

"Everything's yellow," I say as I smile broadly at the beautiful, thoughtful gifts. "And you wouldn't have known, but my hand bag broke tonight on the way in. Everything is so..." I'm lost for words.

"You like it, right?" Alec asks. He's misinterpreting my silence.

"No," I reply, watching his face fall. "I absolutely *love* this. Thank you so much." I place the lid on everything, turn and throw my arms around him, nearly squishing him with my enthusiasm. "No one has ever been so kind. Thank you."

Alec turns his head, finding my lips with his. He laces his fingers through my hair, keeping my head exactly where he wants it. I let go and accept his kiss and his incredibly considerate present.

"Oh, well, I wasn't expecting this," I hear Elise say.

Startled, I pull away from Alec and lower my gaze to my lap. "I'm sorry," I reply as I feel heat settle on my face.

"It's about damned time," Elise replies. "Don't mind me, I'm going to go to my room. Seeing my son getting it on with his girlfriend isn't exactly what I consider prime viewing."

"Oh, I'm not his girlfriend," I say as I point to Alec.

"Yes, you are," Alec replies.

"What?" I turn to look at him as I notice Elise slip out of the room. I wait until she's fully gone, then turn to Alec. "I'm not your girlfriend."

"Yeah, you are," he repeats. Shaking my head, I open and close my mouth several times, intending to say something, but nothing comes out. "Here's the thing, Serena."

"What?"

"You're my girlfriend." I'm still shaking my head, unable to actually verbalize how ridiculous this is. "We're right for each other, so there's no use in fighting it."

I bring my legs up to sit cross-legged on the sofa. "This is happening too fast." I point between him and me. "I always thought once I got Jordan into treatment, that I'd be on my own. I never expected you."

"'Cause I'm a hot fireman?" he asks with a cocky smirk. "In all seriousness, I never expected you either. But now that I've found you, I'm not letting go."

Goosebumps prickle over my skin as my heart rate intensifies. I never thought I'd be in this situation. Basking in his words, I can't help but reach out with a trembling hand to hold Alec's. "Thank you."

Alec presses a kiss to the top of my hand. "You're my girlfriend."

I give him a curt nod. "I'm your girlfriend."

"Great, so we've got that sorted then?" Elise asks as she walks through to the kitchen. "Don't mind me, I was totally eavesdropping on the other side of the kitchen. I wanted to make sure we're all on the same page."

This family is something else.

"I can't wait to move back home." Alec's grip on my hand tightens.

"Oh, yeah. Now that you two are officially a couple I don't want to hear what you're both going to get up to," Elise teases while she grabs a bottle of water from the fridge.

Can my face be any redder? "Um, I think I'm going to go home. I've got a big day tomorrow, and I definitely need my sleep." I lean over and give Alec a chaste kiss on the lips before standing and looking around for my bag.

"It's in the bedroom," Alec says as if he can read my mind. I smile, head into the bedroom and grab my bag with the broken strap then walk out to the living room where Alec is already standing and ready to walk me out. "Here, give me your bag, and you can take the box."

"It's okay, I can balance it on the box."

"Give me the bag," he says again. I do, and he tucks it under his arm, while awkwardly trying to use the crutches too.

"Good night, Elise."

"Night, darlin,'" she calls as she tucks her legs up under her butt, turning the TV on.

I maneuver around Alec so I can get to my car quickly then I can double back and get my bag. But by the time I've placed the box on the back seat, Alec is already at the car. "You're getting much better with these." I indicate to the crutches.

"And thankfully I'll be off them soon. I have this pretty hot physiotherapist who's looking after me."

"Really? Is he any good? Should I use him too?"

"Hey!" He grabs me around the hips and draws me toward him. "I like you, Serena."

"Good. You should."

He kisses my nose, then my forehead. "A lot," he mumbles against my skin.

"I've gotta go. I have to be up early tomorrow. Some of us don't have the luxury of sitting around doing nothing all day."

He smacks me on the butt. "Cheeky." Oh, I like that, *a lot.*

"I've gotta go," I say again. But damn it, it's difficult to leave him.

"I'll call you tomorrow."

"Okay." I finally let go, and get into my car. I really don't want to leave, I want to stay with Alec, and just be with him. The more time I spend with him, the more I like him.

Pulling away from the house, I'm tempted to turn back and spend the night with him. It's not like I have anything but a cold house to return to. A cold house, in a shit area, with a brother who'd sell me if it means he could get his hands on more drugs.

It will be okay. I'm going to get Jordan help. This is why I work my ass off, for my family.

The drive home is quick, and easy at this time of the night. As I pull into the street, there's another huge party happening, and the two guys who live in the house, are sitting on an old sofa out in the front yard. Both have got women sitting on their laps drinking cans of beer. The two guys see my car, and their eyes follow me as I pull into my driveway, get out of my car, and take the box up to the front door.

They've never done anything to me, but the way they watch me is just weird. It's not like I create any problems for them, or call the police, or do anything. So, why are they so interested in me every time they're out the front of their house?

I switch on the hall light and lock the front door. "Jordan?" I call, even though I know he's not here. "Jordan?" I'm met with silence. He's not here. I head to my bedroom, and unlock it before placing the box on my bed. I head over to Jordan's room, just in case he's asleep. But he hasn't been here. His bed is made the way I left it and his clothes are folded the way I left them.

I decide that because I've got such a busy day tomorrow, I better take a quick shower now so I can get out of bed, get ready, and leave for work in the morning. Taking my clothes into the bathroom, I strip and bring the water up to temperature before stepping in. Closing my eyes, I feel the heat of the water pounding down on my back. Jordan consumes my thoughts, I hope he's okay. "Wherever you are, Jordan, I hope you're safe."

All I can say, is I can't wait until Jordan breaks the controlling chains of drugs. Maybe then I can move on and start my life with Alec.

Please, let Jordan be alive. And let Alec be real.

Please.

Chapter 9

ALEC

"YOU TOLD YOUR brothers to be here by five, right?" Mom says as she prepares the salad.

"Yes, Mom."

"And Joanne's not coming, right?"

"No, and neither is Thomas. He's going to one of his friends' house for dinner."

Mom smiles. "I like how easily they've made friends and connections."

"I like Thomas," I say as I grab four plates from the cupboard and place them on the kitchen counter.

"You don't like Joanne?"

"Yeah, I do. She makes Dean happy; you can see it."

Mom smiles widely. "Yeah, she does. Just like how Serena makes you happy."

"She's different," I say not really knowing what else to say.

"In what way?" I should've known Mom would quiz me.

"She doesn't let me get away with anything. Not at all. If I say something stupid, she calls me on it. And I love how she's not afraid to work hard. She's a damn college graduate, and she's willing to clean houses and busk tables just so she can get her brother help. That, to me, is hard-core dedication."

Mom clicks her tongue and lets out a long breath. "She certainly has drive."

"Her brother has been nothing but horrible to her, and yet she fights for him every single day. I mean, how easy would it be for her to throw her arms up and walk away from him? But she chooses to keep fighting for someone who doesn't know enough to fight for himself. I love that about her."

"She has what a lot of people lack." I look over at her as I lean against the counter. "She has hope."

I take the flatware out of the drawer, then turn back to face Mom. "What do you mean?"

"In her world all she's gotten is slammed down, time after time. Her parents passed away together, her brother is a drug addict, all while she refuses to give up hope for her future, and her brother's. That's really inspiring."

"It is. But she's stubborn, and refuses to accept my help."

"What have you offered her?"

"The rest of the money she needs. Do you know, she lives in a shit part of Faith Haven so she can save on rent and put that toward saving for Jordan's rehab? And, she's being evicted soon, too. She managed to get an extension to stay there for another four weeks, but basically, they said she can't stay any longer because the owner is redeveloping the house."

"And what else are you doing to help her?"

"I don't know what else to do, Mom," I say, frustrated with myself.

"Do you know the rehab center she's looking at for her brother?" I shake my head. "It's a good place to start there. How much does she need?"

"She's now got a little over twenty thousand saved, and needs a little under fifteen thousand more."

"Shit, I could give her that."

"Dean and Rhett both said the same thing. We could all give it to her, but she's stubborn and proud, and doesn't want help."

Mom turns down her lips as she nods. "Perhaps you need to show her that right now her brother is alive, but by the time she finishes saving the money, her brother may very well be dead."

"I want her to let me help pay for this."

"Then, you need to figure out a way to get her to take the money." Mom leans over and gently pats my cheek. "You've always been a good kid. Even though I had to kick your ass for saying Serena's chubby." She pointedly looks at me.

"She is, but I like that about her. She's confident and she owns her body shape. I love how she loves her body."

"Hmmm." Mom goes to the fridge and takes the steaks out for the grill.

"Hmmm, what?"

"I think you've fallen in love with this one." Mom seasons the steaks, and doesn't lift her gaze toward me.

"No, I haven't. She's just different."

"And out of all the women you've dated, Alec, for how many of them have you created a gift box filled with things in their favorite color?"

"That's different. She needed some cheering up. She's going through a lot at the moment."

"And how many of your past female companions have you brought over so we can all meet them?" *Female companions?* What are we, in the eighteen-hundreds?

"Again, it's different. You already know her."

"And how many have made you smile the way you do when you see her?" I have nothing to say to that one. "Just as I thought. You're in love with her."

"I can't be, we haven't even had sex yet." I slap my forehead. "And that's too much information for my mother."

"Yes, it is. Don't get me wrong though." She points her finger at me. "I know all three of you are sexually active. I just hope you're being safe."

"Let's not talk about this." *Awkward.*

"You're right, let's not. How about we talk about the woman you're in love with?" I can't help but smile. "See. That right there proves I'm right."

I slowly shrug as I take a piece of cucumber out of the salad and pop it in my mouth. "What do I do, Mom? I want this to work with her. I'm stuck though, I don't know how to get her to relax and loosen the reins."

"Well, I told you what you need to do. Besides, didn't you say she needs to find somewhere else to live? Don't you have room at your place?"

"She won't go for it, because she's damn stubborn."

"Well, son, the only thing I can say to you is, you better figure it out. We'll all help her if it's a question of a few thousand dollars. And when she moves, your brother has a truck, and we can easily relocate her wherever she needs to go."

I hear the clacking of little toenails scraping across the floor. I crane my head to see Dean and his dog, Tripod, coming in. "Hey," Dean says as he enters the kitchen. "Looks intense, what's going on? Are you finally throwing this loser out of the house, Mom?" Dean lightly punches me in the arm.

"Actually, we're talking about Serena," Mom informs him.

"Ah, what's going on? Have you found out where she's sending the brother to rehab?"

"I think she knows I'll go and pay for it, because she's been tight-lipped about everything. But Mom just made a valid point. Her lease has been extended by another four weeks, but when she moves, I'll have to borrow your truck to move her."

"You'll need me to help too."

"I'll volunteer Rhett too," Mom says.

"Shouldn't we ask him?" I ask Mom.

"Nope. He'll do it."

Dean looks at the salad, and picks out some tomato. "I'll go fire up the grill." He takes a step out of the kitchen, the turns to look at me. "You coming, gimpy?"

"Are you talking to me, or your three-legged dog?"

Dean rolls his eyes, and whistles for Tripod to follow him out. Taking my crutches, I lightly put pressure on my foot as I follow Dean out. "You'll be back at work soon. Gotta say, I kinda miss not having you around. I mean, it's more peaceful and shit, but I'd rather have you there than not."

"Aww, look at my big brother. Being all sentimental."

He looks over my shoulder to see where Mom is. "Fuck off," he whispers.

"Mom, Dean swore at me!" I say with a huge smile, teasing him just like I did when we were kids.

"That's nice, dear," she responds.

"How are things with Joanne?" I ask as I head to the outdoor fridge, grab two beers, and hand one to Dean.

He cracks his open, takes a long drink, and sets it down on the side of the grill. He fires up the grill, then picks his beer up again. "We're doing really well. Her house is nearly finished, and once we've moved in, we're getting married in the backyard."

"Shit, I know you've been together for a few months, but marriage, already?"

"When you know, you know."

I stretch my arms up over my head, then knit my fingers together and balance them on top of my head. "I think I know what you're talking about."

Dean's brows rise, and he smirks. "You and Serena, eh?"

"I think so," I say.

"About time you found someone to settle down with. You're getting old, you know."

"I'm ten months younger than you," I bite back.

"What have I missed?" Rhett asks as he walks out, goes directly to the fridge and grabs a water.

"He's finally gotten his head out of his ass and found himself a woman, and I'm getting married in the garden once the house is finished." Dean points to me, then himself.

"Then it's Rhett's turn to find himself a woman, and I'll be one happy Momma." Mom comes out, and places the salad on the table. "Did I hear you say you're getting married in the garden?"

"Yeah, but not until we're in the house."

"Which will be when?" Mom asks.

"It's nearly finished. I think we'll be in there in the next month or so. But we're not exactly sure when we're getting married. We'll settle in first, and go from there."

If he's going to be in the house soon, and Serena needs to be out in four weeks, then it makes sense to get her into Dean's house. "What are you doing with your place?" I ask again even though we've touched on it previously.

"We were going to sell it, but as it turns out, we don't need to."

"Let me talk to Serena, see if she wants it. There may be a week or so overlap, but I'm sure you can move back here, and she can have my place for that week or two." I look at Rhett.

Rhett's face drops, his eyes narrow and he purses lips into a thin line. "Or, I can stay at your place, and you and Serena can move into Dean's place. Now, there's a great thought for you."

"Finally, I'll be free from all this testosterone," Mom says.

I look to Rhett, then Dean. Mom wants her house back? Rhett's face is saying what I'm thinking. I didn't think Mom actually wanted us all gone.

"You'd be okay here by yourself?" Rhett asks the question all three of us must be thinking.

"Not only will I be okay, I'm looking forward to it. But, you're still my boys, and my home will always be your home. So, you can stay for as long as you want, or need. But let me tell you, I'm throwing the biggest party ever once you're all gone."

"I honestly thought you'd want one of us here, for like...ever," Rhett says.

"Darling, I've done my job as your mother, I've raised three incredible men. Now's your turn to go out, and live your lives. Why do you think I insist on family dinner nights? Because I get to have you all back, even if it's only for a few hours. And I'm okay with that. But I only want you to leave when you're ready, and not before."

Rhett smiles as he steps into Mom, and gives her a hug. "I'm giving you my notice," he says. Mom laughs and smacks him on the back.

When Mom pulls away, she sits at the table. "Just so I have this straight. Dean you're getting married within the next year?" Dean nods, agreeing to the timeline Mom's offered. "You're likely going to be moving in with Serena sooner or later." She purposely stares at me. I nod too. "And you're moving out soon." Rhett nods as well. "Will there be a female companion? Perhaps, Pen?"

"Eww, Mom! We've been over this. Pen and I are like this." Rhett holds up his two fingers and entwines them. "And Pen has her on again, off again boyfriend. And, I can't look at Pen and think, oh yeah, I want to be with her." He shivers and grimaces simultaneously. "Besides, I'm not really interested in anyone." Rhett drops his gaze, and half shrugs. I look at Dean whose mouth is open with shock.

"Who is she?" I ask.

"No one," Rhett replies with too much haste.

"Come on, who is she?" It's Dean's turn to ask.

Rhett shakes his head, and avoids the question. Oh yeah, he's into someone. "Wait, is it a he?" I ask.

"What? No." Rhett shakes his head. "Anyway, it doesn't matter. It's not like that between us," Rhett responds vehemently.

"So, there is someone?" Mom asks. "And it's not Pen."

"Will you drop it about Pen? We're like siblings. And it's gross to even think of Pen like that."

"Who is it?" Mom pushes.

"Mom, I promise you, if anything happens, you'll be one of the first people to know."

"You better wash my sheet three times just to get all the jizz out of them," I say.

"Oh, come on. That's revolting," Mom barks. "Anyway, I had to wash all of your sheets when you'd wake up covered in semen in your teenage years."

"Oh my God." The three of us all cringe at the same time.

"Yeah, just remember that." Mom points to each and every one of us. "And let's not even talk about the amount of times the hot water would run out."

I lower my head, dying on the inside of embarrassment, yet laughter too.

"I've had to knock on the door a few times with Thomas," Dean says. "I was never so bad."

"Bullshit you weren't. And your father refused to talk to you boys about everything, and made me do it."

"He talked to us," I inform Mom.

Her face is one of pure shock. "That rascal," she says. "Wait 'til I meet him up there." She points up to the sky. "He's going to get an earful. He *did* talk to you?"

"Yep," Dean answers.

"Uh-huh," Rhett adds.

"Yeah," I say.

Mom narrows her eyes and scrunches her mouth. She throws several small punches into the palm of her hand. "He's going to get it when we reunite. He told me he thought it was my job to talk to you boys. And he knew I didn't want to do it because it's different for boys and girls. That's it, he can sleep on the couch for a week when I get up there." She tilts her head up, looking at the sky. "You hear that, Patrick?" She waves her fist at him. "You're sleeping on the goddamn couch."

"Mom, Mom, Mom." Rhett slings his arm over her shoulder. "You make me laugh, and squirm all at the same time."

"Aww, my job is done then. I figure if you ever need to see a shrink, at least I'll be able to provide you with many sessions worth of discussion." She leans in and gives Rhett a kiss on the cheek.

"Grill's ready," Dean announces.

"I'll go get the meat." Rhett stands and walks into the kitchen to get the steaks for the grill.

"Serena's working down at the restaurant, do you think you can take me so I can drop her off some food?" I ask Rhett when he returns.

"She's at the restaurant?" Rhett confirms.

"Yeah."

A small cheeky smile tugs at his lips. "Yeah, I'll take you," he says, a little too eager. "Maybe we can have coffee while we're down there. Do you know when she's getting a break tonight? We can be there for her break."

Something's going on with Rhett. He's too enthusiastic to drive me to the restaurant. "I'll text her and ask," I say as I take my phone out of my pocket to send her a quick message.

We get on with dinner, but I keep glancing at my phone, waiting for her reply. Something stirs inside of me, hoping she's okay. A part of me wants to get Rhett to take me down to the restaurant right now to make sure she's okay, but I don't want to come across as an insecure stalker either.

I suppose, with the fact her brother is out there somewhere, trolling for drug money, anything is possible. And that's what worries me most. That he'll find her and force her to give him money.

The moment my phone lights up with a message from her, I instantly relax. "Serena just texted back, and says she's on a break in an hour for twenty minutes."

"We'll leave in about forty minutes, okay?" Rhett offers.

I nod. "Sure."

"Thanks for bringing me," I say to Rhett while we head into the restaurant.

"Yeah, no problems, man."

I notice he's craning his head, trying to look inside. "Looking for someone?" I ask.

"No, I'm just seeing if there's a table for us. Does Serena know we're coming?"

"Nah, I thought I'd surprise her."

"Look at you, turning into a giant marshmallow."

"I'll hit you with this crutch." I threaten him with the right crutch.

"Gotta catch me first, and you're like Dean's dog. Hey, maybe your new name should be Tripod Senior." He laughs at his own joke.

I smirk too. "I swear to God, I will hurt you."

He reaches for the door handle to open it, then rolls his eyes as I hobble in past him. "I'd really like to see you try. I am bigger and taller than you."

"The bigger they are, the harder they fall," I say.

"You're such a baby." Rhett looks over the restaurant, searching for someone.

"Who are you looking for?" I repeat.

"No one," he replies defensively, though keeps searching.

No one my ass. I look over and see Serena carrying three plates out to a table. She hasn't noticed me yet, which allows me a chance to watch her work. With all the shit going on in her life, she's still smiling, and being the perfect hostess to the table she's waiting on. And they have no idea that behind her beautiful eyes is a woman who's struggling to keep it together.

As if she senses me, she turns her head to look over toward the door. She looks away, then back to me. Her entire face lights up when she sees me. She quickly looks around, before hastily sneaking off toward me. "Hey, you." She reaches up and gives me a chaste kiss on the lips. "Hey, Rhett." She wraps her arms around me to give me a small hug. "What are you doing here?"

"We came for coffee," Rhett says. "And this." He gives her the plate I've prepared from our family dinner.

"I figure considering you couldn't come to family dinner, we'll bring family dinner to you," I say.

The smile on Serena's face is everything. But she looks like she's about to cry. "You did this, for me?" She peers up from beneath her lashes. My cock stirs, and I want her, right now.

"Of course." Without hesitation, she throws her arms around my neck, nearly knocking me off balance, and gives me a hard kiss. I love how me bringing her a plate of food has made her smile so wide. I know it's not the food; it's the gesture.

"I've got about ten minutes until my break. I'll get you a table toward the back. It's a crappy table no one really likes sitting at, but I'll come join you both when I'm on my break." She starts heading toward the back, and gestures with her head so we follow her.

Rhett is still looking around. "Who you looking for?" I repeat for the umpteenth time.

"Oh my God, Alec, leave it alone! I'm not looking for anyone," he barks over his shoulder at me.

Yeah, right. "Here you go. I'll be out in a few minutes, okay. I'll get Dani to come and grab your order."

"Dani's here?" Rhett asks with a slight crack to his voice.

Oh, I see. He's been searching for Dani. "Yeah, I'll send her over." Serena leans down and gives me another kiss. "I've gotta get back to work. I'll leave this here and have it when I get back."

Serena leaves and encounters Dani walking out of the kitchen with three plates. They exchange some words, and Dani looks over at us and smiles, nodding before Serena disappears back into the kitchen. I want to ask Rhett about it, but I figure, he'll tell us when he's ready. Maybe there's nothing to tell.

"Hey," Dani greets us as she appears at the table. "How are you, Rhett?" Her eyes soften and she smiles wider.

"Yeah, good. You?" Rhett squares his shoulders while staring at Dani.

Whoa, talk about awkward. Dani stands straighter, then tucks some hair behind her ear. Rhett can't take his eyes off her. His mouth is open, and if I didn't know better, I'd say he's drooling over her. "What can I get you?"

"Coffee. And a slice of pie," Rhett responds without moving his eyes to look at the menu.

"What kind of pie would you like, Rhett?"

"Whatever you like." I turn my head to look at him, surprised by his answer. "I mean, whatever you think is good," he corrects himself.

"And you, Alec?"

"Coffee please, and I'll have a slice of pecan pie, please."

"Sure thing." She glances over at Rhett, who's now staring down at the menu trying to act like he's unaffected by her, then leaves.

"Hey, you may wanna wipe your mouth." I nudge him.

"What? Why?" Embarrassed, he wipes at his mouth. "Why didn't you tell me I had food on my face?"

"I think you were drooling and there's dribble on your chin."

He punches me in the arm. "Dick," he mumbles.

"Ask her out," I say as I tilt my head to the side where Dani disappeared.

"Ask who out?" He's playing coy with me.

I just roll my eyes and shake my head. Like two stalkers, I watch Serena as she buzzes around the restaurant, and Rhett watches Dani. Shit, I think Mom's right. I think I'm falling for her hard. There's just something about her, she's an amazing person who fights for what she believes in.

As Serena returns to the kitchen, she holds up five fingers to me, then rubs at her stomach. She mouths the words, *I'm so hungry*. I catch something glistening around her neck, and it thrills me to see she's wearing the necklace I gave her. Yep, she's mine, all mine. She's always been mine, from the moment we met.

I wink at her and Serena drops her gaze, but the huge smile on her face tells me everything I need to know. She's falling for me too. And I love that so much. When she reenters the dining room, she walks over and places the plates down at a table of two guys and a woman. The woman peers down at her food, lifts her chin and crosses her arms in front of her chest.

Serena's smile slowly fades, as she clasps her hands behind her back. The woman hasn't even tasted her food, and already she's complaining.

Serena nods once, then reaches to take the food. The guy sitting to the woman's left, smacks Serena's hand away. I see red. Standing, I grab my crutches, and move forward to have words with that guy.

Serena sees me, and shakes her head. "Leave it," Rhett says as he stands and gets in front of me.

"He fucking touched her." I'm absolutely seething, ready to rip this guy's head from his neck.

Serena steps away from the assholes, and walks over to me. "I've got it," she says as she places her hand to my chest.

"He fucking touched you."

"Trust me, I've got it," she says again, trying to reassure me.

I glare over her shoulder, and the woman has a sneer on her ugly face. "If he touches you again..."

She smiles confidently. "He won't."

With my anger in the danger zone, I back away and sit again, Rhett's teetering on the edge, ready to jump up and intervene.

I watch as Serena walks back to the table, smiles, says something, and goes to take the plate again. The guy raises his hand to smack Serena's away, my eyes zone into him, and I'm ready to rip him to shreds. But, Serena beats me to it, backhanding his hand away, causing him to startle at her reaction. She looks down to him, and with a big *fuck you* smile, she says something.

The guy's reaction is priceless. He inconspicuously looks around to see if anyone saw. When he notices me smirking at him, he lowers his head and avoids all eye contact with me. Serena walks into the kitchen with the woman's plate.

A few moments later, she comes over, drags out a chair, and sits.

"You okay?" I ask as I keep staring at the guy. God, I'd love to treat him the way he treated my woman.

"I'm fine." She shrugs. "But I give them thirty seconds before they stand to leave."

"What did you say to them?" Rhett asks.

"I just said to him, I hope you enjoy your food, I made it myself. Then smiled."

I look at Rhett. "What did you do to it?" My amazing woman is capable of a lot of things, which terrifies and excited me.

"Funny because he asked the same question. And I told him, perhaps he should try it, and then I said, the toilets are out of order." She smiles sweetly as she takes the cling film off the plate, and starts eating what we've brought her.

"Oh shit." Rhett covers his mouth, and starts laughing. "Well, they've all gotten up, and are just about to walk out."

My attention is on them. The guy who touched my woman, takes some bills out of his pocket, throws them on the table, and hurries out of the restaurant. "You might get a bad review," I say.

"What a shame," Serena responds dryly and without an ounce of worry. "I've got too much going on in my life to give a crap about what rude people want to say. The chick's problem was the dinner plate was too large and she didn't want to eat that much. Seriously, get a life."

Rhett laughs some more. But he stops laughing, and straightens as Dani brings over our coffees. "Thank you, Dani," he says. She smiles at him then leaves again.

"You should ask her out," Serena says as she shovels food in her mouth.

"Ask who out?" Rhett asks thinking he's being oblivious to the way he reacts whenever she's near.

"Pecan pie for you." Dani appears and places my pecan pie down. "And my favorite, banoffee pie for you, Rhett."

"Thank you." Rhett stares up her and smiles.

"Thank you," I say and hit Rhett under the table.

"What?" He looks over to me, and widens his eyes. I try to be as unassuming as possible by gesturing toward Dani.

"Anything else I can get you?" Dani asks.

"I'm good. How about you, Rhett? Do you want anything else?" I widen my eyes, teasing him. *Ask her out!*

"No!" he shouts way too loud.

Dani hangs around for a few seconds, nods, and returns to the kitchen. As she walks into the kitchen, she gives Rhett a quick glance. He's too much of an idiot to read the signs and go for it. "If you're scared of rejection, then you're a dick," I say.

"Shut up and eat your pie." He leans his elbow on the table, half covering his face while he rubs at his temple.

"It's like watching two teenagers in high school. Do you want me to pass a note for you, Rhett?" Serena teases.

Rhett glances at Serena and lifts his brows. "I don't need any help getting women."

Serena purses her lips, trying to resist chuckling. "Hey." She holds her hands up in surrender. "It's just she's going to be going on and on about how cute you are, and 'why doesn't he ask me out?' for the rest of the night."

"She says those things to you?" Rhett asks, abandoning his pie and becoming super invested in what Serena has to say.

"You don't need help getting women," she throws his own words back at him.

Rhett pulls his shoulders back and lifts his head. Now he's got that cocky look about him. "Anyway, do you like it?" I look down to the food Serena's half eaten.

"So good. My God, this meat is just..." She brings her fingertips to her mouth and kisses them as she pulls them away.

"Have you heard from your brother?" I ask.

Serena is just about to answer, when Rhett asks, "What facility are you planning on sending him to?"

"It's one in Kentucky. It's called New Dawn. It's one of the best ones I can afford. And by I can afford, I mean I'm killing myself to get the money for it."

I lower my hand and make a fist, Rhett makes a fist too, and discreetly hits my hand. Jackpot, we have the name. Now, we need to figure out how to get her brother there. Paying it isn't a problem. It's the fact we need to physically get her brother to Kentucky. And I'm sure, like every other drug addict, he doesn't think the drug has control over him.

"Serena?" Dani pops her head out of the kitchen, and calls her over.

"Man, I feel like I only just sat down. Sorry, I have to go. Thank you for dinner. I'll see you tomorrow, right?"

"Sure will."

Serena stands, leans over the table and gives me a kiss. "Gotta go."

"Bye," Rhett says.

The moment she's out of earshot, I turn to Rhett. "Good work on getting her to tell us the name. I'll make some phone calls tomorrow, and pay the damn bill."

"Do you need money?"

"I don't, but I know she's going to lose her shit when she finds out I've paid for it. So, I'm thinking, I'll pay the fifteen thousand, and let her pay the other twenty. I don't want to shatter her confidence in the amazing goal she's already achieved." I just want her to know she doesn't have to do everything by herself anymore. She can always rely on me.

"She's strong, and independent and used to doing things on her own. But now she doesn't have to," Rhett says.

"I was just thinking the same thing. She might be angry at me for paying the difference, but if it makes her feel better, she can pay it back."

Rhett snorts. "Like you'd take the money from her."

"I will. Because again, it'll be important to her, but I'll set it aside so we can buy a house. Or buy Dean's house. Whatever."

"So, it's really serious then?"

"For me it is."

"I'm gonna ask, how do you know she's who you want?"

"Serena is everything I've never looked for. She sends me crazy. She's my first thought and my last thought every single day. And when I think about my future, she's in it, still a snarky smart-ass."

"Must be nice to be so sure." He picks his coffee up and takes a sip, before his attention lands on Dani cleaning a table.

"Gotta live in the moment, because tomorrow isn't guaranteed. Look at Dad. He woke up, kissed Mom goodbye, and died in a fire. He just went to work and never returned."

"I can't believe it's been over five years already." Rhett blankly stares down at his half-eaten pie. "Do you think Mom will ever find anyone else?"

I lift my shoulders. "If she does, it'll be a shock to all of us. But she deserves someone who'll treat her well."

"Amen to that, brother." Rhett has the rest of his coffee, and looks over to my now empty plate. "Ready to go?"

"You're not going to ask her out?" I sharply look over to Dani who's now wiping down a different table.

"Not today." He stands, stretches, then adds, "Your shout."

Of course it is. I take my wallet out of my pocket and throw a couple of Jacksons on the table and head out. Serena comes out of the kitchen just as we're heading to the door. She sees me, smiles and blows me a kiss.

That woman drives me crazy.

Chapter 10

SERENA

GOD, I'M SO tired. I think if I sleep for a solid week, it still won't be enough to recharge myself. Thankfully, I'm driving out to Alec's Mom's house, then I can go home and sleep. I'm also grateful the drive from the restaurant to Alec's is less than fifteen minutes. It'll be the drive back home that'll be a killer. But it's okay, I won't stay for dinner tonight, I'm just too tired.

As I'm driving out, I hear a small pop, then the car pulls to right. Crap, don't tell me I've got a flat. I don't have time for this crap. I pull over safely, and get out to have a look. "Shit," I say as I see the completely flat rear right tire. I walk to the trunk, and open the lid. "Shit!" I forgot to get the spare fixed from the last time I had a flat, which was probably a year ago.

I walk around to the front to get my phone so I can call AAA, and lean against the car when I remember I've forgotten to pay them too. Looking down at my phone, I'm struggling with what to do. I'll see if I can get a cab into town, then I can try to get my car towed to a service center to have it fixed. Maybe I don't need to call for a cab. I'll just call to have my car towed. I better call Alec to let him know I'll be late for his physiotherapy session today. Actually, by the time I get there, it'll be really late, and all I want to do is go home to sleep. But I need the money, especially now that I'll have to pay for a tow and two new tires.

I dial Alec's number. "Hey. I bet your ears where burning," he says.

"Nope, they weren't. But, I'm calling to let you know, I'm going to be late today."

"That's okay, did you get stuck at work?"

"No." I look at the back tire, and kick it. "I've got a flat tire."

"I'll come change it, where are you?"

"That would be awesome, if my spare wasn't flat too. And to top it off, I forgot to pay for AAA. I'm about to call for a tow truck to come get my car, and take it to get two new tires. I'm not sure what time I'll be able to get to your house."

"Where are you?"

"Not far from your mom's. Just this side of Oak Tree Parade." I look around trying to figure out exactly where I am. "Near...you know that old church on the corner that's been boarded up?"

"Yeah."

"I'm about fifty yards from there."

"Oh, yeah, I know where you are. Don't call a truck, let me figure it out. Can you do me a favor, on the outside rim of the tires, there's a bunch of numbers, can you take a photo and send it to me, please?"

"You want the size of the tire?" I ask. "Why?"

"So I can call around and see who has it."

"It'll be easier if I call a tow truck, don't worry too much about it. I'm an idiot for forgetting to have the spare replaced."

"I'm already on it, Serena. I'll be there in about ten minutes."

I close my eyes and rub at my temples. "I've got it, Alec."

"Will you let me help you? Stop trying to do everything by yourself," he says with a frustrated sigh.

"I've been doing everything by myself for a long time, and I don't need saving."

"Stop! Just stop. You have to stop saying you don't need saving, I'm not trying to save you, for God's sake. You have to learn to accept help when help is offered. You don't *need* to do this on your own, even though you're fully capable."

Fidgeting with the hem of my t-shirt, I push off the car and slowly pace back and forth. "Fine," I finally capitulate. "Whatever."

"Are you safe where you are?"

"Yeah, I'm on the side of the road."

"How much battery have you got remaining on your phone?"

Awe, how cute. I look at my phone, and see I have plenty of battery life left. "Yeah, I'm good there."

"Okay, we're on our way, we won't be long."

The sound of another call coming through makes me look at my phone. It's Jordan's number. "I've gotta go, Jordan's calling."

Alec exhales loudly, and I know he's now even more worried for me. "Okay. I'll see you soon." I haven't spoken to Jordan in so long, I hope he's okay.

I end the call, and switch it over to Jordan. My heart thumps hard in my chest. "Hey, how are you?" I ask with a shaky voice.

"Where are you, Serena?"

I let out a sigh of relief. *He's alive.* "I'm out. And my tire is flat, so I have to wait until I can get it fixed. Are you okay?"

"Ugh, fuck sake, sis. Where are you? I need some money."

"I don't have any, Jordan. Not now I have to fix my car."

"Who cares about your fucking car! I need money to pay some people."

The hair stands on the back of my neck, and a chill shoots through my body. "Who do you owe money to?" I ask with a tight, and worried voice.

"Just some people," he replies vaguely.

"Who are the people?" I push harder.

"Just some people? I need money, and I need it now."

"How much do you need?"

"Just a couple of grand. Five or six should cover it."

My heart stops with that insanely large number. "I don't have that kind of cash. Where am I supposed to find it? And what did you buy that you needed that much money?" There's silence on the other end of the phone. "Jordan?"

"Just stuff, alright? Jesus, give me the money, Serena," his anger is reflected in his eerily chilling voice. It scares me when he's like this, because even though I hope he wouldn't hurt me, I just can't be sure anymore.

"I don't have it."

"Well, if they kill me, it's on you, you fucking bitch. I hope you can live with yourself knowing you sent your brother to his grave. It's all your fault!" He hangs up abruptly, leaving me shaking and stressed.

A truck pulls up behind mine. Alec and his brother Dean both get out. Alec has better use of his leg, so he's getting around easier with the crutches. He should be off them soon. "What's wrong?" Alec asks, making a beeline straight toward me.

"Is the car open?" Dean asks. I nod my head, unable to answer him. He opens the door, and pops the trunk open.

"What happened? You're shaking and pale. What's going on?" Alec rubs his hands up and down my arms.

I rake my hand over my hair, and through my ponytail. "Jordan called. He owes someone money, and it's quite a lot. He said it's about five or six thousand. He um..." I look away, blinking rapidly trying to keep the tears from erupting. "He um, he said they're going to kill him. I don't know what to do, Alec. Should I give him the money? I should, shouldn't I?" I try to convince myself that giving him the money is the right thing to do. But in my gut, I know it's not.

"God no, you can't give him the money, because that isn't what you're working so hard for."

My entire body is trembling, I'm so confused about what to do. "What if they kill him? I can't let them do that. Not over a few thousand dollars. I've got the money, I can give it to them. Maybe, I can go and tell them to stop selling to him."

Alec wraps his arms around me, pulling me in tight toward him. I lean my head against his shoulder, and I just let every one of my emotions escape. "If he's told them he has a sister who works, then they won't kill him, because then there's no motivation for you to pay. And, if you give them the money, they'll know there's a supply of cash, and they won't stop selling to him."

Stepping back, I sit on the sidewalk and look up to the sky. The sun has fallen and is showing us the prettiest hues painted across the horizon. "I'm not sure I can take too much more, Alec. It feels like it's me against the world."

He struggles to sit beside me, but he does, and places his arm around my shoulder, pulling me in toward him. His warm body calms my frantic thoughts. "Let me help."

"How?" I turn my head to stare into his amazing dark eyes. "I could fall into your eyes," I catch myself saying. "Fall in, and swim away."

Alec cups my cheek, and skims his thumb across my skin. "Let me pay for the rest of his treatment."

My shoulders deflate. "I don't want your money, Alec."

"Okay, I won't give it to you. You'll have to pay me back." He leans in to kiss me, but I turn my head and stare down at the road. "What is it?"

"I don't want to accept it." I fist my hair through my hands, absolutely hating the next part of what I'm about to say. "But I think if I don't take it, he's going to be dead one way or another. If these people he owes money to don't end up killing him, the drugs will."

Alec sighs. "The money is here. Let's pay for his treatment, and get him to New Dawn."

I turn to look at Alec, and give him a small nod and a strained smile. I notice Dean's not here. "Where did Dean go?"

"He took your spare to go get it repaired, and he'll be back soon so he can change it for the flat."

I shake my head, disappointed in myself. "I never wanted to have to rely on anyone."

"You're not relying on us, Serena, we're simply giving you a hand. Besides, the reasons are entirely selfish." He grins. "If we didn't come to fix this, I wouldn't have been able to see you tonight."

"I see. So you're actually using me?" I say in a lighter tone, somewhat relieved. I know Jordan will soon be going into rehab.

"You have no idea how badly I want to use you." My cheeks heat, and I can't help but grin. "But, let's sort your car out first, then we can talk about this whole 'using' business." He circles his finger between us.

"You just want me for my body."

"Ah, yeah! God, yeah," he shamelessly admits. "I love your body." He smirks cheekily.

Huh, interesting. "I think you're nearly be ready to walk without these. We'll do some harder exercises tonight, to really help build the muscles."

He throws his head back and groans loudly. "You mean harder than you've been working me already?"

"Hard enough for you to be sore," I say in a low, seductive voice.

"Oh, well, this is something I like the sounds of. How hard are we talking?" He straightens and stares at me eagerly.

"So hard, you'll feel it right away."

"That hard, eh?"

"You'll be begging me to go harder."

"Shit." He discreetly looks around in case anyone is listening. "Will you go *harder* on me?"

"I'll be going so hard on you, you'll want to..." I catch him hanging off my words. His mouth slightly open, and his chest rising and falling sharply.

"What? Why are you stopping?"

I flutter my lashes at him, and tilt my head to the side. "We're talking about physiotherapy, right?"

"You're a tease." He laces his fingers through the nape of my neck, drags me over and kisses me with heat. His mouth is possessive, and his strong grip confirms how greedy he is. "I fucking want you," he mumbles against my lips.

Shielded by the car, I slip my hand down into his shorts, and subtly grip his warm, hard cock in my hand. "I could wrap my lips around your cock right now, and suck you so hard, you'll blow in my mouth." What the hell's gotten into me? *Not Alec, well not yet.*

His cock hardens in my hand. "I like the sounds of that." I kiss down his chin, where he tilts his head back and I continue peppering kisses down the column of his neck. He grips my hair, guiding me to keep going.

I can feel myself becoming quite flustered. It's getting darker, and a little bit of public indecency could be a bit of fun. I mean,

I won't fully go down on him, but maybe I can make him come with just my hand.

"Jesus," he grumbles as my hand increases movement. His cock is hard, and he's breathing hard.

We both hear someone clear their throat, and I promptly remove my hand from down the front of his shorts. We both lift our eyes to see Dean standing at the back of the car, looking everywhere but at us. "Hey, Dean," I say as casually as possible.

"Yeah, hi!" he replies with an awkward crack to his voice.

Alec starts chuckling, and Dean shakes his head. "Are we in your way, Dean?" I ask.

"Nope, just wanted to let you know that I'm back." He points to me, then Alec, then back to me. "I'll um put the new tire on the car. But you'll need to take it and get this one replaced. I suggest you do it soon." He pinches the bridge of his nose. "I mean the tire. Do the tire...screw it. Do whatever you want." He flaps his hand dismissively.

I've been caught with my hand down Alec's pants, and I'm not even embarrassed.

The moment Dean leaves, Alec laughs. "So, you're an exhibitionist?"

I half shrug, and smirk. "Perhaps," I say as I grab onto his cock through his shorts and squeeze. I push up from the curb, and reach for Alec's hand to help him up. Hesitantly, he takes it, and I haul him up as he heaves himself to his feet. When we're standing, I reach up and give him a small kiss, then grab his crutches. "Thank you."

"What for?"

"For helping me today." I motion toward the car. "And for helping me with my brother."

He opens his mouth to reply, but Dean butts in. "Car's done." He looks over to us, and raises his brows. "Appears like you two are done too."

"Don't know what you're talking about," I say.

"When you were..." he can't bring himself to finish the sentence. He just points, then shakes his head and throws his arms up over his head. "Am I dropping you home?"

Alec glances at me, and raises his brows silently asking for me to take him home. "I'll drop him," I reply.

"I'm out of here. See ya." Dean walks back to his truck, still avoiding eye contact.

"Thank you, Dean!" I call. "Oh wait." I jog up to the side of my car and take my wallet out of my pretty new yellow bag. "What do I owe you?"

He flicks his hand. "We're square. Anyway, I know where that hand has been."

"Actually, it was my other hand." I stick it out and wiggle my fingers.

Dean laughs and shakes his head. "On that note, I'm out." With his tall frame, his strides are long, allowing him to get to his truck quite fast. "Bye," he calls as he takes off down the street.

Turning, I see Alec getting into the passenger side of my car. I get into the driver's seat, and turn to Alec. "I think your brother may think I'm a dirty ho."

"I think you're a dirty ho." He holds his hand up rapidly before I can say anything. "And I freaking love it!" I chuckle. "Anyway, you're *my* dirty ho. So, for me, the dirtier the better."

Something about Alec sets my heart on fire. He's possessive and gentle at the same time. I'd love to pull the car over and just ride him, but that's not exactly very ladylike. Pffft, who am I kidding? Since when have I been a lady? But, I'd better not. Not yet, anyway.

"What's going through your mind?" he asks.

"Nothing!" I nearly shout at Alec. It's not exactly something I want to discuss with him at this stage. "What's going through yours?"

"Well, we could go back to my place for the night, or to yours."

A shudder courses through me. "First of all, you need to get stronger so you can get back to work."

"And second of all?" Alec asks after a moment of patiently waiting.

"I am so embarrassed by where I live, that until I find somewhere else to go, I don't want you seeing it."

"Why?" he immediately questions.

"Because it's a terrible house, in an even worse area. But it was cheap, which meant I could save quicker to get Jordan into rehab."

"You shouldn't be embarrassed by the fact you've chosen your brother's life over somewhere fancy to live. That's one of the things I lo...ike about you."

I glance over to him before returning my focus to the road. "You lo...ike me?"

Alec turns his head, looking out at the inky sky that's now upon us. "No, I didn't say that. I said like. You heard whatever you wanted to hear," he pauses. "I think you're overworked and need a vacation because you've started hearing things." Chuckling, I drive until I pull up front of his mom's house, I turn off the car and rest my head on the headrest. "You okay?"

"I'm tired, Alec. And I'm grateful you're helping me send Jordan to rehab. Now, I just need to get him there. He's not going to go of his own free will. These drugs have taken over completely."

"Do you think an intervention will work?"

"I'm the only person left who cares about him. We've got no other family to help me stage an intervention."

"I can help," Alec offers.

"Don't take this the wrong way, but you mean nothing to Jordan. He's not going to give a crap about what you or your family say." He nods then exhales loudly. "It's okay, I'll figure out a way to get him there." I look up to the sky and exhale. "I'll meditate on it."

"You'll what?"

"Meditate." Alec laughs at me. "What are you laughing at?"

"Really? You meditate. What a load of shit."

Slowly, I lift my head, and with wide eyes, I turn to stare at him. He's chuckling and when he turns to look at me, he sees how serious I am, and his smile rapidly disappears. "We've already gone over this. A load of shit?"

"Come on, you seriously don't believe in all that shit, do you?"

"Not only do I believe in it, I practice it every single morning."

He rolls his eyes, and grunts. "Meditation? Really?"

"Yes, really."

"I don't believe in that hocus pocus crap."

He's about to be bitch-slapped. "I see." I nod my head slowly. "So, what you're saying is, you're highly judgmental of something you haven't tried."

"I don't have to try crystal meth to know it's not good for me."

"And meditation is on par with crystal meth?"

"You're putting words in my mouth," he adds defensively. "I think you've misunderstood what..."

"Hold it right there, Mister." I lift my hand to stop him talking. "You just compared meditation with crystal meth, and you're trying to swing it so I'm in the wrong? You have no idea the benefits meditation can have for the body."

"It's all that new-age crap, and I don't believe in it."

"Wait up a second. You don't believe in meditation because it's new age?" He nods his head, proud of himself. "So, breathing is new age?"

"Breathing? What are you talking about? Meditation isn't about breathing, it's about other stuff."

"Says the guy who's not even tried it."

"I know," he says confidently.

"You know nothing. I *know* you're being a jackass and you have no idea what you're talking about."

"Hey." He rubs the back of his neck. "I know what meditation is about. Trust me, I know."

"Then explain it to me." I cross my arms and wait for him to describe what he thinks it is.

"You sit on the floor cross-legged and chant *aum, aum, aum.*" He places his fingers together, closes his eyes and starts humming.

"You really are an idiot." Alec smirks at me. "Look, either you're wrong about meditation or I'm right. But either way..." I wait for him to catch on to what I just said.

Alec nods, his smile pulled up tight, until he gets it. His eyes widen, and his mouth falls open. "You just said I'm wrong."

"It took you long enough."

He rolls his eyes. "I suppose I deserve that one. Anyway, come on." Opening the door, he swings his legs around, and heaves himself up, hopping on one leg. I get out, and grab the crutches from the back seat. "Thank you," he says as I hand him the crutches.

Reaching in, I take my bag out of the back seat, and close the door. I pull up the calendar on my phone, and make a note to take my car and get the other tire fixed tomorrow. I don't ever want to be stuck like I was earlier again.

"Serena, are you staying for dinner?" Elise asks the moment I'm inside.

"I'd love to, but I don't have time. I'm going home to keep packing."

"That's right, you're moving soon. Alec told me about it. Have you found a place to go yet?"

"I've still got some more time, because they extended the lease by another four weeks. I'm hoping something comes my way."

"You're a successful and hardworking young woman, it shouldn't be too hard for you." Elise smiles, and rubs her hand on my upper back. "If you need any help, don't forget we're here."

This family is exceptionally supportive. They've shown me kindness and support when I thought I needed to do everything on my own. They've proven to me that I'm not alone.

Chapter 11

ALEC

"HEY, LOOK AT you. No crutches," Rhett says as I walk into the firehouse, albeit more cautiously than normal.

"Gone forever."

"When do you come back to work?" he asks.

"Look who's back!" Pen calls from upstairs. "The prodigal son has returned," she dramatically emphasizes by throwing her arms up toward the sky.

"About time. Pen's been driving me crazy," Hugo says as he stands beside Rhett.

Dean appears and Tripod hops over to me, wagging his tail. "I thought you'd never return."

"I've been gone for too many weeks. It feels like years. I'm back at work as of next week."

Everyone disappears except for Dean and Rhett. Rhett stands opposite me, and crosses his arms in front of his chest. He looks down at my foot. "You sure you're good to return?"

"Not only am I good to come back, but I want my house back too. I'm moving tomorrow."

Rhett rolls his eyes and huffs.

"Drills in twenty minutes!" Dean calls out for everyone to hear.

"What?" Hugo complains from upstairs.

"How are you feeling?" Dean asks.

"Excited to get back here. I've missed it. And I've missed my house, too." I look over to Rhett.

"Yeah, yeah, I know, I have my eviction notice. I'm getting out tomorrow. And don't worry, the sheets will be clean."

"Ugh." I screw my nose up.

"TMI, bro," Dean responds. "Speaking of brothers, what's happening with Serena's?"

Rhett steps closer so we're more in a family huddle to keep Pen and Hugo from listening in. "She's got the clinic all lined up. I gave her the rest of the money she needed to book it, but now, we need to get him there. But she hasn't heard from him since the day her tire blew."

"Shit, that was like last week." Dean asks.

I rub my hand over my hair, and massage the nape of my neck. "Yeah, something like that. She's worried he's dead, but I don't think he is."

"I'm sure we can find him. He won't have gone too far from Mulberry Point," Rhett says.

"Does she know where he goes to buy his drugs?" Dean asks while rubbing at his chin.

"She hasn't said. But I'm sure between the three of us, we can find him," I say.

"Drills!" Pen calls.

Rhett jogs backward toward the back of the firehouse. "See you tomorrow. I'll be back at Mom's by about nine."

"In the AM," I sternly insist. Knowing Rhett, he'll try to drag it out all day.

"Yeah, yeah." He flicks his hand at me, then sticks up his middle finger.

"You hanging around for drills, or going?"

I look down to Tripod who's patiently sitting beside Dean. "Nah, I'm gonna go. Just wanted to check in, make sure everything's okay."

Dean winces as he shakes his head. "Yeah, the place hasn't fallen apart without you," he sarcastically states before walking away. "Tripod." The dog turns his head, then scurries toward Dean. "By the way, good to have you back."

I take a deep breath, excited to finally be able to return to work. It's been too long since I've been here, and I can't wait until our next shift. The firehouse is my home, and I've hated having to stay away because of my injury.

"Drills!" Pen yells at the top of her voice.

"Coming!" Hugo screams back. He heads down the stairs, and sees me walking out. "It'll be good to have you back, man."

"Thanks. I'm looking forward to it."

Penelope stands at the side entrance, her hands on her hips, staring at Hugo. "Come on, we're waiting for you."

Hugo rolls his eyes, smirks and gives me a small nod. "See ya."

It feels so good to be back. I've missed being here. A sense of relief washes over me. This is my home.

Opening the door to my car, I get in and start it, ready to pull out onto the street when my phone rings. Taking my phone out of my cargo pants pocket, I look at the name flashing on the screen. "Hello, beautiful." I lean my head back against the headrest and close my eyes.

"Hey, how are you?"

"I'm good. I'm at work."

There's a short pause from Serena. "At work? I thought you were starting back on Friday."

"I am. I came back to talk to Rhett, and tell him I need my house back. What are you doing?"

"I'm on way to work," she says. I start to laugh. "What?"

"You're always at work. Which one of all your jobs exactly are you going to?"

"The restaurant. I'm covering someone who can't come in, and doing my close shift too. So, I'm working until probably nine or ten. Depends how fast we can close."

"I don't know how you do it. I'm in awe of you, Serena." She really is a remarkable person who somehow finds a way to get things done.

"Aww, look at you being all cute again and shit. Compliments will definitely get you laid," she says and laughs. "That's if I don't fall asleep the moment my head hits the pillow." She chuckles again. "I need to go though, I'm just pulling up and I still have to go in and get changed."

"Before you go, what time do you think you'll be finished tomorrow night?"

"Um, hang on, I need to open my phone calendar and see what jobs I have going," Serena pauses for a moment. "Can you hear me? I've got you on speaker."

"Yeah, I can hear you."

"I'm at the hospital all of tomorrow, and then I have the Morrison's house to clean. I should be finished by around six-ish."

"I'm moving back into my place tomorrow morning, so I'm cooking you dinner."

"You can cook more than the meatballs?" she teasingly jests.

"You wound me," I dramatically state while clutching at my chest, which incidentally, she can't see.

"You're such a dork. Okay, you can cook me dinner. I expect a fine dining experience, complete with wine, and of course dancing."

"Dancing?" I ask, my voice cracking in pitch.

"Of course. You have to have dancing when you're at a fine dining establishment."

"As in Studio 54 dancing? Or are we talking pole dancing, because if it's the latter. Yes please!"

"I wasn't aware you're a pole dancer, Alec."

"Not me, I meant you."

She laughs a little louder, and I like when she's free and happy. "I do have to go though. I'll see you tomorrow."

"Okay. Bye."

"Bye."

"I miss you," I say into my phone that now no longer has Serena on the other end. I miss her so damn much. I think Rhett's right, I'm turning into a marshmallow.

SERENA

THE MANAGER LOCKS the restaurant, and I stand beside him, yawning. "You okay to drive home, Serena?" he asks.

"Yeah, I'm fine. I'm so damn tired though. I think I'll be out of it in about two minutes flat when I get home."

"I'll walk you to your car." He turns so he's walking beside me.

"It's okay, I'll be fine. My car is just down there." I point to where it is, down by one of the street lights.

"Alright, I'll see you on Sunday."

"You will. Bye, John." I give him a wave over my shoulder as I walk toward my car. My eyes are burning from how tired I am, and I can't help but keep yawning. I rustle around in my bag for my keys, and find them right down at the bottom. I look up to the darkened sky and search for the moon. There's slight cloud cover, but not enough to hide the moon. The sky is layered with bright stars shining majestically. It makes my heart ache though, because I haven't heard from Jordan in what feels like forever. Now that I finally have the money to send him to New Dawn, he's disappeared and I haven't been able to find him. I wish I could reach him, that way, I could try and convince him to go into treatment. "Wherever you are, please be safe." I look up at the stars for one more moment before I get in my car and drive home.

My stomach is churning, and my hands are shaking as I pull into my street. My mind is overrun with images of Jordan laying in a ditch somewhere, dead. It feels like my every waking moment is taken over by Jordan. I'm killing myself working fourteen- to eighteen-hour days all so I can get him the help he needs. When will this end?

I drive by the party house and the two guys who live there are standing outside, watching as I pull into my driveway. They angle their bodies, and cross their arms in front of their chests as they scrutinize me getting out of the car, then rush to the front door of my house. Although they've done nothing to me, it's still weird how they watch me. My skin chills with bolts of ice as I rustle around for my house keys, busting to get inside to lock myself in.

With my back to the locked door, I close my eyes and take several deep breaths, calming my frantic mind. "They've never done anything to you, so get over yourself," I say trying to find justification. "You've been living here for how long? And they've never said or done a thing to you." It's true, they haven't. It's just their overall intimidating presence.

I walk over to my room, unlock the door, and throw my bag on the bed. I should go have a shower, but I'm just too damned tired. I take my phone out of my bag and plug it in to charge. Looking at the time, my shoulders slump and I rub at my eyes. It's just after ten, and I'm ready to collapse right here. Maybe I can have a twenty-minute nap, then get up and have a shower.

Who am I kidding? If I have a nap, it'll turn into me waking tomorrow morning. Alright, I have to push myself to have a damn shower now. A message comes through as I'm sitting on the bed, trying to motivate myself into getting up.

Let me know when you're home.

I smile like a fool. I think it's so cute how Alec worries about me.

I'm home. Trying to find the energy to go have a shower.

I could come join you. Is the instant reply.

Rain check? I'm really tired.

I haven't had sex with him yet, and I'm already asking for a rain check. Jesus, what a lame girlfriend I'm turning out to be.

"For fuck's sake," I scold myself. I need to get out of my own damn head. Is this what being tired does to a person? Makes them delirious and overthink everything?

Rain check for tomorrow night it is.

I place my phone on the bedside table, grab my pajamas, and head into the shower. Turning on the hot water first, I quickly strip then stick my hand in the stream waiting for the water to heat up. I turn on the cold-water faucet, and wait until the temperature's perfect before standing under the stream.

I stand with the water pelting down on my back, lower my head and close my eyes. I take several deep breaths, trying to steady this bothersome feeling of dread bubbling away in the pit of my gut. "Jordan, I hope you're safe." Although my eyes are closed, several tears roll down my cheeks and mix with the hot water of the shower. "Please, come home to me," I beg in a small voice.

Because if I'm being honest with myself, I'm not sure how much longer I can do this. I want to say I'll keep fighting for Jordan when he can't fight for himself, but I'm not sure I can handle all this pressure anymore. But I doubt I'll ever be able to wipe my hands of him, regardless how long this goes on for.

I allow myself to cry for only a few more minutes. I lift my chin, pull my shoulders back and take one more deep breath. "You've got this," I say to myself. And I do. I'm smart, tough, and I'm doing the best I can.

Forgoing my hair, I quickly wash myself, then turn the water off, grab my towel and wrap it around my body. Walking into my room, I see the screen on my phone dim. Sitting on the edge of the bed in my towel, I pick my phone up and smile as I swipe it to bring it to life. Two missed phone calls and two voice mail messages.

I look at the number, thinking it's Alec, but it's not. Standing, I swipe to listen to the messages as I towel myself dry. Shit, what if it's Jordan and he needs me to go pick him up from somewhere? The message starts playing and I put it on speaker, as I get ready to head out so I can collect Jordan from wherever he is.

"This message is for Serena Whitaker. I'm calling from Mulberry Point Hospital Emergency Department. Could you please return this call as soon as you can?" she then clearly and slowly says the number she wants me to call.

Shit, shit, shit. Something's happened to Jordan. I know it has. Scrambling to get dressed, I dial the number for the hospital. It rings out. Fretting and frantic, I pace my room back and forth. I dial the number again.

No one answers, *again.*

There's no way I'll be able to sleep if I don't get through to find out what it is they're calling me for. I listen to the second message, and again it's the same woman repeating what she did in the first message.

In my gut, I know this has something to do with Jordan. It has to. I dial the number again. No one is answering. I know it's late, and they're all most likely busy, but I need someone to answer so I don't lose my damn mind over here. I try again. Still no answer.

"Screw this," I say as I slip my shoes on, grab my bag and keys and head out of my room. I dial Alec's number on the way out of the house.

"I thought you'd be sleeping by now."

"Alec!" my voice crumbles with stress.

"What's wrong?"

"I was in the shower, and when I got out there were phone calls and messages," I ramble, trying to form a coherent sentence. "I have to get to Mulberry Point Hospital. I've got this really bad feeling, Alec. I think he's dead. I think they've found him. Shit, shit, shit."

"I'm just getting in my car, where do you live, and I'll come to get you?"

Other than the fact that I'm embarrassed by where I live, I don't have time to sit around and wait for him. "I'm on my way to the hospital now." I put Alec on speaker, and reverse out of my driveway like my life depends on it. The two guys who are always out the front of their house, watch as I speed past them and take the corner so fast my tires screech.

But at this stage, I don't care what they're doing, I just need to get to the hospital. "Serena, can you hear me?" a concerned Alec asks, startling me out of my worrying funk.

"I'm here," I say as I speed toward the hospital.

"Talk to me. What did the messages say?"

"Nothing, they just said I had to call them, and every time I tried to return their call, it would ring out."

"Are you sure it was a genuine call, Serena? If you can't get through to them, perhaps it's someone playing some kind of sick joke on you."

My mind is reeling, what if someone is playing some kind of joke? "Well, it's not funny if someone is. But I wouldn't be able to live with myself if it *is* the hospital, and they're calling me about Jordan. I have to go and try to find him."

"I know. I'm nearly at the hospital now. How far are you?"

Considering I'm driving well above the speed limit, I should be there any moment myself. "I'll be there soon. I'm not going to wait for you, Alec, but I'll meet you inside the ER." I pull around the corner, drive straight into the parking bays and find a lot are empty, probably because it's late in the evening. "I'm here. I'm heading inside."

"I'll be there in thirty seconds." By the time I park my car, grab my bag and open my door, Alec is pulling his car into the spot beside me. He's out of his car and next to me within seconds. He drapes his arm around my shoulders, nestles close into me and gives me a kiss on the temple. "It'll be okay, whatever it is."

I can't even think of a response to Alec. "I hope he's not dead."

My body trembles at the mere thought of losing my brother when I'm the one who's supposed to be looking after him. "Hey, come here." Alec stops us just short of the entry of the hospital. He faces me, and wraps me in his arms. "It'll be okay," he says again with more assurance to his voice.

"I should've done more, Alec. I could've, but I didn't."

"You've been amazing, Serena. You've done everything you can, and so much more. But right now, you need to just take a breath and trust that he's okay." Alec rubs his hands all over my back, trying to calm my distress.

He's right, I do need to calm myself, or I'll end up in here with Jordan. "You're right, I need to be strong."

Alec places a soft kiss on my forehead, pulls back, and links our fingers together. "You ready?"

I turn to look at the entrance of the hospital, take another deep breath and nod. *Please don't be dead, please, don't be dead.* I'm not sure I'm strong enough to breathe if Jordan has died.

Alec leads me toward the ER, and we're greeted by the receptionist. "Hi," he says with a smile.

I open my mouth to speak, but find my voice refusing to cooperate. I can't bring myself to say it. I just can't. I look to Alec, and silently beg for him to do the talking. "Has there been a Jordan Whitaker admitted this evening?"

The receptionist taps on the keyboard of his computer, then looks up to us. He opens his mouth to say something, and my stomach clenches as my heart drops. My legs feel like they're collapsing from beneath me. Alec holds me tighter to his body. "I'm his sister, Serena Whitaker," I say in a small voice. This is the hospital I work at, but I've never seen this guy in my life, so there'd be no way he'd know who I am. And I'm all the way up the other end of the hospital.

"Your brother has been admitted into the hospital. He was found by a Good Samaritan who called it in. He'd overdosed, and according to the staff in the ER, the paramedics who were first at the scene administered Narcan."

My breath has been caught in the back of my throat. I've been too afraid to release it. But I find myself pushing out the air and slightly relaxing against Alec, who hasn't let me go. "He's alive?" I ask, my voice painfully quiet.

"He's alive," the receptionist confirms. "You need to head down to the ER, and ask for him there. Do you know where to go?"

I nod. "I work here." He smiles warmly, and both Alec and I thank him before we walk toward emergency. "He's okay," I say on a long sigh.

"This may be the intervention you need to get him to New Dawn."

I nod again, but all I can think is how grateful and relieved I am that Jordan is alive. "If I don't get him over to New Dawn now, I don't think there'll be a next time. Because next time, I don't think he's going to be so lucky."

Once we're in the ER, we're quickly shown to Jordan's room. I recognize a few of the staff, and even though they smile, I'm barely able to keep my emotions and nerves from spilling over. We're told by a nurse that the doctor will be in to see us soon. Alec and I stand outside the door of Jordan's room. I can hear all kinds of painful sounds coming from the other side. Alec stands beside me, holding my hand. "I'll go in first," he offers.

"No, you can't. The Narcan will have blocked any of the drugs going through his system, which means he's detoxing, and if he's detoxing, he's aggressive." Alec squeezes my hand. "He won't hurt me," I reaffirm his unasked, worrisome question.

"Let me go in first, please."

I turn to Alec and stare into his hypnotic, soulfully intense dark eyes. Leaning in, I give him a small kiss on the lips. "Thank you for wanting to protect me, but I have to do this. You can come in, but I need you to trust me to lead, and trust that I know what I'm doing."

Alec breaks our connection and stares down at his feet for a split second before lifting his chin. "I'm coming in, and I won't say a thing. But if he tries to lunge for you, I won't allow him to do that."

"I understand." I nod, then turn to look at the door.

Closing my eyes, I take in a deep breath, before heading into the lion's den.

The moment we're inside, Jordan is moaning, and trying to turn from side to side. I've noticed both his wrists are restrained. He's sweating profusely, and there's a god-awful stench coming from in here. Jordan whips his head to the side to see who's entered the room. He narrows his eyes at me, before replacing the scowl with a smile. "Sis! Thank God you're here. Tell them I don't need to be here and to let me go. And look at this. They have me shackled to the bed like I'm some kind of dangerous animal." His eyes land on Alec. "Who the hell are you?" he angrily spits to Alec. How quickly his mood swings from one emotion to another.

"Don't worry about him," I reply, trying to get the focus away from Alec. Jordan is glaring at Alec, killing him with just his cold, frighteningly angry eyes. I stand in front of Alec, blocking Jordan's view of him. "Hey, don't worry about him," I say again. Behind my back, I flick my hand to Alec, getting him to step back as I move forward. I hear his feet shuffling backward, doing exactly as I've asked of him. I glimpse over my shoulder to find Alec has stepped back, but his focus is still on protecting me.

Jordan moans again, and tries to double over and grasp his stomach. "I'm hurting, sis. You gotta get 'em to let me go. I need some medicine to get better."

"Jordan..." I drag the chair over beside the bed, and sit near his head. A place where I know he can't reach me if he does lunge at me even though he's restrained.

"Just undo this one, I can do the other one." He glimpses down to the restraints then back to me, silently pleading for me to remove them.

"I can't."

"Fuck you!" he screeches. He rapidly changes his tactic, his face softens, and he starts crying. "I just need to get out of here."

"Jordan, I've found a treatment center for you, and I want you to go."

"But I don't have a problem. I can stop any time I want."

"I'm sure every addict says the same thing. But you can't stop, and you need help. I'm sending you to the treatment center."

"You don't control me, Serena. And I can stop. Just loosen this, and I'll come home with you. I just need to go take care of something first, then I'll come home and I'll stop."

"No. I'm taking you to the treatment center," I say again, but firmer. "The only way I'm going to let you get out of here, is if you come to the treatment center with me."

"Please, sis. Please, don't make me go. I don't need to go. I'm fine, there's nothing wrong with me."

"Jordan, you smell like you've shit yourself. And you were found unconscious because of a drug overdose. You're an addict and you need the help."

He starts sobbing, and babbling some shit about no one wanting to give him a chance. "I'm not an addict," he cries between the sobs. "I'm just sensitive."

"Bullshit you're sensitive. You're a fucking junkie," I yell at him. "You're not only ruining your life, you're destroying mine." I lose my cool. "You're sucking the life out of me, Jordan. You're killing yourself and taking me down with you. I'll tell you what. If you don't want to go, don't. But I'm going to sever every single tie with you. I'll move, and you'll never find me."

Jordan's staring at me blankly, his fake tears have now ceased. "But you're the only person I've got," he says in a small voice.

"You don't love me. Not one little bit, or you'd go to rehab and try to help me by getting your life together."

Jordan tries to lift his hand to wipe at his tears, but is jerked back to reality when he can't move his hands further than an inch or two. For a split second, a moment in time, something passes over him. "If I go to treatment, will you move and never see me again?"

"If you go to treatment, I mean, first plane out to Kentucky tonight, then I'll stay in your life forever. Or, I walk out this door and we're done."

Jordan swallows and stares at me with wide eyes. He flexes his fingers several times as he jitters around on the bed. He's agitated, and I'm distraught. "Can I think about it?"

He's just shot an arrow through my heart. I know it's not him, and it's the drugs, but man, this shit hurts. I stand from my chair, and glance over to Alec, indicating I'm ready to walk away from Jordan. "I've spent many days and nights worrying about you. I've taken as many jobs as I possibly can to get the money together to get you into this treatment center. I'm the only one who loves or cares about you. You get from the moment I take my first step toward that door, until I reach it, for you to make your mind up. But once I'm gone, you're completely on your own." I take a step toward the door. My heart is aching from his silence. I take one more step, and feel like I'm about to burst into tears. "I can walk out of here knowing that I mean less to you than you do to me. Because if you don't want to try, then I have no reason to try either."

I place my hand on the door knob. My stomach hardens as a wave of defeated nausea ripples through my body. My legs tremble as I come to the hard realization how much control the drugs have over my brother. It hits me right in the center of my heart.

I turn the handle, and my head spins with disbelief. "Wait," he says in a small voice.

With all my strength, I straighten my shoulders, but don't turn around. "What?" I bluntly croak.

"Don't go. I need you."

I still refuse to turn around and give anything more than he's already taken. "You need the drugs more than me, Jordan." I move to open the door, hoping to call his bluff. I need to know that he's committed to getting help.

"I'll go!" he desperately pleads. "I'll go to rehab. But please, don't leave me."

I shoot Alec a side glance, and give him a small smile. He rubs his hand on my back, and I know I have his support. Right now, Jordan doesn't need a sister. He needs someone who's firm with him. Turning, I look at Jordan. "From here, we'll get the next available flight to Kentucky. You're not to leave my side."

"I'll do anything you want me to." This is the first time that I actually believe him. "Just, please, don't wipe me from your life."

"I'll get us plane tickets," Alec says as he opens the door.

"You don't have to come with us," I whisper.

"Yes, I do." He leans in and gives me a kiss on the cheek. "I'll book us a car too."

"Thank you," I mutter before he walks out the door. Turning, I sit in the chair next to Jordan. He relaxes back, and looks up at the ceiling. "I'm relieved you're doing this."

"I can do it by myself. I don't need a rehab center."

"Nope, sorry." I have to stand my ground. I know statistically, he'll be less likely to fail if he goes through rehab in comparison to doing it on his own. "You made a deal with me."

"Why are you doing this?"

"Because you're the only brother I have and I love you, even though right now, you don't love yourself."

"Yeah, I do."

"That's bullshit. You fucking stink, and you're so skinny it wouldn't surprise me if you're malnourished."

"You've got enough meat on your bones to make up for both of us," he snarls at me.

I know he's trying to be nasty to push me away, but I'm not going to let it faze me. "Yep, and guess what? I love my body. I'm strong, and confident, and I'm digging you out of the shit you've gotten yourself into. So, you're welcome."

He half chuckles. "You think you're better than me."

He's trying to pick a fight so I won't take him to rehab. "I've got you now. And you're going to get the help you need."

"What if I fail?"

"You'll fail if you don't try. But you're going to try, right?"

Jordan hesitates, but slowly nods his head. "I'll try for you, Serena."

"That's all I can ask."

He closes his eyes, and is fast asleep within a few seconds. Alec opens the door, his gaze instantly falling on a sleeping Jordan. He jerks his head to indicate I should follow him out of the room. The moment we're outside, I lean against him and let out a huge sigh as he hugs me tightly. "Everything okay?" he asks.

"As good as it can be. How did you do with the flights and a car?"

"All booked. Do you want me to call New Dawn, or are you going to?"

"I'll email them and let them know we'll be coming. I've just got to wait for the doctor. Wait, we came in two cars. We can't leave one here."

"Already taken care of. Dean and Rhett are coming to get my car, and we'll drive yours to the airport. There's a flight at eight in the morning, which is the one I've booked us on. They've made a note of Jordan's condition and where we're going and have agreed to keep us away from other passengers."

"Thank you, I'm not sure what I would've done without you here."

Alec hugs me even closer, while gently trailing his fingertips up and down my back. "You would've made this work, because you're simply amazing."

I smile against his chest. I could stay like this for the rest of the night. I'm so tired, but I have a ton of emails to send off to various people letting them know I won't be back at work for the next day or two. It's so late, and I don't want to interrupt anyone by calling them. I need to email New Dawn to let them know we'll be in Kentucky tomorrow with my brother who'll be going through some pretty bad withdrawal by that time. I hope the Narcan lasts enough so that the flight won't be bad.

Now, the real work begins.

Chapter 12

SERENA

SITTING IN THE counselor's office at New Dawn, Jordan is beside me, and he's been fidgety since we arrived in Kentucky. Luckily, the drive from the airport to here was less than an hour, and with Alec doing all the driving, I was able to keep Jordan from jumping out his skin, or possibly the moving car.

"How are you feeling, Jordan?" Robert, the counselor, smiles.

Jordan is antsy, it's obvious to everyone in the room. "I'm fine, I don't have a problem, and I don't know why I'm here."

I feel my shoulders droop, and I let out a breath of resignation. This has been on repeat for hours, ever since we left Mulberry Point. "You're here because if you don't take this treatment, then I don't want anything more to do with you," I say, struggling with the words that are so harsh and final. The reality is, I could never walk away and wipe him from my life.

"Seems your sister is worried about you," Robert says.

Jordan's leg is bouncing up and down, and he's looking around the office, remaining silent.

"What would you like to see happen to your brother, Serena?"

"I'd like him to get clean, and find his strength. He's a good person, but right now, any semblance of that is buried under years of drug abuse. And I don't even know who he is anymore."

"We can help with that. Jordan, how do you feel about what your sister has said?"

Jordan shrugs as if he doesn't care. We wait for an answer, but it doesn't appear as if he wants to verbalize one.

"I can't wait until I can come back here for a visit, and see my brother again. Not this version of a brother, but *my* brother. My funny, smart brother who I miss so much," my voice cracks, and Alec reaches for my hand to hold. "The brother I want to be able to talk to, and hug, and want him to hang out with me and my boyfriend. The one I don't have to worry about anymore." A few tears leak and I'm struggling to keep it together. "I want that guy back. Not this one." I point to Jordan.

Alec squeezes my hand to let me know he's here for me. He leans in, kisses my temple, then whispers, "You're so strong."

"Are you ready to live?" Richard asks Jordan

What a daunting question. It makes my stomach churn and my heart race.

Jordan only nods without saying another word.

"We'll need to go through your suitcase," Richard starts.

"This is the only thing he came in with." I pointedly look at the ragged, dirty clothes Jordan is wearing. "But, I'll go to the mall to buy him some clothes and bring them back."

"Excellent. Jordan, if you'd like to follow me, I can introduce you to the treatment team who'll be looking after you and show you to your room." Richard stands. "And Serena, if you don't mind, please wait here a moment so we can have a chat."

"Okay." Jordan stands, and without even looking at me, he follows Richard out the door. "I love you," I call to Jordan, who flips me the bird over his shoulder.

"Don't take it personally," Alec says.

"It's hard not to."

"When we leave here we'll find a Walmart or Target so you can get clothes for Jordan. And I've booked us into a room for the night, not too far from here. We've got a flight back tomorrow at midday."

My head has been in a whirlwind from the moment I listened to that voicemail message last night. "Everything's happening so fast. I'm surprised, because even though I want this, I'm not ready for it."

"This is the best place for him to be. This is what you've been working so hard for. It's his best chance at kicking his addiction."

"Logically, I know this is the best place for him. I'm just frightened. What if this doesn't work and he goes back to using again?" I bury my face in my hands. My chest hurts while my breath becomes short and sharp.

"Come on, it'll be okay." He swivels my chair around easily, pulls me up and sits me on his lap. His arms envelop me while he tries to calm my anxious, wayward feelings. "You're shaking." He kisses my forehead over and over again.

"I feel like a blubbering mess."

"You're allowed to break down, Serena. You've done a miraculous job keeping him alive this long, and you should be really proud of all your efforts."

I clutch at my chest as I crumple against him. "It hurts, Alec. It hurts so bad."

"To be afraid is okay. Be kind to yourself. You've been on the go for how many years, and now he's in the best hands possible."

The door closes, and I struggle to lift my head. "Everything okay?" Richard asks.

"Serena's coming to terms with everything," Alec responds on my behalf.

"I can tell. I know you love your brother, and I know he'll flourish here. And the other thing I know is that I can see how strong a support system you'll be for him once his ninety days are up," Richard says. "Let me put your mind at ease, Serena, and tell you a little about what's going to happen."

I pull back from Alec, and silently thank him for being my rock in my dark hours. I sit again on my seat, and reach for a tissue on Richard's table. "I'm sorry you've seen me like this. I'm usually stronger."

"It's often the times we're feeling our weakest, that we're actually at our strongest."

I suppose that's exactly how I've been feeling. Weak, and empty, unable to help Jordan when he's needed me most. "I feel like I can breathe again."

Richard is an older man, maybe in his late fifties, with a very bad comb-over, but the kindest smile and eyes. "So, he's having a shower right now, and we've got some clothes he can change into. You need to bring some underwear, sweaters, t-shirts, shorts, and pants. Nothing too elaborate, because the withdrawals will be intense once the Narcan is fully out of his system."

"He was hot and sweaty, and quite on edge for the entire flight and car ride over," Alec says.

"Very normal, so don't worry about it. You got him here, and that in itself is commendable. You've kept him breathing, Serena. But now, it's time to trust in us, and to know we'll get him clean and hopefully he'll work hard to stay clean." It's obvious to me that Richard genuinely cares for the patients who come here. He's kind and thoughtful, and speaks with confidence, though gently too.

"When do you think I'll be able to come back to see him?"

"First of all, he'll need to detox before he can see anyone. The physical detoxing is very difficult. However, the hardest part will be the warfare going on in his mind. You see, the receptors in his brain will be telling him for a while that 'just a little bit won't hurt,' and the more he resists it, the weaker those particular receptors become, and the stronger he'll be. He needs to build new, and healthier neural pathways. But, for now, typically, it's around two weeks before I suggest you come to see him. He doesn't have phone privileges to call you, however you're more than welcome to phone us to see how he's progressing. The more we can keep him focused at this massive task ahead of him and limit his distractions, the better it is for him."

I completely understand everything he's saying, and in order to give Jordan the best chance possible, I need to be my strongest for him. "I've done all the research I can, and New Dawn has a success rate of over eighty percent, which is amazing. But what reasons do you find are most typical for relapse?" I ask.

"Old behaviors. If nothing changes, then *nothing changes.* And there are a lot of tools we give every one of our patients to ensure they're successful from the moment they leave here."

"I'll be there to help him," I say.

Richard smiles. "I have no doubt you will be." Standing, he makes his way over to the door and opens it. That's our cue to leave.

"We'll be back shortly with clothes for Jordan."

Richard extends his hand, and shakes my hand, then Alec's. "Take your time."

Alec and I leave his office, walk through the corridor, and we're buzzed out into the foyer. "You were so quiet in there," I say to Alec.

"I'm here for your support, Serena. Do you want to check into the hotel, or find somewhere to buy clothes?"

I can't help but yawn, but my stomach grumbles too. "I'm tired and hungry too. Maybe we can find somewhere to buy his clothes, then grab something to eat and go back to the hotel?" I pull my phone out of my pocket, and look at the time. "It's only midday."

"Actually, we can't check in until two, so we may as well go get his clothes, maybe have some lunch somewhere too." As we walk back to the car, I lean my head on Alec's shoulder while he wraps his arm around my waist. "It's been a big night, and an emotional morning," he says.

There's a stirring of reactions inside my chest and stomach. "A part of me never thought this day would actually come. But now I actually have a moment to think about it, his overdose was a godsend in that he's actually still alive and manageable." We get to the car, and I turn and snuggle into Alec. His strong arms wrap around my body, allowing me to appreciate his warmth and support. "Thank you, Alec. You didn't need to be here, but you are."

He kisses my temple, and takes in a deep breath. "Let's go and find something to eat, and clothes for Jordan." He unlocks the car, and opens the passenger door for me. I slide in and put my seatbelt on. By the time I'm done, he's in the car too. I can't help but stare at how beautiful he is. "What?" he asks.

"I don't know how you do it. You're so nice to look at," I tease.

He tsks, and rolls his eyes. "I'm nice to look at?"

"Yeah, you look awfully fine to a tired woman."

He starts the car, chuckles, then narrows his eyes and slowly turns to look at me. "I'm only fine to a tired woman?" he playfully teases.

"I suppose you're okay to a fully awake one too." I chuckle and jokingly shove him in the shoulder. "But in all honesty, I don't know how you do it. I haven't slept in what feels like days, and I can barely keep my eyes open."

"I'm used to it. At work, our schedule is twenty-four hours on, then forty-eight hours off. So it's something I'm used to."

"Have you ever thought of doing anything else?"

The stern shaking of his head gives me my answer. "We come from generations of firefighters, and I couldn't imagine myself doing anything else. I love it. I think Dean, Rhett, and I were born with it running through our veins."

"But you were hurt; doesn't that frighten you?"

"It's all a chance isn't it?" he says as he glances toward me, then back to the road.

"What do you mean?" I ask, curious.

"At any moment our lives can come to an end. So why not do what you love until that moment arrives?"

"Listen to you, all philosophical and shit." He moves his right hand and places it on my thigh.

"My old man went to work one ordinary day, and never came back. So, I figure, when death is ready, it'll come and get me. But in the meantime, I love being a firefighter, so I'll keep doing it until the day I can't anymore." I turn in my seat to fully appreciate the amazing man he is. Alec seems to sense me watching him, and he sits straighter, with chin held high. "First stop, the mall."

I look out the window to see we're approaching a mall. "How did you find it?"

"I thought I'd drive around for a while, and if that didn't work, I'd look at maps on my phone. Let's find something to eat, and get what you need."

All three of us quite literally jumped on the plane with no luggage. I don't even have anything to wear. We're only here tonight, but I can't be in these clothes anymore. I'll find something for me too while we're here.

Alec's holding one of the bags from the store, and he's got the key to the room. I'm leaning against him in the elevator on the way up to our room, and I can feel my grip loosening on the shopping bags I'm carrying as I struggle to keep my stinging eyes open. "I think I'm going to have a shower and go to sleep for two hours. I don't want to sleep too long, because then I won't sleep tonight," I say in a semi-slurred voice.

"Gotcha. Shower, then bed. Oh, I've booked us a table for the restaurant at seven tonight, and we have to be at the airport by eleven tomorrow morning."

The elevator door opens, and with Alec leading me, we find our room. It's nothing overly fancy, a huge bed, a balcony, a mini bar fridge, and a bathroom. "Wow, look at those views," I say. "Makes up for the shitty reason we've had to come here." I open the door to the balcony and step outside. Alec is behind me, caging me up against the half wall with his body flush against mine. He moves my hair and kisses my neck, as he grips my hip possessively. "God, this feels so good," I say as I close my eyes and lean into him. I can't remember the last time I've been kissed with so much ferociousness. If only I was awake enough to appreciate it more.

He moves back, smacks me hard on the ass, and chuckles. "Go have a shower, and go to bed."

My eyes are seriously closing, and as much as I want him to join me in the shower, I'm way too emotionally and physically spent to truly appreciate him. "Okay, I'm going." Mental side note; when I wake up, I'm so going to show him my gratitude for everything he's done.

Taking my clothes and toiletries out of the store bags, I take the tags off, and bring them into the shower with me. First thing first, I need to brush my teeth. No one likes to kiss someone with furry teeth, and mank breath. *Bleh.*

Stepping into the shower, it's like pure bliss with the hot water, and the pressure of the showerhead. My eyes close, and I can feel myself falling deeper and deeper into a restful and calm state. If I stay here too long, I'm going to fall asleep in no time.

I turn the faucets off, step out and towel dry my body before slipping into the new pajamas I bought. I didn't wash my hair, which means I don't have to dry it. I open the door, and find Alec sitting outside on the balcony with a drink in his hand, gazing over the pretty views of the landscape, greenery mixed with buildings. I head out to him, and wrap my arms around his shoulders from behind. "You smell nice," he says as he kisses my arm. "But you need sleep."

"Don't you too?"

"I'll stay awake until tonight, then I'll sleep well. I'm used to these kinds of hours."

I want to ask him if he'd lay with me, but he appears quite content sitting out here sipping on his drink and relaxing. I give him a kiss on the cheek, then unravel myself from him. "Wake me in two hours please."

"Okay, I will."

I head inside, and lay on the bed, facing the balcony. Alec has the rest of his drink, stands, and comes in. He pulls the covers back, and crawls into bed facing me. "You don't have to come in. You could've stayed out there." I tuck my hands under the pillow, staring into his perfect dark eyes then move my gaze to follow the curve of his strong jawline. There's something about Alec that just speaks to me. "Why are you still single?"

"I thought I had a girlfriend." He smirks.

Cheeky bastard. "You do, and she's awesome, so you better watch it, 'cause she'll kick your ass if you don't say she's awesome too," I say referring to myself in third person. He smiles wider. "But really, why haven't you settled down already?"

"Because I'd relentlessly search for the same type of woman, and I'd always find her. But that type never held my interest long."

"Are you telling me you're going to be bored with me soon?"

"Hmm," he clicks his tongue to the roof of his mouth. "I don't think I'll ever be bored with you. You're nothing like what I thought I wanted." I internally cringe, but I think my face shows my consternation. "You're overthinking it."

"Probably," I agree. "It's just..." I huff in frustration. "I don't know. Maybe I'm just so stupid tired that everything is amplified, and I'm looking at the negative instead of the positive."

He lays his hand on my hip, leans in and kisses the tip of my nose. "You've been nothing but a surprise to me, Serena. It's like when I'd take a lady out for dinner, I'd say to her, what do you feel like eating, and the reply would become tedious to me, because it was the same time and time again. They'd say, *whatever you want is fine.* That's okay every now and then, but when I'm dating someone for a month and we'd go out at least once a week and she could never give me more than that, it felt like she didn't have a voice of her own."

"Well, you know my voice is plenty loud."

"You call me on my shit, and I like that. I love how when we're eating you order what you want and you eat it. Although, I must say, I wasn't impressed about you eating my donut when we went to that cafe today."

"You snooze, you lose, buddy," I say and giggle. "You took way too long to drink your coffee, it was sitting there, mocking me, so I ate it."

"You truly are phenomenal, and I'm so glad we met."

"See, the universe has a funny way of giving us exactly what we need, even if we're not looking for it."

"Here we go again, the whole mumbo jumbo about meditation and crap," he says as he rolls his eyes.

"If you hadn't been hurt in the fire, then we would never have met. Which means, you'd be on your merry-go-round of the same milquetoast girlfriends. I wouldn't have been able to send Jordan to New Dawn yet, and we wouldn't be here, together."

He scrunches his mouth, then lifts his hand from my hip and taps his chin. "Miss Whitaker, it appears you have a point."

"See. The universe knows what it's doing. Maybe I'll even be able to get you into meditation."

He places his hand on my hip again, while laughing. "Yeah, let's not go crazy now or anything." A massive yawn rips through me, causing my eyes to tear. "You need sleep."

"I know, but I like talking to you."

"Close your eyes, or you'll force me to leave."

I close my eyes, and the last thing I remember saying is, "Don't go, I like it when you're near me."

I think I hear him say, "I love it when we're together." Although, that may have been me dreaming.

Chapter 13

ALEC

SERENA IS CERTAINLY not a peaceful sleeper. She snores, and talks in her sleep. I wonder if she knows that? I doubt it. Hmm, she told me to wake her in two hours, but I didn't say how I'd wake her.

She's on her back with one arm over her head, snoring and mumbling while she's sleeping. Her pajama top has ridden up to just beneath her tits, showing me her cute, soft stomach.

God, her boobs are so nice and round. They've got a bit of a sag to them, but my God, I can't wait to get my mouth around her nipples. Perhaps I should help myself. I think she'll love being woken up by my lips all over her. But then, maybe that's a bit creepy. Fuck, I'm overthinking this. I pull the covers back and gently kiss her stomach. Serena only just stirs. I lick her stomach, kissing up toward the hemline of her pajama top.

"Are you trying to have sex with me?" she asks in a croaky, yet sexy, sleepy voice.

"That's the plan." I push her top back, and kiss her tit. Laving my tongue around her nipple, Serena lets out a low deep moan. I smirk against her flesh, loving how she pushes her chest further into my face while making those sexy sounds.

"Keep going," she says.

If the lady wants me to keep going, then that's exactly what I'm going to do. I lift her pajama top over her head, tossing it to the floor beside the bed. "You've got the sexiest tits." I lower my head, taking as much as I can in my mouth. I squeeze the other one hard, making her moan even more. With equal care, I take the other in my mouth refusing to neglect any part of her body.

"Oh man," she murmurs. The sound of ecstasy fluttering past her lips. God, I love her sounds.

Leaving her well-loved tits, I lick my way down to her navel, stopping only to nibble and suck her skin into my mouth. She lifts her hips, and I know what she wants. I hook my fingers into the pajama bottoms, and slide them down her legs, leaving her completely exposed. I sit up in bed, staring at how perfect she is. "I like this," I play with the landing strip of hair covering her pussy.

"Good, because I like it too." She brings the heels of her feet up, and opens her legs. Holy shit. "I'll show you how much I like it." With two fingers, she rubs at her clit while those sexy little sounds keep coming from her. I look up to see she has her eyes closed, and she's biting on her bottom lip, totally enjoying herself.

"Hey, I want in on the fun too." Lowering my head, I swat her hand out of the way, and bury my face into her.

She laughs, then takes in a sharp breath. I've got an idea. I pull away from her and sit back on the bed. It takes Serena a few seconds before she opens her eyes. "You stopped. What the hell?"

Laying on the bed, I hold my hand out to her. "I want you to sit on my face."

"You don't have to ask me twice." She's up on her knees about to forward mount me, when I waggle my finger at her. "What?"

"Turn around."

A cheeky grin creeps up on her face. "Hell yeah, I'm all for giving and receiving." I shimmy out of my sleep pants, my stiff cock ready for action. Serena turns, and backs up onto my face. She sits and I go hard, fucking her with my tongue. She lowers, and the next thing I know, her mouth and tongue is working magic on my cock.

Fuck, my mind is in a state of ecstasy while her tongue swirls around over the head of my hard cock. Serena grinds her hips against my face, while giving me some of the best head I've received in a long, long time. I want to live in her pussy. Park my fucking tongue inside her, and just keep eating her until her cum is all over my face.

Serena stops sucking my cock, and slightly sits up. "Jesus, I'm so close." She tries to move her leg to get off my face, but I grab her hips and hold her down, wanting her to come while she's riding my face. I don't even care that my cock is being neglected, I can take care of that later. For now though, I want her to ride me, and take everything she needs from my mouth. She holds onto my knees, and bucks against my face. "Shit," she groans as if she's out of breath. "Shit!" Her moves sharpen and intensify. She's so close. With small thrusts, she uses me for her own pleasure, and I'm nearly losing my mind. "Fuck!" Serena slows her movements, but I don't let her off that easily. I keep eating, licking, and sucking her, until she tries to pull away. Nope. If I can get a second orgasm out of her, I'm taking it. My tongue buries further into her, Serena straightens and moves her hips like a wave on my face. "Fuck!" She jerks against my face before falling forward, taking my cock back into her mouth.

As much as I want my cum down her throat, I much prefer my cock to be buried deep inside of her. I lift her hips from my face, swing her around so she's facing me, and lower her down. "I've got a condom in my wallet."

"I've got one in my bag." She reaches across the bed, grabs her bag by the handle, and pulls it up on the bed. I'm kinda speechless, because she's seriously impressive. "What? I have to be prepared. Never know when I'll get me some dick," she says as she looks over her shoulder at me while rustling around in her bag.

I smack her ass so hard, it leaves a red hand print. "The only dick you'll ever get again, will be mine."

She glimpses at the red hand print, and bites on her lower lip again. "Do it again." She sticks her butt out toward me.

Fuck, my woman likes it a bit rough. *Hell yeah.* I smack her butt cheek with a little bit more force, and she groans as she jerks forward. "Do you enjoy a good spanking?" She wiggles her butt at me again, telling me the answer. I spank her other cheek. Three brilliant red hand prints are on her ass cheeks. I lean down, and bite her butt.

Serena's keen sigh is music to my ears. "I really enjoyed that. It's made me extremely wet." She's not backward about being forward. Fuck, I love that about her. "Here." With the condom next to me, she grabs my hand, isolates two fingers and sinks down on them so they're inserted. "See how wet I am?" she asks as she grinds her hips on my fingers. "I like being spanked. A lot." Her eyes are watching mine as she keeps slowly rotating her hips.

And I'm about to blow my load at how assertive and confident she is. "Put the condom on," I say trying to hold myself back.

While still riding my fingers, she takes the condom, rips the packet open with her teeth, pinches the top and rolls it on my cock. "I'm done."

"I want you to sit facing me."

She lifts herself off of my hand, takes my cock in her hand, lines us up, and sinks down on top of me. Her tits wobble from side to side as she lifts herself to begin rocking. I bring my fingers up to her mouth, and coat her lips with her juices. "Yum, I taste good."

"Fuck, yes you do." I grab her roughly by the chin, and pull her forward to kiss me. The moment our lips are together, I grab her around the throat, applying the smallest pressure, being extremely careful not to hurt, but to give her the buzz we're both chasing.

Serena and I are perfectly joined, my hand around her throat, her hips moving against me. "Harder," she murmurs. I'm not sure how hard to go, and she must understand my concern, when she reaches up and shows me the pressure she wants around her throat. "I trust you," she says.

I keep kissing her, loving how open she is. Closing my eyes for a moment, I just feel the chemistry between us. An energy surge passes. A complete transfer of power that's raw and animalistic. Serena is one of the strongest women I've ever met, yet right now, she's trusting herself enough to surrender to me for her pleasure. And I can't let this perfect gift go to waste. She wants to surrender, and I want to lead. We're perfect together.

I let go of her throat, tangle my hand in her hair, and pull her head roughly to the side. My mouth bites down at the side of her neck where it meets her shoulder, and I'm rewarded with another long moan. Serena's tempo increases. Her bouncing becomes savage as she's desperate to orgasm again.

With my hand still entwined in her hair, my other hand snakes down between us, and I apply hard pressure on her clit. "Oh shit," she sighs.

She's speeding up, and I'm nearly about to lose my load as she keeps swiveling her hips. "That's it. Take it," I say as I thrust up, play with clit and pull her hair.

"Shit," she moans one more time. Her body convulses over mine. I release her hair, and smother her moan with my mouth. Her orgasm is intense, as her sighs of relief are overpowered by my own mouth. I flip us on the bed, lift her leg as high as I can, and keep pushing into her. I need to be as deep in her as I can be. Closing my eyes, I fuck her, fuck her like I haven't fucked anyone in my life. My hips take over, slamming into her again, and again, and again until finally, I explode. But I don't want to leave her wet pussy. I collapse on top of Serena, who draws lazy movements on my back with her nails.

Catching my breath, I lift myself off her, and give Serena a kiss. "So, you're into a bit of pain?" I ask as I get off the bed, head into the bathroom, take the condom off and roll it up in toilet paper, throwing it in the trash.

"You could say that," she says from the bed.

"You either are, or you aren't." I walk out of the bathroom to find her laying on the bed with sheet half pulled up over her body.

"I am. And a lot of it." An idea springs to mind. "I've never really had a partner who's been willing to explore that with me. If you haven't noticed, I'm a little kinky." She pulls the sheet up, as if she's embarrassed. Her gaze drops and her shoulders sink. "It's okay if you're not. I can learn to live with it, I suppose."

"Learn to live with it? Are you crazy? If you want kink, then I'll make sure you get kink."

Her entire face lights up, as if this is the best thing she's heard in a long time. "You'd do that for me?"

"I'd do anything for you, Serena." Her smile lights up the room, and sparks a flame inside of me too. "But for now, we need to get dressed and head downstairs for dinner. I'm going to take a quick shower."

"Let me pee first." She leaps out of bed in the nude which, incidentally, I fucking love, and she rushes into the bathroom.

I wonder if I can have her totally naked whenever our weekends correspond. "Now that Jordan's in rehab, what are you going to do about all these jobs you have?" My reason for asking this is totally selfish. I want her naked as often as possible.

She opens the door, and strolls over to where her pajama bottoms and top are. She slides them on, then reaches for her hair tie. "I have to find another job is what I have to do."

"What? Why?"

"I need to pay you back, and I need to still find somewhere to go. I've been thinking about asking May if I can rent her stable. It's sitting idle at the moment."

"There's always my place. You can move in with me."

As she ties her hair back in a ponytail, she laughs. "Yeah, we've only just had sex for the first time, and you want me to move in with you. Sure." She snickers and rolls her eyes.

"I'm being serious," I say. "Move in with me."

"How's that going to work, Alec? We're barely a couple. And what if things go south?"

"Wow, you're so optimistic," I say sarcastically as I grab my clothes and stand in the bathroom doorway.

"Come on, you have to be serious now. Can you really see this working out?"

"I wouldn't be asking if I didn't. You know what? You're a pain in the ass."

"No, I'm not. I'm just realistic," she counters.

"Realistic would be for you to move in. Obviously, I want you with me. It would mean sacrifices for both of us. Example, you'd need to be naked when I arrived home from work. And of course, I'd get to spank your butt as often as I wanted." She shifts her stance, and smiles. "And don't forget, I'd have to buy a shit ton of toys to use on you."

"That's not fair, you're using my kinkiness against me."

"Shamelessly," I admit proudly.

"And what if I wasn't naked when you got home from work?" she teases as she nibbles on her bottom lip and lifts her brows suggestively. Oh, she is a tart. She's getting horny again, and I love sparking this fire inside of her.

I simply shrug, then click my tongue to the roof of my mouth. "Well, the only way you'll find out is if you move in with me."

"You just want me for all my skills."

Still naked, I walk over to her, grab her by the nape, and kiss her collarbone before licking up to her mouth. My kisses are ruthless and primal. *I own her.* I dip my hand inside her pajama pants, and find she's wet and ready to go again. "Baby," I whisper against her lips. "You have no fucking idea." Pulling away, Serena is breathless and wanting. I stroll back to the bathroom, and without even turning, I say, "You're moving in. No negotiations." I close the door and don't even bother waiting for a reply.

Turning the shower on, I smile because I know now, I've found my forever girl.

Chapter 14

ALEC

My alarm sounds, waking me. Jumping out of bed, a huge smirk crosses my face. I head into the bathroom, and get myself ready for work. First shift back after having weeks off because of my injury.

Once I'm ready, I head out to my kitchen and make myself a coffee. I lean against the counter, sipping my mug of joe, while scrolling through my phone. I want to message Serena, but it's barely five in the morning, and I don't want to wake her. She works too hard and too many hours for me to message her just because I'm awake.

As I'm scrolling through social media, a message pops up from Serena.

Have fun today and I'll see you tomorrow night.

Why are you awake? You should be sleeping.

I wanted to wish you luck. Anyway, I've got a huge day ahead of me today. I'm at the hospital until around four, then I'm cleaning, then I'm at the restaurant.

I hate how she's working so many jobs. I mean, I commend her for being proactive, but she doesn't need to work quite so many jobs now. But, I also don't want to push her either. She needs to come to this decision on her own. Maybe I can try to persuade her in other ways to drop some of these menial jobs. She's going to wear herself down.

I'll be home after six tomorrow. Come over when you're done.

I will.

Slipping my phone in my pocket, I look around my house. I have to try and clear out some of the shit I've got laying around so I can make room for Serena and her things. I still have no idea where she lives, or even what furniture she has.

Finishing my coffee, I grab the keys to my car, and head out. My first day back at work. The station isn't too far from home, only about a twelve-minute drive. The moment I'm there, I park my car and walk into the station. The guys from the other crew see me walking in. Dean's already here, in a hand-over meeting with the other captain just so everyone is up to date with what's happening. Dean sees me through the office window, and holds a finger up to the other captain.

"You're back," he says when he leaves the office.

"Looks like it," I reply as I stick my hands in my pockets.

Dean looks around, making sure we're out of earshot from everyone. "You okay to be here?"

"Yeah, why wouldn't I be?"

He gives me a small head nod, and smiles. "Good to have you back, brother. I've gotta wrap it up with Graham, then I'll be out. We'll be running drills once everyone is here. Wanna get the gear ready for it?"

"Sure." I walk out the back to the drill tower, and head to the shed where the older equipment that's used for our drills is stored. It's equipment we can't use on the trucks any longer because of wear and tear, or because of damage. No use in throwing it away, we may as well get as much use out of it while we still can, and use it for drills.

"Here I thought you were living the good life, vacationing all around the world, and couldn't be bothered to return to work," I hear Pen call as she walks up to me, and throws her arms around me in a huge hug. "Good to have you back."

"Vacationing all around the world, huh?"

She smirks as she helps me set up for drills. "Put on a bit of beef, Alec. Especially around the middle there. Is that what lying around in the sun for weeks does to a person?"

"You're an ass," I say to Pen while we get everything ready.

"It's good to have you back. I've missed putting shit on ya all the time. I had to put up with all those clowns." She jerks her head to the side. "Heard you've got yourself a woman too."

I smile at just the thought of Serena. "Yeah, I do."

"Tell me she's got a good head on her shoulders and she's not like the other ones you pick up?"

"I think you'll like Serena. Have you and my brother finally hooked up, or what?"

She cringes, and pokes her tongue out. "Rhett will always be my best friend, but as far as the whole part A into part B goes." She screws her mouth up while shaking her head. "I couldn't imagine anything worse."

"I know, I know," I say. "How's it going with Dane?" Pen's shoulders drop and her normal bright eyes, fade into disappointment. "What's going on with the two of you?"

She clicks her tongue, then sighs. Standing, she places her hands on her hips and shrugs. "We just can't seem to make anything work."

"Why?" I ask.

"Because..." She looks around as if she doesn't know what to say. "It's like..." She huffs, then shakes her head. "I don't know," she finally answers.

"He's finished college and working now, right?"

"Yeah, he is. But I don't know what the problem is."

"What do you mean?"

She peers down, her face full of hurt and pain. "I want more with him, Alec, but he doesn't seem like he wants more with me."

"Then maybe it's time to kick him to the curb and find someone who'll want you as much as you want them."

"Maybe you're right. But, it's like when we're together we're so good, and when we're apart, we're both miserable." She lifts her chin, and smiles again, though I can still see the hurt. "Anyway, enough about me. How are you feeling about being back?" When Pen doesn't want to talk about something, she shuts down and won't talk about it.

"I've been looking forward to this day for so long."

"You did have a garage door fall on you. Even though I think there wasn't anything wrong with you, you just wanted a few weeks away from this place. You faked it all, didn't you?" she happily taunts.

"About damn time!" I hear Rhett calling. He jogs over and claps a hand to my back. "So good to have you back."

"Did you miss me?"

"Like a hole in the head," he says. He looks to Pen, and narrows his eyes. "You alright?" he asks with concern.

It's amazing how well these two know each other. Penelope shoots Rhett a scowl. "Yeah, why?"

"You look kinda...off or sad or something."

Penelope drops the heavy hose, links her fingers together and stretches them out in front of her to crack them. "It's on, stud. It's on."

And here we go. The normal competitiveness between Pen and Rhett. "You think you can take me?" Rhett jabs Pen in the shoulder. "Because I think you're just a girl."

"Okay, stud. What's the bet?" They're both as bad as the other.

Rhett taps his finger to his chin, thinking. "I know," he says with a small sly grin. "If I win, you have to clean my new bachelor pad from top to bottom."

"You're finally moving out of Mom's. Good for you. Growing up and being an adult," I say with a chuckle.

"Whatever," Rhett replies. "What do you say, Pen? Like them odds?"

"So, if you win, I have to clean your new place?" Rhett nods his head. "But *when* I win you have to wash my car every week for the next three months."

Rhett screws up his nose. "I don't even wash *my* car."

"That's the bet," Pen says.

"Fine. Because I'm gonna kick your ass." Rhett holds his hand out to Pen and they shake on it.

They both look at the tower, and smirk. Dean and Hugo both join us, and we have a quick meeting about what's happening before we begin drills.

"Boss, can you set up the red flag?" Penelope asks Dean when the mini-meeting is done.

Dean rolls his eyes and shakes his head. "What's the bet this time?"

"He'll have to wash my car for three months," Pen replies with all the confidence in the world.

"And if Rhett wins?"

"He won't." Her strong shoulders and booming laugh are all quite motivating to me. She has so much cockiness. Most people might even think she's smug, but she's not. Penelope is a woman who loves doing what she's doing, but feels like she needs to be at the top of her game because she's in a male-oriented career.

"Then she needs to clean my place from top to bottom," Rhett answers.

"Finally moving out of Mom's," Dean says, surprised.

"That's what Alec said." Penelope points to me and laughs. Rhett rolls his eyes and shakes his head.

"Well, let me set up the red flag. Alec, walk with me."

I jog to Dean as he grabs the red flag from the storage shed and begins toward the drill tower. "You okay?"

"Yeah, I'm good. Why?"

"Being away from here for as long as you've been, could mean nerves about returning."

"Are you trying to make me nervous, because I was fine until now."

Dean laughs. "How's it going with Serena's brother?"

"Nothing more than what you already know. Serena's moving in with me too."

"Makes sense. Anyone can see you love her as much as she loves you."

Love? We're nowhere near that stage. "Yeah, not there yet."

Dean laughs and slaps his hand on my back. "Keep telling yourself that, maybe you'll even believe it." Serena doesn't love me. Just like I don't love her. "Anyway, here." He thrusts the flag into my hands, and looks up to the drill tower.

"You're making me go up there, are you?"

"What a better way to start back." He crosses his arms in front of his chest, and waits. "Up you go." Dean shoos me with his hand.

"You're an ass," I call over my shoulder as I walk away from him. I hear him laughing.

By the time I reach the top of the tower, I can see the crew standing around talking. I wave the flag from the top so they can see I've got it with me, but then shove it in my pocket and make my way back down. Pen and Rhett will be fierce trying to find it, and all along, it'll be in my pocket. *Suckers.*

"Okay, let's get this done. Rules," Dean starts saying.

Penelope quickly interrupts, "Wait, there are going to be rules?"

"We're making it a bit of fun today. Still taking it seriously, but let's throw in a bit of fun too. We'll run proper drills this afternoon."

"Fun?" Penelope mumbles. "I want to kick your ass fair and square," she says to Rhett.

"Shut up, Pen," Dean says to her. She lowers her gaze, embarrassed she's been caught out by Dean. "Rules. The person who brings back the flag, wins." We wait for more of Dean's rules. "Ready?"

"What?" Rhett looks around, confused.

Dean presses the fob in his hands, and the alarm sounds in the firehouse that we're ready to roll. "Thirty seconds!" Dean yells.

We run to our gear, and are dressed and ready by the time Dean calls our limit. The simulated fire is burning through the drill tower, and we're all ready to combat it. "There's someone screaming for help," Dean says through our earpieces. The someone is the flag, which is in my pocket.

It's all part of the drill, but I do feel nervous and anxious about getting back into a burning building again. I know, though, if I don't push past it, I'm never going to be able to do my job again. I'm not going to let that happen. I love my job. I'm also not going to let down my crew.

Hugo is in the truck, backing it up so we can get the aerial ladder up to the top. The moment it's extended, Pen is already climbing her way to the top where she thinks the flag is.

"One and a half," I call the size to Rhett knowing we're on the hose together.

"On it," he responds. Within less than a minute, he's on a knee at the front of the hose, and I'm supporting him from behind as the water shoots out, attempting to extinguish the fire.

"Watch on your left," I call.

"I see it." He hits the fire to the left, trying to control its direction. "Pen, Hugo?"

"We've got a line on the top floor," Hugo responds.

"Mayday, mayday, mayday. I'm out of air! I'm out of air!" Dean calls.

"Pull the line back," I shout to Rhett. "Hugo, survivors?"

"Pulling back," Rhett yells.

"Survivors not found."

"Mayday, mayday, mayday. I'm out of air, I'm out of air! Get out, the roof is collapsing, get out!" Dean yells again.

"Get out now!" I shout over everyone. Although this is simulated and completely controlled, my heart is racing with excitement. I find the adrenaline and energy I've been craving. I've missed this so badly.

Rhett and I retreat, Pen and Hugo are already retracting down the aerial. "Dean, where are you?"

"Back entrance, ten steps to the left, and around the corner."

"I'm on it," Rhett yells as he takes off around the back of the building.

Pen is down beside me, and Hugo finishes retracting the aerial. "You okay?" I ask.

She nods before taking off around the back in search of Dean. Within moments, Dean, Rhett and Penelope all walk around the front. "Response time was good when I called mayday. Where's the flag?"

"That's not fair. I was on the line down here while Pen and Hugo had aerial," Rhett complains as he takes his helmet and turnout gear off his head.

"I didn't get it, so neither of us win," Pen says to Rhett. A satisfied grin decorates Rhett's lips.

I strip out of my turnout gear, and pull the flag out of my pocket and pat it against my forehead. Penelope does a double take when she notices the flag wasn't even up in the tower. "You bastard!" she screams and lunges for the flag.

Laughing, I shove it down the front of my shirt so she can't get it. "Neither of you won. Which means, I've won."

"Don't think I won't go there to get it!" Penelope warns as she shoves me in the shoulder. I respond with the same shove in the shoulder. She scrunches her nose, as she steps back. "Fine, I didn't win. I don't like not winning, Alec."

"I didn't win either," Rhett reminds Pen.

"I swear, Pen, you're the most competitive person I've ever known," Hugo says.

She smiles broadly, quite satisfied with herself. "Good." She pulls her shoulders back, then bends to pick up her gear. "And don't you forget it."

Dean shakes his head. "She is too much sometimes, but God I love that girl," he says.

"I'm a woman!" she barks in return.

Pen is a lot to handle. But she's fiercely protective too. She may be competitive when it comes to being one of us, but she'll have our back each and every time we need her.

Chapter 15

SERENA

I SHOULD'VE JUST stayed at Alec's house tonight, but I didn't bring a change of clothes, and I need to be up early in the morning.

Note to self, take a change of clothes over to Alec's, so if I'm tired, like I am tonight, I can just have a shower and stay. And maybe, I'll get woken up with his mouth on my body. I mean, hello. Hot firefighter going down on me? Hell yes please!

Driving back home, I'm struggling to keep my eyes open, and when I pull into the street, the two guys are sitting out the front smoking something from a pipe as a number of quite scantily-clothed women are sitting on their laps kissing them.

I don't know about them, but I'd rather be getting my freak on instead of getting high from whatever they're smoking in the pipe. What gets me though, is they're quite open about whatever drugs they're using. They're not even trying to hide them. I guess, they can do whatever they like, it's their choice.

I pull into my driveway, and the two guys push the women who are sitting on their laps off them, stand, and both walk to the edge of their front yard, just staring at me. Man, they're peculiar and eerie, but I've been lucky, because other than the odd glares, they've never done anything to me. The quicker I'm out of here, the better. Speaking of which, I need to talk to Alec more seriously about moving in with him. Maybe it's too early to move in together.

I unlock the door quickly, push through, and relock it. Thankfully, now that I know Jordan is in rehab, I don't have to worry about him ransacking my room, looking for anything of value he can pawn in order to pay for his next hit.

Taking my phone out of my bag, I send Alec a quick text telling him I'm home. I throw my bag on the bed, grab my pajamas, and head into the bathroom for a shower. I can't believe how tired I am. Since Jordan's been gone, I feel relieved, but also worried because I owe Alec money and I don't want him to think I'll never repay it. So I've been working every possible shift to earn it so I can pay him back, even though he hasn't asked me for a single dime.

The water is magic against my tired body. It pounds on my shoulders, making my eyes droop shut as the feeling of pure bliss washes over me.

Right now, everything in the world is perfect.

Jordan's in rehab, kicking his drug habit. Alec is my and Jordan's savior by loaning me the rest of the money I needed to get Jordan into rehab. Not to mention, how caring he is toward me. I let out a laugh, remembering the first time I met him. He was angry, and frustrated, and took everything out on anyone who was around him. Including me. Just because he was mad at himself, it didn't mean I was going to let him treat me like crap. I was there to do a job, and I wasn't going to let him speak to me like shit. No matter how badly I needed the money, there was no way I was going to let his behavior stand. *Nope, sorry.*

The moment I'm out of the shower, I towel dry myself, and put my pajamas on. Thankfully, I don't have to wash my hair until tomorrow night. Meaning, I can just jump into bed and go to sleep. I'm beyond exhausted. I know, the moment my eyes close, I'll be out of it.

Sliding into bed, I grab my phone and find a message from Alec.

> ***Sweet dreams. Tomorrow we'll start moving you in here.***

> *Yeah, about that. We need to have a more serious conversation.*

Yawning, my eyes are nearly closing on their own. My phone vibrates, and I look at the message.

> ***No need. You're moving in with me.***

A huge smile stretches across my face. I love how take-charge he is with me. It's comforting. Because for the first time in a long time, someone is taking care of me.

> *Night.*

My eyes close, and before I know it, I'm out.

A loud banging startles me from a deep sleep. I open my eyes, and try to figure out where the banging is coming from.

"Open the fucking door, Jordan!" I hear someone yelling. Afraid, I jump out of bed and run to my door to lock it. "Open the fucking door!" the male voice is deep, and angry.

Quickly, I grab my phone and dial Alec's number. "Hey beautiful," he says in a groggy voice.

"I'm sending you my address, get here quickly," I say, panic coursing through my body. I quickly type out a text, then dial nine-one-one. My hands are trembling as the call is being placed.

"Nine-one-one. What's your emergency?" a calm female asks.

"Someone's breaking into my house. Please, please, be quick." There's another loud bang, this time, I think he's actually breaking down the front door. "He's trying to break in. I can hear him trying to break the front door." My hands tremble as terror surges through me.

"What's your address?" I quickly rattle off the address twice, in case I'm speaking too fast the first time. "What's your name?"

"Um, Um, my name is Serena Whitaker," I'm in such a panic that I'm not even sure if I'm answering questions or just yelling things into the phone.

"Where the fuck are you, Jordan?" I hear the voice is now inside my house.

"He's inside. Oh my God, please hurry. He's inside." I hold my breath, trying to make myself as quiet as I can.

" Are you safe where you are?"

"I've locked myself in my room," I whisper and try to sink against the wall, hoping it'll swallow me and protect me.

"Can you get out through the window?"

"No, there are bars on all the windows. I'm trapped." I hear heavy footsteps down the small hall. "Shit, shit, he's outside the door," I cry into the phone.

"Police are on their way. ETA is five minutes."

He rattles my door handle and finds it locked. "In here," I hear one say.

"Shit, there's more than just one. They're at my door." I don't have five minutes, I barely have five seconds.

"Whatever you do, don't hang up. You're doing really well, Serena. Just don't hang up."

"I won't," I whisper into the phone. The loud thumping echoes through my ears. I know they're at my door, and I'm completely helpless to do anything. I stand from where I'm huddled on the floor, and run to my window. Opening it, I yell with all my might, "Fire! Fire! Fire!" If I yell *help,* in this neighborhood, I might not be taken seriously. But yelling fire, might have people coming out of their houses to at least see what's happening. "Fire! Fire! Fire!" I yell with everything I have. My throat is sore, but I yell it over and over again.

The banging on the door happens once again. The door is nearly at breaking point. One more hit, and there's no chance I'll survive this. Not if they're looking for Jordan. They'll hurt or kill me just to teach him a lesson.

I scream again, and I notice a light flick on from the house next door.

My bedroom door gives way, and there are two men standing at the doorway. One is holding a baseball bat, the other a knife. Neither have a mask over their faces. Shit, I'm gonna die.

I back up against the window, trying to climb out, although it's impossible with the bars on the window. "Where the fuck is Jordan?" the first one says with an eerily calm voice.

"Rehab," I answer without even a second thought.

The one holding the bat looks to the other, and he shakes his head. There's a silent knowing exchange between them, as a dreadful feeling of fear surges through me. It seems like time is moving slowly. The police aren't here yet. No one is coming to help, and these two men are inching closer and closer to me.

"What do you think?" one says to the other.

"I've had worse." He cocks an eyebrow and drags his scary gaze all over my body.

A sickening, gut-wrenching pain overtakes me. I know what's coming next, and it's nothing pleasant. This is where I die...*or worse.* Death would be welcome compared to the knowledge of what else *could* happen. "Please, don't," I plead while shaking my head. I clutch the phone in my hand as I close my eyes and wince at what's just about to happen.

"Who the fuck are you?" I hear an unfamiliar voice. I open my eyes to see one of the two guys from down the street. Right behind him is the other guy. "What the fuck do you want?" He stands taller, a gun sticking out of his waistband.

"Got nothing to do with you. Walk away," the original one with the bat says.

"Get the fuck out." He places his hand on the gun. The other guy behind him has a shotgun pointing at the two who broke in.

"We just want the guy."

"He don't live here. Now, fuck off," the one holding the shotgun says as he moves around the room to stand in front of me.

What the hell is going on?

The two who broke into my house look at me, then back at the two holding guns. They appear completely unfazed, while internally I'm doing everything possible to hold in my tears, and the vomit which wants to make an exit.

They look to me, then to each other and walk out of my bedroom. The one holding the shotgun stays in front of me, while the other stands in the hallway and watches the intruders leave. The one holding the shotgun turns to me, holds his hand out and helps me up from where I've been cowering. He casts a look over my body. "You never belonged in this neighborhood. This isn't a safe place for you. Pack your shit, and leave." I profusely nod, not wanting to anger him. He goes to the door, whispers something to the other guy then turns to me. He looks at my phone, and gestures toward it. I hold my phone out to him, and notice there's no call to the police. I'm not sure how, but I've hung up from them. "We were never here," he says.

"Okay," I say through heavy whimpering.

He and the other guy take off out of my house, and I stand completely still, not sure what the hell just happened. I'm not even sure how long it is before I hear the police sirens. Did this all happen in less than five minutes? Oh my God, I'm going to be sick.

"Ma'am, ma'am, what happened?" a young male police officer asks as I run into the bathroom and hurl my guts into the toilet.

My head is spinning and I don't know what to say. "Two men..." I manage to say before I vomit again.

"Do you know who they are?" I shake my head. "Did they say anything?"

I nod. "They were asking for my brother, Jordan."

"Where's your brother now?"

"Serena?!" I hear Alec calling. "Serena?"

"Alec Morgan?" I hear another male policeman ask.

"Michael, is she okay? What happened?"

"She's okay, she's in the bathroom with Dylan. She's okay."

"I need to see her."

"Alec!" I burst into tears as I push up from the bathroom floor and head straight past the cop into Alec's arms. "Two guys broke in looking for Jordan."

"They didn't touch you, did they?" Alec asks quietly as he holds me close to his rigid body.

"No, they didn't."

"Alec, we need to talk with Serena," the other cop says.

Alec leads me over to the sofa, and sits beside me, his arm possessively around my shoulders. "Where's your room?" Alec asks.

"Down there." I point to the hallway. "The one with the broken-down door." Alec jumps up, and leaves, and returns with the blanket from my bed. He wraps it around me. "Thank you."

"You're shivering, sweetheart." He kisses my temple and drapes his arm around me again.

"I'm Michael Jones, and I'm the sheriff from Mulberry Point. Can you tell me what happened?"

"Um. Yeah." My hands are trembling as I try and recall everything from the moment I woke. "I was asleep, and I woke up when I heard someone banging. Um, two men broke in." I look over to the front door, and it's off the hinges with the wood frame completely broken. "They were searching for my brother Jordan."

"Where is your brother?"

"He um..." I burst into tears, trying to hide my face.

"He recently went into rehab, a place in Kentucky. We both took him there," Alec answers.

"What's the place called?" Michael asks.

"New Dawn Treatment Center," I reply. "Um, they got to my door, and tried it, but I'd locked it before they got in. They kicked it down, and asked me where Jordan was."

Michael is writing things down as he nods. "How many of them where there?"

"Two."

"Did they have any weapons?"

"Yeah, one had a baseball bat, and the other had a knife."

"Can you describe them?"

Blinking rapidly, I wring my clammy hands together. "Both were pretty big and solid. They had dark hair, um, and um." Beads of sweat form on my upper lip and hairline. The intensity is too much. There's a loud noise outside, and I flinch as I turn to look at what's going on.

Dean and Rhett are at my door, both looking around at the aftermath of what's happened. I look at Alec, who gives them a curt nod. "Dean? Rhett?" Michael says.

"We know. We're not touching anything."

Michael nods then turns back to me. "Can you tell me their nationality?"

"Both white men. Stocky in build. Maybe in their late twenties or early thirties," I answer honestly.

"Any tattoos or piercings that you noticed or saw?" I shake my head. "What about haircuts, short? Long?"

"Um, I think they were short. I don't know. I'm sorry." I rub at my temples, desperate not to break down and cry.

"Don't apologize. You're doing well. Did they leave when you told them your brother wasn't here?"

Oh shit. What do I say? I owe my life to the two guys down the road. They told me not to say anything. I can't get them in trouble for saving me. I highly doubt, the shotgun and gun they have would've been legally acquired. I don't know what to do. The right thing to do is to tell the police everything and let them deal with it. But I owe those guys. If they hadn't gotten here when they did, I think I'd have been in a world of trouble.

"I closed my eyes and covered my hand over my ears." I just lied to the police. "But they knew I had called the police."

Michael looks to Alec, then me. "The likely chance is that if your brother is in rehab, he probably owes money to someone. And they came to either collect, or hurt him. And unfortunately, this neighborhood isn't known for security cameras. We'll do what we can, but..." he trails off. "Unless you know who your brother owes money to?"

"I don't, I'm sorry."

"Michael, she works several jobs just so she could save to send him to rehab. Serena isn't involved in that type of lifestyle," Alec adds.

"I can see she doesn't belong here," Michael replies to Alec while looking around this shitty house. "Look, I'll give New Dawn a call and see if I can speak to your brother, but if he's not willing to give me the information, then I'm afraid we don't have a lot to go on. We'll ask your neighbors, and see if any of them heard or saw anything, but without more information, there's not much we can do to find them."

I nod my head. "I understand."

"Have you got somewhere you can stay until you can fix the doors?"

"She's coming home with me," Alec says. "Dean and Rhett are here to clear this place out."

"Okay. Well, here's my card in case you remember anything." Michael extends his hand to give me a business card, and Alec takes it while I sit beneath the blanket, shivering from the trauma of the invasion.

"Thank you," I say.

Michael stands, and gestures for Alec to walk out with him. The moment Alec is up, Dean is beside me, his arms around me. "You okay?" he asks.

I nod without saying anything, and start crying again. "Here you go." Rhett hands me a tissue, and sits on the other side of me.

"Tell us what's coming with you, and what's staying. We'll pack everything you want, and move it tonight, okay?" Dean says.

"There's nothing I want from here. All this stuff is crap. I just need to grab my clothes, and some things from my bedroom."

"Do you want to go now? We'll come with you," Dean asks.

"I'm not sure what to do." I bury my face into my hands, and keep crying. I feel so violated, and sick to my stomach. If those two guys hadn't shown up, I can't stop thinking about what would've happened to me. I owe them more than my gratitude. But, did I do the wrong thing by not telling the police about them? I can't think about that now, I just can't.

There's a movement from beside me, and I instantly know Alec's here. "It's okay. When you're ready, we'll go to your room, and pack your things. If you have nothing here you want, there's no need to ever return again." I lower my hands, and turn to look at Alec. He wipes under my eyes, leans in and gives me a gentle kiss on the cheek. "I've got you."

I know he does. "Thank you." I take a breath, and look around at the mess of this place. "Can we leave soon, please?" This house has never held any kind of joy. The only things I see when I'm here are painful memories.

"As soon as you're ready."

I take several deep breaths, before I stand. With the blanket still wrapped around me, we head into my bedroom. I get a suitcase from my closet and start filling it with my clothes and small keepsakes. I take the tin out of my room, and hand it to Alec. "This is the most valuable thing to me. Please, don't let it go."

"I won't. Are you sure you don't want any blankets, or towels, or the microwave, anything?"

"I don't even want my toothbrush." I finish packing the little I have in one damn suitcase. "I can't believe my entire life fits into this one suitcase." I look around my room, and shake my head. "This isn't a way to live."

"What about Jordan's room? Is there anything in there you want to keep?"

"He pawned anything of value he had. There's nothing in there worth keeping."

"Where are your car keys?"

"In my bag, I think." I motion toward the bag Alec bought me. He walks over, slides the tin into it, then turns to look at me. "Can I go through it to find your keys?"

"You don't have to ask." I try and smile.

"Thank you." He rummages around my bag, finds my keys and holds them in his hand. "Here." I hold my hand out for my bag.

"I'll swap ya." He takes the suitcase from beside me, and hands me my bag. "Are you sure there's nothing else here that you want?" I shake my head. "Okay, let's go." We walk out of the room, and I notice it's just Dean and Rhett left here. They've temporarily fixed the door, but one good kick and the door will be off the hinges again. There's nothing in here of value, if anyone wants anything, they're more than welcome to it. "Can you bring Serena's car back to my house?" Alec asks Rhett.

"Sure." Rhett takes the keys, then comes over to me, and hugs me. "It'll be okay. We're all here for you." He kisses my cheek before stepping back and leaving via the now band-aided front door.

As we walk out in the middle of the night, I notice the two guys sitting out the front of their house, smoking a cigarette. All this time I'd been creeped out by them watching me as I'd come and go, when they were looking out for me. They watch as Rhett gets in my car, and drives down the street waiting for Alec and Dean to fall in behind him.

The two guys give me small nods, to which I reply by mouthing *thank you,* before tears fill my eyes again. I know if they didn't show up when they did, then this whole thing would've gone in a completely different and disastrous way.

Alec places his hand on my thigh, and gently squeezes. What a damn night.

Chapter 16

ALEC

DRIVING HOME, SERENA is sitting beside me, trembling as she chews on her nail. I turn the heat up in the car in case she's cold, but my instincts tell me the trauma of what happened to her is creeping up and she's going to have a full meltdown.

Rightfully so, too.

I can't imagine how traumatizing a home invasion would be for someone, especially a woman alone.

We pull into my driveway, and Rhett pulls up on the front lawn, parking her car. "Wait here," I say as I unbuckle my seat belt, and jump out of the car. I jog over to Rhett who's getting out of Serena's car. "All good?"

"Yeah, no problems." Rhett hands me the keys as we walk over to Dean's truck.

"Hey, thanks for being here," I say to both Rhett and Dean.

"Yeah, of course, man. Whatever either of you need, let us know," Dean replies, and Rhett's nodding his agreement.

Rhett easily jumps up into Dean's truck, and shakes his head. "Where she lives..."

"She never told me where it was, except it was a bad part of Faith Haven. If I knew it was *that* bad, then I would've moved her out weeks ago."

"It's not safe for her to return," Dean says.

"She's stubborn but she's not going back," I say as I cross my arms in front of my chest.

"You can't let her go back there, regardless of what she says. She was lucky tonight, next time, she may not be," Dean says.

"She's not going back," I say adamantly. "As far as I'm concerned, she lives here now."

"Look, go take care of her," Rhett says. "And don't be an asshole to her. Make sure you really look after her."

I roll my eyes at Rhett. "I know."

"Well, you can really be an asshole," Dean echoes Rhett's words.

"See ya." I turn and walk away from them. I hear Dean quietly leave my street. When I get back to the car, Serena is staring out the window, completely devoid of any emotion. Her shoulders have sunken and she's shivering. I open the back door and take her suitcase, then open her door and reach for her hand. "Come on, we're home," I say.

She turns to look at me, and narrows her eyes before taking my hand and climbing out of the car. Serena is an emotionless mess. She's not saying or doing anything, which makes me think she's on the verge of breaking.

I unlock the front door, and turn on the light in the family room. She merely follows me, without saying a word.

"Here you go. Sit. I'll make you something to drink." I guide her over to the sofa, where she sits and draws the blanket up to her chin. I take her suitcase into our room, and remember she also has her handbag, which she must've left in the car. I run back out to the car and grab her handbag before bringing it into our bedroom.

"Can I have a shower? I feel so dirty," she says when I go out to the family room.

"Yeah, of course." I hold my hand out again, and take her to the bathroom. "I'll get you towels."

"Thank you," she says in a small voice.

I hand them to her, and she closes the door to the bathroom. I don't want to hover, but if she needs me, I want to be able to be there for her. She needs some space to process everything that's happened. I'll keep an eye on the time while she's in the shower and if she takes too long, I'll go in there.

Serena turns the water on, and I look at the time. It's just after three in the morning, and I know she'll be tired. I head back into our bedroom, and change the sheets on the bed, then get an extra blanket from the closet in case she needs it. I pace outside the bathroom, stopping every few seconds just to listen. But I don't hear anything.

This gives me enough time to pour myself a whiskey, and down it. I needed that. Leaning against the kitchen counter, I pour two more. One for me, and one for Serena for when she's finished from the shower.

I listen for the water to shut off, but it's still on. She's been in there for what seems like hours, although when I look at the time, it's only been five minutes. My gut is telling me to check on her. I'll give her two more minutes, and if she's still in there, I'll check on her.

Pacing back and forth outside the bathroom, I keep checking on the time. The second I hear her small, smothered wails, I open the door and find Serena sitting on the floor of the shower, her legs drawn up and her head resting on her knees. "Hey," I say as I stick my hand into the shower, turn the water off, then grab one of the towels laid out. "Hey," I say again.

She turns her head to look at me, her eyes are puffy and red, and she's still trembling. "I'm..." She looks up at me, completely broken.

Pulling her up from her shoulders, I wrap the towel around her shoulders, and get her to step out of the shower. With the other towel, I dry her body. Starting from the top, and working my way down. Her hair is soaking wet, sticking to her face and neck, as she stands, lifelessly allowing me to dry her. Once her body is dry, I try to towel dry her hair. I do the best I can, but her hair is long and wet. Like *really* wet. Shit, I think I'm fucking this up.

I'm struggling to even get her hair dry. "I'll do it," Serena says sensing my struggle with her hair.

"Thank you." I notice she doesn't have any clothes other than what she was wearing in here. "Come on," I say when she's wrapped the towel around her hair. Leading her to our bedroom, I go to my drawers, taking out one of my t-shirts and a pair of boxer briefs. I kneel before my queen, and tap her leg so I can get her feet inside the boxers then slide them up her body. They're a bit big on her, but they'll do for now. Then I take the t-shirt, and maneuver it over the towel on her head, as she lifts her arms, and allows me to lower the t-shirt over her torso. Serena stands, staring at me. "Are you hungry?" I ask.

"Nope."

"Thirsty?"

"Nope."

"You need a drink. Sit." I guide her over to the bed, and sit her on the edge. "I'll be back in a second. Running my hand through my hair as I walk out to the kitchen, I take a moment to just take a deep breath. She's been through so much, and right now, she's a mere shell of the person she usually is. I know it's a speed bump in her life, and she's probably thinking about the worst-case scenario of what could've happened. Truthfully, I'm struggling to think of anything else myself.

If I could find the men who broke into her house, I'd tear them limb from limb. And I wouldn't lose a moment's sleep over the hurt I'd bring them.

I bring the two glasses of whiskey into the bedroom, and sit beside Serena on the bed. I hand her the glass. "What is it?" she asks. She slams it down before I have a chance to answer. "Whiskey." Serena winces, and shakes her head then hands me the empty glass.

"Do you want mine too?" I hold it out to her, and she throws that back too. "Better?"

She sits staring at the floor, then pushes back, and leans against the headrest. Looking at me, tears start falling again. She's such a strong woman, but right now, she's a mess. "I can't help but replay it over and over again." She grabs the hem of the t-shirt, and wipes at her eyes. I look around the room searching for tissues. Shit, I don't have any. "I think if those two guys from down the street didn't come when they did, then I'd be..."

"What two guys?" I ask. "What are you talking about?" She told the police it was only two guys who broke in.

Her eyes widen, and she shakes her head. "Nothing, nothing, I shouldn't have said anything."

"Serena, what happened?" Is there more to this than she's already told me?

She lowers her chin, and buries her face into her hands. "I was so scared, Alec. So, scared. It all happened so fast."

"Tell me what happened."

"I can't. I just can't."

"You can trust me. What happened?" I move closer to her, and rub my hands up and down her legs. She remains quiet for a few more seconds. "Serena," I urge her to open up.

She lifts her chin, and wipes at her face again. Looking away again, she brings her hand up and chews at her nails. "It all happened so fast. There was someone bashing at the front door, which woke me." She gulps and takes a breath. "I heard them calling for Jordan to open the door." Serena worries her lower lip between her teeth. "Then the bashing continued, and I knew I was in trouble. Um, they got in," her voice breaks as more tears stream down her cheeks. "And they were looking for Jordan. They got to my door, and they tried it. But, I'd locked it, because Jordan had broken into my room and stole things before to pawn for drugs." Her breathing is labored, short but heavy. Through her tears and talking, I'm trying to piece together what exactly happened. "They broke it down. When they saw me, they...they asked me where Jordan is, and I told them he's in rehab. But then, they looked at each other, and I knew right then, my life was on the line." She grasps her chest with a shivering hand. "And then the two guys from down the street, they came in with guns, and told them to leave."

"Why didn't you tell the police, Serena?"

She shakes her head. "They told me not to say anything, Alec. They helped me when I thought the other two were going to hurt me. I owed them my silence in gratitude."

Shit, this is hard. The right thing to do is to tell the police. But I also understand her insistence on not saying anything too. "We should tell the police, maybe those two from down the road know the other two."

"NO!" she yells. "I promised them, I wasn't going to say anything. I'm not saying anything to the police. They saved me; I'm not saying anything. I'm not. No way," she adamantly repeats.

"What happened after the two with the guns came in?"

"They got rid of the two who were looking for Jordan. Then, one of them turned and told me I'd never belonged in that neighborhood and it's not safe for me. Then they told me to pack my shit and leave." She humorlessly chuckles. "In all the time I've lived there, they'd sit outside on a ratty old sofa, and watch me come and go from home. They'd watch me like a hawk, and they scared me to death. But now I know, they've been keeping an eye on me. And because of that, I owe them, Alec. I can't say a single thing to the police about them. And trust me, it's killing me not to say anything, but it's the right thing to do."

This is a tricky situation. But the fact they've been looking out for Serena means I owe them a debt, too. They were watching out for her when I wasn't. There's a tightness in my chest and a sinking feeling in my stomach. I've got an internal battle going on, but I should push it aside and look after my woman. She's the one who's trying to keep it together. If I don't calm her fears, she could end up scared of her own shadow.

"I feel so hopeless, Alec. I've been working my ass off for so long, trying to do what's best for Jordan, that somewhere along the line, I put myself in danger."

"You didn't do this to yourself, Serena. Unfortunately, you were in the wrong place, at the wrong time. This isn't on you." I don't want to tell her that it's Jordan's actions that put her in danger, not where she lived.

"If I got Jordan help earlier, maybe this wouldn't have happened," she argues back, still trying to take responsibility. "It's playing over and over again." She taps her forehead with the pads of her fingers. "I can't get the look on their faces out of my head."

"You can't torture yourself with this, Serena. It's not your fault, and it's over now. You're safe."

"I just wish I could've helped him earlier. I wish I pushed to get a loan, to have him in rehab twelve months ago, maybe then this wouldn't have happened."

"Stop." I grab Serena around the hips, and move her to sit on my lap. "Listen to me. This isn't on you. Chances are Jordan owes those guys money for drugs, and they came looking to collect. You told the police one had a knife and the other had a baseball bat?" Serena nods. "They weren't going to kill him, they were going to hurt him to teach him a lesson."

"This is fucked," she says in a long breath. "Totally and utterly fucked."

"It is," I agree. "I'm just relieved you're safe, and here with me." I hug her against my body. Serena's posture is rigid. I keep holding her close to me, and over the next few moments, she softens and melts into me.

"I'm tired," she whispers.

"I bet you are." I move her back to the bed, and lay her down. Standing, I go to turn the light off.

"Where are you going?" she asks with desperation.

"I'm just turning the light off."

"Please, don't leave me alone tonight. Please," she pleads.

"I won't." I toe off my shoes, take my jeans off and crawl into bed beside Serena.

She moves so her head rests on my chest, and her arm is draped across my stomach. "Alec?"

"Yeah."

"Thank you."

Even at her worst, she's still putting me before herself. She has to be the strongest person I've ever known. I kiss the top of her head, while drawing lazy patterns on her back. In my arms, she falls asleep. Though the night is spent with Serena tensing and whimpering, and me holding her through each and every cry.

Chapter 17

SERENA

STRETCHING MY ARMS over my head, I'm temporarily lost as to where I am. Opening my eyes, I search the room for anything that might tell me my location. Last night's, or should I say, this morning's events all come flooding back. The break-in, the confrontation, *what could've happened,* and what actually *did* happen.

Alec brought me back to his house, and right now, I'm in his bed, but Alec is nowhere to be seen. The room is dark, too dark. Is it night time already? Did I sleep the entire day away? The window dressings are heavy, blocking out any light from coming into the room. I guess firefighters need to be able to sleep during the day, especially with their work schedule.

I push the sheet and the thin blanket back, and stretch once more before I sit up in bed. My bladder wakes and encourages me to use the bathroom fast.

As I wash my hands, I splash water on my face and look at myself in the mirror. There are dark rings circling my bloodshot hazel eyes. My limp light brown hair falls lightly over my shoulders as it's managed to come out of the towel I wrapped around my head last night.

I look down at the clothes I'm wearing, and shake my head. How sweet, Alec must've put me in his clothes. I don't recall much from when Alec brought me back to his house. I rub at my eyes, and yawn as I open the door to the bedroom, and head out to see where Alec is. "Alec?" I call. I'm met with silence. "Alec?" I walk out to the kitchen and find a note on the counter.

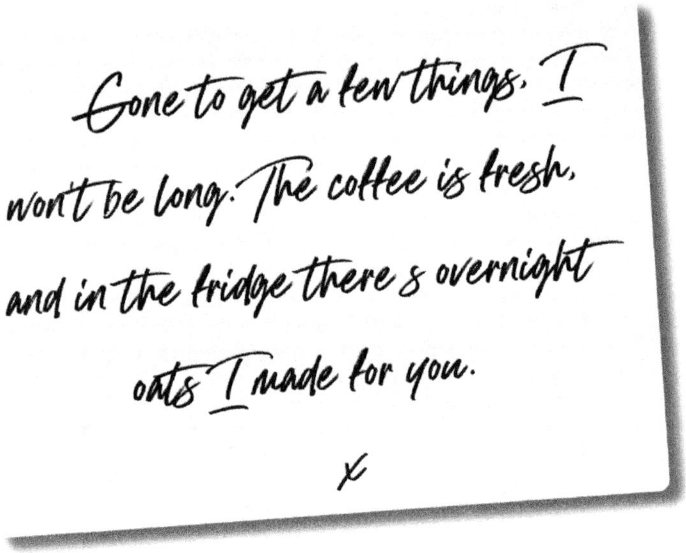
Gone to get a few things. I won't be long. The coffee is fresh, and in the fridge there's overnight oats I made for you.

x

Aww, he made me oats. I can't help but smile at how sweet he's been. I open the cupboards looking for where the mugs are, and when I find them, I grab one and pour myself a coffee.

Leaning against the counter, I close my eyes and appreciate the coffee. There's so much I have to do, including finding somewhere else to live. I know Alec's been trying to get me to move in here with him, but I don't think that's appropriate. Especially considering I'll need to have somewhere safe for Jordan to come home to.

I hear someone at the door, and I instantly freeze. I'm being transported back to earlier this morning. As quietly as I can, I place the mug on the counter, and tiptoe back into the bedroom so I can grab my phone.

"Hey," Alec says, startling me. "You're awake." I grasp at my chest as I take several deep breaths in and out, trying to calm the fight or flight instinct that kicked in. "Are you okay?" He drops the grocery bag on the counter, and rushes over to me. "What is it?"

"I heard you at the door, and I panicked. Truthfully, I was ready to climb out the bedroom window to get away."

"You're safe here, Serena." He envelopes me in a massive hug. I can't help but wrap my arms around his torso, taking deep breaths as I close my eyes.

"I'm such a mess," I say.

"You just had something traumatic happen, of course you're going to be on edge. But, you're safe here," he repeats before pulling back, to place a soft kiss on my lips. "Did you have the oats I made you?"

"I only just woke up about ten or fifteen minutes ago."

He links our fingers and walks us out to the kitchen again. Opening the fridge, he grabs a small bowl, and then opens a draw to retrieve a spoon. "Here."

"Thank you."

"Come on." He heads over to the small kitchen table, and pulls out a chair for me. The moment I sit, he leaves and goes to pour himself a coffee. "How are you feeling?"

"Um..." I puff my cheeks out with air, then let the breath go. "I'm, um." I can barely think. "Surreal. Everything feels surreal."

"You can't go back there."

"I know," I agree with him. "I just need to find somewhere to go." Alec draws his brows together, and shakes his head.

Pinching the bridge of his nose, he looks down to his coffee, before lifting his gaze to stare at me. "What?"

"You don't need to find anywhere. You live here now."

"As sweet as that gesture is, Alec, it won't work."

"Why not? I have a bed, it's comfortable, right?" he asks with every ounce of seriousness.

I smirk, and nod. "Yes, it's comfortable. But, that's not really the issue."

"Then what is? Whatever you think is a problem, we can fix it."

I pick the spoon up, and have a small bite of the oats. I'm not really hungry, but I suppose I should eat something. "In less than three months my brother will be out of rehab, and he'll need somewhere to live. I can't let him go back to the way he was, and nor can I expect him to fend for himself yet. He needs to integrate back into society. But let's face it, he's been antisocial for a long time." Alec patiently listens as I speak. "See, I can't move in here, because I need to find somewhere he can be with me."

He runs his hand through his sandy brown hair and nods. "I know what you're saying, and I understand it's important to you to have your brother close by. But, for how long? He's an adult, Serena. You've been so strong for him, but he also needs to be his own man."

My back straightens as I shake my head in disbelief. "I can't let him fend for himself yet, Alec. He needs me."

Alec wets his lips and nods. "I want you here with me, Serena."

"I'm responsible for him."

"He's not a child," Alec counters.

"I know that, and I know he's going to have to learn to do things on his own." I sigh, frustrated with the whole thing. "Look, I know I can't baby him forever, but these circumstances aren't exactly ordinary. I want him to succeed and stay away from drugs, but I also know I can't watch him forever. And you're right, he's a grown man who needs to look after himself. It's just..." I look down at my barely eaten oats, then lift my chin to look at Alec. "I've worked my ass off to get him into rehab, and I can't just wash my hands of him now and say my job is done. Because it's not."

"Let's try and find a solution that fits all of us. Because you living somewhere else, isn't even an option. It's not going to happen. You and I." He points to himself, then me. "We're together in every sense of the word."

Chuckling, I say, "You make me laugh, Alec. You're so sure we should move in."

"There's nothing funny about it at all," he says with a deadpan expression. "What if we look for somewhere that has either a in-law apartment, or maybe a detached guest house for your brother?"

I'm temporarily stunned and speechless. "But this is your house."

"It's the right size for the two of us, but it's not if we're going to..." he draws the sentence out, struggling to say whatever he's thinking. "It's a good starter home," he finally says. "But, it's not so good for more than two people."

My forehead crinkles and I'm a little lost on what he's saying. Until it dawns on me like a lightning bolt. "Wait, are you talking about a family?" He lifts his hand in gesture, opening and closing his mouth without actually speaking. "Alec?"

He opens his mouth again, then lifts his shoulders slowly. "It's a natural step in a relationship," he says with an unusually high pitch.

I rub at my forehead trying to piece together what he's trying to say. "Wait, you want kids?"

"Don't you?"

This is not how I saw this conversation going. "I suppose, one day. But not yet. Not for a while."

"I didn't say now, but one day, I'd like children. And I've never met anyone who I could imagine carrying my baby..." he pauses for a few seconds. "Until I met you. And now, all I can think about is having a future with you."

"Alec," I start saying, but he holds his hand up to me.

"I know, you have to think about Jordan. And although I'm not overly keen on having him live with us, I know how important he is to you. So, I'm willing to rent my house out, and we'll find somewhere bigger for us that can also accommodate your brother when he's out of rehab." My mouth falls open and I gape as I sit staring at Alec. I'm not sure what to say or do. "Say something."

"This is all overwhelming, Alec. You're willing to change your whole life, move out of here, and buy a house with me, just so my brother can live with us?"

"That's exactly right. Because I don't want to wake up and not have you beside me ever again."

Damn it. He's incredibly beautiful, and so accommodating. "I don't know what to say."

"Is a four bedroom home big enough for us?" he asks.

I chuckle at the absurdity, yet absolute sweetness of this conversation. "I can't ask you to give up your home, Alec."

"You're not. I'm volunteering, because I want us together. And this is the only way I know we can both be happy." I feel my eyes prickling with tears. I wipe at them hoping Alec doesn't notice. "Why are you crying?" Obviously, he does.

"Because," the words get caught in my throat. "You're this amazing guy who's willing to unsettle himself just to give me the world. And I'm feeling so much guilt over it. I feel like I've cornered you into making this massive life decision."

He reaches across the table to take my hands in his. "Hey," he says as he scoots his chair forward, brings my hands up to his lips and kisses my fingers. "I can't help who've I've fallen in love with."

I stare straight into his adoring eyes. His lips part and he leans forward to place his forehead on mine. My heart rate quickens, and all the air leaves my chest. "You love me?" I ask. I haven't heard those words in such a long time.

Alec lifts his hand and places it on my cheek. His warm thumb gently strokes the skin beneath my eye. My stomach flutters with excitement, though deep down inside, I just hope he doesn't laugh at me. "More than I thought I ever could."

I throw my arms around his neck, still blindsided by his admission. He loves me. And it doesn't come with any type of condition. I mean, Jordan would say he loves me after I'd give him a few dollars, but I knew he never meant those words. Not while he was high, or coming down off a high. "I love you," I whisper. Pulling back, I shake my head, trying to dislodge the doubts and fears roaming around in my head. "I feel like I don't deserve this."

"Why?"

"I suppose, it's been such a long time since anyone said they loved me, that I began to think maybe I'm unworthy of love."

"Darlin.'" He hugs me again, his warm body completely enveloping me. "You're so easy to love, it was hard for me *not* to fall in love with you." With my head on his shoulder, I smile. "Even when you're being nothing but a pain in the ass and arguing with me."

"I don't argue," I protest.

"No? Remember when we first met?"

"Hey, you were being unbearable and grumpy. I just had to put you in your place. I wasn't going to let you treat me like crap."

Alec laces his fingers through my hair, leaning in, he kisses my lips. He's shutting me up with a kiss. I smile as he keeps trying to kiss me. "Stop it," he says against my lips.

"What?"

"I wasn't being unbearable and grumpy."

"No, you're right. You were being an asshole. Totally different."

Alec throws his head back and laughs while his fingers are still entwined in my hair. "You're going to be the death of me." He gives me another kiss on the nose. We're interrupted by Alec's phone ringing. "I've gotta get it," he says and pulls away from me. He takes his phone out of his pocket, looks at who's calling, and shakes his head. "Hey," he says and smiles at me. "You okay?" *Dean,* he mouths to me. "Yeah, yeah," he pauses to listen. His brows draw in together, then he nods. "Yeah, we're good." He's listening intently as he begins to pace. "Yeah, sure. The three of us?" Alec's eyes widen then he nods again. "Tomorrow is good. Hang on." He lowers the phone to look to me. "Tomorrow morning I'll be going out with Dean and Rhett. Is that okay with you?"

"You don't need to ask me, Alec. I'll be going back to work. Speaking of, I need to call the hospital and tell them what happened."

"You don't think you should take some time to deal with what happened?" He brings the phone up to his ear. "Hang on."

"If I don't get back to work, the stress will get to me, and I refuse to give those assholes any more power than they've already had over me."

Alec's lips purse together. "Promise me you'll talk to someone about it."

"I already intended to. The hospital can help me find someone."

His smile tells me he's satisfied with my answer. He brings the phone back up to his ear. "Yeah, tomorrow is good. You sure you're alright?" Alec's concerned tone tells me something is going on. I just hope Dean, Joanne, and Thomas are okay. "Okay." He hangs up, and places the phone on the counter.

"Everything alright?" I ask. The distraction from memories of the home invasion is welcome.

"I'm not sure. Dean sounded like something's bothering him. He wants to talk to Rhett and me tomorrow, so we're meeting up for breakfast." He huffs as he looks over to the phone. "You sure you'll be okay to go to work?"

"Your brother needs you, Alec. And besides, I'll be fine. I'm quite resilient."

"And stubborn," he murmurs under his breath.

"I'm not stubborn." Alec glares at me, his eyebrows high and he's shaking his head. "Maybe a little," I surrender.

"A little?'

"That's all I'm saying." I hold my hands up. "Anyway, I have to make a call to work, to let them know what happened." Alec runs his hand through his hair, and turns to stare at the phone again, distracted. "Are you okay?"

"Yeah," he finally responds. "But something is definitely going on. I'll find out what tomorrow."

"Yeah, you will." Standing, I give Alec a hug before heading into the bedroom where my bag is. Opening it, I see the tin with my family memories. I sit on the edge of the bed, and open the lid.

A tight lump swells in my throat as I lift the picture of the four of us out. Jordan poking his tongue out, Dad with his arm around Mom, me looking goofy. Tears well in my eyes as I sit on the bed, staring at the photo. "I'm sorry," I whisper to my parents. "I failed." I drag my thumb over their faces, wishing for just a moment with them.

I'd hold them so tightly, and tell them how sorry I am that I couldn't protect Jordan. That I put myself in danger, and that I'm trying to be a better person for them. "I'm sorry," I whisper again.

A tsunami of emotions spreads rapidly through me. "I miss you so damn much," I say to the photo. My eyes release the emotions coursing through me. The tears are my gateway to how I'm feeling. Damn these stupid tears, why do they have to make me so vulnerable?

"What the..." Alec rushes over to me, and sweeps me up into his arms. "What's going on?"

"I've failed them, Alec. I've let them down."

"Who?" I pull away, and hold the photo out for Alec to take. He sits on the bed, and I sit beside him. "Your parents?" I nod. "You look so much like your mom. She was beautiful."

"Yeah, I do."

"And this is Jordan?" I nod. "The drugs really changed him. He looked happy and healthy here."

"The drugs screwed him over. This box right here is my family's legacy." I take out Mom and Dad's wedding rings, and Mom's engagement ring.

"How did they die?"

Still staring at the photo, I shake my head at the painful memory. I clutch my free hand to my chest, absolutely dreading that I have to relive it. But Alec needs to know all about it if he's going to be part of my life. My heart is heavy, and my hands are shaking. "Jordan," I say with a trembling voice. "Last year of high school, he changed. Started skipping, and hanging out with people he shouldn't. First it was alcohol, then it progressed into pot. I...um, could see what he was doing to our parents, and our family, and I never wanted to put them through what he did. So, I kept my head down, and worked really hard to get into college for physiotherapy. In the meantime, he went from bad to worse. It was awful. *He* was awful."

"Drugs alter people, and even though people think they can stop, they can't. Not when the drug takes over."

I let out a humorless laugh. "Ain't that the truth?" I take another deep breath. "In my first year of college, Jordan just became a statistic. There's really no other way to put it. Mom would call me crying, saying she'd tried to talk to him, but he'd yell at her, and sometimes he'd lash out and hit her." I shake my head. "Sometimes I'd even get phone calls from Jordan just rambling about all sorts of shit. He was incredibly paranoid, and thought the world was out to get him. He was convinced everyone was trying to hurt him, especially our parents. Anyway, one night he'd snuck in at home and stole Dad's car. But my parents knew it was him, and they tried to find him. They um..." I choke up remembering the last phone call from Mom. "Mom called me, and said Jordan had stolen Dad's car, and they were going to go out and try to find him, so they could get the car back." The tears are now flowing unapologetically.

"It's okay, you don't have to tell me," Alec says in a gentle voice.

"No, I do. You have to know." He nods his head and offers me a smile. I take a shaky breath before I continue. "They went searching for Jordan and the car. Mom told me, they were going to drag Jordan home, and put him in rehab, because they feared that the next time it would be a police officer showing up at their door to tell them Jordan had died from a drug overdose." I blink rapidly. "It wasn't even about the car. It was about getting Jordan help." Sweat forms across my upper lip and my hairline. That phone call I received, that was hell. "I tried calling them to find out what was happening, but they weren't answering. I decided I had to go home on the weekend to help them." I weakly shrug. "I had class, and thought I'd leave straight after to go home." I keep shaking my head in disbelief as I stare at the photo. "My phone was ringing constantly, and it wouldn't stop. The number was private..." I hate this feeling of powerlessness, and hopelessness. I never want to feel it again. "I had a sick feeling in my stomach that something was happening. I thought maybe my parents had found Jordan, dead. But..." My voice cracks. "I left the lecture theatre and answered the call. It was the police, telling me my parents had died."

"How?" Alec pushes.

"Mom's car had flipped several times, then hit a power pole that fell on the car, killing them instantly. Dad's car was also there, but there was no driver. They said whoever was driving Dad's car, smashed into the side of Mom's, sending it off the road and rolling into the pole."

"Jordan?" Alec asks.

"There were several different fingerprints in the car. Jordan's was one of them, my parents, and others who were unknown. But whoever was driving would've been badly injured, and when they found Jordan, he was strung out, but didn't have any injuries that reflected he was driving. But someone he was associated with took the car. The police think Mom and Dad tried to stop them, they panicked, and ran my parents off the road. It was probably another drug addict. But Jordan couldn't say who took the car, because he couldn't even remember stealing it to start with. He was arrested, and did some time in rehab, he got clean for zero-point-two seconds, and started using again."

"Shit."

"I think the guilt of what happened to Mom and Dad keeps dragging him back to the oblivion of drugs. He needs to confront what he did and deal with everything, or he's only going to keep returning to his safety net."

"You need to let New Dawn know this."

"I already have. When I was researching rehab centers, I reached out to them and told them about everything. It's one of the reasons I chose them for Jordan, because it's so much more than just drugs. He's dulling all the guilt with drugs."

"Darlin,'" Alec says. "I don't know what to say."

"There's nothing you can say. I just need you to understand why I work so hard, and I'm so focused on making sure Jordan comes through this. Because I've already lost the only family I have, and I can't lose him too. Thing is, as much as I want to blame him for this, I just can't."

"I can't judge you for trying to keep the only family you have left together. I haven't been in your shoes, and although a part of me wants to really knock some sense into Jordan, I also know he's under the influence of drugs. And it's not an excuse, I'm not justifying his behavior. If I'm being honest, I totally agree with you. The drugs are a form of escapism for him because he knows his actions are the reason your parents aren't here. He's likely trying to kill himself subconsciously."

I take several deep breaths, trying to come to terms with what Alec said. He understands now. "This is one of the reasons I never really pursued any type of relationship. I never thought anyone would accept why I fight so hard for Jordan, even after all the devastation his drug addiction has caused."

"I have a question though, did your parents not leave you their house?"

"I wish they had one. They were blue collar workers on just a livable wage that didn't allow for any luxuries, including a home. They were lucky though, the house we lived in was one they'd been renting for many years, and the landlord was happy to have them there. But with only a small life insurance policy, two wrecked vehicles, and the little they did have in savings, I had to put every penny aside so I could send Jordan to rehab."

"Your brother is extremely lucky to have you, Serena. I doubt many siblings would still fight so hard to get them clean, not after everything he's done."

I clutch at my belly. "I can feel it in here. He's going to come out of New Dawn well, and he'll shine so bright once he does. The universe has my back, Alec."

"You're optimistic."

"Hope is my only option."

"Even after this crappy hand life has dealt you, you still remain so positive. I'm so impressed by your outlook."

I pull my shoulders back, and smirk. "I refuse to give up, because I make my own future." I have to be positive; there's no other way forward.

"You're the most headstrong person I've ever met. Who happens to be sexy as fuck, too." He leans in and kisses me on the lips. *Sexy as fuck*...he's such a male. Pulling back, he tucks some hair behind my ear. Holding my gaze, he smiles. "We have three months to find a house, so we better start looking today."

"Okay," I respond.

"Get dressed, let's head into Mulberry Point and see what houses are on offer." Standing, I take myself into the bathroom to have a shower. I had one last night, but I need to wash away those harrowing moments, and look forward to a life of happiness instead of reverting to the bleakness I've been living with.

But that's a lot easier said than done.

Chapter 18

ALEC

"I'M GOING TO work, but I'm finishing early, because I need to head down to the mall and buy some clothes," Serena says to me as I make us both a coffee.

"Do you want me to come with you?"

"No, it's okay. I'll go straight after work. And, I spoke to my supervisor yesterday. Tomorrow I'll be seeing a counselor about…" She circles her hands. "Everything."

My chest swells with pride as I sit, staring at Serena. "I can't tell you how proud I am of you. So many people would just bottle all this shit up, and think they could deal with it on their own. But not my woman. She's a tough warrior."

There's a gleam in her eyes as she leans in to give me a kiss. "Thank you." I reach for her but she steps back. "You have breakfast with your brothers, and I have to get to work. But I really want to do a meditation first. I'm going to close the bedroom door, is that okay with you?"

That's right, she believes in that mumbo jumbo crap. If it's what she needs to get herself through her day, then who am I to shit on it? "How long will you be?"

She looks at the wall-oven clock and winces. "I've got about twenty minutes before I have to leave."

I turn to look at the clock too. I need to leave in about forty. "Yeah, I'll just put the TV on, and wait until you're done."

"Okay." She smiles brightly, although I can see she's barely holding it all together. This last week has been unbelievably hard on her. Serena's brother went into rehab, her home was invaded while she was there, and her memories of her parents were brought to the surface. Oh man, I can't imagine how overwhelming all this is for her. I'm glad she's getting mental health help. She needs it.

The door to our bedroom closes. I walk out to the sofa, and pick up the remote. Slumping into the sofa, I turn the TV on, and start flicking through the channels. Nothing is really catching my interest, until I happen upon the tail end of a home renovation show. This is the least boring thing I've found. I'll watch it until Serena is finished in the bedroom and I can get ready to leave.

My mind starts spinning as the host stages the house ready for it to go on sale. We've still got at least the next month here, and I know Serena loves her mumbo jumbo shit, so why don't I make the spare room into a space for her to do it in there?

I know she loves yellow, so after breakfast with my brothers I'll head to the store to get a bunch of shit to make her feel comfortable in there. Crap, what does someone need to be able to meditate? I don't want to ask her, because I want it to be a surprise for her.

I turn the TV off, and grab my phone. I open the search engine, and stare at it blankly. What do I type in? Meditation rooms? Seems like a good place to start.

I click on the photos to try and find something that'll work in the room I have. Thankfully, it's large enough that I can move my home gym to one side, and Serena can have a meditation area on the other side. Oh, an eight panel, rice paper room divider. It's got flowers all over it. It says it's a zen garden room divider. That's gotta be good, right? I make a mental note of where I can get this. Another image has this huge round meditation pillow in yellow on the floor. Shit, what the hell is a meditation pillow? Is a meditation pillow different from a regular pillow? What the hell is this? A chakra tapestry? Aren't tapestries something old women do? Is a chakra tapestry even a thing? Does she need one of those to meditate?

There are candles and indoor water features I can get. Wow, who knew there was so much stuff people can buy? Maybe I've got no idea what I'm talking about, but here I thought mediation was closing your eyes and say *aum, aum, aum* over and over again. There are a few links to places where I can buy this stuff, and I'm pleased to see there's a place in the local mall. I wonder how long they've been there? I don't recall ever seeing any of this hippy stuff at the mall. I'll swing by after breakfast and grab things for the room.

"What are you doing?" I hear Serena asking.

She's caught me browsing the mumbo jumbo stuff, so I quickly flip my phone face down. "Just looking at stuff." As I stand, I shove my phone in my pocket. "You look beautiful," I say as I walk over to her and wrap her in my arms. I love it when she's near me.

"I'm just dressed for work." She sighs loudly. "I've been thinking, maybe it's time I give up waitressing. It's too much on me."

"Thank God," I reply as I hold her closer to me. "Give all of the jobs up, except the physiotherapy. Keep that one."

"Nah, I can't give up the cleaning, not yet. Let me get ahead a little bit, then I'll look at letting them go. I've got a mountain of debt, Alec."

"Like what?" I ask, genuinely curious.

"Well, there's the loan I took out to finish college, there's my car loan, and I have to pay you back."

I flick my hand at her casually. "That can wait."

"No, it can't. You helped me to get my brother into rehab, I need to return your money. You don't owe us anything."

Here she goes again, stubborn, and proud. "Serena, we're going to be buying a house together. How about for now you don't worry about what I've loaned you, and we can figure it out after we buy the house." She opens her mouth to argue, but I silence her with a kiss. When I feel her body soften in my arms, I pull back. "And what other debt do you have?"

"Well, nothing really. I don't even have a credit card. But I feel like what I owe you is sitting on my chest like a hundred-pound gorilla."

"So, what you're saying is the loan is a major thing because it's my money?" In all honesty, I have no intentions of ever asking her for it.

"Money is important to everyone, Alec."

"Okay, then let's open up a joint account, and what we both have will go into it."

She drops her hands from around my waist and steps back. "Don't be ridiculous, we can't do that."

"Why?"

"Because even some married couples don't do that."

"My parents did. There was never an issue between them. I can't see why there'd be an issue between us," I counter.

"I'm not comfortable with that, Alec. Your money should be your money. Anyway, I've gotta go to work. Do you think you'll be home for dinner?"

Hell yeah, I will be. Hopefully, I'll have my gym room ready with her voodoo stuff. I can't wait to surprise her. "Yeah, I will be."

"Okay. I should be home about six-ish. I haven't given my notice at the restaurant yet, but I'm taking a couple of days off from there. Tonight will be an early night for me." She slings her yellow bag over her shoulder, reaches up and gives me a kiss on the lips.

"See you tonight," I say as I walk her to the door, and wait for her to leave before I head back into the bedroom to get ready.

"The pancakes here at Elle's Café are the best," Rhett says as the three of us sit in a booth toward the back of the café.

"It looks good in here since they made it over," Dean says as he nervously looks around the café.

"Hey guys, how are you?" Dani greets as she hands us all a menu. Rhett's eyes widen, he pulls his shoulders back and gives her a nod. Dani's cheeks turn pink before she lowers her gaze. "I'll give you a few minutes," her voice seems to have softened.

"Rhett?" I say in a low voice so Dani can't hear us. "Are you two...?" I don't finish the implied sentence.

"What? No," Rhett says in a huff. "What are you eating?"

Hopefully Serena tonight. I look down at the menu, but can't help notice how Rhett keeps lifting his gaze to search for Dani every few seconds.

"I'll get the pancakes," Dean says and shoves the menu to the side.

"Yeah, same," I say. "And a coffee."

Rhett is pretending to peruse the menu, but he can't take his eyes off Dani. Something is going on between them, and he's refusing to say anything to us about it. Dani is behind the counter, talking to the older guy cooking, but she keeps turning to look over in our direction too. She casually strolls over, and stands at the end of the booth. "Are you ready?"

"Three pancakes, all with a side of bacon and hash browns. Three coffees," Rhett says in a clipped and almost rude tone.

"Anything else?" Dani asks with a chirp.

"Nope." Rhett picks all three menus up, and hands them to Dani barely acknowledging her.

What the hell is happening?

"Sure thing." She smiles warmly toward Rhett.

The moment she leaves, Dean says, "If Mom was here with us, she would've clipped you on the back of the head. Since when do you talk to any lady like that?"

Rhett lowers his gaze, obviously embarrassed by his behavior. "I don't know what came over me. I'll apologize when she returns."

"So you should," I say. Turning to Dean, I wait for him to tell us why we were summoned here to start with. "What's going on?" I ask.

"Um." He pinches the bridge of his nose, and closes his eyes. "Um." Shit, I've never really known him to be frazzled by anything.

"Are Joanne and Thomas okay?" I ask, as I sit straighter.

"Yeah, yeah. They're good." He blinks several times, but is still avoiding eye contact with Rhett and myself.

Dani's holding three mugs by the handles in one hand, with the coffee pot in the other. Rhett sees her, jumps to his feet, and takes the mugs out of her right hand. She smiles warmly at him. "Thank you," she says.

"I'm sorry for being a jerk to you. I shouldn't have snapped." Rhett isn't afraid to say he's being a dick, and I admire that about him.

"Apology accepted. Do it again, and it won't be," she replies.

Holy shit, Dani's making it clear that she's not going to put up with his shit. With a tight smile, Rhett nods. Once our coffees are poured, we all thank her in unison. There are small glances exchanged between Dani and Rhett before she turns to leave.

"I can cut the tension in the air with a knife," I say.

Rhett shakes his head, and briefly glances over at Dani before returning his attention to us. "Anyway, what's going on?" He pointedly glares at Dean. "If Thomas and Joanne are okay, then it must be something else. Are you alright?"

Dean sucks in a deep breath, and turns to make sure no one is listening. "Joanne and I have been trying for a baby."

"Congratulations, man," Rhett happily cheers.

But Dean doesn't appear so happy. He shakes his head, and lowers his eyes. "Nah. I wanted to talk to you both, and um..." he stops talking, puffs out his cheeks and blows out the air. "We...um."

"What the fuck is happening?" I ask.

"Go get yourselves checked, because I can't have kids." His eyes redden, and for a moment I'm stuck on what he's said.

"What?" I ask, still trying to process.

"I'm sterile. I can't have kids. Joanne is fine, but, I'm not. If either of you ever thought about kids, get yourselves tested."

Rhett lifts his hand and scratches his head. I'm sitting opposite Dean, and next to Rhett, unable to comprehend the actual words Dean's spoken. "You're sterile?"

"Yep." He nods, but anyone can see this is bringing him a world of hurt.

"Are you sure?" Rhett asks.

"Yeah, I'm sure. Which is why I wanted to talk to the both of you."

"But, how?" I ask.

He slowly lifts his shoulders. "We don't know, and the worst thing is, we may never know why I'm sterile. I don't have the risk factors that can make a man sterile, drugs, alcohol, weight, cancer, there are so many things. You both will likely be fine, but like I said, if you're considering kids in the future, then go get yourselves tested."

"Shit," is the only thing I can say.

"Kids aren't something I really want," Rhett says. "So, I'm good. If I'm sterile, I'm sterile." He shrugs. "I really don't care."

"Yeah, you might not care because you're only twenty-two. But if you meet someone you love, and she wants kids, then you will care," Dean says. Rhett sits up straighter, his eyes follow Dani behind the counter.

"Yeah, I doubt that'll happen," he adds. Rhett picks his coffee mug up, and takes a sip before placing it on the table again.

Both Dean and Rhett refocus toward me. "I think I want kids. Serena and I are going to start searching for bigger houses with more space for whatever happens in the future."

"Are you? How's she doing after what happened?" Rhett asks.

Dani interrupts us again, balancing three plates stacked high with pancakes, hash browns and streaky bacon. "These look good." Dean sits back and peers down at the plate she's slid in front of him.

"Really good," I say when she places my plate down.

"It does look delicious. Thank you." Rhett hasn't taken his eyes off Dani, not once since she's been at the table. Why is it I think he's not talking about the food?

Dani smirks. "Enjoy."

"I can't wait to eat it," Rhett shamelessly flirts with Dani. He's definitely not talking about the food. He's an enigma. One moment he's ignoring her, and the next he's flirting.

Dani walks away, and I turn to Rhett. "Ask her out."

"What? Who?"

"We're your brothers. We can recognize you flirting. Just ask her out," Dean says. "I'd be happy to call her over and ask her for you."

"What?" Rhett shrieks. "Just eat your food and shut the fuck up."

I can't help but smile. Picking up one of the slices of bacon, I chew it as I watch my brothers be idiots. "As I was saying," I interrupt their stupid disputes. "She's doing okay. Serena's at work today, and they've set up counselling sessions for her, too."

"Have you heard anything about her brother, or is it too early?" Rhett asks.

"Nah, nothing yet. But you know," I place my elbows on the table and think about her. "She's had to be strong for so long, that now she feels like she has to keep being strong. She has moments of vulnerability, but those walls are pretty high."

"She works how many jobs?" Rhett asks. "All so she could give her brother the best possible help." He clicks his tongue to the roof of his mouth. "Most people would've washed their hands at that, and moved on with their lives."

"Her parents died because of her brother's addictions, too."

"What?" Dean asks.

"Basically, he stole the father's car, they tried to find him, someone else was driving the father's car and ran the parents off the road. They slammed into a power pole, and died. That's the short version."

Dean's eyes widen as he sits opposite me staring. "And she still has his back?" He shakes his head. "That right there shows you how committed she is. Serena is a powerhouse, Alec, and you're damn lucky to have her."

"I know," I agree.

"So, you're looking for a new house? Are you going to sell yours?" Rhett asks. He's asking because he wants out of Mom's house and probably into mine.

"Rent it."

"Yeah? When do you think this'll all be happening?"

"We'll be looking at a house that can accommodate her brother too. And we need to be in it by the time his rehab is done. So, three months."

"Huh." Rhett crinkles his forehead. "Three months you say?"

"Yes, Rhett. You can rent it." I know this is where his casual conversation is heading.

He smiles broadly, incredibly pleased by my offer. "Will the furniture stay?"

"You're a pain in the ass. Eat your breakfast." Dean's snicker reminds me why we're actually here. "What are you going to do? Is there some kind of medication to help you with your little problem?" I hold my pinky finger up and wiggle it.

"I'm sterile, not impotent, you idiot. But, besides that, there's nothing much they can do. I suppose, we have Thomas, and I'm grateful for him, but at the same time, I would've loved a child of my own."

I slyly look over to Rhett, he shakes his head and shrugs. "Is there anything we can do to help? Shit, man, I don't know if there is anything we can do." I nod in agreement with Rhett.

"Nope, not really." Dean's chin lowers to his chest as he breathes out a long, low sigh. I feel for him, he appears beaten and so sad. "It's okay." His vacant eyes and toneless response tells both Rhett and me, it's far from okay.

"Whatever we can do to help, just let us know," I offer.

"I mean if you want a kid, everyone says you and I look so similar...you know," Rhett's high-pitched offering is met with Dean staring at him like he wants to kill him. Rhett's holding in the chuckle, but if I was Rhett, I'd be running fast.

"Oh man, what song do you want at your funeral?" I ask.

"He has to catch me first."

Dean narrows his hard stare to Rhett, who's completely avoiding him. "You're lucky I need you at work," Dean says in a deadpan voice.

"You know I was joking, and I love Joanne, but not like that. Anyway, in all seriousness, if you need anything, let us know."

"I know. Thanks."

"You okay?" I ask as I continue to eat my breakfast.

"We'll be fine," he replies. Dean's words sound confident, but I know him well enough to know this is killing him.

There's nothing more we can say about it, so we leave it alone. "Anyway, how's your new house?" I ask Dean.

"It's massive. Like, way too big. But Joanne loves it, and it's ample enough that when her parents come to visit, they're comfortable."

"Yeah, how are they with you now?" Rhett asks. "Her old man still trying to pay you off to get rid of you?"

"He's good now." Dean finishes the last of his food, and sits back in the booth, throwing one arm up over the back of the seat. The door opens, and two women walk into the café. As they walk past us, they both do a double take, staring at Rhett and giggling. "What the hell?" Dean says when the two girls sit a few tables away. "Do you know them?" he asks Rhett.

Rhett's in his own world, not even paying attention to the two women, who I'd put in their early twenties. "Who?" Rhett's completely oblivious to them. Dean discreetly gestures to the two women who keep staring over at our table. Rhett isn't subtle at all, he looks at them, then turns back to us. "I have no idea who they are."

"Well, they're certainly checking you out," I say.

Rhett instantly searches for Dani, who's standing at the counter with a tight jaw and a devil glint in her eye. Shit, what is going on with them? They can't keep their eyes off each other, yet neither have said more than five words. "Are you two fucking?" Dean bluntly asks.

"No, we're not."

"Funny, because Dean didn't mention a name," I say, catching Rhett out.

Rhett shoves the rest of the food in his mouth, downs his coffee then stands and sighs. "I'm out of here. See you at work tomorrow." He opens the door and walks past where we're sitting, he taps on the window with his keys, and sticks his middle finger up at us.

"Bastard left so he wouldn't have to pay," I say.

"Why do you think he sits on the outside? Smart boy, that one." Dean chuckles. "You done?" He looks over at my empty plate, takes in a large breath, then lets it go. "Thanks for listening." Standing, he walks over to the counter and pays for all our breakfasts. We head out of the café, and I drive straight back over to Mulberry Point Mall. I need to find this hippy store so I can buy Serena her new age stuff for the room.

Chapter 19

SERENA

TODAY'S BEEN NOTHING but long and stressful. The counselling session was intense although I'm relieved and grateful I did it. I've got another five sessions booked, and all I can think of is how much I didn't know I actually really needed them.

Driving back to Alec's, I'm looking forward to dinner, a shower, and bed. My body feels like it's been hit by a truck, and my eyes are stinging from how tired I am. At this point I think it's more mental exhaustion than physical.

I pull up outside Alec's small house, and sit in the car for a moment as I try and gather my thoughts. I know I desperately need to meditate just so I can put my feelings into the right headspace. But, I also feel bad for locking Alec out of his own room in order for me to meditate. Thankfully, he's understanding, even though he calls it mumbo jumbo and doesn't believe in it.

What's there not to believe in? We all breathe. That's what meditation is—purposeful breathing.

Grabbing my bag, I get out of my car, and walk up to the front door. Alec opens it, as if he was waiting for me. "Hey," I say as I instantly crave the warmth of his arms around me.

"You look tired." He slings my bag off my shoulder, links our fingers together and leads me into the family room. I plonk down, melting into the back of the sofa, completely relaxing.

"What's this?" I can't help but notice the dining table has two plates, four flickering candles, and two wine glasses already set for us. A delicious smell of something incredibly familiar wafts through the house. "Did you cook me dinner?"

"Cook is such a strong word." He flinches. "As we know I can cook, and what I do cook I'm very good at, but I've had an eventful day, so I didn't cook tonight."

"Tell me about your day," I ask.

"Tell me about yours first. What happened at the counselling session?" He holds a finger up. "Wait." He ducks off into the kitchen where he pours us two red wines and brings them over. "Okay, go on." Aww, how sweet, but I don't have the heart to tell him I don't like red wine. He's gone to so much effort. I take a sip, and my face automatically contorts. "You don't like red wine?"

"I'm sorry. But I actually don't like wine at all. I'd rather have a beer than this." Alec's eyes widen. "But I'll drink it, because I really appreciate you doing this for me." I take another sip, my right eye half closes as I try to welcome the flavor. But seriously, yuck.

"Thank God!" he proudly announces. "I can't stand wine either. And, as it turns out, I have beer." Taking both glasses over to the sink, he dumps them out and turns the faucet on to rinse them out. He returns with two beers, one for me and one for himself. He takes a sip. "Yep, *so* much better. Anyway, tell me about your day."

I drink a good third of the beer, really savoring the robust taste. "Work was good, I was based at the hospital all day. I do have to go out and see May on Monday. The counselor is fantastic. I've got five more sessions booked with her, and I'm looking forward to them." I feel myself scrunching my brows as I shake my head. "You know, I never thought I was holding on to so much garbage, but clearly I was. It's only been one session, but I felt like a weight had been lifted once I left her office."

"If she's helping, then you should stick with her."

"I will. Anyway, how was breakfast with your brothers? Did you have a good time with them?" He shrugs. "It would be nice to have a positive relationship with siblings. I'm holding on to hope that I'll have that with Jordan once he finishes rehab."

"You will." He places his hand on my thigh and gently squeezes. "Well, the reason Dean wanted to talk to us was to tell us he's sterile, and we should go get ourselves checked if we're considering having kids."

Sterile? "How do you feel about that?"

"Him being sterile?" I shake my head. "Um, well, I want a family, Serena. And I want that family with you." My heart swells with more love. Alec and I are really only just getting to know each other, but he's already talking long term with no end in sight. "I was hoping you'd be okay if I went and got myself tested."

"I...it's not, I, um." I place my hand to my chest. "I don't know what to say to you, Alec. This is something only you can decide."

"No. We're a couple now and we do things together. Especially something so big. It's not fair to you if we don't discuss these things first."

"You're something else, you know that? I think if it's something important to you, then I'm on board for whatever you want to do."

He takes my beer out of my hand, and places both mine and his on the small wooden table in the living room. "Okay, I will. But, before we have dinner, I want to show you something."

"Oh? What?" I ask, as he pulls me up.

"Just, come." Alec takes a step ahead of me, and I wrap my arms around his waist from behind, my front pressing firmly into his back. "Fuck, your tits feel good on me." I lean my head on his back and I chuckle. The walking is a bit clunky, but we manage it. He stops outside his gym room. Turning, his huge smile says he's done something extreme. "This is my gym room."

"I know," I say.

He opens the door and waits for me to peer inside. "But now, it's *our* room."

My hands drop from around his waist, and come up to cover my mouth. "Are you kidding?" I say. He's separated the room into two sections with this beautiful, light yellow rice paper divider. On one side is his home gym, on the other side he's created a sanctuary for me. There's an oversized, yet not overly fluffy yellow pillow on the floor, a large rock salt lamp with several sizes and types of crystals. There's even a chakra tapestry on the wall. "You did this?"

"Yeah, I wanted you to have a space for yourself, even though we'll only be here for a few weeks until we find our own home. I know meditation is important to you, and I wanted you to be able to feel comfortable. Is it okay? I mean, I don't understand that chakra stuff, but the women said they're good. And those rock things, she told me those different colored rocks all do different stuff."

I turn to face Alec. "It's perfect, thank you so much." I smash my mouth to his, kissing him for so many reasons. "You're perfect, do you know that?"

"I just want you happy."

Kiss. "I." *Kiss.* "So." *Kiss.* "Am." I couldn't be happier.

"Oh, and by the way, I went to a different kind of store today too." He smacks me on the butt, hard.

A sudden urge of desire floods me with warmth. The hair on the back of my neck rises, craving a deeper connection to Alec. "What did you buy?" He entwines his fingers through my hair, and pulls my head back, putting my mouth a perfect position for him to take. "Oh," I murmur, and a shiver tears through me.

He releases my hair, turns me around, and spanks me even harder making me jump forward. "Dinner time," he says, his voice dangerously sexy and low.

Help my soul. When he drops his tone, and speaks with confident authority, fuck me dead. Holy shit. I try my hardest to hold it together. "What's for dinner?' I ask, hopeful it'll be me.

"You'll see." *Please let him eat me, please, please, please.* The moment we're in the kitchen, his hands are already taking my pants off. He shimmies them down my legs, kneels and waits for me to use his shoulders to steady myself so he can take them off. "I kneel before my queen," he says. Once out of the pants, he turns his head, and starts eating me. *YES!* But stops after only a few licks. *NO!* "Just wait." He jumps to his feet, throwing my pants on the back of the sofa.

"Like I can go anywhere with my bottom half exposed."

I hear his laugh as he disappears down the small hallway into his bedroom. "Okay, I need you to sit." I try to see what he's hiding behind his back. He pulls a dining chair out for me, and indicates I should sit. I ain't arguing. No, ma'am. Not if I'm going to get to orgasm. Hopefully around his mouth, or his cock. Whichever. I'm perfectly fine with either.

I sit on the chair. Standing behind me, he grabs my chin, and arches my neck to the side. Alec's mouth is all over my neck, biting, licking, kissing around my collarbone. This isn't sweet, or tender. My heart is beating heavily, and I can feel myself throbbing while I wait for him to do whatever he wants to me.

I'm his for the taking. He can fuck me any way he wants. I trust Alec.

He pulls away, and I let out a soft moan, missing his mouth. "Arms up." I lift my arms, and he takes my work shirt off over my head. He unclasps my bra, and tosses it aside as if it's offensive. Something soft touches my eyes. It takes me a second to figure out he's blindfolding me.

Oh. My. God. *This is awesome!*

I try to close my legs, trying to find some relief. "Don't you dare," he commands. My legs stay open, but damn, I'm desperate for whatever he's going to do to me. His hot breath skims across my neck, before rapidly disappearing. "There's nothing more beautiful than you sitting in front of me, naked and exposed." From the sound of his voice, Alec has moved and is in front of me. I swallow the lump forming in my throat. My breathing is rapid and I need him to touch me. "Grab the edge of the chair." I want to touch him, but God damn, all I want to do is submit to him.

"Like this?" I ask as I tuck my hands under my butt. Alec doesn't respond. He grabs my left leg and lifts it, placing it on the edge of the dining table. He does the same with my right leg, totally exposing me. A sudden urge of dignity courses through me, and I want to hide. "I can't do this, Alec," I say as panic thumps through me.

"What? Why?" he asks.

Lowering my legs, I shake my head. "Because, even though I've never hated my body before, right now I do." I reach to take the blindfold off.

Alec steadies my hand, refusing to allow me to untie it. "Don't," he says.

Shaking my head, I feel self-conscious. "I know you've been with women who have perfect bodies."

"Stop," he says again. Pushing my legs open, I feel his mouth on me. His tongue darts in and out, licking, and lapping while he groans. "This is perfect," he mumbles against me, before taking another mouthful of me.

"But, my stomach is..." I try to argue with him.

"Is just perfect as it is." He eats me again, shoving his tongue into me, then teasing by licking my clit, bringing me to the very edge of an orgasm under his mouth.

Desire ripples through my body, causing me to shiver as I hold off coming on his face. Jesus, if he does that again though, I'm not sure I'll be able to control it. "Please," I beg, forgetting about my own stupid self-consciousness.

"What do you need?" he asks in a low sultry voice. Alec's mouth is reminding me I'm exactly where I belong. He pulls away, and I want to reach out, fist my hand in his hair, and pull his face back into my pussy. "You need this, don't you?" I feel something hard enter inside me, and I suck in a breath when the hard thing inside me, starts vibrating. I squirm, trying to rotate my hips to get the vibration on the very spot I need so I can orgasm. "It appears you're enjoying this."

"Hell yeah, I am," I reply, my voice unusually rough, on the verge of cracking. He turns the vibration up, and all I want to do is close my legs, and get it to that perfect spot for my own pleasure. Alec turns off the vibrator, takes it out, and I'm blessed to have his mouth on me again. "Ohhh," I moan. I can't help myself. I reach forward to find his head, clutch his hair, and use his mouth to bring myself to the point of explosion. God, I wish I could see him. But there's something extremely erotic about having a blindfold on, not knowing what's going to happen next.

With me right on the edge and Alec feasting on me, I grind my hips hard. I'm half hanging off the chair, but I don't care. I feel the resistance as he pulls back, and spanks me on the pussy. "Fuck!" He startled me. He spanks me once again, then his tongue is inside me. He pulls back, spanks me for a third time, then roughly licks me, playing with and nibbling at my clit. He spanks me again, then his tongue fucks me hard. I can't even get my head around what's happening inside my body. I want him to do that again, and again, and again.

My body trembles as Alec's mouth assaults me, making my breath quicken as every nerve tingles with need. Licking my lips, I feel myself opening my legs wider, hungry for more of what he's doing. Alec is moving his mouth all over my pussy, bringing me to my limit. My mouth dries, and my body tenses. "Yes!" With the blindfold still on, I reach for his head, hold it in place and ride him until I physically can't take another lap of his raspy tongue. Letting go, I sink against the chair, my arms falling limp to the side. I hear his zipper, then I feel him inside of me. He moves my legs to clamp around his hips, I'm in an unnatural position, but he's deep inside, and I'm loving it.

"Beautiful," he says. His thumb rubs my clit, hard. He's about to bring me to the edge again. Another orgasm? Jesus, how fucking lucky am I? "Fuck," Alec grunts. One hand is possessively gripping my hip so hard he's going to leave a mark. The other, rubbing my clit, brings me right to the point of orgasm. "Fuck," he groans again. His speed increases, and with only a few more firm pumps he comes hard. "Jesus, that wasn't my best performance."

I take the blindfold off. I'm in the most unusual position, but for some reason it works. "Your performance was fantastic. And, if you happen to want to do that thing with your mouth again sometime, then I'm good with it." He thrusts, then pulls out of me. I notice the glistening condom as he steps backward and leans against the dining table.

"You liked that, did you?"

"All I'm saying is if you come home from work, and I happen to be asleep, or if I'm cooking, and you want something to eat, or even, if I'm in the shower and you're a bit peckish, by all means, please feel free to feast on me."

Alec throws his head back and laughs. He pushes off from the table, and starts walking toward the bathroom in our room. "By the way, I don't want to use these." He points to the condom on his still-hard dick. How can he still be hard? *How?* "When you're comfortable, I'll get rid of them."

Ah well, I know he's been with other women, just like I've been with other men. He's probably had more partners than I have, but I think it's best if we both get tested. "I'm happy to do that, but I want us both to be tested." I stand and follow him to our room, naked.

He walks out of the bathroom, also naked while drying his hands on a towel. He stops when he sees me, drops the towel to the floor. Alec's eyes widen as he stares at my body. A smirk slowly stretches across his face. He grabs his hard cock and slowly rubs it up and down. My eyes are drawn to Alec pleasuring himself while he stares at my body. "Round two." Grabbing me by the hips he pulls me toward him, our mouths colliding.

Fuck yeah, round two here we come...*and cum.*

Chapter 20

ALEC

Two Weeks Later

SERENA IS WRINGING her hands together as I drive her out to New Dawn. "What's wrong?"

She shakes her head while looking out the front window. "Nothing."

Yeah right, *nothing* my ass. She's nervous about seeing her brother. From the moment I booked the flights to Kentucky, she's been buzzing with excitement. But last night she became rigid and withdrawn. "Don't lie to me," I say.

Serena draws out a low breath. "I'm nervous."

"What about?"

"I know this is the best place for him, but what if...?" Serena shrugs. "I don't know. Part of me can't wait to see him, and another part of me is terrified of how he'll be." She wipes at her eyes and sucks in another deep breath. "What if? I don't know."

I grab her hand, and link our fingers together leaving my other hand firm on the steering wheel. "You're right, he *is* in the best place. Remember, this is what you've worked so hard for. Whatever Jordan's reaction is going to be, that's on him. You've done everything in your power to get him here."

"The worst part is, logically, I know this. But, I'm just so nervous. When Jordan was high, I always knew what to expect from him, and that was anger and lies. But now, I don't know. I can't remember the relationship we had before he turned to drugs." Shit. Serena is terrified of a family she's never really known. "I think it's time I look to the future as opposed to what I never had in the past. I just hope Jordan doesn't hate me."

"I'm sure he's going through an array of emotions, and hate would likely be high on the scale early on."

She turns to look at me, her brows up, her nose crinkled. "You're not helping my anxiety here."

Fuck. "I just mean..."

"I know. If I'm being truthful, it's just that I'm frightened for what might happen today."

"There's more than one step to recovery, and he has to go through all of the emotions before he can finally make it out the other side." God, I hope that was the right thing to say. "And of course you'd be nervous. When was the last time you saw your brother sober?"

Serena taps her finger to her mouth as she stares at me, thinking hard on my question. "I can't even remember. I know it was before I left for college." I pull into the parking lot of New Dawn, and Serena sits straighter in the seat and looks out at the massive, sprawling building with several wings. The sign reading New Dawn, looks more like it's announcing a resort than rehabilitation center. The extensive gardens are green with pops of color from blooming flowers.

I turn the car off, and wait to take my cues from Serena. She's always had to be strong, but right now, she's completely vulnerable. "When you're ready," I gently remind her.

Serena nods once, takes another deep breath, and opens the car door. I get out and rush around to her side, waiting for her to take the first step. She's fidgeting, and wrings her hands around the bottom of her t-shirt.

I take her bag off of her shoulder, place it on the seat, and envelop her in my arms. Beneath my touch, I can feel her trembling. "It's okay," I reassure Serena. I wait for her to stop shaking, pull back and give her a soft kiss on the forehead. "You've got this, because you're tough."

Serena's eyes are wide as she stares at the building. "I feel like I'm going to be sick." She takes a deep breath, pulls her shoulders back and lifts her chin. "I have no idea why I'm feeling like this. But, whatever happens, I put him in there because I love him."

There's my girl. "And you'd do it again if you had to."

She abruptly turns to look at me. With the most confidence I've seen in her in today she says, "I won't, because when he walks out of here, he'll be a changed man."

I love how positive she is. "Yep, you're right." *I hope so too.*

She grabs her bag again, and takes the gift bag from the back seat. "I'm ready." I hold her hand as we walk up to the front door of New Dawn. Once inside, she looks around. "Wow. It feels so different now than when we were here nearly three weeks ago. I was so consumed with Jordan that I never really took it in. It's quite pretty." She looks around as we approach the nurses at the front desk.

"Hello, we're here to see Jordan Whitaker," I say.

The male nurse smiles. He looks to Serena and says, "You're his sister, Serena?" Serena nods. "Jordan's been waiting for you to arrive. He's been talking about you nonstop."

"He has?" Serena asks, her eyes fill with tears as she smiles.

"He has." The nurse notices her handbag, then sees the gift bag. "I'm going to have to search through your bag, and is that for Jordan?" He gestures to the gift bag. Serena nods. "I'm going to have to search through that too."

"Of course." Serena takes her bag off her shoulder, and gives it to the nurse, then hands him the gift bag.

"Alternately, you can lock your handbag in one of our lockers, but the gift bag I need to search."

Serena looks to me as to what to do. "We'll wait," I say taking the pressure off Serena to have to think in this moment when she's super anxious to see her brother.

"We'll wait," Serena confirms.

I like how she trusts me and what I say. The nurse takes both her bag, and the gift bag, and after a thorough search, he hands them both to Serena. "Let me see where he is." The nurse sits in front of his computer, and looks on their security system. "He's in the courtyard. It looks like he's sitting with Hannah." He stands, says something to the other nurse, and comes out from behind the desk. "I'll show you the way."

"Thank you." I take Serena's hand in mine.

The nurse takes us through two doors that require a swipe card, and walks us to where Jordan is. The closer we get to our destination, the more Serena squeezes my hand. And I'm here to support her. But I'm also leery, because even though the nurse has said Jordan is excited to see her, he may still lash out. And I don't care if he's in rehab or not, I won't let him hurt my woman.

"Here he is," the nurse says when he opens the door leading us to a tranquil garden with water features and beautiful trees shading part of the outdoor area. Serena squeezes my hand even tighter when she sees her brother. "Jordan, your sister is here."

Jordan turns from where he's sitting, sees Serena, jumps to his feet and runs straight to her. Serena drops my hand, her bag and the gift bag, and runs to Jordan. He towers over her, but his frame is so skinny in comparison to my girl. He's looking healthier, even after just a few weeks in rehab. I swoop up her bag and the gift, and take a few steps toward them.

Jordan is holding her tight, but I'm close by in case something goes horribly wrong. "I'm so sorry," Jordan repeats over and over again.

"It's okay," Serena whispers.

They stand holding one another for a long moment. I can hear them both crying. A lump forms in my throat as I watch this intimate and clearly difficult connection they're sharing. I look over to the girl Jordan was talking to, and notice she's rather young. She can't be older than her late teens. She gives me an awkward smile, then lowers her gaze as she writes something in her notebook.

"Oh man," Jordan says as he pulls back, and wipes his eyes with the hem of his t-shirt. He looks at me, and crinkles his brows. "I know you," he says.

Serena steps backward, standing by my side. "This is Alec, my boyfriend."

"Boyfriend?" Jordan's eyes widen. "Good for you, Serena." He moves forward and offers a handshake. It's a step in the right direction in my eyes. "I know we've probably met in the past, and I'm sorry for anything I may have said or done to you."

"We have, and don't sweat it. You haven't done or said anything too offensive." I shake his hand.

"I'm going to go back to my room, Jordan," the young girl says.

"No, hey. Before you go. Serena, this is my friend, Hannah. And Hannah this is the person who saved my life. My sister, Serena."

"Nice to meet you," Hannah says. She stands, and grabs her book. "Come find me when you're ready."

It blows my mind how young this girl is.

"I will," Jordan says.

I have so many questions, because if he and she are *involved,* I don't think that's a good idea. Especially considering they're both addicts, and she's just so damn young. She heads inside, leaving just the three of us at this table. There are other people out here, but they're not close enough to disturb us.

"Sit, sit." Jordan pulls out a chair, and waits for Serena before he moves to the next chair to offer it to me. I can tell by the look on Serena's face, she has the same questions about Hannah that I do. Jordan picks up on it fast. "No," he starts. "Hannah and I are friends."

"Um," Serena says. "She's very young."

"You have no idea. There's something about her, I feel protective of her. Like, I'm her big brother. She got herself involved with the wrong man, and he got her hooked on meth. She thought he was the love of her life, as it turned out, he was her nightmare." He shakes his head, and runs his hand through his shaggy hair. "She's such a nice person."

"But there's nothing going on, right? Because she's really young, Jordan. And, two addicts." Serena makes two fists and bumps them together. "That's a disaster in the making, you can't..."

"No! No, it's nothing like that. We're just friends," Jordan reaffirms. He leans forward and clasps his hand over Serena's. "Thank you," he says. He looks over to me. "How do I know you?"

"I'm a fireman at Mulberry Point. You came to one of our cookouts."

Jordan narrows his eyes, trying to recall the interaction. "I don't remember."

Shit, what do I say? "You weren't your normal self." I try to be as dignified as I can without reminding him he was so strung out.

Ashamed, he lowers his gaze. "I haven't been a good brother," he says in a small voice. "Or a good person." Serena opens her mouth to say something, but I place my hand on her thigh and squeeze. When she looks over to me, I slightly shake my head. Jordan needs to start making amends with his sister. And an apology is only the start.

Serena crinkles her brows, before giving me a strained, knowing smile. She turns to look at Jordan, and nods. "You haven't been a good brother at all," she says. Although her voice is strong, her bouncing leg and death grip on my hand over her thigh speaks a secret language only I'm privy to.

A tear runs down Jordan's cheek. "I don't think me saying 'sorry' is enough for everything I've put you through. And Mom and Dad…"

The air around us is thick, and tense. "It'll be a start toward reconciling and rebuilding a relationship between us, Jordan."

He wrings his hands together, still looking down and not lifting his eyes to look at Serena. "And I owe you more than the money keeping me in this place costs."

"You owe it to yourself not to let this opportunity to get clean be wasted. Because, you're right, this place has cost me so much. And I'm not talking about the money aspect of it."

He nods, lifts his hand and wipes the tears, still avoiding direct eye contact. "I feel like I'm under a constant dark fog, fighting with the person I was only a month ago to be the person I want to be."

"No one ever said recovery is easy. But you got yourself into this mess. I got you this far, now it's your turn to do the rest." Serena's firm with her words.

"I'm trying," he says. Jordan lifts his head slowly, his eyes are red, and tears are freely falling. "I'm sorry, Serena. I know I've done and said horrible things to you, and you didn't deserve any of them. I'm going to fix this. I'm going to fix everything."

Serena purses her lips together, and nods. She takes in a sharp breath before letting go of my hand and reaching across for Jordan's. "I want you to fix yourself. Because if you leave here, and go back to the way you were, I'm sorry, but I'm washing my hands of you."

Jordan's forehead creases as his chin trembles with worry. Serena may have been hard on him, but he needs to hear it. "I understand," his voice croaks and breaks. "I won't let you down." They stare at each other for a long moment, neither saying anything to the other.

Finally, Serena's strained smile eases and she replies, "If you're serious about helping yourself, then I'll be there to help you every step of the way."

"I don't want to lose you."

"You won't, as long as you never go back to the drugs."

Jordan sits a little taller, obviously comforted by Serena's answers. "I've been thinking about something."

"What?" Serena asks, still holding hands with Jordan.

"You know Hannah?"

"The young girl who you were talking with?" I ask.

"Yeah, her." Jordan smiles. If he tells me he loves her, I'm not sure I'll be able to stop myself from telling him what I think. I'm fairly certain Serena feels the same way. "She's young, like late teens, and she's ended up in here because of a man who manipulated her. I think I want to do something where I can help teenagers like Hannah before they end up dead."

I see the evident relief on Serena's face. "How do you want to help?"

"I know I need to go to college, but maybe I can be some kind of counselor for teenagers." Jordan eagerly stares at Serena. He's hanging on her words, waiting for her approval.

"I think that's a wonderful idea, and seeing as you've had first-hand experience, you'll really be able to support these kids in finding a better way."

Jordan's wide smile speaks volumes. "You think I can do it?"

"You've always been smart, Jordan. But the drugs kept you from being what you could have been. I'm so happy you're back."

"I'm going to do this, Serena. I'm determined."

"Good." She looks to me, tilting her head to the side as she wordlessly asks if it's okay to tell Jordan about something. There's nothing she should hold back from him, so I give her a reassuring nod. She lets Jordan's hand go, and links our fingers together. "So, there's something I have to tell you."

"What?"

"We no longer live in that crap house."

Jordan clears his throat and rolls his neck. "Well, I'll say this. I'm glad, because you never belonged there. I know you did it so you could help me. I should never have put you in the position compromising your safety because of my drug addiction."

"Damn straight," Serena replies. "But, that's in the past. Anyway, Alec and I are buying a house together."

Jordan's reply is nothing more than a shocked expression. "We'll be buying something that can accommodate you too," I say.

Jordan stares at me for a moment, before turning his attention to his sister, then back to me. "You do realize, I'm a drug addict?"

"I do," I reply earnestly.

"And, you're okay with me living with you?"

I need to make sure my reply is honest, but also boundary setting. "There'll come a point in your life, Jordan, when you won't want to live with us. Until you're ready to be on your own, you'll have a place to call home with us."

"But rest assured, I'll kick you out if you go back to using," Serena's eerily calm voice is confident, and she's being straight with Jordan.

"I understand," he repeats. "Thank you." Jordan looks to me and nods. "I know you don't have to do this, and I'm thankful you are."

"This isn't a free ride, Jordan. You'll owe us," Serena says. Wow, talk about tough love.

Jordan stands, walks over to Serena, lifts her and holds her. "Thank you." He kisses her on the cheek. "Thank you for always fighting for me, even when I gave up on myself."

"You're my brother. It's what family does."

Jordan pulls away from Serena, steps to the side and holds his hand out for me. "I owe you so much."

"You don't owe me anything, Jordan."

He shakes his head. "I owe you both my life, and my future. I'm one hundred percent sure, if I didn't have you, it would only be a matter of time before I'd become just another dead junkie."

"I have to say, I was nervous coming here today," Serena says. Jordan walks back over to where he was sitting. "I didn't know how you and I were going to be with each other."

"I'm more embarrassed and ashamed of everything I put you through. I was thinking if you never wanted to see me again, I would've respected that, because I know I put you through hell."

"Yes, you did. Anyway, how's it going here? Do you like it?"

"It's hard. And every moment of every day all I can think about is trying to get back to where I was. But, at the same time, I know this is exactly where I need to be. The first two weeks were absolute hell. I struggled with detoxing, and the need to get high. It was the most difficult thing I've ever done. The counselors are amazing. Some of them have been addicted themselves and have turned their lives around, which gives me so much hope. If they can do it, I can do it too."

Serena smiles proudly. "Yeah, you can."

"It was when I met Hannah that I really started thinking how I wish there was a way I could do something to help kids like her. She's so young. And her story is mind-blowing. And when I was talking to my counselor, he said if I apply myself, I can do what he does. I want to be more than just an ex-junkie."

"If you want to, then you can do anything," Serena encourages.

"Tell me about you two." Jordan changes the topic, not wanting to talk about himself anymore. "How did you meet?"

"I hurt myself at work, and needed to keep my strength up. Guess who was my physiotherapist?" I pointedly look over to Serena.

"He was an asshole," she bluntly says.

"No, I wasn't."

"Yes, he was. He called me fat."

I slowly close my eyes, a massive smirk stretching across my face. "In my defense, I was hurting."

"You mean you were an ass?" Serena corrects. I cock my head to the side, and deliberately raise a brow. "Admit it, you were an ass."

"Whatever." I can't help but smile. "But you weren't exactly a ray of sunshine yourself."

"I was professional."

"You called me an asshole."

"If you didn't act like one, I wouldn't have called you one," she counters.

I wave my hand, dismissing her words. "Ridiculous allegations," I say. "I'm always courteous to everyone."

Serena rolls her eyes at me.

Jordan chuckles and sits back in his seat, crossing his arms in front of his chest. "I can see how this goes."

A glow radiates off Serena. The moment the laughter fades away, Serena says, "I love him, Jordan, and Alec loves me too."

"I can see that. He hasn't taken his hand off you once the whole time you've been here. He's protective of you, and it makes me happy to know you've found a good guy like Alec." He looks over to me and nods slowly. "Thank you, for being her rock. Because since we lost Mom and Dad, she's always been on my side, regardless of how I've treated her." He switches his gaze back to Serena. "You need someone who's on your side, and now I'm certain you have someone who is."

Serena chokes back tears, wiping at her eyes before they fall. "I need Alec, Jordan. For me, nothing is more important than the two of you getting along, because I love you both. Obviously, in different ways."

"I would hope so." Jordan wrinkles his nose up.

I lean in and kiss Serena on the cheek. Overprotectively, I snake my hand up to the back of her neck to hold and massage her nape. When Serena turns to look at me, her eyes light up with so many emotions. No words are needed because we both know how I feel for her.

"Where are you looking at buying a house?" Jordan asks, interrupting our nano-moment of intimacy.

"Mulberry Point. My work is there, and Serena is at the hospital, so it makes sense to stay in the area."

"Is there anything I can do to help?" Jordan asks.

"Yes, get clean, and stay clean," I say.

"That's exactly what I'm going to do. I'm not going to let you down again, Serena. I promise you that I *will not* let you down."

"On that note, I bought you a present." Serena hands the gift bag over to Jordan.

"For me?" He pulls the bag over to him, and opens it, peeking in the top. "You got all my favorite candies. Thank you." Standing, he leans across the table, and gives Serena a quick hug. "Do you mind if I share some of these with Hannah?"

"It's yours to do with what you want," Serena replies.

"Just so we're clear, the peanut M&M's are mine and mine alone." Jordan chuckles. "Thank you." A man walks out, and places his hand to Jordan's shoulder, startling him. Jordan turns, and the moment he sees the man, he smiles. "Jack, this is my sister, Serena. Her partner, Alec. This is my counselor," Jordan proudly announces.

"I've heard a lot about you, Serena. Nice to meet you." He shakes Serena's hand, then mine. "You're late for your session," he says to Jordan.

"Shit! I'm sorry. I got caught up talking with my sister."

"We can reschedule it for this afternoon," Jack offers.

"No, please. Alec and I have to leave." Serena and I both stand to our feet. "But we'll be back tomorrow before our flight."

Jordan's shoulders drop, but he hesitantly nods. "Okay," he says. I'm sure he wants to keep talking with Serena, building on their fractured relationship. "Thank you for coming, and thank you for this." He looks down at the gift bag.

Serena walks over to him, and throws her arms around him. "I'm proud of you for trying, Jordan. So, damn proud." They embrace tightly for a few moments, until Jack clears his throat. "We'll be back tomorrow." She kisses Jordan on the cheek.

"I love you," Jordan says. He then looks over to me, and holds his hand out, waiting for me to shake it. "Thank you," he mouths.

"I love you." Serena reaches for my hand, grasping it tight as Jordan and Jack head back into the building. When he disappears inside tears stream down her cheeks and she turns to bury her face into my chest. "I'm so happy," she says.

Kissing the top of her head, I hold her so tight she'll never doubt the love and support I have for her.

"Are you ready to go back to the hotel?" I ask.

"Absolutely."

Holding hands, we head out and back to the car.

Chapter 21

SERENA

I'M EMOTIONALLY AND mentally exhausted. The drive back to the hotel was a whirlwind.

Now, I'm standing in the shower under the hot stream of water, reliving the time I had with Jordan. With my forehead to the wall, the therapeutic flow of the water is calming every one of my nerve endings. My head is jumbled though. Seeing Jordan like he was makes me so happy, but also conflicted.

If I had borrowed the money earlier, he wouldn't have overdosed, and he'd be a good month ahead with his treatment. I should've done it sooner, so he'd be even healthier today than how he is now.

"What's wrong?" Alec asks surprising me.

I lift my head, and wipe over my face. "I didn't hear you come in. Nothing's wrong."

"Then why have you been in here for the last ten minutes with your head on the wall and your eyes closed?"

He caught me in my own head. "I'm thinking," I admit.

Alec strips down, opens the door and pulls me into his arms. "What about?" He laces his fingers through my soaking wet hair, and peppers kisses from my forehead down the bridge of my nose.

"If you do that, I'll be too distracted to tell you what I'm thinking about."

"Hmm, is that right?" Alec skims his nose down the column of my throat, his mouth lightly touching the sensitive skin.

"Aha." I close my eyes and lean into him.

"What are you thinking about?" He takes my earlobe into his mouth, sucking and nibbling.

"I was thinking how I failed with Jordan." He bites on my earlobe, a complete contrast to how gentle he's being. "Why did you do that?"

"Because you need to be reminded how phenomenal you actually are."

Alec makes me smile. He has a way of focusing on what's important, and not what I can't control. "I know," I say.

"You make me crazy." Alec backs me up to the wall, reaches down, and lifts my leg over his hip. He pushes into me, causing me to suck in a deep breath.

"I light up when you're near." He places his forehead to mine, staring straight into my soul.

As he thrusts up into me, my eyes are glued to his. "You're mine now, Serena, and don't ever think you'll have to go through anything alone again."

Sorrow fills my heart. Tears well in my eyes and my body trembles. "You have no idea how much I need you, Alec."

"I know, baby, I know." He kisses my nose. "No one can ever take you from me." He pushes into me harder, though slowly. Our connection is deeply emotional. "I'm your man."

"I'll never find anyone else like you." Alec holds one leg over his hip, and with the other steadies himself on the wall. He places his lips over mine, kissing me tenderly. Our hips dance together, swaying in perfect rhythm. He keeps thrusting into me, and even though I'm nowhere near ready to orgasm, I know Alec won't let me go without me getting my happy ending too.

Alec groans as he speeds up, nearing his own orgasm. "Fuck!" The veins in his neck protrude as he pumps his hips hard into me. "Fuck," he says and follows it with a groan. When he's done, he pulls out of me, and pins me with his body up against the wall. "You didn't come."

"Nope."

He crinkles his brows, and nods. "Okay." Alec lowers his mouth to mine. Kissing me with passion and heat. I take his hand and guide it down toward my pussy, where I'm desperate for his touch. Pulling his hand back, a cheeky smile crosses his beautiful face. "I'm hungry," he says.

"And I'm horny. You owe me an orgasm."

He throws his head back and laughs. Stepping back, he shrugs, opens the shower door and leaves me completely unsatisfied. "Hurry up, we have dinner reservation." Alec wraps a towel around his hips, and heads out of the bathroom. What an asshole! He pops his head back in, and smirks again. "Oh, and by the way, don't think of trying to make yourself come either."

Oh, it's like that is it? *Hell yes!* "You can't stop me," I challenge as he disappears again.

He pops his head back in. "Want to make a bet?" he asks in a dark and seductive voice.

Yes. "No." What? I meant to say yes.

"I thought so." He vanishes again. Damn him. "Hurry up," he calls from the bedroom.

Sulking, I turn the water off, wrap my hair in a towel, then wrap one around my body. Screw you, Mister. You want to play, then let the sex games begin. If he won't get me off, then I'm going to make dinner incredibly uncomfortable for him too. Pulling my shoulders back, I walk out of the bathroom and strut past Alec who's sitting on the edge of the bed looking at his phone.

"I'm hungry too," I say as I head over to my suitcase and rifle through it for what I'm wearing tonight. Although Alec is on his phone, I notice how he keeps turning his head, his eyes hard on me.

My body is hyperaware of how he's discreetly watching me. And I fucking love it. Smirking, I take out the dress I brought and look at my underwear. Nah, no underwear is needed tonight, just my bra. "Do you like this dress?" I ask as I hold it up against my body.

Alec's focus shifts from his phone to me. "Yeah." He looks at his phone again.

"Yeah?" I'm so not needy, but if he wants to play, then hell with it. By the end of the night, he's going to have blue balls, because right now I have the female equivalent of that. "I'm not sure." I walk around to stand in front of the full-length mirror on the wardrobe, drop my towel and hold the dress up to my body. "You sure?"

Alec's trying not to smile. "It's fine," his voice slightly roughens.

Yes, I'm affecting him.

Bring. It. On.

"If you say so." I sway my body from side to side, and can see Alec staring at my butt. Turning, I drape the dress across the end of the bed then position myself so I'm closer to Alec. I bend at my waist, flipping my hair out of the towel to roughly dry it.

"I know what you're doing," he says.

"Pardon?" Without straightening, I look at Alec upside down. "What are you talking about?" My butt is right there, only inches away from him.

"It's not going to work. You're not going to get a reaction from me."

Game on, buddy. "I'm not?"

"Nope."

"Okay." I keep towel drying my hair, and when it's not dripping wet, I flick my head back. "I need my bra." I head over to my suitcase again, and grab my black lacy bra. I bought this bra and panty set only a few days ago. I know putting this on will send Alec crazy. But hey, he said I can't provoke a reaction from him. *I'm sure I can.* Putting my bra on, I clip it in the back, then grab the dress, lift it over my head, and wiggle into it. "Do I look okay?" I ask as I smooth the dress over my hips.

"Where's the underwear?" He looks to my suitcase, then back to me.

"I don't need them."

"Yeah, you do. That dress only comes halfway down your thigh."

"So? I often don't wear underwear when I wear dresses. I don't like the panty lines. It's okay, I've done this millions of times before." No, I haven't. I always wear underwear; I just enjoy teasing him.

"I'd feel more comfortable if you put them on."

"You can put them on if you're into wearing my underwear. I mean, I'm not gonna judge."

He scrubs his hand over his chin, stands and grabs the black thong that goes with this bra. "Wear them," he says.

Jesus, he makes me so damn hot. That wicked tongue, I need it inside of me. "Okay, I will." Alec walks over to me, and dangles my underwear from his finger. I lean in, kiss him on the mouth, and take the underwear, making sure to slide them on as seductively as I can and praying I don't topple over and make a fool out of myself, I bend again, sticking my butt out to him, and slide the underwear slowly up my legs. Straightening, I head over to the mirror and look at my body. "Panty lines. See."

I smooth the dress, accentuating the line of the underwear. I've never given a shit about panty lines before, but hey, if it makes him crazy, why not?!

"I don't care. I don't want you without underwear."

"Fine." *Just watch me, Mister.*

Alec drops his towel; I lean against the wall and watch as he dresses his tall frame. Dress pants, a button-down shirt and he finishes with a black tie. Hello there, sexy! "I think this should be required attire," I say as he finishes adjusting the tie.

"Do you?"

"I have an idea. You should wear your fireman outfit and when you come home you should change into this." I wave my hand around his incredibly delicious body. Fuck, I want to lick him so bad.

"Fireman outfit?" he asks and chuckles.

"Yeah you know. What you have to wear at work."

"My turnout gear? Or my dress uniform, or my tactical gear?"

"Yes!"

"Yes, what? Which one?" he asks confused.

"Just yes."

Alec laughs loudly. "You have to tell me which one you want to see me in."

"I am. I'm saying yes. Which means, wear them all. Sex me up good and proper wearing all of them."

Alec runs his hand through his hair, laughing. "Sex you up, eh?"

"Yes! Jeez, Alec, I thought I was being fairly clear here."

"In other words, I'm just a sex object."

I clap my hands together. "Finally, he's got it," I tease.

"You want me to fuck you while I'm wearing my uniform?" He saunters over to me, grabbing me possessively on my hips and squeezing.

"I think you should throw me on the bed and fuck me right now. I mean, it would be nasty to leave me high and dry while we're at dinner," I say, trying to convince Alec.

Alec walks me back until my legs find the bed. He gently pushes my shoulders so I fall on the mattress. "Is this what you want?" He kneels before me, grabs my ankles and pulls me toward his face.

"I want to use your face as a chair," I say.

He flips the skirt up, and buries his face in my underwear. "Like this?"

"Just move my thong to the side so you have better access," I say.

He moves the lacy material and continues eating. "Delicious," he murmurs around me. His tongue is magic. I lean up on my elbows to watch him eating me. The moment I do, he rocks back on his heels and stands. "There you go."

"What the hell just happened?" I refuse to get up, laying there with my bottom half exposed.

"A preview of what's to come."

"I want to *come* right now!"

With his fingertip, he wipes his bottom lip then sexily sucks on his finger. "I will say this, Serena, you taste so good."

"Then get over here and finish." He smirks and winks at me. "You make me crazy. You know that, right?"

"Hurry up or we'll be late for dinner."

Murmuring, I stand, fix my dress and sulking, I head into the bathroom. Right. This is war. Serious World War III kinda war. The moment the door is closed, I shimmy out of my underwear and stick it in my bra. I'm so going to give him the bluest balls of his life. He has no idea what I'm capable of.

I quickly run the comb through my damp hair, then grab the hotel hairdryer and dry it enough to be able to put it up in a high ponytail. I'm not a makeup sort of girl, so I don't even bother with that, I mean, I look at the mascara wand coming toward me and my eye is instantly watering. And as far as all that other stuff women put on, I have no idea about that. My repertoire of makeup consists of lipstick and maybe eye shadow. Sometimes I wish I was more girly, but then I remember that kind of stuff isn't really me. I truly admire a woman who has the time, and patience to learn about it and put it on, but, it's just not me.

I flush the toilet, and wash my hands as I head out of the bathroom. Alec is standing by the door, holding my cardigan. He holds it out so I can put it on. "Thank you," I say as I hold my head high, knowing what I'm going to do to him.

"You seem quite composed."

"Do I?" I grin as I give him a kiss on the cheek. "I'm really looking forward to dinner." *And to teasing the hell out of you.*

"So am I."

He closes the hotel door behind us, slips the key into his wallet, then takes my hand and leads me to the elevator. He turns, and casts a critical eye over me. "You look beautiful."

"Thank you."

"I like your hair like this. It's cute."

"The high ponytail?"

"Yeah. I like it. Something for me to grab on to when I fuck you from behind."

I close my eyes and swallow the lump. Maybe not wearing underwear wasn't a good idea. This may come back to bite me. Nope, you've got this, girl. Get it together. I sneak a peek at Alec, and he's so proud of himself for what he's doing to me. *Am I really that obvious?* Clearly.

I shrug, as if I'm not totally turned on. "That's if I let you fuck me from behind."

"You'll let me," he responds without missing a beat. *Bastard.*

The elevator door opens, and there's another couple in there. He's scrolling on his phone; she looks bored. Alec and I step in, and I smile at the woman. She returns a smile, then her eyes go instantly to Alec. Her brows rise then rapidly lower as she stares at him for a moment too long. Her entire posture begins to change. She pulls her shoulders back, and lifts her chin as she keeps glancing over at my man.

Hell no, not on my watch.

I look to Alec and notice he's completely oblivious of this chick who keeps stealing looks at him. Alec, though, is watching me, and can see how I'm uncomfortable at how she's looking at him. He turns to me, grips my jaw and smashes his mouth to mine. His kiss owns every part of me. My heart races at Alec's greedy, yet incredibly controlling kiss.

Holy shit. Is it possible to combust right here in the elevator?

The door dings open. Alec pulls away from the kiss, lowers his left hand to curl around my waist and brings me in tight to his body. I catch the woman rapidly walking out to the foyer.

"Why did you do that?" I ask.

"Because I didn't like how she was looking at you."

"She was looking at you, Alec, not me."

"She needed to know, I'm yours and no one else's."

Aww, he makes my heart flutter. "Good. You need to know you're mine and no one else's too." I squeeze his butt cheek.

"You're in so much trouble, Miss Whitaker." He gives me a small tap on the behind.

Bring. It. On.

"What are you ordering?" I ask as I look over the menu.

"I think I'll go with the steak." Alec places the menu down. "You?"

"I'm hungry. I think I'll get the steak too." He smiles widely. "What?"

"One of my absolute favorite things about you is how you eat."

I feel slightly taken aback by his statement, though I know it's not meant it to be critical. "What do you mean?"

"You eat unapologetically."

"Why should I apologize for having an appetite? I told you a long time ago, I'm comfortable in my skin. I have hips, and boobs, a butt and my stomach isn't flat. If someone feels uncomfortable with my body, I suggest they look away."

Alec sits back in his seat and crosses his arms in front of his chest. "Have I told you how much I love your body?"

I roll my eyes and look away. "Not enough to make me orgasm before our dinner reservations tonight," I shameless say.

Alec laughs a little too loud, causing one of the other diners at a table nearby to glance over. "You can't say things like that in public, Serena."

"Why? Do you want people to think you're a hot *virgin* fireman?" He shakes his head and runs his tongue along his bottom lip. "Do that again," I say as I watch his mouth.

"Do what again?"

"Lick your lip."

"You're a hussy," he teases. Then proceeds to lick his bottom lip.

"And damn proud of the fact that I'm getting boned by you."

He rubs at his forehead, still chuckling. "Do you not have a filter tonight?"

"I left it back in Mulberry Point. No one knows me here, so I really don't give a crap what they think of me. Of course, I generally don't really care what people think of me."

"You're simply amazing."

"Oh, hey, before I forget..."

"Hi, I'm Antony and I'll be your waiter tonight. Are you ready to order?" this cute, tall, dark-haired guy announces.

"Oh, hello," I say brazenly flirting with Antony, noting Alec's displeased reaction.

"Hi," Antony replies, so oblivious to my lackluster flirting. Alec, on the other hand, is not impressed. "Are you ready to order?" My gay-dar is in the red zone. But that's okay, 'cause he's seriously cute.

"We'll have two of the steaks, both well done." Alec picks both our menus up and hands them back to Antony. "And two beers, please." Alec hasn't taken his eyes off me. He's been staring at me while giving our order. I lean back in my seat, watching him watching me. I cock an eyebrow while smirking.

"Thank you," I say as Antony starts to walk away.

"I think you need reminding of where you belong," Alec says in a low voice.

"Is that right?" I sit forward, lean my right elbow on the table and with the lightest touch outline my bottom lip all while staring at Alec. "I already know where I belong, Alec."

"Where's that?" his voice is sultry and dark. His eyes are commanding and domineering.

"You know?" I say as let my fingertips trail down my chin to gently skim across my throat. Alec keeps his eyes locked on mine, though we both know I'm teasing him right now. I can see his chest heaving faster than normal. "Did I forget to tell you that..." I slide my hand down the front of my body, careful to make sure no one other than Alec is watching. I sneak it under my dress, and skim it across my pussy. Bringing my finger up to my mouth, I watch as Alec keeps watching me. I lick and nibble on the tip. "Hmm, I do taste good."

Alec's smirk slowly fades. He looks around the restaurant, and leans in to me. "Did you take your underwear off?" I shrug and raise my brow. "Did you?" his voice cracks.

"I don't know, did I?"

Alec looks around the restaurant again. "Open your legs," he commands. I slightly spread them, not enough for him to see, just enough to tease him. He knocks his cloth napkin off the table, and ducks to pick it up. He's such a perve. Straightening, he narrows his eyes at me. "I didn't see anything."

"No? Oh." I play with the top of my cleavage, and untuck just the smallest amount of the black lace of my thong.

Alec's eyes lower, then bulge when he realizes what I'm subtly showing him. He shakes his head and closes his eyes. Though his elevated breathing and huge smile tells me all I need to know. "Even if I wanted to stand, I wouldn't be able to."

"Really? Why's that?"

Antony returns with our two beers and two beer glasses. "Thank you, Antony," I say as I pick my beer bottle up and slowly bring it to my lips, forgoing the glass.

"You're welcome." He places Alec's down in front of him, then leaves.

"Will you stop flirting with him?"

"Is it making you uncomfortable, or is it turning you on?" I lick the rim of the beer bottle, before taking another sip.

"Because all I want to do is use that beautiful mouth of yours. But not before I lick you to the brink of desperation."

"So, if I spread my legs for you right here, do you want to crawl under the table and eat your dessert before your dinner?" I honestly can't believe the things coming out of my mouth. But, fuck it, I love him and I want him to know he can have me any time he wants.

He tilts his head to the side, picks his beer up and takes a long drink from it. Placing his beer bottle on the table, he clicks his tongue against the roof of his mouth twice. "You're being quite naughty."

"Yeah?" He nods. "I'm enjoying myself." I'm challenging him, seeing how far I can push him before he loses that control he always has.

"I bet you are." While his gaze is firm on mine, he smirks wide. "What am I going to do with you, Serena?"

"You brought this on yourself. So really, you only have yourself to blame."

Antony approaches the table with two large white plates. He places the first one in front of me, then he walks around and positions Alec's in front of him. "Cracked pepper?" he offers from a huge pepper mill he had tucked under his arm.

"No, thank you," I say.

He looks to Alec who shakes his head, still watching me. "No, thank you."

"Enjoy your meal." Antony looks to Alec, then me. Without moving my head, I glance to Antony and nod while smiling. Antony leaves, and I take a large breath before picking my fork and knife up.

I cut into the meat, and examine it for a moment. "Is there a problem?" Alec asks.

"Not at all. Look, it's so moist and juicy." I hold the fork out to Alec. "Like me."

He chuckles and shakes his head. "What am I going to do with you?"

"I've already told you what you can do with me. But, no, you decided not to. So, for now, I'll eat my moist dinner and walk out of here pantieless and wet. Then, when we get back to the room, I'll strip off completely, and go to bed."

"Go to bed?"

"I'm getting quite tired." I feign a yawn adding a small stretch.

"Then I'll head down to the bar to get myself a nightcap."

Oh, he's trying to play me. I cut another piece of meat, pop it in my mouth and chew. When I'm done with it, I look down at my plate and cut another piece. "Lucky I'm really good at taking care of myself. I wonder how many times I can make myself come while you're having a nightcap? Three? Maybe even four times."

"No, you won't," his voice barely rises over an audible whisper. "You'll wait until I return."

"But, will I?"

"I'm fighting the urge to throw you over my shoulder and take you back to the hotel right now."

"Neanderthal."

"When it comes to you, yep." I love how possessive he is. I squeeze my thighs together, becoming increasingly flustered with Alec. He cuts into his steak, and I find myself hanging on his every word. "This." He makes a circular motion, gesturing between us. "This is going to get you so fucked when we're back at the hotel."

I swear to God, I'm ready to leave this awesome steak behind, just so he can do what he's promising. "Hmm, we'll see." I shrug, trying to downplay the effect he has on me.

"Yes, we'll see." He looks over to my plate and notices my steak is only half eaten. "You better hurry up. Because we're leaving in twenty minutes." I take my phone out of my pretty yellow bag he bought me, set the timer for twenty minutes and place it face down on the table. "What are you doing?"

"Setting my timer for twenty minutes."

He pinches the bridge of his nose and laughs. "You're going to be the death of me."

"Hey, I have to eat this whole plate in under twenty minutes. I'm not wasting a perfectly good steak. Now, if you said to me, leave the steak we're going back to the hotel so we can fuck, then this steak would go cold. But, because you said I have twenty minutes, I ain't leaving it. I'm hungry, and I need my energy. So, imma eating it."

Alec's been laughing quite a lot tonight. "I fucking love you."

"As opposed to, I love fucking you?"

"I love that too. You know, I love how big your tits are."

"I love how hard your cock gets."

"I love that you have hips I can grip."

"I love how you tongue fuck me." I'm so happy no one is so close they'd be able to hear this dirty conversation.

"I love how you wrap your thighs around my head," he spars.

"I love using your face as a seat."

"I love spanking your ass and leaving my hand print on it."

"I love, love, *love* when you lick my body," we both rapid fire.

"I love licking your body."

"I love when your hard cock is in my mouth, with my lips stretched around it."

Alec's eyes widen, and his mouth snaps shut. *Game, set, and match.* I've got him. He slowly lowers his fork and knife. Looks at my plate, then my phone. "We may need to stay here a little bit longer."

"Why?" I ask innocently, though I already know the answer.

"Don't talk anymore. Just hurry up and finish your steak."

"What? I can't talk anymore?"

He holds a finger up to me. "Eat." Like a ravaging animal, he demolishes everything on his plate, then looks over to me. I've just finished the steak, when he places his knife and fork down, stands and untucks his shirt from his dress pants trying to conceal his quite prominent bulge. "You're done," he says.

"No, I'm not."

"Yes, you are." He grabs my phone, takes my hand and starts lifting me out of the chair. Luckily, I have a few seconds to grab my bag. He closes the gap between us, and whispers, "You're going to have to stand in front of me."

Yes! Light bulb moment. "Okay." I kiss him on the cheek. "I wouldn't want you to be uncomfortable."

I lead us toward the front to pay our check, and as we approach the maître d,' Alec hands me his credit card. I look at him and shake my head. "Take it," he says.

"I can pay."

"I know you can, but I don't want you to."

"How was your meal this evening?" the maître d' asks as he hands us our bill.

"Positively divine. Thank you," I say. From behind yet slightly to the side, Alec hands the guy his card. "I've got it," I sigh.

"I know you do." He leans into me. "But I want to take care of you." My heart flutters with his persistence.

"Okay." I take out a twenty from my purse, and leave it in the tip jar.

"Have a good night," the maître d' says as we head out of the restaurant.

"I know I will be," Alec says under his breath so the maître d' doesn't hear. We walk out, and wait for the valet to bring our rental around. I stand in front of Alec, while he kisses down my neck. I make sure to grind into him, my butt hard up against his bulge. I can feel his excitement. Alec flips my ponytail out of the way. "No one has ever sent me as crazy as you have."

"And no one but me ever will again," I say.

He flicks me around, staring into my eyes. "I don't ever want anyone but you, Serena. You're my girl, for now, and forever." His sweetness makes my entire body want to crumble into his arms. I love how he can be sweet, yet firm. He's not afraid to tell me what he thinks, and I just love that so much. "You're made only for me."

"Thank you." I tilt my head up, giving Alec a kiss on the mouth as we wait.

"What for?"

"In my twenty-seven years, I've never felt this way about another man. I love you so much."

He holds me tighter against him. His hands are traveling up and down my back, but he settles to leave them on the curve of my ass. "You walked into my life and turned it upside down. I thought I had a type, but I think I was treading water until you came along."

"Manwhore," I say and pinch his hip. "But, that's okay, because now you're *my* manwhore."

The car pulls up in the front, the Alec walks me over to the passenger side, where he opens the door for me. He turns and gives the valet a tip. The moment he's in the car, he merges onto the street. Placing his right arm on the back of my seat, I notice his speed is faster than it was on the way here. Thankfully, the hotel isn't too far.

He parks the car in our designated spot. "Wait here." He jumps out of the car, and with long, quick strides, he appears beside me. Opening the door, he holds his hand out to me. "Miss Whitaker."

"Mr. Morgan." I place my hand in his. Alec gently pulls me out of the car and into his body. We stand beside the car, just staring at each other. His jaw tightens as something dark passes through him. His chest is rising and falling quite fast. Mesmerized by his hypnotic eyes, I find myself speechless. He grasps the back of my neck, his fingers a powerful grip.

My body trembles from this exhilarating moment. An unexpected connection erupts between us. Something deeper than what I've ever felt before. My skin itches with desire. My heart thrums with a lustful need. With his dominating grip on the back of my neck, he pulls me closer to him. Alec lowers his head and kisses me. The kiss is soft, yet intense. He owns every part of me. My body, my mind, *my heart.* Breathless, and completely submerged in this sensual moment, Alec stops kissing me.

"You set my heart on fire, Serena."

I don't say a single thing, because I don't think there's anything I can say. I might set his heart on fire, but he ignites my entire soul. He closes the door, and leads me into the hotel. My head is spinning, and I can barely think straight.

The elevator dings open just as we arrive to it. The moment we're inside, Alec pushes me up against the wall, kissing, licking and nibbling all around my neck. "Jesus," I whisper.

"I've never shown my affection toward anyone in public, but when it comes to you, I can't keep my hands off you. I love everything about you."

Seems we're both crazy for the other. The elevator dings again, and we know we're on our floor. Alec and I walk to our room, and as he takes the key out of his wallet, I can't help but hug him, and kiss the back of his neck. I just need to be as close as I can to him.

He opens the door, pulls me inside, and pushes me up against it. Falling to his knees, his mouth wastes no time licking me. "Jesus," I repeat. He hooks my leg over his shoulder, and reaches up to place his hand on my stomach. Closing my eyes, I let go and just feel what he's doing.

"...me," he mumbles while still fucking me with his tongue.

"What?" I run my hand through his hair, and guide him to keep going.

"Marry me."

I try to push his head away. "What the hell did you mumble?"

He pulls back, looks up at me and repeats, "Marry me." His glistening mouth pulls up into a wide smile before he returns his mouth to my pussy to keep going down on me.

"What?" I push his head away again, and move back from him. "Am I hearing things?"

Standing, he wipes his mouth and moves to me. "I've given this some thought, and I want to marry you. So, marry me." It's not even a question, more like a sure-thing statement.

I straighten the bottom part of my skirt, then look around the room. "Are you pranking me, Alec?"

He casually walks over to the small bar fridge, grabs a beer, cracks it open and takes a drink. "I want you to be my wife," he says coolly.

"You want to marry me?"

"Yes, so marry me."

I place my hand to my hip. "And you've thought about this?"

"I've given it a lot of thought, yes."

"You have?" He confirms with a nod. "Where's the ring?" I ask as I tilt my head. His hand stalls in midair as he was bringing the beer up to his lips.

"I haven't had time to buy you one."

"Then my answer is no, Alec. I'm not marrying you. Because if you haven't had time to buy me a ring, it means you haven't really thought it through about us getting married."

"I have," he counters as he places his beer on top of the bar fridge and walks over to me.

"Look," I start saying. "Marriage, to me, is serious. I don't want to become a divorce statistic. I want us both to be sure, because once that piece of paper has been signed. I never want to sign another saying we no longer love each other."

"But I do love you. And don't forget, we're buying a house together." He leads me to the bed, sits and guides me to sit on his lap.

"I know you love me, and I love you. But you haven't thought about this for long? It's easy to sell a house. A marriage isn't something I ever want to consider dissolving. I'm sorry, Alec, but my answer is no."

"It's no because I don't have a ring?"

"It has nothing to do with a ring. It's 'no' because you haven't really thought about the long term. I know who I am, and I also know jumping into a lifelong commitment takes serious thought."

Holding me, Alec nods. "Meet me in the middle, Serena. Say yes, and we'll have a long engagement. As long as you want. A year, two years, five, ten. I just want the world to know you're my woman."

"I'm not saying yes, Alec. Not until I know you've really thought about it. As far as the world is concerned, I don't give a rat's ass what they have to say. I know I'm your woman, just like I know you're my man."

"I want a ring on your finger."

"When you buy me one, then it'll be there."

He nestles into my neck, kissing me. "I'll buy you the biggest damn ring I can find."

I lean back to look at Alec. "I don't need anything large."

He smiles, then places a gentle kiss on my lips. "Okay. Nothing too big." A knowing glint sparkles in his eyes. "I promise."

He's up to something. I don't know what, but the cheeky smirk tells me he's definitely conjuring something.

Chapter 22

ALEC

"YOU READY?" I call through the bathroom door.

"Really? You're banging on the door and asking me if I'm ready? If I was ready I'd be out there, wouldn't I?" Serena replies sassily.

Pacing inside the bedroom, I stop to stare at the door. She's such a smartass. "Hurry up."

"Yeah, yeah." I head out to the kitchen to grab my car keys, and my wallet that's sitting on the counter. "You're quite impatient, you know that, right?" Turning, I can't believe how beautiful Serena is. She truly takes my breath away. "Why are you looking at me like that?"

"How am I looking at you?"

She peers down at her clothes, and flattens the pretty top she's wearing over her hips and her jeans. Her heels elongate her legs, and right now, I'd really like to have them wrapped around my head. "Like something's wrong."

"Oh no, there's definitely nothing wrong. Quite the contrary, I was thinking how I'd like to have those legs of yours over my shoulder."

"You really do like having your mouth full, don't you?"

I walk over to her, and grab her pussy through her jeans. Damn clothing always in the way. "As long as this is wet, I'm happy to have my tongue buried in it."

"You're a dirty bastard," she says, but allows me to keep feeling her up. "Although, if you want, I'm happy to duck into our room, strip and let you eat."

Her sexual appetite matches mine, and I fucking love it. "I can't believe I'm going to say this, but I'll have to take a rain check for when we return from Dean and Joanne's."

"Then, can you stop trying to rub me through my jeans please?" She turns and heads straight back into our room. I spank her butt before she's out of arm's reach. "Stop trying to make me hornier."

Hornier? I'm gonna fuck her when we get to my brother's. I need to be inside of her. "Hurry up," I call again.

"Can you put this on me?" She brings out the necklace I bought her. Handing it to me, she turns, holds her ponytail up and waits until I clasp it on her. When I do, Serena turns, gives me a quick kiss and rushes back into our room only to emerge a few seconds later with her yellow bag.

"Are we ready to go?" I ask once again.

"Unless you want sex, then yeah, we're ready."

My lips thin in frustration. Yeah, I want sex. But we're going to be really late for my brother's housewarming. And I know, I'll never hear the end of it from Mom if we're not there soon. "Hurry up," I playfully snap.

Serena walks ahead of me down the hall, and I can't help but watch her ass jiggle in front of me. "Stop staring at me, you freak."

"I like watching your butt."

She sways her hips a little more, making her butt wobble that little bit extra. Fuck I love her ass. "Do you still like it?"

"Now, I just want to fuck it." She turns to look at me over her shoulder, her mouth open in shock. "What, you think I don't?"

"You've never told me you enjoy *that*."

I lock the front door, and reach for her hand as we walk to my car. "If I could have my cock inside of you twenty-four hours a day, seven days a week, I would."

She turns to look at me. "I'd be quite chafed if you did." I shrug. "Anyway, you want butt stuff?"

I open the passenger door for her, and wait until she's in before I head over to the driver's side. When I get in, I put my seat belt on, and start the car. "Yeah, I want butt stuff with you. Have you had butt stuff before?"

"I have to say, other than the spanking, nope, no butt stuff. Have you given or received butt stuff in the past?"

"I have not had the pleasure of giving butt stuff."

"But you've received it?"

I glimpse at her and shake my head. "I'm a giver, not a receiver," I say.

"I'll remember that the next time you attempt to guide my head down to your cock."

I start laughing. "That's not what I meant."

She chuckles as she looks out the window. "It's a pretty night tonight, don't you think?"

"There are so many stars out." Suddenly, my nerves spark to life, because in my pocket is the ring I'm going to give to Serena tonight. I try to push those thoughts to the side and focus on anything else but the proposal. "When do you want to see your brother again?"

"I think if we can get out there every three weeks, that would be good."

"Okay, I'll book our flights for next week then." Serena knits her hands together, then pulls them apart and slides them under her thighs. "What's wrong?" I ask.

"I haven't spent much time with your family, Alec."

"Are you afraid they won't like you?"

"We're moving along by leaps and bounds. What if they want us to slow down?" I laugh out loud. "What?"

"Dean and Joanne are engaged, and they barely knew each other for five minutes before they decided to get married. He's in the process of adopting Thomas. Maybe it's a Morgan thing to do. Although, I'm not sure about Rhett. Maybe he was adopted." I shrug.

Serena stares at me, with a wicked cheeky smile. "Dean and Rhett look like brothers, and you look like the odd one out. You sure you're not the adopted one?"

"Shut up," I scold. "As I was saying before you rudely interrupted me." Serena laughs again, and turns to keep looking out the window. "I know Rhett likes Dani, it's so obvious to everyone. But, for some reason, he's not doing anything about it."

"Maybe he wants to live the bachelor life. He is hot, and he is a fireman. He probably can get whoever he wants."

"Did you just call my brother hot?" my voice holds a tinge of irritation.

"Oh, come on. All three of you have been blessed in the looks department. Not to mention, you're all tall. And really easy on the eye. And have great bods. And oh my God, so nice to perve on."

"You've mentioned our looks three times in one sentence."

"Well, you interrupted me, I was going to keep saying how sexy the three of you are."

I briefly hold my hand up to her. "How about you talk about me and not my brothers?"

"I can appreciate a beautiful person, male or female. Doesn't mean I want to use their face as a chair. You, on the other hand, any time you want to hold your breath, you're more than welcome to. Unless I'm on my period, or sick. Then it's a no-go zone."

"I'm agreeing with you on both of those instances. But, fucking you on your period, then, you know."

"Eww, that would be messy."

"Not if we have sex in the shower." She turns her head slowly to stare at me. "What?"

"I've never had sex on my period."

"I read something once that says when women orgasm while they're on their period it actually helps with cramps. I mean, we could try it." I can sense her still staring at me. "If you want," I quickly add.

"I'm kinda grossed out right now. But, in saying that, I've never done it, so I suppose we can try. But the caveat will be it's gotta be in the shower."

"Deal." I hold my hand out to her.

"Uh, we don't need a handshake, Alec. What is this, a business transaction? A gentleman's agreement?" I place my hand back on the steering wheel, but chuckle to myself. I round the corner where Dean and Joanne live, and pull up outside their house. "Wow, this house is massive." Serena's wide eyes take in the enormous house. "It's so damn pretty too."

"Dean's shown us pictures of it, but I haven't seen it myself either. I think Mom helped them move in. And FYI, Mom's gonna be helping us too when we buy our house."

"Elise doesn't meddle, so I don't mind. Anyway, I like your mom. She's really chill." She shifts in her seat, then opens the door. "Well, let's go." She's out of the car before I can stop her.

I meet her around the front of the car, and take her hand. Serena takes a step forward, but I pull her back toward me. Her forehead crinkles, as she silently questions why I've pulled her back. "For me, you're it." A huge smile pulls at the edges of her lips. Her nose slightly wrinkles, as she sucks in a deep breath. "I love you."

"I love you too."

There are cars everywhere, and we can hear music coming from the back of the house. We walk to the front door, where we knock, but I doubt anyone will be able to hear us over the music. I try the lock and find it's open. "About time you guys got here," Rhett says as he's walking toward us. "Hey, Serena." He leans in and gives her a kiss on the cheek. "Dick," he says to me and holds out a fist.

"It's bigger than yours." I fist pump his balled-up hand. I look at the drink he's holding. "Whatcha drinking?"

"Bourbon." He waggles his brows at us. "Everyone's out in the back."

"Better be careful, Rhett. You're a lightweight when it comes to bourbon."

"Fuck off," he teases.

Serena chuckles. "I'm gonna go find your mom, and say hello." She loosens her grip on me, but I tighten my fingers around hers.

"I'll come with you. I don't need to hang out with this loser." I punch Rhett in the shoulder.

"That's abuse," he says. "Personal space, *dick*."

"The joys of brotherly love." Serena shakes her head. "Come on."

"What are you doing?" I ask Rhett.

"Just waiting for Pen. She's not here yet." Rhett opens the front door, and heads out.

"Hey, where is everyone?" I ask before he closes the door while he waits for Penelope.

"Follow this long ass hallway, and to the left, then down the back."

"Thank you," Serena says. We make our way down the wide, bright hallway. "Wow, this place is awesome!" Serena looks around. "It's so light and gorgeous."

"Yeah, it is." When we get to the end of the never-ending hallway, it opens up to a massive family room. We walk in, and Mom's in the kitchen making something. She looks up, and smiles widely. "Hey, Mom."

"Hey. Here's my boy. I didn't know if you were coming." She leaves whatever she's making, comes over and throws her arms around me. When she's hugged me, she grabs Serena and hugs her too. "Serena, you look so beautiful."

"Thank you."

"How's your brother doing?" Mom rubs her hands up and down Serena's arms.

"I'm going to find Dean," I say to Serena, then lean in and give her a kiss.

"Okay." She smiles at me like I'm her entire world.

Fuck, I love how she makes me feel when she looks at me like I'm her everything. I hover for a moment, just in case she's uncomfortable. "I'm not going to bite her, Alec. Piss off." Mom flicks her hand at me.

"I'm going." I hold my hands up in defeat. Heading out the back, I search for Dean. There are quite a few people here, maybe about fifty or so. Most of whom I know through either Dean, or being a firefighter. "Hey," I say when I find Dean. He's drinking a beer, and talking with Hugo.

"Hey. Where's Serena?" Dean asks and looks behind me. We both turn to see she's still speaking with Mom. "I knew it wouldn't have taken Mom a long time to get her claws into Serena."

"Beer?" Hugo offers.

"Yeah, thanks," I reply. Hugo walks away, leaving Dean and me. "Where's Joanne?"

"She's upstairs." He shakes his head. "What do you think of the house?"

"It's massive. But you have to give me a tour."

Dean squints at me. "Go have a look yourself." He flicks his head to the side.

"Yeah, I'm not about to go wandering through your house," I say.

"Here." Hugo hands me a beer. "The wife is summoning me." He looks over to his wife where we both wave to one another.

Dean lifts his beer, and gestures toward Serena. "How's it going with you two?"

"Yeah, pretty good. I proposed," I say.

"What the fuck? Congratulations, man." He comes in for a hug, but I step back. Stopping himself, he reads my deflated expression. "Oh shit, she said no."

"Yeah, she said I haven't thought about it long enough to actually make such a big decision."

"Ouch." He clenches his jaw in a wince. "What happened?"

"I was going down on her, and I asked her to marry me."

"Fuck, you didn't. Did you?"

"Yeah, I did. She asked me for a ring. I told her I didn't have one yet."

Dean attempts to conceal the chuckle. "So, let's get this straight. You were eating her out, and you asked her to marry you, and she said no?"

"Yeah."

He shakes his head, and pinches the bridge of his nose. "No wonder she said no. She probably thought it was just the high of having sex with her. You gotta do something grand. Or at the least thoughtful."

"How did you propose?"

"I asked Thomas if he'd be okay with me marrying his mom, and she lost her shit. Started crying and all that kind of stuff."

"Wow, you paint such a romantic scenario." I take a drink from my beer. "Punch me if I ever come to you for relationship advice."

"Says the guy who was going down on his girlfriend when he proposed."

"What's going on?" Rhett asks as he nurses his bourbon.

"Actually, I'm glad you're both here. I have a question for the two of you," Dean says when Rhett joins our conversation.

"What?" I ask suspiciously. He better not say anything about my proposal to Rhett. Rhett would never let me live it down.

"You both know that Joanne and I are engaged, right?" I look to Rhett, trying to figure out where this is going.

"Yeah. Even though there's no date set yet," Rhett says. "Maybe she's come to her senses and would rather have the hot brother than the boring brother." He points to himself, then to Dean.

"Shut up, Rhett," Dean snaps. "Anyway, I'd like to know, if you two would stand by my side as my groomsmen?"

"I should be your best man," I say almost offended. "You've known me longer than him." I point toward Rhett.

"He may have known you longer, but it doesn't mean he likes you more," Rhett retorts.

"You're both my best men then. Jesus," he mumbles something inaudible under his breath. "I need to know if you'll both be my best men?"

I smack him on the shoulder. "What a stupid question."

"Dude, seriously uncool," Rhett says. "Of course, we'll be your best men. Why are you even asking? We *are* your best men. Who else did you think would be by your side when you two *finally* get married?"

"You two are killing my brain cells." Dean looks to me, then to Rhett. "Follow me inside, we need to talk about something." He begins walking inside while Rhett and I follow him.

Serena is still with Mom, and when she sees the three of us heading past her, she squints and lifts her shoulders, silently asking where we're going. I lift my hands in resignation. *I don't know,* I mouth.

Okay, she replies then blows me a kiss.

Dean takes the steps two at a time, and when we're on the landing upstairs, I look around, noticing how massive the upstairs is. "Dean, is this the never-ending house?"

"Joanne wanted a big house. So we've got a big house." He opens a door and steps inside. Once Rhett and I are in there, he closes the door, walks over to the walk-in wardrobe, and comes out holding two black suits. "Here, yours." He hands me a suit. "And yours." He hands Rhett a suit too. "Put it on."

"What's going on?" Rhett asks.

Dean disappears back into the walk-in wardrobe, and returns with a third suit. He takes his t-shirt off over his head, and starts placing his arms through the crisp white shirt. "Holy shit!" I say.

Dean's face lightens, his smile wide and proud. "What?" Rhett says.

"They're getting married now," I say to Rhett.

"Joanne's next door in our room getting ready. Her parents are downstairs too. No one knows this is happening now, except us, and Thomas. And just so you know, Thomas is standing beside the two of you."

"Fuck man," I say as I grab him and hug him. "Fucking congratulations!"

Stepping back, I take my shirt off, and put on the one Dean wants me to wear.

"Jesus, this is awesome! About time," Rhett says. He hugs Dean too. "This is totally cool too. Spring it on everyone."

"Joanne didn't want anything fancy. She decided she only wanted the people who are important to us to be here." He does his buttons up, then puts on his suit pants. "Rhett, when we're ready, I need you to check on Joanne."

"Got it." The three of us dress quickly. The perks of being a firefighter and having to work well together under pressure. Rhett fixes his tie, and looks at himself in the mirror. "You ready?"

"As ready as I'll ever be," I say.

"Right, I'll go check on Joanne."

Rhett leaves the room, and I notice Dean pacing back and forth in front of the door. "You okay?" I ask.

"Nervous. I've never done something like this before, and I'll never do it again." He stops to look at his reflection in the mirror. "But it feels right, you know? I can't imagine going through a day without her."

Yeah, buddy, I know how that feels. At the risk of sounding pussy-whipped, I need Serena. "Yeah, I get it."

"When are you going to propose again?"

I was going to propose tonight, but I refuse to steal the spotlight from my brother and his family. Tonight is about them, not about Serena and myself. "Soon, real soon."

Dean paces some more, waiting for Rhett to return. "You have to do something."

"Whatever you need," I reply.

"When we're ready, I need you to go downstairs, and get everyone to gather on the north side of the pool. The moment you do that, I've got the remote for the music system to start. The celebrant is already down there, and they'll stand in place. Just stay where you are, Rhett, Thomas. and I will join you."

I clap a hand to his shoulder. "Consider it done," I say.

The door opens, and Rhett steps inside. "She's ready." He smiles. "And she looks perfect."

Dean takes a deep breath, pulls his shoulders back and smiles. "She's ready?"

"Yeah, she is," Rhett says.

"You know what to do?" Dean looks to me.

"I've got it." I hold my hand out to him. He takes it and we shake. "I'm proud of you, Dean. Really proud of you."

He pulls me in for another quick, brotherly hug. "Let's do this."

I head out of the bedroom, walk down the stairs and find Mom and Serena still in the kitchen, talking easily. Serena sees me before Mom does. "You've changed?" Serena approaches me, and wraps her arms around me. "You look sexy. Wait, why did you change? Wait," she pauses. "Wait?" she says in a lower voice. "What's happening?"

"What's going on, Alec?" Mom asks.

"Dean and Joanne are getting married right now," I say.

"AHHH!" Mom screams, jumps off the seat and claps her hands together. "What? Why didn't they say something?"

"They wanted to keep it a secret. So, I need you outside." Serena pulls away from me, her eyes are teary, and she's wearing a huge smile.

Mom is already a mess, crying. Serena slings her arm around Mom's shoulder. "Come on, Elise."

"Oh my God, I would've dressed nicer," I hear Mom saying.

"You look perfect to me," Serena replies.

I walk ahead of them, and look for the sound system to turn the song off. Dean beats me to it, turning the music off completely. "Ladies and gentlemen. It appears we were brought here under false pretense tonight. Dean and Joanne didn't invite us for a housewarming." I see people's smiles fading, and everyone appears confused. "Would you all please come to this side of the pool?" I boom loud enough so everyone can hear me. The celebrant must be a woman, because she stands alone, at the front, while everyone gathers together. I turn to see Rhett and Dean approaching. "Dean Morgan, our groom," I introduce.

There's a sea of *awws,* and *ahhs,* and a ton of clapping. Dean stands beside me, Rhett on my other side. Quickly, Thomas follows. I hold my fist out for Thomas, who returns a fist bump.

Dean takes a small remote out of his pocket, and presses it. The moment the song starts, all I can do is look for my girl. She's standing beside Mom, holding her hand while Mom sniffles into a tissue. Serena doesn't even notice me staring at her. She's too busy consoling my blubbering Mom. Serena looks up to see Joanne, her eyes widen and her right hand flies up to her heart. She's staring at Joanne with admiration and happiness in her eyes. I can't tear my gaze away from my girl. She's so perfectly beautiful. She catches me staring at her, and she smiles at me. *I love you,* I mouth the words.

She smiles widely, then wipes at her eyes.

"Ladies and gentlemen, I'm pleased to welcome you all here to the secret wedding of Dean and Joanne." The celebrant looks at Dean and Joanne. "Rascals, aren't they?" she asks.

An eruption of laughter echoes the backyard.

For the next twenty minutes, I can't take my eyes off my girl as the celebrant speaks words of love and adoration.

There's something in Serena's love that I'll never have enough of. I need to make her my wife, so the world knows she's mine. The celebrant wraps the ceremony up quickly, ending with Dean grabbing Joanne and dipping her as he kisses her.

I make a beeline for my girl, grabbing her and kissing her with complete control. "I'm addicted to you, Serena." Lacing my fingers under her top, I trace my fingertips across her lower back.

"I love you." She places her head to my chest, and I kiss the top of her head.

I want to slide that damn ring on her finger, but I also know I can't do it here. Not now. I'm not enough of a prick to do this to my family. Holding Serena, I watch as my mother fawns over Dean and Joanne. This night has not been what I expected it to be.

Serena crawls into bed wearing nothing but my t-shirt, and a pair of the worst underwear I've ever seen. I flick her t-shirt up to see the underwear. "These are horrible," I say.

"It's not the underwear you want to fuck, is it?" she teases. I remain quiet. "Thought so," she says.

I grab the hem of her t-shirt, and rip it off her head. "Come here." Gripping her hips, I start taking the atrocious underwear off, and throw them to the floor. "Note to self, get you sexier underwear. Thongs all the way. Easy access for me. I can move them to the side and fuck you, or eat you."

"They're not always the best underwear to have on." I take my boxer briefs off, already hard and waiting for her.

"Why not?" I move her so she's hovering over my hard cock.

As she sinks down on me, I try to hold it together. Serena starts swiveling her hips as she rides me. "Because they're not always convenient, especially when I have my period and I'm heavy."

I take her tit in my mouth, sucking on it as she continues to her pacing of how she likes feeling me. "Serena?"

"Yeah." I still her hips and clasp her face between my hands. "What is it?" She looks confused.

"I'm addicted to you." A small smile begins to stretch her mouth. "I love you."

"I love you." I lower her face to meet mine, and kiss her hard. She's lost in the moment; her hips take over and she fucks me. Serena reaches across and grasps the headboard of the bed, using it to steady herself while she keeps the rhythm of our bodies. I trail my hand down her stomach, and find her clit, rubbing it with my thumb as she increases the tempo.

Jesus, I have to let her orgasm first, or I'll lose myself and come before she does. She increases her hip movement, closes her eyes and throws her head back. "Shit," she moans. "Shit." I rub harder. "Yes. Shit. Fuck." Her breathing increases as her body convulses around my cock. With a deathly grip on her hips, I thrust up, fucking her until I lose myself, and come inside of her.

She kisses me, then swings her leg over and gets off of me. She heads into the bathroom, and I keep looking at the drawer where her ring is.

Serena returns into the room, and looks for her underwear and t-shirt. "Leave them off," I say to her. She shrugs, gets into bed and turns the small night light off on her side.

"Love you." She wiggles her butt close to me. I open the drawer, take the ring out of the box, then turn the light on my side off. I sidle up so my front is to her back. She moves her butt into my crotch. My cock likes her ass against me. I hold her ass cheek open, and nestle my cock between her cheeks. "Oh, are we doing the butt stuff now? I think we better buy some lube if you want to try." She shoves her butt back, and lets out a small moan.

I wrap my arm around her, holding her hand. Kissing her back, I try and slide the ring on her finger. "I love you."

"What are you doing?" She reaches across to turn the light on. Looking down at the ring that's half on her finger, she stares at it, then me. "What's this?"

"It's an engagement ring, Serena. A yellow diamond engagement ring." She looks at the ring, then me. "I can hear your heart beat from across the room. When you laugh, your nose does this cute little wrinkle. You send me crazy with how stubborn you are. You're the only person I ever want to be with. I need you more than I think you need me. And I don't want to go another day without you wearing this, so say yes to the next thing I'm about to say."

Serena's eyes water as she sucks in a deep breath. "Well then," she says. "What are you waiting for?"

"Marry me." I slide the ring down her finger.

She stares at the ring while I wait for her answer. "On one condition," she says.

"What?"

"Never stop loving me."

"Abso-fucking-lutely." I flip her over, and kiss her as she wraps her legs around me, and I push into her.

About fucking time, she said yes.

Epilogue

ALEC

SERENA'S NOT HOME from her cleaning job yet. I head into the kitchen and grab my phone off the kitchen counter. Calling, I wait for her to answer.

"I'm on my way," she says.

"Where are you?"

"About two minutes from home. Don't worry, we won't be late."

"I know, I was checking that you're okay." Yeah, I am a bit worried. Serena has a way of leaving things until the last minute. I like to be super organized; she's always had such a tight rein on everything that now she's learning how to relax and go with the flow.

"I can hear it in your voice, Alec. Your crazy ass discipline is stressing out right now, right?" I lean against the counter and shake my head. "You're shaking your head too, aren't you?"

"No," I snap.

"Aha. Anyway, open the door, I'll be there in a minute."

"A minute? As in a Serena minute, or an Alec minute?" I walk to the front door, open it, and wait out on the small porch for her. "You're not here yet."

"You're so impatient. I can see you, so stop your stressing." I turn to look to my left and see her car approaching. Hanging up, I head out to meet her at the car. "See," she says as she gets out. I lean in to kiss her, and she pulls away. "I'm sweaty and dirty. So, don't."

"I don't care." I pull her toward me, and kiss her with everything I have. I love this woman, and I want the world to know she's all mine.

"Eww, get off me, you freak," she says as she pushes me away.

Laughing, I let her go, and help her with whatever she has in the car to bring in. "You're right, you do stink."

As she's walking ahead of me, she swings around to walk backward, glaring at me. "I never said I stink. I said I'm sweaty and dirty, not smelly."

"I thought we were adding adjectives about the aroma coming off of you." I wave my hand in front of my nose playfully. She narrows her eyes. "Today is not a good day to die. Especially considering we have to be over at Mom's for Rhett's birthday is less than two hours."

"And you were going into controlling freak mode because I wasn't home yet. Plenty of time for me to shower, meditate, and get ready."

"I'll join you in the shower," I say once we're both inside.

"No, you won't because then we'll definitely be late. And I still want to do a meditation."

"You mean, hocus pocus, mumbo jumbo," I murmur. Deservedly, I get a smack on the shoulder. "Ouch, you hit hard."

"You see, I've got this feeling in my bones that you deserved it." She smiles widely, as she begins stripping off and heading into the bathroom.

Like a horny teenager, I follow and watch her perform her little striptease for me. Serena doesn't even have to try to be sexy, she just is. She moves her hips with seduction, and she has no idea she's even doing it. I sit on the edge of the bed, and watch as she unclasps her bra, and drops it in the laundry hamper. She hooks her thumbs around the top of her leggings, and slides them down her legs.

Jesus, my cock hardens, and it's taking all my control not to strip off and join her in the bathroom. I can't take my eyes off of her.

"Enjoying the view?" she asks as she opens the shower door, and turns on the water.

"Immensely." Fuck it, I'm going to join her. I don't care if we're late for Rhett's twenty-third birthday. I can't pass up an opportunity to be buried balls deep in my girl.

Serena has her back to me as I strip. She's completely immersed under the water when I open the glass door. She shakes her head and smiles without even opening her eyes. "I knew you couldn't help yourself."

"What can I say. I want to fuck my hot fiancée."

Her smile widens. "I like the sound of that. Hmmm." My hands are all over her body, my mouth trailing down the column of her throat. "I like that too."

My right hand skims down her cute, soft stomach straight between her legs. "I like this," I say as I continue to kiss as much of her as I can. I tease her before plunging a finger inside. She sucks in a breath, and embraces me tighter. Her mouth opens as a heavy breath escapes past her lips. As much as I want to fuck her mouth and make her lips swell with my cock between them, I know we need to be relatively quick. Especially if she's going to do one of her meditations. I know how important they are to her.

Serena hooks her leg over my hip giving me the perfect opportunity to fuck her while we're in the shower. Removing my fingers from her needy pussy, I slide my cock into her. "You waste no time, do you?" She opens her eyes and stares into mine.

"You still need to do a meditation." I kiss her, silencing her small groans. "You have no idea how much I'm in love with your body."

"So, you only want me for my body?" she jokes. I push up into her, showing her exactly how much I love her.

"Hold on, baby." She grips me tightly, and I fuck her hard and fast. Just as I'm about to finish, I make sure to rub her clit and get her to come seconds before I do. "God, I love you." I pull out of her, and kiss her nose. "But hurry up, because you're going to make us late."

"You're a fiend."

I quickly wash myself, and get out of the shower. With my towel hanging on my hips, I turn to see Serena staring at me. "What?" I ask.

"You have that delicious V women go crazy for. How have I never noticed it before?"

"Delicious V women go crazy for?" I look down at my torso. "You mean this?" I slink the towel lower, highlighting it.

She licks her lips, and cocks a brow. "Yep, that one," her voice brightens. "I can't believe I've never noticed it. Now, I have to lick it. I mean, I can't pass up an opportunity to lick every part of you. Especially that part." Her eyes are lowered and staring at my hips.

"You haven't made eye contact with me once."

"Are you crazy? I'm ogling you."

Smirking, I stand with my legs apart and start skimming my fingers across the top of the towel. Serena's mouth opens further, before she visibly swallows. "Am I only a sex toy to you?" I ask, pretending to be hurt.

"Yep," she responds without missing a beat. "Can you just drop the towel? I don't have such a great view from over here." I tease her, playing with the edge of the towel as I walk backward into our room. Serena steps forward, pressing her face into the glass shower door. "Don't go!" she calls as she tilts her smooshed face into the door.

"Hurry up!"

"Party pooper!"

I make sure to stand so she can only just see me as I get my clothes organized before I towel dry and change. "Hurry up!" I call again when I have my jeans and t-shirt on.

The water turns off, and within a few moments, she comes into the bedroom with a towel around her head, and one around her body. "You distracted me. So, it's your fault. And if we're late, I'm telling everyone it's your fault." She pokes me in the shoulder as she gets her clothes ready. "I'm thinking of wearing jeans too."

"What about a dress? Easy access for me."

"We're going to your mom's so, no sex for you while we're there."

"Not even a little feel?" I argue. "Just a finger or two?"

"Not with your entire family there."

"And about another thirty-odd people."

"Definitely not then. Jeans it is." She opens the drawer, and takes out a pair of blue jeans.

"If you're going to wear jeans, do me a favor and wear the black ones."

"But they're a bit tight." She places the blue ones back in the drawer, and takes out the black ones holding them up to me. My cheeky smile, tells her why. "Oh, you like these?"

"I love how your body looks in those. Reminds me what's beneath the clothes that I get to fuck whenever I want." I walk over to her, and grab her ass. "Wear the black ones."

"How can I deny you when you're so greedy for my body."

She seriously has no idea how much I adore her body. All her soft parts are incredibly fucking perfect. I clear my throat, because I'm getting hard again. "I've gotta go do something. Hurry up." I spank her butt again, she yelps and hops forward. When we get home tonight, I'm so using the vibrator on her while I spank her ass. I know how much she loves it. But right now, I have to remove myself from her or we won't even make it to Rhett's birthday party.

Mom has one arm around my waist, and the other around Dean's. "My boys. I'm so proud of you. Now, we need Rhett to find someone, and my life will be complete. Then. I can wait for grandbabies." I look to Dean whose features slightly drop.

"Back up a bit, Mom," I say making sure Mom doesn't see Dean's sadness. "Let us have a bit of a life with our women first."

"Not yet, obviously. Maybe in three or four years." She reaches up and gives Dean a kiss on the cheek, then gives me a kiss. "Where is your brother? Have you seen him?"

"He's been drinking hard since we've been here. Which means he's going to have the worst hangover ever tomorrow," I say.

Mom shakes her head and sighs. "That boy is a lightweight when it comes to drinking. But, it's his birthday, and he is twenty-three, so let him go." She shrugs. "Just keep an eye on him, okay?" she turns to ask us both.

"Yeah, of course," Dean says. The moment Mom turns her head, he mouths *no* and shakes his head to me.

"Elise, do you need any help with anything?" Joanne asks when she sees Mom has her arms around Dean and me.

"Oh no, darling. I think I have everything covered. Go, take your husband and enjoy yourselves." She pushes Dean out of the kitchen. "Go with your wife."

Dean leaves Mom and me in the kitchen. A flurry of people are coming in and out of the house from the back. Mom's smile is large as she bops along to the songs blaring from the sound system in the backyard. "You okay, Mom?"

"I'm so proud of my boys. I just wish your father was still alive to see how amazing you all turned out." She blinks rapidly, her eyes becoming misty. "Anyway, it's time for cake. Can you go find that brother of yours and get him up here ready for us to sing to him?"

I turn to look out at the patio, but don't see him. "He and Pen will probably be passed out drunk somewhere."

"I'm not drunk!" I hear Penelope call from outside. She staggers inside, holding a drink that's sloshing around. *At least she can walk.* "Who said I'm drunk?" She approaches Mom and throws her arms over her. "I love you, Elise."

"I love you too, Pen."

"You're like my second mom."

"Yes, I am." Mom is stone cold sober while Pen is drunk and slurring. Mom gives Pen a kiss on the cheek. "Thank you for being the best friend to Rhett anyone ever could be. I just wish you two would end up together."

Pen sticks her tongue out, and pretends to vomit. "That's like me and Alec being together. No thanks, the only man I want is Dane, and he doesn't want me." Her smile quickly fades, and the drunk sadness is about to take over.

Mom quickly hugs her. "It's okay, sweetheart, you'll always have us."

Penelope goes from sad drunk to happy drunk in three seconds. "Yay!" she cheers.

"Go find your brother," Mom says to me. "Come on, Pen, let's get ready for cake. I'm going to take you outside, so you can sit and wait. But you have to stay there, okay?" I hear her instructing Pen as I walk out.

"Hey, have you seen Rhett?" I ask Serena who's talking with Dean and Joanne.

"Nah, I haven't. I'll come with you to find him though." She smiles at Joanne. "Excuse me." Serena has molded into our family so easily. She's a Morgan through and through. "Have you checked his room? He's been drinking so hard, he may have gone in there to pass out."

"Not yet." We both walk to his room and open the door. Nope, no one is in here. "He's probably passed out down in the back somewhere," I huff.

We head out and down the back of the yard. The further we get away from the patio, the less light there is. "Wait, I think I can hear something," Serena says. We both stand still and can hear soft voices coming from further down.

As quietly as we can, we both tiptoe in the direction of the voices so we can hear what the hell is going on. The closer we get, the louder the voices become, though still they're merely above a whisper.

We stop walking when we hear Rhett mumbling about something. Then, as clear as day he says, "I've always loved you, Dani." Serena places her hand on my shoulder, stopping me from walking further.

"I've never loved anyone but you, Rhett," she replies.

What the fuck did we just hear?

There's more drunken murmuring and mumbling happening. "I love you," she says.

"I love you more."

"What do we do?" Serena asks.

I had no idea they loved each other. Why the hell are they hiding down here? "Rhett?" I say.

"Shhh, it's my brother." There's lots of giggling, and shhh-ing.

"Rhett, Mom wants you so we can have cake," I say, not knowing what the hell to do here.

He laughs out loud. We hear something scrape, then more laughing. "I can't get up," he slurs. He must be so damn drunk.

"Hang on." I look at Serena and lift my shoulders. Heading toward where he is, I help him up. Dani is now lying flat on the ground, sleeping. "Serena, can you come give me a hand." Serena comes over with the torch on her phone. She looks at Dani and a slumped Rhett. "Yep, they're both so drunk. Can you help with Dani?"

"Sure." She rouses Dani, and helps her up.

"Come on, buddy. We've got a cake for you."

"Yum, I love cake. But not as much as I love Dani," Rhett says. His words are becoming jumbled as he stumbles alongside of me back toward the patio.

Mom sees me half carrying Rhett, and Serena helping Dani up. She starts laughing, but lights the candles on top of Rhett's cake.

"Sit him here. My God, he's so bad," Mom says between laughter. "He's gonna be so much worse tomorrow."

"I love you, Mom." Rhett points to Mom.

"I love you too, son." She brings her hand up to cover her snicker.

The moment we sing happy birthday, Mom manages to get the candles out of the cake before Rhett face-plants into it, passing out. The loud laughter rouses Rhett, and he lifts his face with half of it covered in cake.

I take my phone out, snapping photos of him with cake all over his face. He's laughing and swaying from side to side.

"So, Rhett and Dani, huh?" Serena says.

"I have no idea what's going on there, and for now, I don't want to know," I say.

She wraps her arm around my waist, and leans her head on my shoulder. "In case I forgot to tell you, I love you."

"I love you too."

Keep reading for a preview of Rhett

Rhett

Prologue

Past

"Hey, have you seen the new girl?" Pen asks as we both sit in the cafeteria at school.

"Nah, why?"

"She's cute," Pen replies. She places her bag on the chair beside her, and looks around the cafeteria. "There she is." Pen gestures toward the entrance.

I turn to look at who she's pointing out, and I see *her*. Shit, I can't help but stare as she walks in and timidly glances around before heading over to the line to get some lunch. Pen's right, she's really cute. Her light brown hair is pulled back into a messy bun, she's wearing a long t-shirt and leggings with chunky Doc Martin boots.

Pen smacks me on the shoulder. "What?" I drag my eyes away from the pretty new girl, to scowl at Penelope. "What?" I repeat.

"You're drooling." She wipes at her mouth. "You look like a stalker goob."

"A goob? What the hell is a goob, Pen?"

"Out of what I said, you heard goob? Not stalker, but goob?" She rolls her eyes at me.

"Just, whatever." I look back to the girl standing in line. She appears nervous, as she looks around the cafeteria, worrying her lip in between her teeth. Standing, I head over toward her.

"Where are you going?" Pen grins and waggles her brows.

I turn and smile. I go to the girl and tap her on the shoulder. She flinches as she turns. Looking up at me, she holds her head high. "Hi," I say. "I'm Rhett." I hold my hand out to her.

Her line of sight falls to my hand. She takes it, and slightly nods. "Dani."

"You're new, right?"

"Uh-huh." She shyly glances down at her clutched hands.

"Would you like to sit with Penelope and me." I point over to Pen, who waves at Dani eagerly.

Dani looks past my wide shoulders to see Penelope standing enthusiastically watching us. "Um." She crinkles her brows, and mashes her lips together. "Thanks," she says with a small crack.

"Great." I stand beside her as we move up in the line. She's nervous, because she's barely talking. "Where are you from?"

"Um, just around. We move a lot."

"Army brat?"

"Nah, nothing like that. Just we move, you know." She shuffles up a step as the line progresses.

"How are you liking Mulberry Point?"

"Yeah, it's okay." She lowers her gaze, and takes a long breath. "We probably won't stay for long. But it seems nice." She shrugs as if moving around is a normal thing her family does.

"So, you move around a lot then?"

She scoffs. "You have no idea." It's clear she's not a fan of it. If she's not an army brat, then why does her family relocate so much?

"So, do you have any brothers or sisters?"

"Nope." She shakes her head. "You?"

"Yeah, I have two older brothers."

"That's cool. Do they come here too?"

"Nah, they've finished and are training to be firefighters."

"Firemen?" She smirks. "That's super cool." Dani is the next one in line, and she grabs what she wants to eat. I take the tray once she's got what she wants. "I can carry it."

"I know." I keep a hold of it as we walk over to where Pen is sitting, now joined by Louis and Brent. "Hey, guys, this is Dani and she's just moved to our school," I say as I place her tray down opposite me.

"Hey," she says to everyone.

"This is Penelope." I point to Pen who smiles widely. "Louis and Brent." I point to them.

"Hey," Brent says as he looks at Dani and arches a brow.

Shit.

I notice her cheeks pink when he looks her way. *Oh, right.*

She sits and starts picking at her food. "Where are you from?" Pen asks.

"Around," Dani replies elusively.

Pen looks at what I've got for lunch, and helps herself to whatever she wants. "Yum. Is this your mom's mac and cheese?" Pen asks as she opens the container.

"It is."

"Excellent." She shoves her food toward me, takes mine and inhales it. "This is so good, Rhett."

"That's why I brought it for lunch, Pen."

"You snooze, you lose."

Dani giggles, and when I look over to her, I notice the cutest dimple in her cheek when she's smiling.

"What do you like to do?" Brent asks as he directs his attention to Dani.

I can't help but notice how Dani's eyes downcast for a moment when she looks at Brent. "Um, I, um..." She swallows, and tucks some hair behind her ear. I hang on every one of her movements, and I notice, Brent does too. "I'm pretty basic," she says.

I highly doubt that. There's nothing basic about her.

"Do you like watching movies?" Brent asks smoothly.

The small smirk on her pretty face breaks my heart. She likes him, and he likes her. "Yeah, I do," she says.

Fuck. He's going to make his move, and I'm not the type of guy who'll stand in either of their way. It's clear to everyone, she's digging on him as much as he's digging on her. "There's a new horror movie playing."

"Oh my God." She places her hand to her chest. "Horror is my favorite genre," she says excitedly. "Especially slash 'em up, jump scare, in-your-face gory movies."

Great, that's the type of movies I *don't* like, and the exact type Brent does. They'll make a good couple. Dani slides over on the bench seat and begins a more in-depth conversation with Brent. I spend my lunch talking with Pen, but trying to listen to what Dani's saying. When lunch is finished, Brent and Dani walk out of the cafeteria, having made a date to go to the movies.

"Sorry, man," Penelope says as we walk toward our next classes. English for me, and math for Pen.

"What? Why?"

"You like her, and she likes Brent. That's gotta be hard."

I try to downplay it, pretending it doesn't matter. "There are plenty more chicks," I say casually.

"Don't bullshit me, Rhett. I'm your best friend, and I can see you like her. Fight for her."

"Nah." I shake my head. "She's into Brent, not me. No use in fighting for someone who didn't even see me." Pen turns and pokes me in the shoulder. "Ouch." I rub at the spot.

"Don't be a dick. If you like her, go after her."

"Nah." I shake my head. "She's into Brent. Anyway, he's a good guy, and he'll treat her well. So, that's it."

"Rhett..."

"No!" I say with authority. "No more, Pen. We're not talking about this anymore."

"But..."

I stop both of us walking. Looking into her eyes, I shake my head. "I said enough." She opens her mouth and points her finger at me. "No more."

Pen huffs. "Fine, but she may very well be the love of your life, and you'd be letting her go with Brent. I know he's a good guy, but what if..."

"Stop." I run my hand through my hair. "Are you coming over after school today?"

"Duh."

"I'll wait for you out the front. See ya." I don't give Pen the chance to say anything else about me asking Dani out.

If it's meant to be, then it'll happen. But judging by the way Dani's eyes lit up while she was talking to Brent, then it's obviously *not* meant to be.

Maybe one day, just not today.

Addiction

I CAN STOP ANYTIME I WANT

NEW YORK TIMES BESTSELLING AUTHOR

MARGARET MCHEYZER

Prologue

"Is she dead?"

Groaning, I try to roll over so I can see where the voice is coming from.

"She's moving. We have to help her," someone else says. Their voice is breathy, sounding panicked.

My limbs are heavy, my head is fuzzy, and I swear I can hear my mother's voice.

"Hannah, are you high?" She aggressively holds my chin and stares into my eyes.

"No, Mom," I respond, and giggle.

"Your eyes are bloodshot, and you're barely looking at me."

"I'm just tired," I say and giggle again.

"What's so funny?" she asks as she lets go of my chin and steps backward.

Shrugging, I look around the room.

"We need to call an ambulance," someone says, reminding me that my mother isn't here with me.

My vision is blurry. I can't focus on anything at all. Turning my head, I look straight into the eyes of a girl. She's probably around my age, but I bet she hasn't seen half the stuff I have. She kneels beside me, and behind her are another two girls and three guys. One of them looks bored; he's scrolling on his phone.

"What do you want?" I bark toward her, but my voice comes out broken, and slurry.

"Jasmine, she's a junkie. Look at her. Just leave her. She's not our problem," the bored guy says.

"We can't just leave her," she snarls back at him.

Suddenly, my stomach starts contracting, and my breathing becomes challenged. Gasping for air, my body tightens with spasms, trying to get oxygen into my lungs.

"Shit, she must be overdosing. We gotta get out of here before anyone finds us," bored guy says.

"I'm not leaving her. She's just a kid."

"She ain't my problem. I'm outta here," the bored guy says and takes off, the others going with him.

The girl stays with me, and as I try to focus on her, all I can see is the pretty chain around her neck. It looks like it's worth a lot, I'm sure I could give it to Edgar for some crystals. Man, maybe a few days' worth. I need money big time.

"I'm going to call an ambulance," the girl says as she takes her phone out of her pocket and dials it. "What have you taken?" she asks.

Everything is fuzzy. Her voice sounds disjointed and almost robotic.

Reaching for my pipe, I scream in pain. But she doesn't seem alarmed by my screams, maybe I'm actually not moving. Everything hurts.

"I need an ambulance…" her voice is frantic as she tells the operator where she is.

My eyes keep drifting shut, and she screams at me to open them again.

"She's frothing at the mouth, and she's barely moving."

I try to turn over, but whatever those fuckers gave me was strong. It's weighing me down. I can barely move.

"Her breathing is shallow…"

If I can just get up, I'll find my way back to Edgar's. He'll look after me. He always does. Sometimes he asks me to do stuff for him. "I'm alright," I mumble.

"She's trying to say something," the girl says into the phone. "Okay, I won't touch her." Her eyes are filled with pity and sadness. I stare up at her, and can see how concerned she is. I can see her. Can she see me?

"There's a syringe beside her. I think she might have injected something. There's a pipe, too. Maybe she smoked crack or meth?"

Yeah, baby. Crystal meth. Meth. Crystal. Ice. Tina. Glass. I love it. I love getting iced. It's the best feeling in the world. Being invincible, even when there are a million people in the room. Being free. Floating. That floating is what I love best. Anything can be happening around you, and when you smoke a bit of ice, you're floating above everyone. Free and happy and high.

"I'm here!" The girl jumps up and waves her arms frantically.

"Thank you for calling, we'll take it from here," another woman says to the girl.

The girl steps back and continues to stare at me. I'm being rolled over, and talked at by someone in a uniform. "What's your name?"

"Hannah," I respond.

"She's unresponsive," the woman says as she looks up to someone. She presses into my chest plate with her knuckle, and a shooting pain rips through me. "She's barely coherent. Heart rate is down, pulse is weak. She's overdosing."

"Get me back to Edgar's," I say.

"She's crashing. Administering Narcan."

There's a tightness in my chest. Pain soars through me, every part of me is like someone is stabbing multiple sharp knives into my body.

A darkness overtakes me.

A blanket of warmth is thrown over my entire body. My last breath escapes past my chapped lips.

Suddenly, I feel weightless. This must be what heaven feels like. It's so peaceful.

"We're losing her!" I hear someone yell.

Who's losing who? What's happening?

"ETA sixty seconds," someone else says in a calm voice.

I'm not sure what's happening, all I know is I like the quiet.

"Breathe, damn it, breathe!"

"Great, another dead junkie," someone snickers.

"I haven't lost her yet."

"She's just a junkie, Sally. Who cares if she dies? It's another one off the streets."

"Hey, she's someone's daughter. You want to be the one to knock on her parent's door?"

I hear a grumble from behind me. More like a pained sigh.

Who's talking?

What the hell is happening?

As it turns out, this is far from the end of my story.

Also by MARGARET MCHEYZER

Dean

He risks his life for others. She's tortured by her history. Will their timid bond flourish into a lifelong love?

Dean Morgan is an everyday hero. A well-respected firefighter in a small community, he believes everyone deserves compassion. So when he daringly rescues an unconscious teen from a burning building, the boy's troubled mother immediately sets his heart ablaze.

Joanne Hamilton fears she'll never escape her imprisoned husband's abuse. But when the handsome ladder-man plucks her son from the jaws of death, she's surprised when his presence stirs more than gratitude. And when she witnesses the gorgeous guy's kind soul in action, she feels her shattered spirit might just have a chance to mend.

As Dean forms a fatherly connection with the boy, his protective instincts naturally pull them all closer. But when Joanne's toxic baggage rears its ugly head, she's terrified her budding attraction isn't the only thing in danger.

Can they survive a dark past and fan the flames of happiness?

Healing Hearts

We started out as friends with benefits, we were never meant to be anything more.

I was content with how we were, but feelings developed and Charlie was asking for something I couldn't give.

However, my past is standing in the way. He wanted all or nothing...

Losing him isn't an option, but is the possibility of having my heart broken a risk I'm willing to take?

Our Chance

We started out as friends.

But as time goes by I find myself developing a crush on Jake.

I'm fairly certain our attraction is mutual. When we're together we're dynamic, our chemistry is undeniable. But something is stopping us from acting on our feelings.

Resisting him is nearly impossible.

The problem is, I'm running from my past.

Jake's the Sheriff of Hope River, and it wouldn't be hard for him to uncover my secrets.

Do I risk telling him the truth, or do I run again?

Hope's River

Working with my hands has always been my passion, so now I flip houses for a living. I love what I do.

I was happy where my life was heading.

Although I knew he wasn't the one, I was even content with my long-term relationship… until suddenly I wasn't.

I needed a change. So I got in my truck and asked the universe to help a sister out. It was then that I stumbled upon a cute small town called Hope River. Ironic really...

Not only did the name of the town hold significance from my past, but it led me to find something I thought was once lost.

Little did I know how significant this town would be for my future…

Perfectly Thin

When I'm thinner, no one will make fun of me.

When I'm thinner, I'll be accepted.

When I'm thinner, I'll be beautiful.

When I'm thinner, I'll be happy.

When I'm thinner, I'll be loved, and adored.

When I'm thinner, I'll like myself.

I can't wait until I'm perfectly thin.

Echoes of You

At seven I was adopted by the most loving parents in the world.

In this perfect family, I also found my best friend, and sister Tina.

Throw into the mix my boyfriend Dylan, and my dog Zhen, life was good... until it wasn't.

A catastrophic incident unearthed echoes of my past.

It left me no choice but to confront my inner demons.

Will I be able to live through this again?

A Bump in the Road

Pregnant at 15.

These are the words I didn't think I would ever have to live with.

Alex and I thought we were careful.

Becoming accidentally pregnant was obviously written in the stars for me.

I can't know what the future holds, or if Alex will even stick around.

But the one thing I know for sure; I'll turn this hardship into a blessing.

With or without anyone else.

Luna Caged

I often stare at the walls and wonder what's beyond them.

The Elders tell me that nothing but sin, sadness, and disease lie beyond the wall.

Sometimes I hear things, noises that are strange to me. They're often faint, and when I ask the Elders what those sounds are, they tell me they are the tortured souls of thousands of people behind the gates of hell. I don't know what they mean.

I dream of leaving these walls, but the Elders insist this is the only place we're safe. They talk about danger, hatred, and the devil himself waiting just beyond. They tell us the walls were built to keep us safe.

Although I believe the Elders, I want to see the outside world for myself.

But there's no way out.

Or so I thought...

Luna Freed

I often stared at the walls and wondered what was beyond them.

After my first escape, I realized that everything I'd believed, everything the Elders told us, and everything I thought I knew were all calculated lies.

Now I know the truth will set me free.

Addiction

Drugs ruin people's lives.

I should know, they destroyed mine.

I'm Hannah and I got hooked on ice. What started as a trickle, ended with a tsunami washing everything away; my family, my life.

I'm not sure you're ready to read my story; it's real and confronting.

Open the book, read the pages and see how easy it is for anyone to get addicted.

Ice affects all types of people. It doesn't discriminate.

It will SCREW. YOU. UP.

Drowning

I'm a cutter.

I cut because I find solace in it.

I cut because it helps calm my frantic mind.

I cut because the voice inside my head tells me to.

I cut because this is the only way I know how to handle life.

The Gift

I have something people want. I have something they cannot take or steal. I have something they'd kill for.

The something I have, isn't a possession, it's more.

Much, much more.

It's a gift.

It's part of me.

The Curse

It's been the butterfly effect.

I changed the course of my life because I warned a man.

I thought what I had was a gift, but it's quickly turning into my curse.

Now I realize I'm much more than a girl with an ability.

Because now... I'm becoming a weapon.

Dying Wish

I have three major loves in my life: my family, my best friend Becky, and ballet. Elijah Turner is quickly becoming the fourth.

He's been around as long as I can remember. But now he's much more than just the annoying guy at school.

My life was working out perfectly...until it got turned upside down.

Mistrust

I'm the popular girl at school.

The one everyone wants to be friends with.

I have the best boyfriend in the world, who's on the basketball team.

My parents adore me, and I absolutely love them. My sister and I have a great relationship too.

I'm a cheerleader, I have a high GPA and I'm liked even by the teachers.

It was a night which promised to be filled with love and fun until…something happened which changed everything.

Ugly

This is a dark YA/NA standalone, full-length novel. Contains violence and some explicit language

If I were dead, I wouldn't be able to see.

If I were dead, I wouldn't be able to feel.

If I were dead, he'd never raise his hand to me again.

If I were dead, his words wouldn't cut as deep as they do.

If I were dead, I'd be beautiful and I wouldn't be so...ugly.

I'm not dead...but I wish I was.

Chef Pierre

Holly Walker had everything she'd ever dreamed about - a happy marriage and being mum to beautiful brown-eyed Emma - until an accident nineteen months ago tore her world apart. Now she's a widow and single mother to a boisterous little 7-year-old girl, looking for a new start. Ready to take the next step, Holly has found herself a job as a maître d' at Table One, a once-acclaimed restaurant in the heart of Sydney. But one extremely arrogant Frenchman isn't going to be easy to work with...

Twenty years ago, Pierre LeRoux came to Australia, following the stunning Aussie girl he'd fallen in love with and married. He and his wife put their personal lives on hold, determined for Pierre to take Sydney's culinary society by storm. Just as his bright star was on the upswing, tragedy claimed the woman he was hopelessly in love with. He had been known as a Master Chef, but since his wife's death he has become known as a monster chef.

Can two broken people rebuild their lives and find happiness once more?

Smoke and Mirrors

Words can trick us.

Smoke obscures objects on the edge of our vision.

A mirror may reflect, but the eye sees what it wants.

A delicate scent can evoke another time and place, a memory from the past.

And a sentence can deceive you, even as you read it.

Grit

****Recommended for 18 years and over****

Alpha MC Prez Jaeger Dalton wants the land that was promised to him.

Sassy Phoenix Ward isn't about to let anyone take Freedom Run away from her.

He'll protect what's his.

She'll protect what's hers.

Jaeger is an arrogant ass, but he wants nothing more than Phoenix.

Phoenix is stubborn and headstrong, and she wants Jaeger out of her life.

Her father lost the family farm to gambling debts, but Jaeger isn't the only one who has a claim to the property.

Sometimes it's best to let things go.

But sometimes it's better to fight until the very end.

Yes, Master

***** THIS PROLOGUE CONTAINS DISTRESSING CONTENT. IT IS ONLY SUITED FOR READERS OVER 18. *****

ALSO CONTAINS M/M, M/M/F, M/F AND F/F SCENES.

My uncle abused me.

I was 10 years old when it started.

At 13 he told me I was no longer wanted because I had started to develop.

At 16 I was ready to kill him.

Today, I'm broken.

Today, I only breathe to survive.

My name's Sergeant Major Ryan Jenkins and today, I'm ready to tell you my story.

A Life Less Broken

****CONTAINS DISTRESSING CONTENT. 18+****

On a day like any other, Allyn Sommers went off to work, not knowing that her life was about to be irrevocably and horrifically altered.

Three years later, Allyn is still a prisoner in her own home, held captive by harrowing fear. Broken and damaged, Allyn seeks help from someone that fate put in her path.

Dr. Dominic Shriver is a psychiatrist who's drawn to difficult cases. He must push past his own personal battles to help Allyn fight her monsters and nightmares.

Is Dr. Shriver the answer to her healing?

Can Allyn overcome being broken?

My Life for Yours

He's lived a life of high society and privilege; he chose to follow in his father's footsteps and become a Senator.

She's lived a life surrounded with underworld activity; she had no choice but to follow in her father's footsteps and take on the role of Mob Boss.

He wants to stamp out organized crime and can't be bought off.

She's the ruthless and tough Mob Boss where in her world all lines are blurred.

Their lives are completely different, two walks of life on the opposite ends of the law.

Being together doesn't make sense.

But being apart isn't an option

HiT Series Box Set

HiT 149

Anna Brookes is not your typical teenager. Her walls are not adorned with posters of boy bands or movie stars. Instead posters from Glock, Ruger, and Smith & Wesson grace her bedroom. Anna's mother abandoned her at birth, and her father, St. Cloud Police Chief Henry Brookes, taught her how to shoot and coached her to excellence. On Anna's fifteenth birthday, unwelcome guests join the celebration, and Anna's world is never the same. You'll meet the world's top assassin, 15, and follow her as she discovers the one hit she's not sure she can complete - Ben Pearson, the current St. Cloud Police Chief and a man with whom Anna has explosive sexual chemistry. Enter a world of intrigue, power, and treachery as Anna takes on old and new enemies, while falling in love with the one man with whom she can't have a relationship.

Anna Brookes in Training

Find out what happened to transform the fifteen-year-old Anna Brookes, the Girl with the Golden Aim, into the deadly assassin 15. After her father is killed and her home destroyed, orphan Anna Brookes finds herself homeless in Gulf Breeze, Florida. After she saves Lukas from a deadly attack, he takes her in and begins to train her in the assassin's craft. Learn how Lukas's unconventional training hones Anna's innate skills until she is as deadly as her mentor.

HiT for Freedom

Anna has decided to break off her steamy affair with Ben Pearson and leave St. Cloud, when she suspects a new threat to him. Katsu Vang is rich, powerful, and very interested in Anna. He's also evil to his core. Join Anna as she plays a dangerous game, getting closer to Katsu to discover his real purpose, while trying to keep Ben safe. Secrets are exposed and the future Anna hoped for is snatched from her grasp. Will Ben be able to save her?

HiT to Live

In the conclusion to the Anna Brookes saga, Ben and his sister Emily, with the help of Agent rescue Anna. For Anna and Ben, it's time to settle scores…and a time for the truth between them. From Sydney to the Philippines and back to the States, they take care of business. But a helpful stranger enters Anna's life, revealing more secrets…and a plan that Anna wants no part of. Can Anna and Ben shed their old lives and start a new one together, or will Anna's new-found family ruin their chances at a happily-ever-after?

Binary Law (co-authored)

Ellie Andrews has been receiving tutoring from Blake McCarthy for three years to help her improve her grades so she can get into one of the top universities to study law. And she's had a huge crush on him since she can remember.

Blake McCarthy is the geek at school that's had a crush on Ellie since the day he met her.

In their final tutoring session, Blake and Ellie finally become brave enough to take the leap of faith.

But, life has other plans and rips them apart. Six years later Blake and his best friends Ben and Billy have built a successful internet platform company 3BCubed, while Ellie is a successful and hardworking lawyer specializing in Corporate Law.

3BCubed is being threatened with a devastatingly large plagiarism case and when it lands on their lawyers desk, it's handed to the new Corporate Lawyer to handle and win.

Coincidence or perhaps fate will see Blake and Ellie pushed back together.

Binary Law will have Blake and Ellie propelled into a life that's a whirl wind of catastrophic events and situations where every emotion will be touched. Hurt will be experienced, happiness will be presented and love will be evident. But is that enough for Blake and Ellie be able to live out their own happily ever after?

Printed in Dunstable, United Kingdom

81974537R00178